An Irish Country Village

An Irish Country Village

PATRICK TAYLOR

A Tom Doherty Associates Book

New York

AN IRISH COUNTRY VILLAGE

Copyright © 2008 by Patrick Taylor

Maps by Elizabeth Danforth

A Forge Book
Published by Tom Doherty Associates, LLC
175 Fifth Avenue
New York, NY 10010

www.tor-forge.com

Forge® is a registered trademark of Tom Doherty Associates, LLC.

Library of Congress Cataloging-in-Publication Data

Taylor, Patrick, 1941–
   An Irish country village / Patrick Taylor.
      p. cm.
   "A Tom Doherty Associates book."
   ISBN-13: 978-0-7653-2023-0
   ISBN-10: 0-7653-2023-1
1. Physicians—Fiction. 2. Country life—Northern Ireland—Fiction. I. Title.

PR9199.4.T36 I75 2008
813'.6—dc22

                                                            2007040871

First Hardcover Edition: February 2008
First Trade Paperback Edition: February 2009

Printed in the United States of America

0   9   8   7   6   5   4   3

To all rural GPs everywhere

ACKNOWLEDGMENTS

Doctor Fingal Flahertie O'Reilly made his first appearance twelve years ago. His gradual development was gently supervised by Simon Hally, editor of *Stitches*. O'Reilly's growth to maturity has been nurtured by two other remarkable people: Carolyn Bateman, who edits, advises me about, and polishes all my manuscripts before submission, and Natalia Aponte of Tor/Forge Books, who has had unswerving faith in the inhabitants of Ballybucklebo and has constantly encouraged me.

During the preparation of *An Irish Country Village* I was fortunate enough to be able to call upon the expertise of two physicians, Doctor Jimmy Sloan, pathologist, and Doctor Don Griesdale, neurosurgeon. Their helping a broken-down old gynaecologist to understand the finer points of myocardial infarction and Parkinson's disease was invaluable.

To you all, O'Reilly, Laverty, and I tender our unreserved thanks.

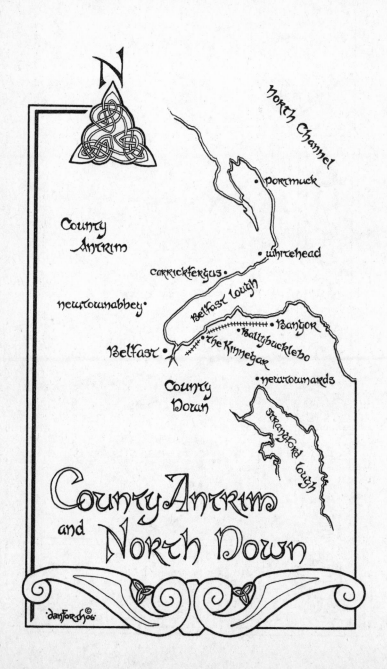

N

North Channel

• portmuck

County
Antrim

• whitehead

carrickfergus

newtownabbey •

Belfast Lough

• Bangor

Belfast •

the Kinnegar

• Ballybucklebo

• newtownards

County
Down

Strangford Lough

County Antrim
and North Down

danforth ©

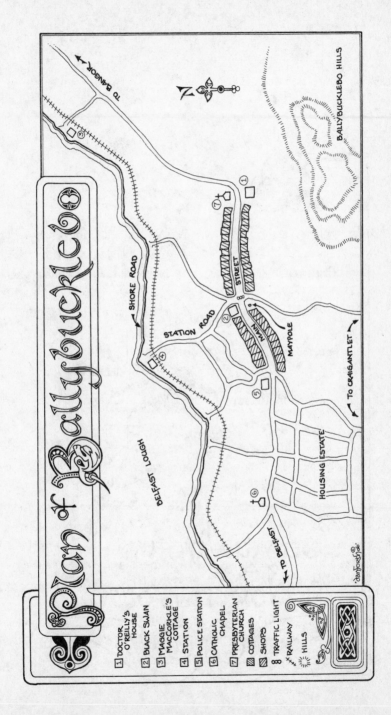

1

This Bodes Some Strange Eruption to Our State

Barry Laverty—Doctor Barry Laverty—heard the clattering of a frying pan on a stove and smelled bacon frying. Mrs. "Kinky" Kincaid, Doctor O'Reilly's housekeeper, had breakfast on, and Barry realized he was ravenous.

Feet thumped down the stairs, and a deep voice said, "Morning, Kinky."

"Morning yourself, Doctor dear."

"Young Laverty up yet?" Despite the fact that half the village of Ballybucklebo, County Down, Northern Ireland, had been partying in his back garden for much of the night, Doctor Fingal Flahertie O'Reilly, Laverty's senior colleague, was up and doing.

"I heard him moving about, so."

Barry's head was a little woozy, but he smiled as he left his small attic bedroom. He found the Cork woman's habit of tacking "so" to the ends of most of her sentences endearing and less grating than the "so it is" or "so I will" added for emphasis by the folks from his native province of Ulster.

In the bathroom he washed the sleep from his blue eyes, which in the shaving mirror blinked at him from an oval face under fair hair, a cowlick sticking up from the crown.

He finished dressing and went downstairs to the dining room, passing as he did the ground-floor parlour that Doctor O'Reilly used as his surgery, which Barry knew an American doctor would have called his "office." He hoped to be spending a lot of time here in the future. He paused to glimpse inside the by now familiar room.

"Don't stand there with both legs the same length," O'Reilly growled from the dining room opposite. "Come on in and let Kinky feed us."

"Coming." Barry went into the dining room, blinking at the August sunlight streaming in through the bay windows.

"Morning, Barry." O'Reilly, wearing a collarless striped shirt and red braces to hold up his tweed trousers, sat at the head of a large mahogany table, a teacup held in one big hand.

"Morning, Fingal." Barry sat and poured himself a cup. "Grand day."

"I could agree," said O'Reilly, "if I didn't have a bit of a strong weakness." He yawned and massaged one temple, his bushy eyebrows moving closer as he spoke. Barry could see tiny veins in the whites of O'Reilly's brown eyes. The big man's craggy face with its cauliflower ears and listing-to-port nose broke into a grin. "When I was in the navy it's what we used to call 'a self-inflicted injury.' It was quite the ta-ta-ta-ra yesterday."

Barry laughed and wondered how many pints of Guinness his mentor had sunk the previous night. Ordinarily drink would have as much effect on O'Reilly as a teaspoon of water on a forest fire. Barry still wasn't sure if the man's magnanimous offer, made in the middle of what had seemed to be the hooley to end all hooleys, had been the Guinness talking or whether O'Reilly was serious. When he'd first woken he'd thought he might've dreamed the whole thing, but now he clearly remembered that he'd vowed before laying his head on the pillow to muster the courage this morning to ask O'Reilly if he had meant it.

He knew he could let the hare sit, wait for O'Reilly to repeat the offer under more professional circumstances, but damn it all, this was important. Barry glanced down at the table, then back straight into O'Reilly's eyes. "Fingal," he said putting down his cup.

"What?"

"You were serious, weren't you, about offering me a full-time assistantship for one year and then a partnership in your practice?"

O'Reilly's cup stopped halfway to his lips. His hairline moved lower and rumpled the skin of his forehead. Pallor appeared at the tip of his bent nose.

Barry involuntarily turned one shoulder towards the big man, as a pistol duellist of old might have done in order to present his enemy with a smaller target. The pale nose was a sure sign that fires smouldering beneath O'Reilly's crust were about to break through the surface.

"Was I what?" O'Reilly slammed his cup into his saucer. "Was I *what*?"

Barry swallowed. "I only meant—"

"Holy thundering mother of Jesus Christ Almighty I know what you meant. Why the hell would you think I wasn't serious?"

"Well . . ." Barry struggled desperately to find diplomatic words. "You . . . that is, we . . . we'd had a fair bit to drink."

O'Reilly pushed his chair away from the table, cocked his head to one side, stared at Barry—and began to laugh, great throaty rumbles.

Barry looked expectantly into O'Reilly's face. His nose tip had returned to its usually florid state. The laugh lines at the corners of the big man's eyes had deepened.

"Yes, Doctor Barry Laverty, I was serious. Of course I was bloody well serious. I'd like you to stay."

"Thank you."

"Don't thank me. Thank yourself. I'd not have made you the offer if I didn't think you were fitting in here in Ballybucklebo, and if the customers hadn't taken a shine to you."

Barry smiled.

"You just keep it up. You hear me?"

"I do."

O'Reilly stood and started to walk round the table until he stood over Barry. O'Reilly stretched out his right hand. "If we were a couple of horse traders we'd spit on our hands before we sealed the contract, but I think maybe a couple of GPs should forgo that in favour of a simple handshake."

Barry rose and accepted O'Reilly's clasp, relieved to find it wasn't the man's usual knuckle-crushing version of a handshake. "Thanks, Fingal," he said. "Thanks a lot and I will try to—"

"I'm sure you will," said O'Reilly, releasing Barry's hand, "but all this serious conversation has me famished, and I'm like a bull with a headache until I get my breakfast. Where the hell's Kinky?" He turned and started to amble back to his chair.

Barry heard a loud rumbling from O'Reilly's stomach. He did not say, "Excuse me." Barry had learned that the man never apologized; indeed his confession of being short-tempered in the morning was the closest Barry knew O'Reilly would get to expressing regret for having roared at Barry moments earlier. The man rarely explained himself and seemed to live entirely by his own set of rules, the first being "Never, never, *never* let the patients get the upper hand."

Barry heard a noise behind him and turned to see Mrs. Kincaid standing in the doorway. He hadn't heard her coming. For a woman of her size she was light on her feet.

"You're ready now for your breakfast, are you, Doctors?" she said, moving into the room, setting a tray on the sideboard, lifting plates, and putting one before O'Reilly and one in front of Barry. "I didn't want to interrupt. I know you're discussing important things, so." Her eyes twinkled and she winked at Barry. "But you get carried away sometimes, don't you, Doctor O'Reilly dear? I hear that kind of thing is very bad for the blood pressure."

"Get away with you, Kinky." O'Reilly was grinning at her, but with the kind of look a small boy might give his mother when he knew he'd been caught out in some peccadillo.

Barry turned his attention to his breakfast. On his plate two rashers of Belfast bacon kept an orange-yolked egg company. Half a fried tomato perched on a crisp triangle of soda farl. A pork sausage, two rings of black pudding, and one of white topped off the repast. He felt himself salivate as the steam rising from the platter tickled his nostrils. If professional reasons weren't enough to keep him here, Mrs. Kincaid's cooking certainly tipped the scales. "Thanks, Kinky," he said. "When I get through this, I'll be ready to go and call the cows home."

He saw her smile. "Eat up however little much is in it, and leave the cows to the farmers, so." She turned to go, her silver chignon catching the sun's rays as they slipped through the room's bay window to sparkle in her hair and plant diamonds in the cut-glass decanters on the sideboard.

"Thanks, Kinky," said O'Reilly, tucking a linen napkin into his shirt-neck. He waved his fork. "Begod I could eat a horse, a bloody Clydesdale, saddle and all." He shoved most of one rasher into his mouth.

Barry swallowed a small piece of tomato.

O'Reilly speared a piece of black pudding and chewed with what appeared to be the enthusiasm of a famished crocodile feeding on a fat springbok. "I can't face the day without my breakfast. Once I get this into me, I'll be a new man."

As Barry sliced his bacon he heard the front doorbell, Kinky's footsteps, and a man's voice. Kinky reappeared in the dining room. "It's Archibald Auchinleck, the milkman."

"On a Sunday morning?" O'Reilly growled through a mouthful of soda farl.

"He says he's sorry, but—"

"All right," O'Reilly growled, ripping the napkin from his throat. "Between you making breakfast late with your questions and the patients interrupting it," he said, eyeing Barry, "I'll die of starvation." He stood and walked down past the table. Mrs. Kincaid moved up the other side. The pair of them look like partners in a slip jig, Barry thought.

"I'll pop this back in the oven. Keep it warm, so." She lifted O'Reilly's plate.

Barry nodded and returned to his meal. Suddenly a roar shattered the morning.

"Do you know what bloody day it is, Archibald Auchinleck, you pathetic, primitive, primate? *Do you?*" O'Reilly's shout made Barry's teacup rattle. "Answer me, you pitiful, pinheaded parasite."

Barry was glad he wasn't on the receiving end. He strained but couldn't hear the milkman's reply.

A line echoed in Barry's head. *Never, never, never let the patients . . .*

"Sunday. Well done. Pure genius. You should get a Nobel Prize for knowing that. Not Monday. Not Friday. *Sunday.* Now I know what it means in the good book, in Genesis chapter one, verse twenty-five, that on the fifth day God made "every thing that creepeth upon the earth. Relatives of yours, no doubt, Archibald Auchinleck. But what . . . what does it say in chapter two, verse two, about the seventh day? Tell me that."

Muted mumbling came from across the hall.

O'Reilly continued his rant. "It says, and please correct me if I'm wrong, 'And on the seventh day God ended his work . . . and He rested.' And what did he do?"

Barry could just make out the reply: "And he rested, sir."

Never, never, never let the patients

Barry could hear O'Reilly resuming his diatribe. "Yes, he rested. *He bloody well rested.* Now tell me, Archibald Auchinleck, if the Good Lord could put his feet up on the Sabbath, why in the hell can't I? What in the name of Jesus H. Christ possessed you to come to annoy me today, Sunday, with a simple backache you've had for bloody *weeks?*"

. . . get the upper hand. It might be O'Reilly's first law of practice, Barry thought, grinning widely, but the corollary, the first law to be obeyed by O'Reilly's patients, was "Pokest thou not a rabid bull mastiff in the eye with a blunt stick."

O'Reilly's voice dropped in volume and seemed more placatory. "All right, Archie. All right. Enough said. I know you only get Sundays off from your milk round. It's probably all the stooping and bending to deliver the bottles that's giving you gyp, and having a boy in the British army must be a worry. Tell me about your back, and I'll see what I can do for you."

Barry mopped up some egg yolk with a piece of soda farl. That was O'Reilly in a nutshell, he thought. A temper and a tendency to erupt like a grumbling volcano, wedded to an encyclopaedic knowledge of his patients and a sense of obligation to them that made the oath of Hippocrates sound as trite as a Christmas-cracker motto.

Barry pushed his plate away, stood, and looked out through the bow window. It was a beautiful day, and as O'Reilly had said he could have today off, he was free from any responsibility to the practice.

He intended to enjoy his freedom to the full. Tomorrow would mark the start of his assistantship to Doctor Fingal Flahertie O'Reilly.

2

Full Many a Glorious Morning Have I Seen

A grumbling O'Reilly was back in the dining room finishing his reheated breakfast. Archibald Auchinleck, milkman by trade, had left clutching a prescription, still full of profuse apologies for having disturbed the great man on the Sabbath.

Kinky adjusted her Sunday-best hat in front of the hall mirror before leaving to attend morning service in the Presbyterian church across the road from O'Reilly's house. "It'll be grand with the new minister. I heard his sermon last week, and you could feel the spits of him six pews back."

"Maybe you should take your umbrella for a bit of waterproofing?"

"Go on with you, Doctor Laverty. Wouldn't I look the right eejit in church with a brolly?" Kinky giggled.

The image conjured up made Barry chuckle. "Enjoy yourself, Kinky," he said. "You deserve a little entertainment after cooking such a champion breakfast as that." Sitting through an interminable sermon dodging spittle was not his idea of a cheerful way to spend a glorious Sunday morning.

"Entertainment, is it?" said Kinky, drawing herself up as if to engage him in combat, but then she sighed. "You young people. You think everything should be like those Beatles nowadays. Sometimes I think they must believe they're more popular than Jesus himself. It's a disgrace, so."

Kinky readjusted her hat and swept out the door.

"You're right, Kinky," Barry called after her, hoping he hadn't offended her. He was sure he hadn't. Any woman who could stay on as housekeeper with Doctor Fingal Flahertie O'Reilly since shortly after the Second World War would be hard to offend. Nevertheless, a wise man would do well to keep her on his side. He'd think of a way to make it up to her, just in case.

But not now. He had other plans.

He'd not be spending the day exactly as he'd hoped, but as O'Reilly was fond of telling patients, "What can't be cured must be endured." Barry wondered if Fingal knew the quote came from Robert Burton, a morose English vicar who'd penned a seventeenth-century book with the priceless title of *The Anatomy of Melancholy*. He probably did. Not much got past O'Reilly.

Barry had other plans, but they didn't include Patricia Spence, the shining girl he'd met by chance last month on a train journey to Belfast. The twenty-one-year-old civil engineering student who had burst into his cosmos as brightly as a supernova. The young woman who was so committed to her studies she'd told him ten days ago she wasn't ready to fall in love. He hadn't seen her since then, but yesterday afternoon she'd miraculously shown up unannounced at the Galvins' going-away party. She'd cooked him dinner last night in her flat. He could still remember the taste of their good-night kisses. And the taste of the lasagna. For an engineer, she wasn't a bad cook at all.

But today Patricia was off visiting her parents in Newry, about forty miles south of Belfast. She had promised to phone him soon. He'd have to lie content with that promise, although he was aching to tell her about his prospects here in Ballybucklebo.

It was a beautiful day, he thought, so why not get out and enjoy it? He hadn't had time for a walk in weeks, and the exercise would do him good.

He stuck his head into the dining room. "I'm nipping out for a while, Fingal."

"You're what?"

"Nipping out. You said . . . you said yesterday I could have today off."

"Jesus. Half an hour ago you said you knew you'd have to satisfy me that you were worth taking on as a partner. The practice isn't a Butlins Holiday Camp."

Barry muttered to himself, "The way you're going on today, O'Reilly, it's sounding more like a forced labour camp."

"What?"

"Nothing." Barry took a deep breath. "Do you not want me to go?"

He saw O'Reilly shake his head. "It's all right. I didn't mean to spoil your day off. I was just thinking about Archie Auchinleck."

"With the sore back?"

"That's what he says."

Barry stepped through the doorway, interested in spite of himself. "Do you think he's swinging the lead?"

O'Reilly shook his big head. "Not Archie. He's not missed a day on his milk round for God knows how many years."

"Then what is it?"

"His boy." O'Reilly looked up from the plate. "He's only got the one, and he joined the British army."

Barry remembered seeing something on television about some British troops with a United Nations peacekeeping force. "He's not in Cyprus, is he?"

O'Reilly nodded. " 'Fraid so. And the Turks or the Greeks or some other silly buggers have been shooting at them. Poor old Archie's worried sick." O'Reilly rose. "I shouldn't have yelled at him. There's not a bloody thing us doctors can do until his boy gets back home. It's frustrating as hell."

And, Barry thought, you get angry when you get frustrated, don't you, Fingal?

"Go on with you then. Make the most of your time. Pity it's a Sunday."

"Why?"

"Any other day you could get a haircut."

"But I don't need one."

"You will soon. I'll be working you so hard from now on you're not going to have time."

Barry saw the laugh lines deepen at the corners of O'Reilly's eyes and knew it was a hollow threat, although if the patients kept coming the way they had in the last month there would be plenty of work to do— and he was looking forward to it. "Sure when it's down over my collar you can tell the customers I'm trying to get a job with the Beatles."

O'Reilly laughed. "Look, if you're going to do a job, do it right. Really let it go. You can try to join the Rolling Stones. I saw them on the news. They looked like a bunch of perambulating haystacks."

"I've never heard of them."

"I think you're going to," said O'Reilly. "They make an interesting sound."

Barry watched as O'Reilly peeled an orange and somehow managed to keep the rind intact in one long, continuous spiral. "I'll take your word for it."

"Do, and you can take my word for something else." O'Reilly grinned. "I promised you today off, so away off and enjoy yourself."

"Thanks, Fingal."

Barry let himself out through the front door and started to walk along Ballybucklebo's Main Street. Across the road he could see the doors to the Presbyterian church standing open, the black-robed minister on the steps welcoming his flock.

The August sun had climbed over the crest of the Ballybucklebo Hills and shone down from the sky, blue as a robin's egg. The listing steeple of the church opposite cast an asymmetrical shadow over the yew trees and headstones in the little churchyard.

Barry watched people hurrying along Main Street towards the church, men in black suits, women in summer frocks and hats and white gloves, children neat and clean. As he remembered from being taken to church every Sunday in Bangor as a boy, they were going for their weekly dose of hellfire and brimstone. The Presbyterians could be stern. John Calvin and John Knox and that lot. They didn't put up with any nonsense.

Barry recognized some of the worshipers. Julie MacAteer with her long blonde hair swinging under a little straw hat, the young woman from Rasharkin, County Antrim, who'd moved here recently. She smiled at him. "Morning, Doctor."

"Morning, Julie."

Maggie MacCorkle, who'd first presented with a complaint of headaches—two inches above the crown of her head—wore an outlandish hat. Barry had to stare because every day she put different flowers in the hatband. Two maroon antirrhinums today. "Morning, Doctor Laverty."

"Morning, Maggie. And how are you today?"

"I've a toty-wee headache," she said, motioning to a spot exactly two inches above her head. "But it's nothing for you to worry about, Doctor."

"And Sonny?" he said, making a mental note not to ask patients how they were on his day off. Sonny was in the Bangor convalescent home recovering from pneumonia.

Maggie grinned her toothless grin. "The old goat's on the mend now, thanks, Doctor. I'll be getting him home any day." Both in their sixties, Sonny and Maggie were to be married soon.

"I'm pleased to hear it. Give him my regards when you see him again."

"I will."

"And say hello to the General." General Sir Bernard Law Montgomery, Maggie's one-eyed, tattered-eared cat who, being an Ulsterman like his famous military namesake, enjoyed a good scrap and bore the scars to prove it.

Barry smiled. Knowing these people, not just their names or their diseases but about their lives, and having them greet him as a friend warmed him as much as the morning sun.

He was in no hurry as he strolled on, listening to the sounds of the village.

Blackbirds were singing in the churchyard yews. A song thrush's treble voice, repeating each note twice, soared above the lower registers. Pairs of collared doves perched on the telephone wires and cooed their love. The birds' songs had to compete with the faint pealing of church bells coming from the steeple of the Catholic chapel at the other end of Main Street.

Barry saw a couple approaching. The man, black-suited and

bowler-hatted, was short and rotund. He stamped along, accompanied by an equally dumpy woman wearing a floral dress. He was scowling, and she was clearly out of breath trying to keep up with his hurried pace. "For Christ sake, Flo, get a move on."

Councillor and Mrs. Florence Bishop, the wealthiest couple in Ballybucklebo. Barry hadn't met Mrs. Bishop before, but as he knew from his dealings with the councillor, Bishop was the most grasping, conniving weasel in the Six Counties.

"Morning, Councillor. Morning, Mrs. Bishop."

Barry was rewarded with a weak smile and a "Morning, Doctor" from the missus and a growl from the councillor. Well, he thought, O'Reilly was right. Not all your patients are going to love you, and Councillor Bertie Bishop had good reasons for disliking his medical advisors. Until last week he might have thought he was the craftiest man in the village. He wasn't the first and he certainly wouldn't be the last man to underestimate how wily O'Reilly could be.

Barry turned the corner and passed between whitewashed rows of single-storey cottages on either side of Main Street. Some were thatched, some had slate roofs, and the little buildings, one attached to the other, jostled together like a group of neighbours lining the thoroughfare to await a parade.

He reached the central crossroads in the middle of the village where the permanent maypole, painted in red, white, and blue spirals, leant companionably beside Ballybucklebo's only traffic light. A horse and cart on rubber-tired wheels waited patiently for the green light. The roan mare's eyes were well protected from the glare by a pair of leather blinkers and a straw hat with holes cut for her ears. She nibbled from a feedbag, lifted her tail, and dropped a pile of horse apples to steam on the tarmac.

"Morning, Doctor Laverty," said the driver, a man Barry did not recognize. "Grand day."

"Indeed it is," said Barry, pleased to be recognized by a stranger. "Indeed it is."

He crossed the street. The breeze that bore the scent of salty seaweed from Belfast Lough made the hanging sign of the nearby public house, the Black Swan, known to the locals as the Mucky Duck, sway. Its hinges creaked rustily.

As he walked under the single-arch railway bridge, he heard the Bangor-bound train rattling overhead, smelled the diesel fumes. He'd ridden that train daily from his home to Queens University in Belfast when he was a student. He'd met Patricia Spence on it, purely by chance, when he made a trip up to Belfast a month earlier. He had reason to regard the thing with affection, just like the locals who said it was mentioned in the book of Genesis. They used the very same verse O'Reilly had quoted that morning: "And God made . . . every thing that creepeth."

The train was slow, right enough, but didn't that fit in with the pace of life in a place like Ballybucklebo? Rural, sleepy, and at peace with itself? A village that seemed divorced from the internecine hatred that flowed under the surface of much of the rest of Ulster.

Barry started to climb a low dune that separated Shore Road from the foreshore. He knew that in the winter when the great northeasterlies raged it was only the dunes that kept the waters of the lough from tearing at the houses behind.

He picked up a pebble and chucked it across a narrow beach into the water.

Of course, he didn't need to worry about sectarian strife here. O'Reilly had assured Barry of that and as proof had offered evidence. Seamus Galvin, a Catholic, was the pipe major of the Ballybucklebo Highlanders pipe band. Barry had seen the band in the recent Twelfth of July Orange parade, and neither Seamus nor the Orange lodges had seemed to object. The local Catholic priest and the Presbyterian minister played golf together every Monday. Barry wondered if other golfers could feel the spits of the minister some distance up the fairways.

The image made him laugh to himself, made him grateful that O'Reilly was giving him the opportunity to settle here where the Orange and the Green simply didn't seem to matter.

He lengthened his stride and followed the crest of the dunes, sorry that Patricia wasn't with him to stroll among the marram grasses and clumps of sand seawort. He decided he'd walk for an hour, then head back to O'Reilly's for lunch. No, he corrected himself. He'd have to start thinking of the greystone house at Number 1 Main Street as his house too. In a year, "Dr. Barry Laverty, M.B., B.Ch., B.A.O., Physician and Surgeon" would, he hoped, be inscribed on another brass plaque beside the front door.

"Grand day," the stranger on the cart had said. Barry danced a little jig. By God, it was. This *was* his home. He felt completely at home here in rural Ballybucklebo, much more so than he had ever done during his student days in bustling Belfast. He was going to hear from Patricia soon, and most important, Barry had decided the direction his career should take.

He heard a mewling overhead, stopped, and looked up to see gulls soaring down the wind, wings rigidly outstretched. Now that he was committed to an assistantship, he looked forward to stretching his own professional wings. O'Reilly was bound to see that and give Barry more independence because . . . because in just one year he was going to be a full partner here in Ballybucklebo.

Perhaps, he thought, half an hour more would be enough before he headed back, because he was really looking forward to his lunch and the prospect of a lazy afternoon. Unless, of course, as was often the way here, something unexpected cropped up.

3

The Unkindest Cut of All

Barry sat in O'Reilly's upstairs lounge, his feet up on a footstool and another of Kinky's fine meals in his stomach. He'd almost finished the *Sunday Times* cryptic crossword. He wondered when O'Reilly would be back. The pair of them had almost collided as Barry came in through the front door and O'Reilly rushed out, muttering about "bad pennies turning up again" and cursing the bad pennies because visiting them was going to make him late for his second meal of the day.

Ah, Barry thought, the joys of rural practice—and the pleasure for once of not having to respond to an emergency, particularly if it involved one of O'Reilly's problem patients. Barry wondered briefly who it could be, then turned his attention back to his puzzle.

He frowned at the clue for twelve across: "Ran amok in prison causing great loss of life (7)." His concentration was not being helped by the attentions of Lady Macbeth, O'Reilly's pure white cat, who, perched in Barry's lap, kept dabbing with one paw at the end of his pencil.

Barry stared at the grid. By solving some of the down clues, he now had three letters, c–n–e, but he'd be damned if he could understand what the poser of the puzzle was after. That was the trouble with the things: somehow you had to get inside the mind of whoever had set them. It was like trying to do the same with Doctor Fingal Flahertie O'Reilly.

"Ran amok in prison . . . ? Ran . . . ?"

The front doorbell rang. Barry heard Kinky answer the door, and from downstairs came the sounds of her voice and a child's sobs. Barry shoved a complaining cat to the floor, rose, and headed downstairs.

Kinky met him in the hall. "It's little Colin Brown and his mammy. The wee *muirnin*—that's darlin' to you, Doctor dear—the wee dote's cut his hand, so. Mrs. Brown says she's stopped the bleeding, so I've put them in the surgery to wait for himself to come back. I told them you were on your day off."

The unexpected had happened. "I'll see to them," he said, knowing that was precisely what O'Reilly would have done, and headed for the surgery at a trot.

Mrs. Brown, wearing her Sunday hat and coat, knelt in front of O'Reilly's old rolltop desk, trying to comfort her six-year-old son. Barry recognized the little boy, Colin. Yesterday he'd been happily playing in O'Reilly's garden, howling with laughter. Today his howls were accompanied by tears, and runnels of snot from both nostrils. His right hand was wrapped in a bloodstained tea towel.

Barry knelt beside the mother. "What happened?"

"I'm not sure," she said. "I think he was playing with one of Derek's tools. The poor wee lad came running in from the toolshed bleeding all over the place, so I wrapped his hand," she nodded at the tea towel, "and brung him right here, so I did."

"All right," said Barry, turning to the boy, "can I have a look-see, Colin?"

The little boy hunched his shoulders, cocked his head to one side, and held his wounded hand close to his chest. "No." He sniffled and glanced up at his mother. "My mammy says you don't have to. My mammy says—"

"Maybe Mammy could help?" Barry waited.

Mrs. Brown moved closer. "Come on, Colin. The nice doctor's going to make it better, so he is. He's not going to hurt you."

Barry wished her last remark could be true, but judging by the amount of blood on the towel the cut was deep and was going to need stitches. He was always torn when working with children, hated the fact they couldn't understand why he was hurting them.

Colin wiped his upper lip with the sleeve of his shirt and then held his hand to his mother. Seeing the trust in the child's eyes cut into Barry as deeply as the tool must have sliced into the little hand. "It's sore," Colin whimpered.

Mrs. Brown made gentle shushing noises and slowly unwrapped the tea towel. "Go on," she said, "show it to the nice doctor man."

Colin held his hand palm up to Barry. He could see little but blood. "I think," Barry said, "I'll have to give it a clean." He stood and moved across the room to stand beside the examining couch where it was tucked against the green-painted wall. "I'm going to ask your mammy to bring you over here. Okay, Colin?"

Barry waited until Mrs. Brown had led the lad over and lifted him onto the couch. At least, Barry thought, the poor wee fellow has stopped crying. He pushed an instrument trolley beside the table. A presterilized pack lay to one side of the green-towelled top. "Can you put your hand on there, Colin?" He waited until the boy stretched out his arm. "Good boy."   ·

Barry opened the outer wrapping of the pack. Inside, a sterile hand towel and a pair of rubber gloves lay beside a roll of instruments and two shining steel gallipots. He lifted a bottle of saline from the trolley's lower shelf, unscrewed the cap, and poured some into one metal cup. Dettol next. The fluid splashed into the second gallipot. He was going to have to wash the wound with the disinfectant but shuddered to think of how the solution would sting and burn—unless . . . yes. It might work.

"I'm just going to wash my hands," he said, moving to the sink and turning on the taps. As he scrubbed he could sense the boy's eyes boring into his back.

Barry heard footsteps behind and turned to see O'Reilly standing watching. The man looked flushed and frown lines creased his forehead, but he gave Barry a reassuring nod. "I just got back. You carry on."

Barry turned back to finish scrubbing. He was disappointed to have O'Reilly here, supervising as if Barry were still a student. Still, he was going to need some assistance. If nothing else, Barry's being here, working, should show O'Reilly that despite his crack earlier, young

Doctor Laverty was well aware that he wasn't at one of Billy Butlins Holiday Camps.

Barry returned to the trolley, dried his hands, and slipped on the rubber gloves. "Now," he said, unwrapping the pack and removing balls of cotton wool and a pair of forceps, "let's get this cleaned." He grasped the cotton wool in the forceps, soaked it in the saline solution, and gently sponged the palm of the boy's hand. It was going to need stitches. The wound, two inches long, ran diagonally across the palm from the web between the thumb and first finger towards the boy's wrist.

Barry turned to O'Reilly. "I need a hand." Barry made a rapid motion with his right wrist, showing O'Reilly in dumb play the action that would be needed to place a suture.

O'Reilly nodded. "Local?"

"Please."

Barry stood so his body blocked Colin's view of the hypodermic. He drew back the plunger, drawing air into the barrel.

"Here," said O'Reilly. He held a bottle of Xylocaine in one hand, wiped its rubber top with a swab soaked in methylated spirit, inverted the bottle, and waited as Barry thrust the needle through the rubber cap and injected air. The pressure forced the local anaesthetic out of the bottle and into the syringe. Barry set the hypodermic on the sterile towel.

Barry held out a small metal cup. "Could you pour a bit of local in there?" This was the technique that moments earlier he had hoped might work.

Barry saw O'Reilly's brows knit as he poured. He'd bet the older man hadn't seen this trick. Barry'd learnt it a year before from a senior registrar in the Casualty Department. Not speaking, he lifted the cup, turned, and poured a trickle of the solution directly into the wound.

Colin whimpered and tried to pull his hand away, but his mother had taken a firm grip on the boy's forearm. "It'll only be a wee minute, son. Only a wee minute more."

"I'll be damned," said O'Reilly. "I wonder why we didn't think of that. I suppose the local's absorbed directly?"

"Aye, and the wee one won't feel the Dettol or the . . . ," Barry mouthed the word "needle."

"Weird and wonderful are the workings of a wheelbarrow," said O'Reilly, with a vast grin. "Do you know," he remarked, turning to Mrs. Brown, "it's a grand day for Ballybucklebo since Doctor Laverty came."

Barry felt himself blush. "Now, Colin," he said, hoping he'd let enough time elapse for the local to have done its job. "I'm going to paint the cut brown."

Barry used forceps to soak a cotton-wool ball in Dettol. He hesitated, then dabbed experimentally, steeling himself for a shriek. Dettol in an open wound usually burned like the blazes. Not a squeak. The local was working. He swabbed the cut liberally with antiseptic, the brown stain shining in the light from the window.

"Now, Colin, your mammy's going to keep holding on." Barry dropped the forceps on the table and, still blocking the child's view, lifted the syringe. He used forceps to lift one lip of the wound, exposing the yellow fat under the dermis, the red strands of muscle below. There was some blood in the wound—that was to be expected—but no severed artery pumped and spurted. Good.

"You may feel me pushing a bit, Colin." Barry drove the needle in under the fat at one end of the wound and steadily advanced its tip until it was close to the other end. Then he slowly withdrew it, squeezing on the plunger as he did. The edge swelled and blanched as the local anaesthetic solution was forced into the tissues. He pulled out the needle. Now for the other side.

"Right," he said when he'd finished. "We'll give that a minute or two to work."

Barry dragged the back of one forearm across his brow. It was warm in the surgery and he'd started to sweat, but he wasn't perspiring simply because of the heat.

"You all right, Colin?" Barry asked

"Yes, sir." He'd stopped crying.

Barry smiled at the boy's mother and was gratified when she smiled back. "Right," he said, loading a curved needle, to which was attached a black silk suture, into the jaws of a needle holder. The instrument was like a pair of scissors but with short, deep, blunt-nosed jaws, which could be locked by a ratchet between the handles.

He lifted one wound edge with forceps and used the needle holder to push the suture through all the layers until he could see the tip shining in the depths of the wound. Then he transferred the forceps to the other lip, lifted it, and with the same wrist-twisting action he'd used to show O'Reilly the boy needed stitches, flicked the needle through the tissue. When its sharp tip appeared above the skin, he grabbed it with the forceps and pulled it through.

Now there was a length of black silk suture through the wound. Barry grabbed the loose end with the forceps and wound a loop round the tip of the needle holder. Then he used the forceps to place the end of the silk in the jaws of the needle holder, closed them, and pulled it and the silk through the loop. Gentle traction on both ends of the silk tightened the first throw of the knot. He repeated the process. A tight reef knot lay over the wound, and the lower part was snugly shut. He used a pair of scissors to clip the ends short, but not too short—the stitches would have to be removed in a few days, and there had to be enough of each stitch left to lift it so the loop could be cut. "Nearly done," he said.

In less than five minutes Barry had placed four neat stitches, the wound was shut, and there was no more bleeding. "Finished." He dropped the instruments and smiled at Colin.

"I never felt nothin'," the wee lad said, eyes wide as he stared at his hand. "Wait 'til I tell Jimmy Hanrahan and them others at Sunday school this afternoon that I got stitches."

Barry could hear the pride in the boy's voice, knew how his injury was going to put up his stock with the other boys, and marvelled at the resilience of children.

"Thanks very much indeed, Doctor Laverty sir; and you on your day off too." Mrs. Brown tutted. "We don't want to keep you. We'll be running along, so we will."

Barry smiled. "Not so fast. I have to dress it." He rummaged under the trolley for a box of Elastoplast adhesive strips, selected one, and stuck it over the wound. "You might want to give Colin an aspirin every six hours for the next couple of days. It's going to sting a bit when the local wears off."

The mother nodded sagely. "I will, so I will."

"Bring him back on Friday to have the stitches out." Barry pushed the trolley over to the sink and started putting in the dirty instruments.

"Friday? Right enough, we'll be here, won't we, Colin?"

"Yes, Mammy. Can I get down now?"

Barry heard the gentle thump of the boy's feet hitting the floor.

"Say thank-you to the nice doctor, Colin."

"Thank you, Doctor Laverty," the boy piped. "Do you know what? When I grow up, I'm going to be a doctor too."

"Away on with you," Barry said, grinning from ear to ear, knowing it wasn't only the thirty-five pounds a week O'Reilly paid him that made him want to stay in Ballybucklebo. "And don't cut yourself again."

As soon as Mrs. Brown and Colin left, Barry turned to O'Reilly, half expecting him to say it had been a neatly done job, but the big man's face was expressionless. Why, Barry asked himself, should I be looking for praise for a routine job? If I'm going to take my share of the work, stitching up a cut is no more than I'll be expected to do. O'Reilly's lack of comment pleased Barry.

He finished tidying up, dropping the soiled cotton-wool swabs in a pedal-operated Sani Bin.

O'Reilly had parked himself in his office chair and turned to look out the window. "Leave the rest for Kinky," he said, rising. "I need to have a word with you, Barry." There was an edge in O'Reilly's voice. "Let's go up to the lounge."

Barry felt a sinking feeling in his stomach and turned towards the door. "What about?"

"The emergency I'd to go to." There wasn't the faintest glimmer of a smile on O'Reilly's face.

Had it been someone Barry had seen recently? Had he made a mistake? Before he had time to ask, he heard O'Reilly's growl, then realized it wasn't directed at him.

"What the hell are you doing here, Donal Donnelly, and how did you get in without ringing the doorbell?"

4

A Horse of a Different Colour

Barry turned to see Donal Donnelly, a gangly youth with a shock of carrot red hair and buckteeth, filling the surgery door frame. He was obviously dumbstruck by O'Reilly. He held his cloth cap in both hands. Barry knew that he was the betrothed of Julie MacAteer, and a good thing too. Julie was pregnant, and Donal, the father-to-be, was soon going to make an honest woman of her. Pregnancy out of wedlock was more than frowned upon in some circles in rural Ulster in 1964.

"I'm waiting, but I'm not waiting much longer, Donal Donnelly," O'Reilly bellowed.

Donal swallowed. "I'm sorry, Doctor. I'm not sick nor nothing. I just came to ask a wee question. I slipped in when Mrs. Brown was going out."

"Well, you can bloody well slip out again. I've not had my lunch, and I've important things to discuss with Doctor Laverty."

Barry felt O'Reilly brush past. Look out, rosebushes, he thought. If Donal wasn't careful, he'd be on his way into them just like Seamus Galvin. Watching O'Reilly hurl Seamus out bodily had been Barry's introduction to his senior colleague. He wished Donal would go away. Barry didn't want O'Reilly to be made angry. Not now. Not when he'd something—God alone knew what—to discuss.

"I'm not sick, sir," Donal squeaked. He took a step backwards, holding his cap in front of him. "I've come about a racehorse." His tones rose a full octave. "I could make a few bob for Julie and the baby."

O'Reilly halted. "A horse?" Barry heard an interested edge in his voice. "A horse is it? Which horse?"

"Arkle, sir," Donal whispered.

Barry had vaguely heard of the animal. He paid little attention to the world of horse racing. He knew Donal had a racing greyhound called Bluebird. O'Reilly had won four hundred pounds betting on her, but what did Donal have to do with a racehorse?

"Arkle? Away off and feel your head, Donal. You might be able to rig a race with a dog, but you'll have as much chance of getting near Himself as you would trying to whistle and chew meat."

"Excuse me," Barry said. "Excuse me. Who's Himself?"

He was surprised when both Donal and O'Reilly laughed. O'Reilly explained. "Arkle's a steeplechaser, the best animal ever to come out of Ireland. He's owned by Anne, duchess of Westminster. He's so well known in this country that we just refer to him as Himself."

Now Barry understood. "Isn't that the horse that won the Cheltenham Gold Cup on Paddy's Day this year?"

"Aye," said Donal, "and the Irish Grand National thirteen days later."

"All right, Donal," O'Reilly growled. "You've got my attention. What's this all about?"

"Can I come in, sir?"

O'Reilly stepped aside. Donal sidled into the surgery and shut the door behind him. He glanced round and lowered his voice. "I've a wee notion how to make a few quid with Arkle, so I have. For me and Julie, like."

"Go on."

Barry watched Donal rummage in his pants pocket. He produced a silver coin. "See that there, sir?" He handed it to O'Reilly. "That's a half crown from the Republic, so it is."

Barry knew the coins well. One side bore the image of a harp; the reverse showed the horse known as the Irish hunter.

"I reckon when I go to the races I could sell them to the English punters for a pound a piece, so I could."

O'Reilly laughed. "How in the blazes could you do that?"

Barry saw Donal's eyes narrow. "I'd tell them they'd pay two pounds for one in Dublin. Folks'll always bite if they think they're getting a bargain, and they love putting one over on a daft Ulsterman."

Certainly, Barry thought, and Donal would have no difficulty looking the part.

"But why would anyone pay twenty shillings for something that's only worth two shillings and sixpence?" O'Reilly demanded.

"Because, sir, the writing on the coins is in Irish. An Englishman couldn't read that, but he would see the horse." Barry saw Donal's skinny chest swell. "You see, sir, I'd tell them the florins were specially coined Arkle medallions. I've a pal at the Ulster Bank. He can get me fresh minted ones straight from the Bank of Ireland."

"You'd say they were what?" O'Reilly's eyebrows rose.

"Arkle medallions, sir."

Barry watched the big man's sides shake, his eyes water. "Oh, dear," he finally managed to gasp. "Oh, dear me." He rummaged in the pocket of his tweed pants, pulled out a handkerchief, took off his half-moons, and wiped his eyes. "That's bloody ingenious. That's nearly a five hundred percent markup, less the two and six face value of the half crown. You'd be making seventeen shillings and sixpence per sale. Oh dear, oh dear."

"Aye. I know that, sir, but what I don't know, and that's what I want to ask . . ."

O'Reilly was still chuckling. "Go on."

"Do you think it would be legal, sir?"

O'Reilly shoved his half-moon spectacles back on his nose and stared over them at Donal.

Barry asked, "Why are you asking us, Donal?"

Donal shuffled his feet. "You're the only ones I can trust to keep it a secret. You know what gossip's like here, sir."

Barry did indeed.

"And," Donal winked and held one finger beside his nose, "youse doctors have to keep anything a patient tells you in the surgery to yourselves. I know that, so I do, and amn't I a patient and amn't I in your surgery?"

"Indeed you are," said O'Reilly, with a glance at Barry.

"So, like I asked, would it be legal?"

O'Reilly shook his head. "Probably not, Donal . . ."

"Oh." Donal's shoulders sagged.

". . . but I'm damned if I know what you could be charged with if you got caught."

Donal straightened up, and Barry watched as a hint of a smile played on his lips. How could O'Reilly be so utterly irresponsible? He was as good as encouraging Donal to commit fraud. "Fingal," he said, "are you sure it's a good idea?"

"No," said O'Reilly, "but it has the makings of an amazing joke. I wish I'd thought of it." He turned to Donal and adopted a more serious tone. "Doctor Laverty's right, Donal. I can't encourage you to go ahead." Barry noticed how O'Reilly's left upper eyelid drooped in a slow wink.

"Thanks very much, sir," Donal said, smiling. "I'll be running along, so I will."

"Off you trot," said O'Reilly, "and close the front door after you."

"Och," said O'Reilly, head cocked to one side, smiling gently. "I wonder if I would do a thing like that to a poor unsuspecting Englishman?"

"I should hope not," Barry said, immediately recognizing how prim he must have sounded. "But I'm damn certain Donal'll be off like a whippet to the next race meeting to sell his memorial medallions."

"And why do you think that is?" There was a hint of seriousness in the question.

"Because Donal's moral compass is a bit out of line with magnetic north?"

"That," said O'Reilly, "is a given, but he's only a degree or two off. If he was a really bad *bashtoon*, he'd not have asked our say-so. He'd have simply up and done it. Why do you think he wanted our opinion?"

"I hadn't thought of that." Barry had earlier taken the query as a token of Donal Donnelly's trust but hesitated to say so. Somehow that might seem a bit conceited.

"Because Donal's a simple chap, but he respects learning. All the locals do." O'Reilly leant forward. "And I reckon he thinks he can trust you, and that, above all, is what you'll need to make a go of it here. I've watched you for the last month, and I'll tell you what I think . . ."

"Go on."

"You're well on your way, son." He smiled, a little sadly, Barry thought.

Barry felt as though he'd just been presented with a gold medal, perhaps even a specially minted Arkle medallion. "Thank you, Fingal," he said quietly.

"But you've a ways to go yet . . . I still need to have that word with you, Barry." The edge had returned to O'Reilly's voice.

Barry took a deep breath. The little bit of drama with Donal's scheme had temporarily made him forget. O'Reilly clearly hadn't.

"I've been out to see an old patient of ours. His wife phoned in a panic. She couldn't reach her own doctor . . . Doctor Bowman from the Kinnegar."

"The Fotheringhams?"

"I'm afraid so."

Major and Mrs. Fotheringham were a pair of aging Anglo-Irish gentry whose hypochondria had caused O'Reilly many a late-night emergency call.

Barry vividly remembered going alone to see the man when he was complaining of a stiff neck. Barry had been in a hurry to see Patricia, assumed the stiffness was yet another of Major Fotheringham's imagined ailments, and had rushed the examination.

"They're not our patients anymore," Barry said, immediately regretting it. O'Reilly would no more refuse to see anyone who was sick than the tide would refuse to flood. Still, Barry wished Fingal hadn't gone. Barry had failed to diagnose that Major Fotheringham was bleeding into his brain from a ruptured, thin-walled artery and was having a subarachnoid haemorrhage. The mistake had almost cost the man his life. No wonder the major and his wife had transferred to the care of another physician. He said, hoping it were true, "I suppose poor Mrs. Fotheringham was having another one of her attacks of the vapours."

"No," said O'Reilly, "she wasn't. Sit down, Barry." He indicated his swivel chair.

Barry sat looking up at O'Reilly and trying to read the expression on his face.

"She phoned to say she couldn't wake him up." O'Reilly paused. "When I got there, he was dead."

"He was *dead*?"

"As mutton. I'm sorry."

"Jesus Christ."

"Aye," said O'Reilly. "I think the pair of us need to have a chat about this . . . about what it's going to mean for you going on working here with me. You heard what Donal said about how rumours spread here."

Barry couldn't tell from O'Reilly's voice what that meant. Was he going to withdraw his offer? He hung his head and waited.

"Come on," said O'Reilly, "you could probably use a drink. I could, so we'll finish this upstairs." He turned and left.

Barry stood and followed, feeling like a fourth-form pupil at Campbell College, his old boarding school, a pupil who has been summoned to the headmaster's study for a caning.

For no apparent reason the answer to the crossword clue he hadn't been able to solve came to him with great clarity. "Ran amok in prison causing great loss of life"? The answer was "carnage."

5

Confidence Is a Plant of Slow Growth

"Here." O'Reilly handed Barry a half-full Waterford glass that, judging by the peaty smell, contained Irish whiskey. "Park yourself."

Barry took the glass, although he would have preferred a small sherry, and sat on the edge of an armchair in the upstairs lounge. Through the window he could see past the steeple and over the roofs to Belfast Lough. He sighed when he realized how much he was going to miss Ballybucklebo.

"Get to hell out of that." O'Reilly shooed the kitten from his usual chair and sat. She jumped onto the nearby coffee table. "*Slainte.*" He took a pull on his drink.

Barry hunched forwards, nursed his glass between both hands, and waited. O'Reilly fumbled for his pipe, filled it from a tobacco pouch, and took great care lighting it. Barry fidgeted in his chair. He recognized that this was O'Reilly's way of playing for time before he said something difficult.

O'Reilly exhaled a cloud of blue smoke and said, "So? What are we going to do about this?"

Barry saw tiny ripples in his whiskey. His hand trembled, so he set the glass on the coffee table. "I'm sorry."

"Aye, no doubt, but 'sorry' won't butter any parsnips."

Just get it over with, Barry thought. Tell me you've changed your mind about the offer. "It's my fault. If I'd sent the major to hospital sooner—"

"Jesus Christ," said O'Reilly. "*If*. If boars had tits they'd be sows.

What's done's done. There's no profit ploughing the same furrow twice." He stood. "I told you when it happened there was no point blaming yourself." O'Reilly moved closer and dropped a hand on Barry's shoulder.

"But—"

"No bloody 'buts.' In the first place, anyone could have missed the diagnosis, particularly in a man with the major's history of screaming for intensive care every time he had a runny nose. In the second, aneurysms hardly ever bleed again once they've been treated, unless the neurosurgeon made a bollocks of the surgery."

"I don't think that's very likely."

"You never know, and anyway, something else could have killed the man."

"I doubt it," Barry said. "How often does one patient have two lethal diseases at the same time?"

"True," said O'Reilly, looking Barry straight in the eye. "But we won't know that until after the postmortem."

"Postmortem?" Barry frowned. "Why a postmortem?"

"There'll have to be one." O'Reilly's gaze never wavered. "I couldn't sign a death certificate. I hadn't seen the man as a patient recently enough. You know the rules."

Barry did, but he was sure O'Reilly was wrong. Given the major's recent history of brain surgery, certainly the government department responsible for registering births and deaths would have had no trouble accepting O'Reilly's word if he had chosen to write, "Aneurysm of a cerebral artery." Had he withheld his signature so that the case would be referred to the Home Office? Was there a remote chance the statutory coroner's autopsy would turn up something to exonerate Barry? Not that it mattered. The damage was done, and not only to the Fotheringham family. If Barry stayed, O'Reilly's practice could lose patients—a lot of patients—once the word was out in the village. He took a deep breath and said levelly, "Doctor O'Reilly, perhaps . . . perhaps it's not such a good idea for me to stay here. Perhaps I should look elsewhere?"

"Aye," said O'Reilly, shaking his head. "Or you could borrow a carving knife from Kinky and commit seppuku while you're at it."

"Do what?"

"Hara-kiri. Ritually disembowel yourself like a disgraced Japanese samurai . . . and we agreed, it's Fingal, not Doctor O'Reilly." He took another drink. "Do you really want to leave?"

"Do I have any choice?" Barry glanced at O'Reilly and saw that the man's face was puce, his nose tip turning pallid, as he roared, *"Of course you have a bloody choice, Laverty."*

"You mean you'd keep me on?"

"Only if you want to stay." Colour was returning to O'Reilly's nose. "It's up to you."

Barry hesitated. He knew it was only a matter of time before tongues started to wag, before people who had been prepared to forgive him his youth and obvious lack of experience would refuse to see him. "Well, I—"

"Good," said O'Reilly. "That's settled then." He smiled at Barry. "You'll stay. We'll wait for the postmortem results; they could take a couple of weeks, and even if it was the bloody aneurysm, two weeks'll give you time to get your feet back under you."

Barry swallowed the little lump in his throat. "That's very generous of you, Fingal."

"Away off and feel your head . . ." Barry had learnt that to suggest openly that O'Reilly might be well motivated was something the big man could not bear. "Nothing generous about it. I'd be an eejit to let a man go who can put in stitches for wee Colin Brown the way you just did. That was a clever business, pouring the local directly into the wound. Strange as it might seem, medicine's changed since I graduated. Maybe, just maybe, I might learn a thing or two from you." O'Reilly sat and idly shoved the cat off the table. He handed Barry his glass and raised his own. *"Slainte."*

"Slainte mHath, Fingal." Barry sipped his neat whiskey, tasting the peat, feeling the warmth of it. "And thank you."

"Bollocks," said O'Reilly, but Barry could see the big man's grin. "Right. Now that's decided, we need a plan of attack."

The "we" pleased Barry.

"I think," O'Reilly said slowly. "I think we've a bit of rebuilding to do. The divil of it is you were getting yourself accepted here by the locals."

"I know."

"Ah, sure," said O'Reilly, "there was a while there when the Israelites gave up on Jehovah and put their bets on a golden calf—"

"Fingal, I'm hardly the Deity."

"No, you're not. Neither was Moses, and as soon as he turned his back the Israelites started having ideas of their own. It'll be the same here. Tongues are going to wag."

Barry felt his newfound pleasure at being asked to stay ebbing. "Do you think I'm up to it?"

"Come here," said O'Reilly, rising and heading for the door.

Barry followed him to the landing, where O'Reilly stood staring at a photograph of a dazzle-painted *dreadnought*. "Do you know what ship that is?"

"HMS *Warspite*. You and my dad served on her in the war."

"Right," said O'Reilly. "She was launched in 1913. Took a powerful battering at the battle of Jutland in the Kaiser's war, but . . ." He jabbed Barry with his pipe stem. "But she came back. The navy didn't write her off because she was badly wounded."

"Fingal, I'm not Jehovah, and I'm certainly not a battleship."

"No, but when I told you the major was dead, it hit you like a twelve-inch shell. You should have seen your face."

Barry let his head droop.

"You're wounded, but if you're half the man I think you are, Barry Laverty, you'll get over it, just like my old *Warspite*. When she was refitted, she came back as Admiral Cunningham's flagship in the Mediterranean in the Second World War. She was the most successful battleship in the British navy. You'd have been proud of her. Your dad and I were."

And Barry wanted the senior man to be proud of his assistant.

"So," said O'Reilly, "you're going to need a bit of repair work to get your confidence in yourself back. It'll take time."

"I know."

"And we'll have to get the customers back to trusting you."

"How?"

O'Reilly let go a blast of tobacco smoke. Barry thought he looked as his old ship must have when she vented her furnaces.

"Pianissimo, pianissimo," O'Reilly said. "Very, very softly. And damn it, it's going to slow things up."

"How?"

"I'd hoped to let you off the leash a bit." O'Reilly turned back to the lounge. "It's not very efficient having the pair of us working together all the time." He planted himself back in his armchair.

Barry followed.

"I'd hoped that now you know your way around, I'd be able to run the surgery while you were making home visits and vice versa."

"I'd been expecting it," Barry said, thinking of the free-flying gulls he'd seen that morning.

"Huh," said O'Reilly, "you shouldn't buy a dog and bark yourself, but I don't see we've any choice."

"So you can keep an eye on me? Be my Moses?"

"Not at all. I'm only fifty-six," O'Reilly said. "I'd not suit a long grey beard, and the only tablets I'm going to be handing out'll come from the chemist."

Barry smiled at the thought of O'Reilly in a long robe, solemnly pronouncing the Ten Commandments, and yet he recognized that in many ways that was exactly how O'Reilly behaved with his patients.

"If we stick together and the patients see that *I* trust you, it'll work wonders. You wait and see."

"I suppose," Barry said doubtfully. For six years as a student and one as a house officer, he'd always had someone more senior keeping an eye on him. He'd thought those days were over for good.

"Have you a better idea? Or should we ask Kinky for the carving knife right away?"

"No. I don't fancy seppuku. So . . . it'll be like my first month here?"

"That's right," said O'Reilly, pulling on his drink. "There's only the two of us, but we'll be like the Three Musketeers. 'All for one . . . ' "

" 'And one for all.' " Given O'Reilly's girth, Barry had no difficulty casting him as Porthos.

Barry moved to take his own seat, failing to notice that Lady Macbeth had fallen asleep near his chair. His foot landed on the tip of her tail. He was almost deafened by her screech, and he stood, mouth open, as a white blur shot across the room and up the curtains at what seemed to him a speed approaching that of light.

"Jesus," said O'Reilly, staring at where the cat perched on the pelmet, looking to Barry like a gargoyle on some mediaeval cathedral. "Would you come down out of that, Your Ladyship?"

The cat spat, and Barry wasn't sure if her vituperation was meant for him or O'Reilly. "Sorry, Lady Macbeth," he said.

"Push-wush," said O'Reilly coaxingly. "Pushy-wushy-wushy."

The cat hissed and flattened her ears. Barry thought he could see red lights flashing from her green eyes.

"Come down this instant, you *cat fiáin*." He set his glass on the table. "You what?"

"*Cat fiáin*. Wildcat," said O'Reilly, pushing a chair in beneath the curtains. "If you don't, I'll come up after you." He started to climb on the chair. "Will you steady me, Barry?"

Barry hesitated, watching O'Reilly standing on the chair, teetering as he reached up towards the cat. "Perhaps if you left her alone, she'd find her own way down?"

O'Reilly ignored the advice and made a grab for the animal. She bit his finger. He roared, the chair tottered, and he whirled his arms trying to regain his balance.

Barry set his drink down, strode forward, and grabbed O'Reilly's thighs, steadying the big man. "Hang on, Fingal." Barry peered up in time to see O'Reilly take the animal between both his hands and, after a short struggle to loosen her claws from the material, pull her to his chest. "Right," he said. "Got her. You can let go."

Barry stepped back out of range as O'Reilly jumped to the carpet, bent, and released the squirming animal. "Off you go, you." He sucked his bitten finger. "Only a love bite," he said.

"I think," said Barry, "you might have been better leaving her to come down on her own."

"Och, she's only young," said O'Reilly, reaching for his whiskey.

"Sometimes youngsters do need someone a bit older to help them out."

For a moment Barry wondered if O'Reilly was referring to kittens—or young doctors.

"Thanks for the hand with Her Ladyship. I couldn't have done it without you, Barry," O'Reilly remarked, studying his drink. "Here's to us," he said, finishing the whiskey.

Barry took a sip and nodded.

"So it all starts again tomorrow at nine, in the surgery. It's Monday and we're going to be busy."

Barry Laverty surprised himself by realizing that, despite the present crisis, he was looking forward to working in close harness with O'Reilly once more.

6

Reflections in a Golden Eye

"Salt-mine time for the pair of us," said O'Reilly, rising and dumping his napkin on the table.

Monday's breakfast was over. Barry had eaten little. Despite O'Reilly's reassurances the day before, he was nervous. He pushed his chair back.

O'Reilly strode through the open dining-room door. "Come on. Time, tide, and the weary, walking wounded wait for no man."

Barry followed. He heard a murmur of voices coming from the waiting room. By their volume he knew it was going to be a busy morning. At least some patients had shown up. He straightened his tie and went into the surgery.

O'Reilly had taken his customary place in the swivel chair, pulled out his half-moon glasses, and stuck them on the bridge of his bent nose. So, Barry thought, it was clear who was going to be in charge. Well, it was what they'd agreed on yesterday.

"Nip along, Barry . . ."

"I know, and see who's first." Why couldn't Kinky do it? He'd been anticipating working medically, not as a glorified receptionist. He walked along the hall and opened the waiting-room door. Every seat was taken. He recognized most of the patients. Julie MacAteer smiled at him. Usually there would be a chorus of "Good morning, Doctor Laverty." But apart from Julie's voice there was silence.

He swallowed. "Good morning," he said. "Who's first?"

A man he did not recognize stood. "Is himself in?"

"Of course."

"Right, then. I'm your man." The questioner, who looked to Barry to be about forty, was dressed in jodhpurs, a collarless shirt, and an old black waistcoat with a gold chain leading to the fob pocket. He was tiny—Barry reckoned about four foot nine—and had bowlegs. He sported a camel-hair cap and held one hand over his left eye.

"Come with me, please, Mr. . . . ?"

The patient did not give his name and did not remove his cap.

So that's the way it's going to be, Barry thought. I'll bet the hat comes off the minute he sees O'Reilly.

"Good morning, Doctor O'Reilly, sir," the man said, clutching his cap in his right hand.

"Morning, Fergus Finnegan. Sit down on a chair."

Barry hoisted himself onto the edge of the examining table and sat swinging his legs.

"Mr. Finnegan here's a jockey," O'Reilly remarked. Then he asked the now seated patient, "And what can we do for you today, Fergus?"

Barry heard the "we" again, just like last night. At least O'Reilly was trying to include him in the consultation.

"My eye feels like it's full of all the sand on Ballyholme beach. It's been like that for two days."

"Did you hurt it? Get anything in it? Horse dander maybe?" O'Reilly leant forward.

"No, sir."

"Right," said O'Reilly. "Let's have a look."

Finnegan took his hand away. "I can't look at the light. It hurts, so it does."

Barry stopped swinging his legs and listened. The man's symptoms suggested inflammation of the conjunctiva, the thin membrane that covers the front of the eyeball.

O'Reilly peered through his half-moons at the eye, sat back, and said to Barry, "Take a look at this, Doctor Laverty."

Barry slipped off the couch to stand beside O'Reilly. Finnegan's eye was flaming red. All the small blood vessels stood out. The inside edges of the eyelids were swollen and scarlet. The eyeball looked dry.

"What do you reckon?" O'Reilly asked.

"Acute bacterial conjunctivitis."

"It is *not*. It's pinkeye, so it is, and it's been hurting something chronic." Finnegan stared at Barry. "Acute conjunctivitis, my Aunt Fanny Jane." His good eye was wide. His infected one kept blinking. "I don't believe a word of it. What do *you* think it is, sir?"

"I don't think," said O'Reilly. "I don't have to. You're right, Fergus, but Doctor Laverty's right on the money too."

"Makes a change," Finnegan muttered.

Barry clenched his teeth. He might have suspected it from the way the patients in the waiting room had behaved towards him. Now he knew. He glanced at O'Reilly, who peered at Barry over his spectacles.

"Remember the *Warspite*," said O'Reilly quietly.

Barry took a deep breath. "There's a germ in your eye, Mr. Finnegan. It's infected."

"Are you absolutely certain?"

Barry came close to snapping, "Of course I'm bloody well certain!" O'Reilly would have, but instead he said calmly, "No, Mr. Finnegan. Nothing's absolutely certain in medicine, but . . . you're a horsey man?"

"Aye."

"I'd give a hundred to one on that I'm right."

Finnegan whistled. "I'd not like to bet against them odds, so I wouldn't. A hundred pounds down just to win one?"

"Nor," said O'Reilly, "would I. Have you not heard how smart Doctor Laverty is, Fergus?"

"I heard different," the man muttered.

Barry clenched his fists, tightened his lips.

"Did you now?" O'Reilly said calmly. "There's a thing. And do you believe everything you hear? Would you believe it if I told you there was a plague of frogs in Ballybucklebo last night?"

He's being Moses again, Barry thought.

Finnegan bowed his head. "No, Doctor."

"I'm glad to hear that," said O'Reilly. "Treatment, Doctor Laverty?"

"Penicillin ointment every two hours for the infection, dark glasses so the light won't hurt, and . . ." —Barry remembered how country patients put great faith in potions—one percent yellow mercuric oxide ointment." He knew it was only a weak antiseptic and would have little if any real effect. It was the penicillin that would clear up the infection. "The last stuff's called golden eye ointment," he said, stressing the word "golden." "It's an awful colour, but it's very strong. I'll write you a script."

"Boys-a-dear," said Finnegan. "Strong?"

"As a horse, Fergus," said O'Reilly with a tiny wink to Barry. "And speaking of horses, never mind Doctor Laverty's hundred to one on; I'll give you ten to one the eye'll be better by Friday."

"Ten to one? For a pound?" Finnegan scratched his chin, sucked air between his teeth, and said, "I'm your man, Doctor." He held out his hand, and O'Reilly shook it to seal the bet.

Barry handed the man the prescription. "Take that round to the chemist."

"Come back on Friday," O'Reilly said. "And Fergus, don't forget the pound note. Now just let yourself out, and close the door behind you."

Finnegan crammed his cap on and turned to leave.

"I beg your pardon?" said O'Reilly.

"I never said nothing, so I didn't."

"Strange. I could have sworn I heard you say, 'Thank you, Doctor Laverty.'"

"Aye. Thanks."

When the door was closed, O'Reilly rose, put a hand on Barry's shoulder, and grinned. "You done good, son, particularly with the golden ointment."

"Thanks, Fingal," Barry said. "And thanks for the support. But if all the patients are going to treat me like that, do you not think I was right last night?"

"About what?"

"About leaving." Barry's voice was flat.

"I don't know," O'Reilly said, "but you'd better be right about the penicillin. If he's got one of those new penicillin-resistant bugs, I'll be out ten quid on Friday."

You haven't answered my question, Barry thought, and if I am wrong about the treatment I'll have another black mark against me. He said, "I'll pay the ten pounds if that's all you're worried about."

"Indeed," said O'Reilly, as if he could not care less. He nodded his head towards the door. "Now be a good lad—"

"And nip along and see who's next." Barry left and walked to the waiting room. What was the point of staying here if all the patients were going to treat him with suspicion? "Next, please," he said, hardly paying attention to who it would be.

"That's me, Doctor Laverty." Julie MacAteer rose.

He noticed she was wearing a loose blue dress and sandals. Her corn-silk hair was tied with an Alice band, and her blue eyes smiled at him. He noticed the flush in her cheeks and wondered why women in early pregnancy all seemed to glow. "Good morning, Julie." At least Julie still trusts me, he thought.

He led her along the hall. "How's Donal?"

"He's up to something. He was so full of himself when he came home yesterday . . ."

The Arkle caper, Barry thought.

"But he's very busy too, Doctor. He's on the roofing job at Sonny's old place."

"I'm glad to hear that."

"I don't think Councillor Bishop's too happy."

Barry stood aside to let her precede him into the surgery.

O'Reilly rose. "Did I hear you say Bertie Bishop's not happy? What a pity." O'Reilly chuckled. "I don't know what got into him to agree to fix Sonny's roof for free . . ."

The hell you don't, Barry thought. We blackmailed the councillor into doing it and into settling five hundred pounds on Julie when she left her job as the Bishops' housemaid. No wonder he growled at me yesterday.

". . . But sure it's a fine Christian thing he's doing. It might even be ready when Sonny gets out of the convalescent home, I hear."

Julie smiled. "You know me and Donal are getting married?" She dropped a hand to her tummy and coughed. "Have to actually."

"And that's why you're here?" O'Reilly asked.

"The last time I was here you gave me the laboratory forms to take to Bangor this afternoon, so I thought I'd kill two birds and come in for my first checkup before I go down there. My last period was ten weeks ago, on May twenty-third. I brought a sample." She handed O'Reilly a small bottle. "I'd like Doctor Laverty to examine me," she said. "He was very kind when I first came here."

Barry smiled at her. He pulled a folding screen in front of the couch. "Nip in there, Julie," he said. "Lift up your dress and take off your panties. There's a sheet to pull over yourself. I'll be in in a minute."

When he went behind the screen, Julie lay with her lower abdomen and legs partly hidden under the sheet. He quickly ran through the routine prenatal questions. "Blood pressure," he said, wrapping the cuff round her arm and sticking his stethoscope in his ears. "Fine." He deflated the cuff and put on a pair of rubber gloves. "I'm going to have to examine you. Can you draw up your knees?"

Between one hand on her abdomen and two fingers in her vagina, he could feel the uterus, tilted forward and enlarged. It seemed to be about the right size for ten weeks, the time elapsed from her last period, but as he knew, estimating uterine size in the first three months was inaccurate at best. Was the organ softer than it should be? He wasn't sure but there was no point worrying Julie unnecessarily.

He pulled the sheet up to cover her. "Everything looks fine, Julie. You'll be due on . . ."—he added nine months to the date of her last period and subtracted one week—"on February thirteenth."

"If I'm a day late it'll be Saint Valentine's Day." She sat up. "Thank you, Doctor, and thanks for being kind. It's my first and I suppose all women get a bit antsy about it," she said, twisting a corner of the sheet in one hand.

"Of course they do."

"Aye, but you make it easy, so you do. I hear you did a great job for Maureen Galvin." She put a hand on his arm. "Will you deliver the baby?"

Barry smiled. The jungle telegraph might be efficient, but at least it was a two-way street. "If you like," he said. Then he thought, If I'm still here. "But we'll have to get you seen at the Royal Maternity first."

She frowned. "Why? Is there something wrong?"

He shook his head. "It's routine. First babies *are* usually fine, but the specialists like to see every first pregnancy once to make sure it's safe to deliver you at home."

"I'll be quite safe with you, Doctor Laverty. I know that." Her blue eyes sparkled. She lowered her voice. "Don't you pay no heed to what some of the folks are saying."

"Thanks, Julie." A few more patients like her and he might change his mind. "Now get yourself dressed." Not all the folks in Ballybucklebo thought he was useless, and it was good to know.

"Urine's fine," O'Reilly said.

"Good," Barry said, and sat down at the rolltop desk to fill in the necessary referral forms.

Julie came out from behind the screen.

"The folks at the Royal Maternity will send for you, and I'd like to see you in a month." He'd deliberately not said, "We'd like to see you." He glanced at O'Reilly, who said nothing.

"I'll be running on," she said. "See you in a month, Doctor Laverty and . . ." She hesitated. "Donal and me hope to see you both at the wedding."

"We'll be there," said O'Reilly. "Give our best to Donal."

"Nice girl," he said when she'd left.

"And don't worry about the ten quid. If you've fixed Fergus Finnegan's eye, he'll owe me a pound, and if he's properly grateful he'll look after you too."

"Look after me?"

"There's a horse race at the Ballybucklebo course in a week. If Fergus can't tip you the wink, nobody can."

"We'll see," said Barry, less interested in making a winning bet than having been right about the jockey's eye.

"We will indeed," said O'Reilly, "but we have to finish this morning's surgery first."

"Right," said Barry, wondering how the rest of the surgery would go.

The only patient who stood out in Barry's mind among all the routine ones was a woman with a case of scabies, caused by the female of the mite *Sarcoptes scabiei hominis*, which burrowed under skin folds and laid her eggs to set up a violent itch and inflammation. As he examined the patient, Barry felt himself itching.

"Jesus Christ," O'Reilly said, after the woman left. "No bloody wonder she's infected with a parasite that flourishes in dirty bed linen." His nose tip was ashen. "Can you guess where that one lives?"

"The housing estate?" Barry had made several home visits to the rows of jerry-built terrace houses on the far side of the village. He knew that the dwellings had been thrown up as cheaply as possible, and with as much profit as possible to the builder, by none other than Councillor Bertie Bishop.

"Give the boy a prize." O'Reilly ground his teeth. "How the hell is anyone meant to keep sheets clean when there's hardly enough hot water to wash their faces?"

"I don't know, Fingal."

"There's nothing wrong with that place," he said, as Barry scrubbed his hands thoroughly, "that a bit of the fire that consumed Sodom and Gomorrah wouldn't cure."

Barry dried his hands. "Do you want Mrs. Bishop turned into a pillar of salt too?"

"I do not," said O'Reilly. "Flo's a decent woman. And that family doesn't need any more humans turned into anything."

"Pardon?"

"Bertie Bishop's already the biggest pile of horseshite in the village," he said, but Barry noticed the big man's nose had returned to its usual colour. Perhaps, he thought, still trying to understand O'Reilly, the man's ranting and raving is like a safety valve on a steam engine. Interesting idea.

"Och, bugger it," said O'Reilly. "There's no point you and me taking the head staggers over something we can't fix. Come on. Grub, and then we'll see what Kinky has for us for home visits after our lunch."

Barry's stomach rumbled and he realized he'd eaten very little breakfast. He was hungry, and the prospect of food combined with the satisfaction of having survived this morning's surgery made him feel less anxious about making the home visits with O'Reilly.

7

Be Fruitful and Multiply

O'Reilly shoved his now empty plate aside. "All right," he said, from his seat at the dining room table. "Let's see what Kinky has for us today." He picked up a piece of paper on which Barry knew Mrs. Kincaid had written a list of patients who had requested home visits. "Just one," he said. "Myrtle MacVeigh. She says her kidneys are acting up again, but Kinky doesn't think it's too serious."

"Then why didn't she come to the surgery and save us a trip?"

O'Reilly laughed. "You'll see when we get there." He stood up and stretched. "And anyway, she lives out near Sonny's place. Do you fancy dropping by to see how the work on his roof's coming along? Make sure Councillor Bertie Bishop's kept his word?"

"Why not?"

"So we'll see Myrtle first, then pop in at Sonny's."

"Is your car in the garage or out in front?"

"The garage."

"Thought so." Barry glanced down at his corduroy pants and wondered how they would fare when he crossed the back garden to O'Reilly's dilapidated garage and had to run the gauntlet of Arthur Guinness's inevitable amorous advances. Every time O'Reilly's black Labrador spotted Barry, he'd make a beeline for him and wrap Barry's leg in a fond embrace, usually to the ruination of his trousers.

"We haven't all day," said O'Reilly, striding past the table. "And get your coat. It's raining out."

Barry nipped into the surgery, and picked up his black bag. Then he grabbed his raincoat and went into the kitchen.

Mrs. Kincaid was hoisting a loaded clothes-drying device, three parallel wooden bars suspended from the ceiling by a rope and pulley. "It's too wet to put the clothes out for a good blow," she said. "Monday's washing day." She pointed at Barry's corduroys. "Try to keep those clean like a good lad."

"I will, if Doctor O'Reilly can keep Arthur away."

O'Reilly had already opened the kitchen door. "Can I trouble you to join me?"

"Coming."

The moment Barry set foot in the garden he heard a series of delighted yips and saw Arthur Guinness charging across the lawn, tail going nineteen to the dozen. Not again. Maybe the skirts of his raincoat would protect him.

O'Reilly stuck two fingers in his mouth and produced a whistle that sounded like a cross between a shipyard siren and a steam engine.

Arthur skidded to O'Reilly's side, halted on the wet grass, slammed his backside on the ground, and tongue lolling, stared up at O'Reilly.

O'Reilly sniffed. "Jesus, Arthur, you stink. Back in your kennel and keep dry, you buck eejit."

The dog obeyed.

Barry's pants were safe. He caught up with O'Reilly at the back gate.

"Come on," said O'Reilly, turning up the collar of his raincoat, "we're getting soaked ourselves." He crossed the lane and opened the garage door. "Hang on. I'll get the car out."

Barry waited as the engine of the old long-bonnetted Rover caught; then the car backfired and was reversed into the lane. He climbed into the passenger seat and immediately was thrust backwards like an astronaut in an acceleration sled as O'Reilly took off.

Barry had to brace his arms on the dashboard as O'Reilly slammed to a halt where the lane joined the main road. While O'Reilly, drumming his fingers on the steering wheel, waited for a tractor towing a cartload of manure to go by, Barry stared up at the lopsided steeple of the Ballybucklebo Presbyterian Church. The slates, ebony black from the drizzle, were punctuated with colons and commas of dark green moss. Looking ahead, he could see over a low stone wall and into the churchyard filled with the headstones of generations of villagers.

The family markers, Barry thought, brought continuity to the seasons of Ballybucklebo. There were worse places to spend a lifetime and finally settle in with your friends and neighbours.

"Right." O'Reilly roared off down the road.

Barry wondered why he hadn't yelled, "Charge."

The car bounced over potholes and listed as O'Reilly took the bends. Barry hardly dared to look ahead and instead distracted himself by staring out the window. Across a narrow strip of sea pink–spotted dune grass lay a shingle beach. Beyond, the battleship grey waters of Belfast Lough were sullen under curtains of drizzle.

He recognized Maggie MacCorkle's seaside cottage as they approached and wondered if the "toty-wee headache" above her head had improved since yesterday. She hadn't been to the surgery for some time. "Should we call on Maggie, Fingal?"

"She'll be out," O'Reilly said. "Down in Bangor visiting Sonny. She's daft about the old goat. We'll drop in on her next week . . . but it was a good suggestion."

Barry knew that O'Reilly didn't only visit the sick on his rounds. He made it a practice of keeping an avuncular eye on his older patients as well.

O'Reilly slowed, indicated for a right turn, and started to drive inland. Accelerating, he took a shallow curve with the wheels of the car well over the centre line. Coming off the crown of the bend, he narrowly missed a cyclist stolidly pedalling in the same direction. Barry glanced back in time to see the unfortunate rider hurl himself and his bicycle into the ditch. He recognized Donal Donnelly, but the bicycle, which had been black and covered in rust patches the first time Barry had encountered Donal, had been transformed. Barry tried to see how many different colours adorned the machine, but O'Reilly was already well into another bend.

"You nearly hit Donal, Fingal."

"I never pay any attention to cyclists. They know my car. They get out of the way."

Which, Barry thought, was true enough. How many times had he seen one take to the ditch like Donal? O'Reilly's total disregard for the other occupants of the road was a price that simply had to be paid for having O'Reilly in Ballybucklebo. In Barry's opinion it was a fair trade, even if Donal Donnelly might not think so. He glanced behind to see Donal clamber out of the ditch and remount.

"Good Lord," Barry said. "Donal's painted his bike. It looks like a wheeled version of Joseph's coat of many colours. I wonder why?"

"Sounds like Donal," O'Reilly said. "No doubt we'll find out, all in good time." O'Reilly slowed and turned left onto a farm lane, then stopped in a farmyard. "We're here. Out."

Barry grabbed his black bag, heaved himself out of the car, avoided the border collie that seemed to be standard equipment for all Ulster farms, and walked to the farmhouse, a two-storey, grey stone building with brown trim on the frames of its sash windows. Like Maggie's cottage, the windowsills were adorned with flower boxes, the bright petals softening the drabness of the building. To one side, turf was piled against the gable end, drying under a corrugated iron roof. He could smell cow manure.

O'Reilly knocked on the door.

It was opened by a child of about four. "Ma. The doctor's here."

O'Reilly tousled the girl's hair and said, "How are you, Lucy?"

"Ma's sick again," she said. "Come on in."

Barry followed O'Reilly into a high-ceilinged kitchen. A turf-fired Aga range radiated a pleasant warmth and the country scent of burning peat. Children's toys were littered around a tiled floor: an eyeless teddy bear half buried under a pile of Leggos; two tricycles; a discarded cowboy suit with a pair of six-shooters; four dollies, one with an arm missing; a doll's pram.

A baby was crying somewhere in the house.

"She's in here," Lucy said, opening a door for O'Reilly.

It led to a ground-floor bedroom where thrown-back bedclothes lay on a double bed.

Barry went in. Lucy stood in one corner, eyes wide, sucking her thumb. Three identical cots, two of them occupied by sleeping babies, were ranked along one wall. So, Barry thought, no wonder O'Reilly had said he'd understand why Myrtle MacVeigh couldn't come to the surgery. She had four kids, three of them about six months old.

"Thanks for coming, Doctor O'Reilly," she said. She was sitting in an armchair, a dumpy woman with frazzled hair. "The ould trouble's back again."

It was after two o'clock, but she still wore fluffy slippers, and a pink dressing gown half open over a flannel nightie. She was giving a bottle to a baby. The crying he'd heard earlier had stopped. She shivered and he could see a sheen of sweat on her brow.

"Myrtle had a postpartum urinary infection after the triplets were born. I thought we'd got it cleared up," O'Reilly said.

"Who's he?" she asked, nodding in Barry's direction.

"Myrtle, this is Doctor Laverty, my assistant."

"Aye," she said. "I've heard all about him, so I have." She refused to meet Barry's eye.

O'Reilly made no comment. Instead he asked, "So what seems to be the trouble?"

"It's my kiddleys, so it is." She sounded certain.

O'Reilly agreed. "It probably is," he said. "Would you like to tell me how they're bothering you?" As he spoke, he dropped a hand to her wrist.

"It come on the night before last. I took the shivers something fierce. I feel dead rotten and . . ." She lowered her voice and spoke directly into O'Reilly's cauliflower ear.

"Mmm," said O'Reilly, "dysuria and frequency."

Barry realized that O'Reilly, who usually avoided using medical jargon in front of patients, was letting Barry know that the patient was experiencing a burning pain every time she urinated and was passing water very often. They were both classic symptoms of infection of the bladder. She'd be embarrassed discussing such personal functions in front of a strange man, even if he was a doctor, and O'Reilly was trying to spare her that.

O'Reilly leant over Myrtle, and Barry saw him put a hand in the small of the patient's back. "That sore?"

She gasped.

So it was probable that her kidneys were affected as well as her bladder.

"Your pulse is a bit quick too." O'Reilly stood up. "What do you reckon, Doctor Laverty? *I* think Myrtle's right."

So O'Reilly wasn't going to pretend he was seeking Barry's advice. Barry had to agree with his colleague's diagnosis. "Kidney infection," he said, deliberately avoiding using words like "acute pyelonephritis."

"And have you been treating yourself, Myrtle?" O'Reilly asked.

"I have indeed," she said. "My granny's cure. Two ounces of sweet nitre, one ounce of oil of juniper, half an ounce of turpentine, and grated horseradish . . . mixed in a pint of good gin. One wineglass three times a day."

Barry eyes widened. It sounded like a pretty toxic concoction, but after a month here he was getting used to hearing about a lot of bizarre country remedies.

"Powerful stuff," O'Reilly said, "but I doubt if it's working." He rummaged in his bag. "Here." He produced two bottles. "I think a bit of this sodium citrate and sodium bicarbonate will help." He put the bottle on the night table beside her bed.

The mixture was used to render the urine alkaline and inhibit the growth of coliform bacteria, the commonest cause of urinary infections.

"And these are sulphamethizole."

She squinted at the second bottle. "Is them the same ones you give me last time?"

O'Reilly nodded.

"Great," she said. "They done me a power of good."

Barry coughed. Not as well as they might have if, as seemed probable, the infection had recurred. He hesitated, then said, "I've some nitrofurantoin with me." He waited to see how O'Reilly would respond to the unasked-for suggestion to use a more modern antibiotic.

"Have you, by God?"

"In my bag."

"Then give them here."

Barry handed the bottle to O'Reilly.

"I want them sulphur-what-do-you-me-callums Doctor O'Reilly said," Myrtle insisted.

Barry bit his tongue.

"No," said O'Reilly levelly. "No, you don't. Sulphas are old-fashioned. It's a good thing Doctor Laverty's here. He's up on all the new stuff."

"I like the old stuff," she said, taking the bottle from the baby's mouth.

"I know," said O'Reilly, "like your granny's cure . . . and it didn't work, did it?"

"No, sir."

"There you are then. You do like the pair of us say, and you'll be right as rain in no time."

She managed a weak smile. "I'll need to be with my lot. It's a good thing wee Peter's out with his da today."

Good God, Barry thought, the poor woman has *five* children. It was a miracle she was coping at all. And typical of O'Reilly to visit her at home.

"Where is Paddy, then ?" O'Reilly enquired.

"Sure you know what farming's like. The crop's early, and he has to get the hay swathed. Him and Peter'll be back when they're finished, so they will."

"Fine," said O'Reilly. "I'll have a word with the district nurse. Have her pop round and give you a hand 'til you're on your feet again."

"Thank you, sir." She stood and laid the baby in the empty cot. She winced and put a hand in the small of her back as she straightened up. "I hope you're right about them nighties-fer-aunties, young man," she said, looking directly at Barry for the first time.

"He is," O'Reilly said. "I promise."

Barry waited as O'Reilly gave instructions about how the medication was to be taken. O'Reilly continued, "And remember, Myrtle, it's not uncommon for a woman to get her kidneys infected during labour, or for the damn things to flare up again. I want you to drink lots of fluids, especially orange juice, and keep your kidneys well flushed out."

"I will, sir."

"Right," said O'Reilly. "One of us will pop round tomorrow, but don't be scared to give Mrs. Kincaid a ring if you need us sooner."

"I will, Doctor O'Reilly," she said, "and I hope it'll be yourself that comes, so I do."

"We'll see," O'Reilly said. "Now we'd better be running along. We'll let ourselves out."

Barry waited until the Rover was jolting back down the lane. "It doesn't look as if anyone's going to take me seriously."

"Rubbish. Just keep on sounding confident, and do your job as best you can."

Barry sighed. "I hope you're right."

"I am," said O'Reilly, turning left onto the tarmacadamed road. "Sure it hasn't been that long since the MacVeighs have been back to trusting *me*. For a while I thought they'd never speak to me again."

"Why ever not?"

"Contraception," said O'Reilly, putting two of the Rover's wheels up on the verge to pass a hay wain drawn by a pair of Clydesdales. "Or rather failure thereof."

Barry waited.

"Before Peter, their eldest, was born, Myrtle came to see me because she and Paddy wanted to space their family, didn't want to start having kids too soon after they were married. There was none of your pill back then."

"I know."

"Aye," said O'Reilly, "but other things were available. The Easter Rising in Dublin wasn't the only thing that happened in nineteen sixteen."

"You've lost me, Fingal."

"Nineteen sixteen. That's the year Margaret Sanger opened the first birth control clinic in New York. Bit before your time."

Indeed, Barry thought, and you, Fingal, if I've done the math right were a ripe old eight-year-old.

He had to grab the dashboard as O'Reilly suddenly braked for no apparent reason. As far as Barry could tell, there was nothing in the way, but then a cock pheasant appeared at his side of the car, strutting proudly across the road, followed by two dowdy hen birds.

"Be a shame to hit that big fellah," O'Reilly said, "at least with a motor car. But I'd not mind getting a shot at him when the season opens."

"You baffle me, Fingal. You pay no attention to cyclists, but you brake for game birds?"

"Of course," said O'Reilly. "There's no sport in shooting cyclists." He moved off. "Now about Myrtle. I suggested she and Paddy use condoms, and they did; and eleven months later Peter was born."

"Had you explained to her that condoms could leak?"

"Of course, and her husband Paddy has a right sense of humour. He nicknamed the wee lad "Leaky.""

Barry smiled.

"So next time around I fitted her with a diaphragm."

Barry remembered the little girl, Lucy. "No," he said. "I don't believe it."

"You'd better. I explained diaphragms could work loose—"

"So they called the girl Lucy?"

"Aye. So they wouldn't trust barrier methods and asked me for advice again."

"So you told them about the rhythm method?"

"Right." O'Reilly made a left turn. "You saw the result. Triplets. That was the end of them trusting me."

"But it was hardly your fault."

"Do you think I don't know that? It's what I've been trying to tell you. No matter what you do, some patients will be dissatisfied."

And some of them will be dead, Barry thought, suddenly remembering Major Fotheringham.

"You have to learn to live with it," O'Reilly said.

Barry understood what O'Reilly was trying to say, but as the car narrowly missed a stray sheep, instead of agreeing, he yelled, "Look out, Fingal!"

"Pay no heed," said O'Reilly, "it's only a sheep. And that's the trouble with the human race. I think they're all related to sheep. One takes the lead and the rest follow willy-nilly."

"So if Myrtle MacVeigh refuses to trust me, she'll tell her friends?"

"Probably. But by the same token, if she gets better on the drugs you suggested and if Fergus Finnegan's eye gets better, who knows? You could have a whole new following."

"I suppose so."

"I bloody well know so. Take the MacVeighs, for instance. They left the practice as soon as she knew she was having triplets."

"So why did they come back to you?"

"Pure chance. She had to have the babies in the Royal Maternity Hospital. No GP in his right mind would confine a woman with triplets at home."

"True."

"Two days after they discharged her, she blew up the urinary infection. She phoned her new GP. Two o'clock on a Saturday morning. He said it wasn't his problem, she'd have to go back to the hospital. He refused to go see her."

Barry felt the car slowing down.

"Paddy phoned me."

"And you went?"

O'Reilly turned and stared at Barry as if he were a simpleton. "Naturally. I got her sorted out, *and* I got her to a gynaecologist up at the Royal Victoria for a tubal ligation. He fixed her up, they've been with me since, and we get along grand."

"So sometimes they do forgive you?"

"Of course. It's trite but it is true: time is often a great healer."

"So you think I just need to be patient?"

O'Reilly laughed. "Right. Patient with the patients. I like the ring of that." He started to slow down. "It didn't hurt that Paddy sees the funny side of almost anything. Do you know what he said to me last week?"

"No."

" 'You know, Doc,' says he, 'we dote on our kiddies now, but we were annoyed with you. We thought you'd let us down. I'm sorry the missus took a scunner to you for a while, but you know, we're the only parents who've five kids with great names for a rock-and-roll band . . . Leaky, Lucy, and the Three Rhythm Boys.' "

As Barry laughed, O'Reilly pulled up at the side of the road. "Here we are," he said. "Sonny's. Let's go and see how the great work's progressing."

8

Raise High the Roof Beam, Carpenters

As far as Barry could tell, not much had been happening to Sonny's place. Ivy straggled up the walls of the roofless two-storey house. A spin dryer and television set squatted silently on the grassy verge. The front garden was overgrown with brambles and cluttered with old cars, motorcycles, farm machinery, and a yellow caravan.

Ever since Sonny had taken ill, been admitted to the Royal Victoria, and subsequently discharged to a convalescent home in Bangor, Maggie MacCorkle had adopted Sonny's five dogs. They usually lived in the caravan while Sonny slept in his car, because his house had been roofless since a dispute years ago about the installation of new slates.

Councillor Bishop's building firm had been engaged to repair the roof and had removed the slates. Bishop's sudden demand at that point for payment in advance, contrary to the way things were usually done in Ulster, had riled Sonny, and he'd balked and refused to pay. According to O'Reilly, Bishop had told Sonny he could bloody well whistle if he thought the job would be finished without the cash, and Sonny, a normally reserved man, had suggested that Bishop do something O'Reilly described as physiologically impossible.

There matters had stood until O'Reilly, with Barry's help, had accused Bishop of being the father of Julie MacAteer's unborn child, said he could prove it, and threatened to let the word slip out. This had proved sufficient coercion for Bishop to agree to rebuild the roof—at no cost to Sonny.

Unfortunately, Donal Donnelly had come forward, confessed his sins, and asked Julie to marry him, leaving O'Reilly with no hold over Bishop. Since then he and Barry had been worried that Bishop might renege on his promise.

Barry could see that scaffolding had been erected at the nearest gable end, and ladders ran from the ground to the highest level of the spidery structure of rusty iron tubing. A man stood on the upper platform holding an old, weathered roof beam, which he tossed off the edge to land with a thump in a nettle patch below.

Barry walked round the car to stand beside O'Reilly. The rain had stopped. The land smelt fresh, and wisps of vapour drifted from the road's tarmac as the sun warmed it. "So, what do you think's going on up at the house, Fingal?"

O'Reilly pushed at a black-painted iron gate in the low blackthorn hedge.

Barry heard the gate's hinges screech.

"Wonders will never cease. Bertie Bishop's keeping his word," O'Reilly said. "Of course, he'd have to."

"Why?"

"Didn't he make a great public song and dance about doing it as an act of Christian charity when we told him the citizenry might put up a statue to him?"

Barry laughed, remembering the conversation vividly.

"A man like Bishop's too bloody conceited to back down from a thing like that." O'Reilly stared at the man on the roof. "If I'm not mistaken, that's Seamus Galvin up there." O'Reilly shook his head. "Seamus Galvin, the greatest skiver unhung, is doing an honest day's work. Can you believe it? I suppose he's trying to get a few more quid together before he and Maureen head off to the States."

"Why don't we go and ask him?" Barry went in through the gate, and O'Reilly followed. That makes a change, Barry thought. Usually I follow in his wake.

They walked along a path of uneven concrete slabs where grass and clumps of black horehound had forced their way through the cracks. The horehound gave off an unpleasant, acrid smell when the leaves were crushed underfoot. A pair of cabbage white butterflies drifted over the tangled bramble bushes at the path's edges.

Barry halted at the foot of the scaffolding. Nearby a rusty brazier supported two fire-blackened soup cans sitting on top of a heap of cold ashes. Twisted strands of wire formed loops over the cans' open mouths. The Ulster labouring man's tea kettles. No job could be completed without liberal doses of stewed tea.

"Is it yourself up there, Seamus Galvin?" O'Reilly roared.

The man peered over the edge of the platform. "It is, Doctor O'Reilly, sir. Hang on. I'll be right down."

Barry watched Galvin clamber onto the ladder and begin his descent, accompanied by flakes of rust from the wobbly structure.

"Lo," said O'Reilly, "in the words of an old hymn, 'He comes with clouds descending.' "

Galvin jumped off the last step. "Afternoon, Doctors," he said, landing heavily.

"The ankle's all better now, is it, Seamus?" O'Reilly enquired.

"Indeed, sir. Indeed. Right as rain."

"And how's the job coming?"

"It's a bugger, Doctor O'Reilly." Seamus said. "The roof beams is rotten from appetite to arsehole. Every one of them'll have to be torn out and replaced, so they will. It's going to cost Mr. Bishop a right wheen of do-re-mi."

"What a crying shame," said O'Reilly, smiling broadly. "Couldn't happen to a nicer man."

"How long," Barry asked, "will the job take?"

"Hard to say, sir, but I'll tell you one wee thing. We'd get it done a damn sight quicker if Donal Donnelly didn't keep going home for his lunch."

"Donal? We passed him on our way here," Barry said, remembering Donal's rapid dive into the ditch. "Seamus, do you happen to know what Donal's done to his bike?"

Seamus laughed. "Indeed I do, sir. He decided it needed painting before he gets married. There was a clatter of half-used pots of paint

An Irish Country Village   69

lying about his place. On Saturday night, after the party, he set to. He says it's art."

"Art?" Barry laughed.

"Aye. He says he seen a picture in a magazine by a Yankee fellah." Seamus scratched his head. "The man was called for a fish." He frowned, then his face lit up. "Haddock. That's it. Jason Haddock."

"Could you mean Jackson Pollock?" Barry enquired gently.

"The very man himself, although here in County Down we call them pollocks 'blockan,' so we do. That's why I got it mixed up." Seamus picked at one tooth and lowered his voice. "I think Donal just took a fit of the head staggers, or maybe he had a bad bottle at the party."

Head staggers was a disease of sheep caused by a parasitic worm invading the affected animal's brain, and as far as Barry knew, it did not affect humans. The mythical "bad bottle" of beer seemed an equally unlikely explanation, but it was frequently invoked to explain away overconsumption, the daft things men did while under the influence, and usually, the next day's inevitable hangover.

"Sometimes," Seamus said, "Donal's so mean he'd wrestle a bear for a penny, so when one pot of paint ran out he just opened another. He made a right bollocks of it, in my opinion, but he thinks it's the greatest thing since sliced bread. Here he comes, sir. See for yourself."

Barry turned and watched Donal Donnelly wheeling his gaudy machine along the path. It did look like something painted by Jackson Pollock.

"Was it lunch you were having, Donal, or did you stay for your supper too?" Seamus yelled.

"Away off and chase yourself, Seamus." Donal kept walking, propped the bike against the gable end, and knuckled his ginger forelock to O'Reilly. "Good day, Doctor."

"Good day yourself, Donal."

Is he not going to greet me? Barry was wondering, when Donal remarked, "And you too, Doctor Laverty."

Barry noted there was no respectful knuckling in his direction.

"Are you coming to work, or are you just going to stand there flapping your jaw?" Seamus demanded.

"Take your hurry in your hand. I need a wee word with the doctors."

"Jasus," Seamus muttered. "Don't take all day." He turned to the ladder. "One of us had better get going," he said, and with that, he started to climb.

"More to do with Arkle?" Barry asked, with a sideways glance at O'Reilly. But Fingal missed the enquiring look. He was too busy studying Donal's bike.

"Not at all," said Donal. "That's coming on bravely. Never you worry about that." He hesitated. "But seeing as how you and himself there were right decent about giving me advice on that, I have another wee question."

"Go ahead."

Donal frowned. "I'm powerful worried, so I am."

"What about?"

"What does 'endow' mean, sir?"

Barry was about to answer that it was just a big word meaning 'give,' but O'Reilly interrupted.

"Why do you want to know, Donal?"

Donal looked longingly at his bike. "Me and Julie went to see the minister to run through the wedding ceremony."

"And?" said O'Reilly.

"There was a couple of bits I didn't understand, like." He shifted from one foot to the other. "You being learned men, I thought maybe you could explain."

"Explain what?" Barry asked.

Donal's brows knitted. He picked at the edge of one thumbnail. "There's a bit I've to say, 'With all my worldly goods I thee endow.' I don't like the sound of it one wee bit. Not one bit."

"Why not? It simply means to—"

"What's bothering you about it, Donal?" O'Reilly interrupted.

Donal bit his lower lip with his buckteeth, then blurted, "Does it mean I've to give Bluebird—my greyhound—and my bike to Julie?"

O'Reilly laughed. "Not at all."

"Oh."

Barry could see the way Donal's face relaxed.

"At least," O'Reilly continued, with a quick glance at Barry, "not immediately."

Donal's frown came back.

"No," said O'Reilly. " 'Endow's' a lawyer's word. It's what you do in a will."

"A will, sir?"

"Aye. It's how the dear departed instructs his lawyer to make sure people get their bequests. 'And to my daughter, Sheila, I leave my rosebushes.' That's an endowment."

And it's not true, Barry thought, but looking at Donal's grin he thoroughly approved of O'Reilly's minor deception. He realized that possessions that to him would seem trivial could mean so much to a man like Donal Donnelly. They were probably all he had.

"That's not much of a bother, Doctor O'Reilly. By the time I've fallen off the perch, the oul' bike'll be long gone" He sighed. "And so'll Bluebird. She's a grand wee dog, so she is."

"She is that," O'Reilly said.

"Thanks for the advice, Doctor. It's a great load off my mind." Donal turned to Barry. "It's all a bit awkward, like, but I've a question for you too."

"What is it, Donal?"

"On Saturday, at the party, my Julie had great *craic* with your Miss Spence."

"Patricia?" He'd been so preoccupied with trying to reestablish himself in the practice he'd hardly given her a thought. And she'd promised to phone.

"Aye. She's filled my Julie's head with all kinds of hobbyhorse shite, so she has."

It was Barry's turn to frown. "What?"

"It's like this. The minister was telling Julie she had to promise to love, honour, and obey, and Julie says, 'I'll have no trouble with the first two, but . . .'—and I nearly filled my pants when I heard her—'. . . Miss Spence told me I wasn't to say I'd obey anybody.' "

Barry couldn't help laughing. He could picture Patricia, eyes bright, seeking another convert to her cause. "Sure," he said, "two out of three isn't bad."

"Aye. But—"

"But nothing, Donal. If that's what Julie wants, humour her."

"You think so?"

"Of course. Patricia has a lot of newfangled notions about women. Maybe she's right."

Donal looked doubtful. "If you say so, sir, but it seems odd to me."

A voice came roaring from above. "You'd talk the hind leg off a donkey, Donal Donnelly. Will you get yourself up here this minute?"

"Coming." Donal put one foot on the bottom rung, hesitated, and then asked O'Reilly, "Will I be seeing the pair of you at the races?"

"Indeed," said O'Reilly.

Donal lowered his voice. "My pal at the bank'll have a brave wheen of Irish half crowns for me by Friday."

O'Reilly glanced at Barry.

"Get up here, Donal Donnelly, or by Jesus I'll come down to you," Seamus Galvin roared.

Donal started to climb. "Thanks to you both for explaining all that stuff. It's a great comfort to a fellah to have the likes of you two doctors in Ballybucklebo, so it is."

"Away on with you, Donal," Barry said, but his step was lighter as he and O'Reilly began to walk to the Rover.

"I wonder how long it'll take before the roof's as good as new again." O'Reilly mused aloud; then without seeming to be speaking to Barry, he continued: "Like a lot of things, it's amazing what a bit of time and hard work can do."

Barry glanced at O'Reilly, who was staring across the road to a small field where a herd of black-and-white Friesians grazed contentedly or lay chewing the cud.

"Right," said O'Reilly. "Let's get home. Maybe we can both put our feet up for a while."

"That would be grand," said Barry, not paying attention to where he was going. He felt something tugging at his leg. Stopping, he found that a thick, thorny briar had snagged the left leg of his corduroys. He tugged hard and felt the material rip. Blast! He'd heard about places being called the "graveyards of ships." For him, Ballybucklebo was well on the way to becoming the last resting place for every pair of pants he owned. He trotted to the gate, closed it, and got into the Rover.

O'Reilly was staring at the old house. "It seems to me," he said, "that God is in his heaven and all is right with the world. Bertie Bishop's doing the job for Sonny, Seamus and Donal are both at work, and you"—he leant closer to Barry—"seem a damn sight more cheerful than you were at breakfast." He started the engine. "But," he said, "one of us had better be on call tonight."

Barry waited, hoping that O'Reilly would want the night off.

"It had better be me," O'Reilly remarked, driving off as if he were intent not so much on breaking the sound barrier as shattering it beyond any hope of repair.

Barry sighed and clutched the armrest on the door panel.

O'Reilly winked at Barry. "And if you're not working, maybe you could nip over to the Kinnegar and see that Miss Spence who's given Julie MacAteer such food for thought."

Barry was damned if he could decide whether O'Reilly had volunteered to work because he was hesitant to leave his assistant unsupervised, or whether it was a measure of the big man's innate generosity that he was willing to give Barry time to spend with Patricia. He'd phone her as soon as he got back to Number 1 Main Street and see if she would be free tonight.

9

Nor Its Great Scholars Great Men

"Come in." Patricia held open the door to her flat and stood aside.

Barry kissed her chastely as he passed.

"I am sorry about yesterday," she said. "I didn't get away from Newry 'til all hours, and I've been going round today like a bee on a hot brick. I should've phoned."

"It's all right; I've been a tad busy myself. I'm glad you're able to spare me an hour," he said, feeling his disappointment that it wouldn't be longer. When he'd phoned earlier from O'Reilly's, she'd been pleased to hear from him, would certainly see him for a while, but had made it clear that this was very much a working day and evening for a civil engineering undergraduate taking extra summer courses.

"Sit down, Barry. Make yourself at home. Sorry the place is a bit cluttered." She lifted a pile of textbooks from her two-seater sofa and stacked them on her small dining table to keep company with other tomes, ring binders, two slide rules, and loose sheets of paper. He noticed an angled draughtsman's table in one corner of the room. A sheet of architectural plans was fixed to the surface with drawing pins. An Anglepoise articulated lamp hung over the table's face.

He parked himself on the sofa. "Looks like you've been busy," he said, remembering his own student days when it had seemed that the knowledge to be mastered was limitless and the time in which to master it impossibly short. He pointed at the drawing table. "Tools of the trade?"

"Yes." She came and sat beside him, half turned to face him, knees together, hands in her lap. "We're learning about stresses on bridge supports. We have to be able to read structural plans."

"You remember Jack Mills? You met him on Saturday at O'Reilly's hooley?"

"The junior surgical registrar from Cullybackey? The one with the blonde with enormous bristols?" She held her hands cupped in front of her breasts, but a good six inches away.

"That's Jack." Barry laughed at Patricia's use of rhyming slang. "Bristol cities" for "titties." "That's Jack, all right. Anyway, when he and I shared digs, we had one of the tools of our trade, an articulated skeleton, hanging in our room. We called him Billy Bones."

"Like the pirate in *Treasure Island*?"

"The very lad. Mind you, being Jack, he had the poor thing dressed in ladies' underwear." He moved closer.

"And I'll bet," she said, "every piece was from one of his conquests."

"How did you know that?"

"I watched him with the blonde." She took his hand. "He seemed like a decent enough chap but—"

"He's my best friend," Barry said.

"Well, I'm not sure I'd want to go out with him."

"I'm damn *sure* I'd not want you to. I'd be too jealous." The thought of Patricia with anyone else, particularly Jack, made his stomach tighten.

She squeezed his hand. "Not many men I know would admit to being jealous," she said. "I like that . . . now your Jack—"

"What about Jack?"

"I'll bet you he believes buying a girl a cheap dinner is the price of admission to her bed."

Barry frowned. "Now that's not fair."

"It is. Most men are like that. But you're not, and it's another thing I like about you. I feel safe with you."

Barry was sure he was blushing. "I'm a regular Prince Charming," he said, to cover his confusion. He smiled. "It's because I'm much too sensitive."

"Sensitive?"

"Yes. Absolutely. A good slap in the face brings me out in great red welts."

She laughed, a throaty chuckle. "You think I'd slap your face?"

"No. I think you're probably a judo black belt who'd tear my arm off and beat me to death with the soggy end."

"Barry!" She bent forward and kissed him. "I'd do no such thing."

"I'm very glad to hear it," he said, seeing how lovely she looked even in old jeans and a baggy sweater. Her black hair was highlighted by the setting sun's soft light as it slipped shyly across Belfast Lough and past the Esplanade, seeming to hesitate outside her window to ask permission before coming into the room.

He held her to him, breathing in the subtle scent of her. "Much better," he said softly, "than a slap." He moved back, put his hands on her shoulders, and looked into her eyes, sloe black, slightly tilted, set above Slavic cheekbones. "You are very lovely," he said, and he watched the dimple in her left cheek deepen as she smiled.

"Thank you." She put her head on his shoulder. "And thank you for coming over tonight."

"I thought I was interrupting your studies."

"You are, but sometimes I need to be interrupted. Sometimes"—she swallowed—"I think I've got myself in out of my depth."

Barry stroked her hair. "You're not the only one," he said. He wondered if he was thinking of how deeply he felt about Patricia, or how even now, with her head on his shoulder, thoughts about his uncertain future with O'Reilly kept intruding. "I'm feeling a bit that way right now about the practice."

"Why?"

He hesitated, not wanting to burden her with his troubles. Then he said, "O'Reilly's keeping me on. He's offered me a partnership in a year."

"That's wonderful." She kissed him. "I envy you, and I'm so pleased for you . . . if it's what you want."

"I'm pretty sure it is. I could settle in Ballybucklebo, but I'm in a bit of bother."

"What?"

"A bit of loss of confidence in me by the patients." He could see the sympathy in her eyes. "O'Reilly reckons I can work my way through it."

She squeezed his hand. "I'd trust that man's opinion."

"I hope you're right. I feel . . . I feel like I'm sitting my final exams all over again."

She stood and crossed her arms in front of her breasts. "That's why *I'm* worried. I've one coming up next week."

"An exam?"

"Mmm."

"You'll murder it, I know." Barry scratched his chin. "Funny time of year. I thought examinations were held in June."

"They are. This is a special one. For a scholarship."

"A scholarship?"

"And I have to win it." She bunched her fists. "I have to."

He didn't know what to say. "Of course you will" would be trite. "Just do your best" was the kind of advice given by a mother who suspected her son was going to fail. "But if you don't win, it's not the same as one of your normal professional exams, is it? I mean . . . it wouldn't set you back? Make you lose a year?"

"No. It wouldn't." He detected a note in her voice that sounded defeated. "Not me personally."

"Then who?" Barry frowned. There had been special awards and scholarships in the medical faculty, but most of the average students, including him, hadn't even bothered entering. They left that to the few budding geniuses. Undergraduates like him and Jack Mills were very happy, thank you, to squeak passes and finish the course in the allotted six years. Some of the dimmer ones had taken longer to qualify, had had to repeat years of study. "I think," he said, "if it's upsetting you, perhaps you should withdraw."

"I can't."

"Why not?"

"Because I'm a woman."

Barry resisted the temptation to remark he'd never have guessed if she hadn't told him. Instead he said, "What's that got to do with anything?"

"Barry." She stood squarely in front of him, shoulders braced, face taut. "I told you how difficult it was for me to get into a professional school . . ."

"I remember."

"Half the other students, aye, and some of the faculty too can't wait for me to trip up." She crossed the room her gait awkward as a result of her childhood polio, turned, and faced him. "If I do, they can smirk and say, 'I told you so,' and then it'll be even harder for girls to get in. I have to win for them, not just me. Do you not see that?" Her head drooped.

Barry had a fleeting memory of a TV documentary about votes for women and the suffragette movement—and Emily Davison throwing herself under the king's horse at Ascot in 1913. "I suppose," he said, "but I don't like to see you getting yourself upset." He stood and crossed the room, put one hand under her chin, lifted her face, and looked her straight in the eye. "Look," he said, "I still haven't got to know you very well, but I do know some things." He'd learnt the technique in an early psychology course. When someone is discouraged, build on their known strengths. "You had polio . . ."

He heard her gasp. He knew how she hated to have attention drawn to her handicap, but he ploughed on. "You haven't let it slow you down one bit . . ."

Her face was expressionless.

"You did get into the Faculty of Engineering . . ."

"I suppose . . ." She sounded hesitant.

"How many in your class are going to sit the scholarship exam?"

"Ten, and I'm the only—"

"I know. Girl."

"Woman."

"Right. You're the only woman. My God, girl, you should be proud of yourself for that alone."

"You mean that, don't you?"

"Of course I bloody well mean it. And . . . and . . ." They'd taught him in the same course never to try to comfort patients by telling them personal things about yourself, but Patricia wasn't a patient. "You may not succeed . . ."

"That's what I'm scared of." Her eyes were moist. She sniffed.

". . . but you'll have to carry on. I've had to."

"I don't understand."

"It's the lack of confidence I mentioned. Two weeks ago I muffed a diagnosis. The patient nearly died but the neurosurgeons fixed him; at least I thought they'd fixed him."

"But they hadn't?"

"I don't know. I do know O'Reilly went to see him yesterday. The man was dead."

"Barry." Her hand covered her mouth. "No."

He nodded. "I'm afraid he was." He took her hand in his. "I'm going to have to face that, my first big failure, if I'm going to stay on working with O'Reilly."

"I didn't know."

"Of course not. I hadn't told you." And I'd no intention of telling her, he thought, except it seemed the right thing to do if it could help her get over her funk. "I just didn't want you to think you were the only one who could fail at something."

He felt her arms go round him as she held up her face to be kissed, and he hugged her and kissed her and then held her at arm's length.

"Thank you," she said, "for telling me. It does help." Her eyes glimmered, but he could see it was from the light not tears. "And it helps when you're serious about important things."

"Yes, I can be," he said quietly, looking into her face.

"So can I, Barry," she said softly. "So can I."

Barry knew they each had come within a whisper of saying, "I love you," but he'd not rush her. He could hear O'Reilly's voice; "Pianissimo, pianissimo."

"Look," he said, "you have to be getting on with your studies, and I have to be running along."

"I suppose so," she said. "I'm not sure I want you to go."

God knew he'd sell his soul to be able to stay. Perhaps he wasn't being fair to her, but his own inner voice said, "Barry, this time it's your turn to play a little hard to get."

"I don't either," he said, "but I want to be able to boast that my girl has won a civil engineering scholarship at Queens."

She made no demur at his calling her "my girl." But she let his hand go, closed her eyes, and took a deep breath. "It's not to Queens, Barry. It's to Cambridge. Starting next term."

10

Some Enchanted Evening,
You May See . . .

O'Reilly was in the upstairs lounge, sitting in an armchair with his back to the door, booted feet propped up on a stuffed footstool, a large glass of what Barry knew would be John Jameson's Irish whiskey clutched in his right paw. He was listening to the crashing chords coming from the Phillips Black Box gramophone.

Barry half recognized the symphony that O'Reilly was conducting with his left hand. Lady Macbeth lay curled up on his lap, nose hidden under her tail tip.

"Evening, Fingal," Barry said to the back of O'Reilly's head.

"Pom-pom-pom-pom-pom-pom," O'Reilly boomed, waving his hand in time with the beat with the enthusiasm of a drunken semaphore signaller.

Barry moved round and stood in front of the chair. "Evening, Fingal."

O'Reilly held his index finger to his lips. "Tiddle-tiddle-*pom*." O'Reilly's left hand oscillated to each "da." "Da-da-da-da-da-da-*pom*." At the "pom," his clenched fist bludgeoned the air.

He grinned at Barry, who stood waiting until after a final "pom." O'Reilly said, "Be a good lad and switch the thing off. I'm heavily encatted"—he indicated the sleeping kitten—"and I don't want to disturb Her Ladyship."

Barry switched off the machine.

"Grand stuff, old Ludwig van B," O'Reilly said. "That's his Fifth Symphony."

"I didn't recognize your version of it."

"Philistine," said O'Reilly. "Never mind. Help yourself to a sherry." He finished his glass. "And top that up while you're at it. A bird—"

"I know . . . can't fly on one wing." Barry took the glass, went to the sideboard, refilled it from a decanter, and poured himself a small glass of Shooting Sherry.

"Here." He handed O'Reilly's glass back and sat in the chair opposite him.

"You're home early," O'Reilly said. "How's your Patricia?"

Barry sighed. "She's fine but—"

"But what?" O'Reilly bent forward without disturbing the cat. His shaggy eyebrows moved closer. "But what?"

Barry hesitated. "She rattled me a bit."

"How?" The eyebrows drew closer until it looked to Barry as if a single hairy-bear caterpillar were crawling across O'Reilly's forehead.

"She's trying to win a scholarship to Cambridge." It was, he knew, something in which he should take great pride, but if she won it, she'd be there in England—and he'd be here.

"Is that a fact? Good for her." O'Reilly's frown disappeared, and he raised his glass. "More power to her wheel."

Barry sipped his sherry. "I'm not so sure," he said, wondering if he should leave O'Reilly and try to find an assistantship in Cambridgeshire or apply for a specialist training position in Addenbrooke's teaching hospital.

"Why ever not?"

Barry's head drooped. "She'd be going next term." He looked up into O'Reilly's face. "I'll miss her, Fingal." He'd more than miss her. He was terrified that he would lose her.

"I know how you feel," O'Reilly said. He stood, decanting a complaining Lady Macbeth to the carpet, and walked over to stare out of the bay window. "I'd to leave a girl once."

Barry said nothing. Mrs. Kincaid had sworn him to secrecy when she'd confided in him about O'Reilly's loss during the war.

"A lot of the men in the services did." O'Reilly's voice was low.

"My dad was away for five years," Barry said. "But I was too young to know."

O'Reilly kept his back turned. "He came back to your mum, didn't he?"

"Yes." Barry'd been five when a strange, gruff-voiced, bearded man in a naval uniform had burst through the front door of the house on Victoria Road in Bangor. He would never forget his mother's excitement.

O'Reilly said softly, "There was nobody here for me."

Was there a catch in the big man's voice? If there was, Barry could understand. Kinky had explained how the love of O'Reilly's life, a young nurse, had been killed by a bomb when the Luftwaffe raided Belfast in 1941.

"I'll mebbe tell you about it one day." O'Reilly turned to face Barry and said, very deliberately, "I know you've been having second thoughts about staying here."

"Well . . ."

"And now you're wondering about looking for a post in Cambridge?"

How the hell did O'Reilly know he was? Dear God, they'd only known each other for a month, but O'Reilly seemed able to peer directly into Barry's mind.

O'Reilly walked back from the window and stood in front of Barry's chair. "I'd not be the one to stand in your way."

"That's very generous of you, Fingal. I've seen how much help you need with the practice."

O'Reilly laughed. "Not at all," he said. "I know you're in love with the girl . . ."

Barry felt himself blush. Those were the kind of sentiments Ulstermen kept to themselves, and yet O'Reilly hadn't hesitated to come right out with it. "Well, I—"

"Did you ever see *South Pacific*?"

"Yes."

O'Reilly sang gently in a deep baritone. " 'Once you have found her, never let her go.' Take my advice on that, son."

"Thanks, Fingal."

"Of course," said O'Reilly, "you're the one who'll have to decide."

"Decide what?" Barry heard the double ring of the telephone in the hall downstairs.

O'Reilly raised one eyebrow. "If you're going *from* or going *to*."

"I don't understand."

"Yesterday you talked about leaving because you felt you weren't going to succeed here. That would be going *from*. Tonight you have a notion to follow the girl you love. That would be going *to*."

Damnation. O'Reilly was absolutely right. And when he looked in his heart, Barry couldn't decide which would be the most important reason. "If you put it that way . . ."

"I do, Barry," O'Reilly said, "because it's the truth of the matter."

"I'd need to think on that." Barry knew he was playing for time. He heard the door opening.

"Do, because if you go *from* you'll always wonder if you could have made it here."

"I know."

"But then if you don't go *to*, you could end up regretting it for the rest of your life." O'Reilly looked back at the window and seemed to find something interesting in the middle distance.

Someone coughed in the doorway.

Barry turned to see Kinky, dressed in her best coat and hat and clutching a pair of gloves. She held a handbag in her other hand. "I don't want to interrupt," she said, "but I'm on the way to my Women's Union meeting. That was Ethel O'Hagan on the phone, so."

O'Reilly turned to face her. "The usual?"

"Aye. It's her Kierán again. He's blocked."

Barry heard the Cork lilt. Ulsterfolks would have called the man Kieran. Kinky pronounced it "Keer-awn." "I told her one of the doctors would be round."

"Right," said O'Reilly. "You trot on, Kinky. Enjoy your meeting. We'll see to it."

"Thank you, sir." She left.

"Bloody waiting lists," O'Reilly growled. "Kieran O'Hagan's been needing a prostatectomy for nine months."

"It's not malignant?" Barry knew that cancer cases were not kept waiting long.

O'Reilly shook his head. "Benign hypertrophy. I've told his wife what simple things to do if he gets retention. They musn't have worked, and the daft bugger won't do as he's told to try to prevent it. He likes his pint too much. His bladder fills up and he can't piss."

"It's not Friday."

"Friday?"

"When I was working in casualty in the Royal Victoria, Friday night was catheter night. The old boys would go to the pub, sink a few pints, and end up with urinary retention."

"So you're a dab hand with a catheter?"

"I've done my share."

"Good," said O'Reilly, bending over his shelves of records. "Kieran's eighty-six, and Ethel's eighty-one. They live in the housing estate in Number 17 Comber Gardens, next door to the Finnegans."

"Declan Finnegan? The man with Parkinson's disease who has a French wife?"

"You remember them?"

"Of course." Barry felt a tinge of pride in remembering the patient's name and not just the disease.

"Good." O'Reilly stood straight, holding a long-playing record. "There's a sterile catheter pack in the drawer of the instrument trolley. It's labeled, so help yourself."

"You mean you want me to go . . . You're not coming?"

"Lord Jasus." O'Reilly lifted the Beethoven from the turntable and put another record in its place. "He's a big man is Kieran O'Hagan, but his willy's not so big it'll take the pair of us to pop a thin rubber tube through it."

"Right," said Barry, pleased to have been distracted from their earlier discussion and more pleased to be sent out on his own. He was going to say more, but O'Reilly was staring out the window again.

"I'm off," Barry said, setting his half-finished sherry on the sideboard. He ran downstairs, pausing only in the surgery to collect the sterile pack.

Coming from upstairs he heard the first bars of Mozart's Requiem, sad, ponderous, and solemn, and he wondered if O'Reilly had selected a piece to reflect his mood. The loss of the girl he was daft about had indeed hit the big man sore. It must have cost him to refer to it, even obliquely, and to say he might tell Barry the story one day.

Barry went out through the front door and round the house to the back lane where Brunhilde his elderly Volkswagen was parked. Arthur Guinness barked once from his kennel as Barry approached. Fooled you this time, dog, Barry thought as he drove away.

The sun had gone and was painting the few clouds with pastel pinks. The first star was up above the village, a silver sequin on a velvet sky. Barry stopped at the traffic light just in time to see Seamus Galvin, one arm round Donal Donnelly's shoulder, heading through the doors of the Mucky Duck.

The light changed and Barry drove to the housing estate. He had no difficulty finding Comber Gardens and Number 17. He parked, grabbed the pack, and walked to the O'Hagans' front door.

He noticed how the sandstone of the single front step was spotless. On any morning of the week, all the women would be out with buckets of hot, soapy water and stiff brushes, down on their hands and knees, scrubbing away at the steps like the crew of a man-of-war holystoning the deck. But unlike sailors, who were bound to strict silence, the women would be jabbering away like a flock of jackdaws, gossiping, arguing, and weaving more tightly the fabric of their corner of Ballybucklebo.

Barry knocked on the door and waited until it was opened by a diminutive woman wearing a calico pinafore and pink, fluffy carpet slippers. She was tiny, wizened. Her hands were gnarled, blue-veined, and discoloured with liver spots.

"Mrs. O'Hagan?"

"It is."

"I'm Doctor Laverty."

"Could himself not come?" she asked in a thin, raspy voice.

Here we go again. "I'm sorry," Barry said, knowing what O'Reilly would say, "but he's been called out to another emergency."

"You'll have to do," she said. "Come on in."

He followed her into a thinly carpeted hall and up a narrow staircase.

"Kieran's in here." She pushed open a narrow door to a tiny room. A medicine cabinet with a cracked mirror hung from a wall whose paper had peeled away to reveal the cheap, pink plaster behind it. The room smelled of mildew.

According to O'Reilly, the housing estate had been built by Councillor Bishop, who had cut as many corners as possible to increase his profit. Bastard. He made money while these folks had to live in damp, jerry-built slums.

Both taps were running into a chipped, enamelled washbasin. A man, who must have been at least six foot six, sat hunched on the seat of a porcelain toilet beside a tiny, half-filled, cast-iron, claw-foot bathtub. He wore only a striped shirt. He was completely bald, and his face, creased as dried chamois leather, was screwed up. His breath came in short puffs.

"This here's Doctor Laverty, Kieran," Mrs. O'Hagan said. "He's come to fix you, so he has."

"Just . . . get . . . a . . . move . . . on," Mr. O'Hagan begged through clenched teeth.

Barry could see the swelling above the man's wiry, grey pubic hairs. The skin of his belly hung in thin folds. "Can we get you along to the bedroom, Mr. O'Hagan?" It would be impossible to have him lie on the floor here.

"Aye . . . just . . . hurry." He rose unsteadily and put an arm round Barry's shoulder. "You'll . . . have . . . to oxtercog me."

Barry knew that in Ulster oxter was the armpit, and cog meant to carry.

"Right." For a man of such height O'Hagan was remarkably light. "Which way, Mrs. O'Hagan?"

"First door on the right. Do you need a hand?"

"I'll manage up here," Barry said, "but can you go get a big bowl or a bucket and some towels?"

"Yes, sir."

Barry heard her leave. Clutching his pack in one hand, he manoeuvered the tall man to the bathroom door and along a narrow landing.

Behind him, over Mr. O'Hagan's grunts, Barry could hear the taps still splashing water in the sink.

The bedroom door was open. He groped for a light switch, found it, and switched on a bare, overhead bulb. A brass bed was crammed against one wall. He set the pack on a dresser next to a framed sepia tint of a young couple in wedding clothes. As he helped the patient onto the bed, Barry wondered how long the O'Hagans had been married.

"Won't be long now," Barry said.

"Thank Christ for that." Mr. O'Hagan held his lower belly with both hands.

Mrs. O'Hagan came in carrying two threadbare towels and a large porcelain basin. "Here y'are."

Barry took both towels. "Can you lift your backside?" As soon as there was clearance under the man's buttocks, he spread the towels on the counterpane beneath. "Right. Now can you put your legs apart?

"Basin, please." He set the receptacle in the space at the top of the patient's thighs; then he took the pack from the dresser, set it on the bed, and opened the outer wrapping. "I'll just go and wash my hands." When he returned from the bathroom, he dried his hands on a sterile towel and slipped on a pair of rubber gloves. Presoaked antiseptic swabs were loaded in sponge forceps. Barry cleansed the tip and shaft of Mr. O'Hagan's penis, dropped the forceps on the towel on the bed, and wrapped the organ in a second sterile towel.

Mr. O'Hagan had started to whistle through his clenched teeth. It was an old hymn, "Nearer, My God, to Thee."

A red, India-rubber catheter was coiled neatly around a small sterilized tube of K-Y Jelly. Barry unscrewed the cap, lubricated the tip of the catheter, and grasped it in his right hand. He lifted the penis with his left. "This may hurt a bit," he said, as he began to thread the slightly angled, rigid tip of the catheter through the urinary meatus at the tip of the penis.

Mr. O'Hagan's hymn rose an octave, but he made no other sound.

Barry fed in more of the catheter until he felt the tip hit something solid. He took a deep breath. This would be the tricky bit: getting past the obstruction of the enlarged prostate where it clasped the urethra at the neck of the bladder. He nudged the near end of the red rubber tube over the basin's lip.

Next he used his left hand to lift the flaccid organ to a vertical position, and he pushed with his right. The second he felt any advance, he dropped his left hand and pushed harder with his right.

Mr. O'Hagan's single note climbed the scale as the catheter slipped in and bright urine gushed into the basin.

Barry couldn't help thinking of Madame de Pompadour's words, "Aprés nous, le déluge."

Mr. O'Hagan sighed, and Barry glanced up to see a toothless smile.

He used his left hand to exert gentle suprapubic pressure and then waited; when the flow into the basin finally stopped, he slipped the catheter out.

"Boys-a-dear," said Mr. O'Hagan. "I've had that there done a brave wheen of times, but . . . It's Doctor Laverty?"

Barry nodded.

"Well, young fellah, you've a quare soft hand under a duck, so you have."

Barry smiled, not only at the quaint Ulsterism meaning gentleness, but also because the procedure had gone so smoothly.

"Aye," he heard Mrs. O'Hagan say from over his shoulder. "And nary a drop spilt on my clean counterpane neither."

Barry tidied up his equipment, stripped off his rubber gloves, and said, "Try to have a decent night's sleep, Mr. O'Hagan. And if it happens again don't hesitate to ring before it gets too bad. I'll give the hospital a call in the morning to see if we can get them to speed things up."

"I'd appreciate that, Doc," the old man said, "but never you worry. If I need it done again, you can come round anytime, so you can." He smiled.

"Fair enough." Barry picked up his bundle. "Time I was off."

"I'll see you out, Doctor Laverty." Mrs. O'Hagan left, carrying the half-full bowl. "I'll just flush this and turn off the taps."

Barry had wondered about the running taps. He waited in the hall until she came downstairs.

"Would you like a wee cup of tea in your hand, Doctor?"

"No thanks, Mrs. O'Hagan." Barry was gratified to have been invited. "But I do have a question."

"Fire away."

"Why was the bath full and the taps running?"

"Och, Doctor dear," she said, "we don't like to disturb people at night, and Doctor O'Reilly had taught us a few wee tricks that work for my man sometimes, so we were giving them a go first."

Barry waited.

"Aye. Sometimes if Kieran hears the taps running he sort of comes out in sympathy."

Barry smiled. He'd seen the same trick used to get a patient's slow bladder going in the hospital, particularly on the gynaecology ward.

"Sometimes if I sit him in the bath . . ."

That was a new one.

"But tonight, divil the bit of use was either." She beckoned with her finger, and Barry had to bend to hear what she was whispering. "I shouldn't be telling you this, but you're a doctor and all, so you are."

Yes, I am, Barry thought, and it's nice to have someone notice.

"Well, last week we'd the plumber in to fix the kitchen sink. There was a wee air lock in the water pipe, so there was."

Barry frowned. Air lock?

"I reckoned maybe Kieran had one . . . now you'll not tell nobody?"

"Of course not."

"I tried what worked for the plumber, so I did. I took hold of Kieran's willy . . . you're not to laugh . . . and I tried blowing up it . . . the way the plumber did."

The mental picture of this tiny old woman huffing and puffing into her husband's penis was almost too much for Barry. He just managed to control himself.

"It didny work so we'd to send for you. We're main glad you come, so we are. I hate to see my man suffer." There was a tear on her cheek.

"Glad to help," Barry said, opening the front door.

"Another wee thing, Doctor Laverty . . ."

"Yes?"

"Don't you pay no heed to what folks is saying about you. Me and Kieran'll tell them they're full of shite, so we will."

"I appreciate that, Mrs. O'Hagan. I really do. Now," he said, starting to leave," I really must be running along."

He opened Brunhilde's door, chucked the used pack on the passenger seat, and climbed in. He knew he was smiling broadly, certainly because he could still picture Mrs. O'Hagan's dramatic attempts to ease her husband's suffering, but also because of what she had just said.

As he started the engine, Barry wondered had O'Reilly simply wanted to be on his own for a while after confiding a little to Barry about a loss that still troubled the big man? Perhaps. Or was he being devious? O'Reilly would know there were few more grateful patients than those suffering from acute urinary retention once the pressure was relieved. Was that why he'd sent Barry out on his own?

He pulled away from the kerb. If that had been O'Reilly's plan, it was working. It wouldn't take many more grateful patients like the O'Hagans to start getting him back on his feet with the locals—and by Friday he'd know how well Colin Brown's cut had healed and how the treatments of Fergus Finnegan's conjunctivitis and Myrtle MacVeigh's pyelonephritis had turned out. Perhaps he'd have a couple more supporters by then.

Barry left the housing estate and drove along Main Street past the lighted windows of the tobacconist's, the shop that stayed open later than any of the others, and past the darkened windows of the greengrocer, the fishmonger, and the hardware store. He stopped at the traffic light.

The windows of the Mucky Duck were frosted glass, but illuminated by the lights from within he could read the words etched in the glass:

Black Swan
William Dunleavy, Proprietor
Licensed for the Sale of Porters, Stouts, Ales,
Fine Wines, Spirits, and Tobaccos.

He'd half a mind to pop in for a beer, but he hesitated. It was too soon to risk going in, hearing the conversation die, and feeling every eye on him.

He drove on through the green light. O'Reilly was almost certainly right. Patience and a few more grateful patients, and Barry wouldn't need to feel he had to go *from*.

He sighed as he parked in the dark back lane. The trouble was, if he was successful in reestablishing himself here in Ballybucklebo, he was going to find it a damn sight more difficult to go *to*.

11

Rich and Rare Were the Gems . . .

"Oh Lord," O'Reilly groaned, peeping through the crack as he held the waiting room door ajar. "Not him. Not on a Tuesday."

Barry couldn't see past O'Reilly. "Who, Fingal?"

"The all-high mucky-muck of Ballybucklebo, His Serene Highness, Worshipful Master of the Orange Lodge, Great Panjandrum, and probably first cousin to the Lord of the Flies . . ."

Barry smiled. "Would that be Beelzebub or Councillor Bishop?"

"Bishop. In the flesh," said O'Reilly, just before he opened the door. "If only *that* lump of 'too too solid flesh would melt.' "

Hamlet, Barry thought. He heard the chorus of "Good morning, Doctor O'Reilly," and O'Reilly asking, "Right, who's first?"

"Who the hell else would it be, O'Reilly?" Barry recognized the councillor's voice. "Me and the missus have waited long enough, so we have."

"It's not *quite* nine yet," O'Reilly remarked, "but I'm sure your time is precious. Do come along."

Barry went into the surgery and sat up on the examining couch. Whatever small start he might be making to reestablish his reputation in the village would not be improved by this consultation. He waited until O'Reilly took his seat in the swivel chair. Fingal's nose tip was pallid, reflecting like the upper tenth of an iceberg the dangers lurking beneath the surface.

Councillor Bishop strode in, much, Barry thought, as it is given to a man of five foot four and a good fourteen stone to stride. He wore his customary black suit and across his belly a watch chain from which a miniature, gold Masonic set-square pendant swung. The councillor did not have the courtesy to remove his bowler hat. He sat down hard in one of the wooden chairs, tucked his thumbs under the lapels of his jacket, and without bothering either to turn around or to acknowledge Barry's presence, snarled, "Would youse get a move on, Flo? I haven't got all day."

"Coming, dear." Mrs. Florence Bishop's voice was expressionless and as grating as cinders under a door. Kinky had described Florence as one of "nature's unclaimed treasures" in an effort to explain why a basically decent woman would have settled for marrying a man like Bertie Bishop. It was no secret why he'd married her—for the money she'd inherited.

Florence was probably in her early forties but looked ten years older. Her hair was short, listless, and a peculiar red that could only have been achieved by the liberal use of henna. Her left eye had difficulty remaining aligned with her right, and her floral dress must have been tailored by a company specializing in bell tents. She had calves, Barry thought, like a Mullingar heifer's, and the flesh of her ankles bulged over a pair of low-heeled brogues.

Barry heard the second wooden chair complain when she sat. From where he was perched, the couple reminded him of Sir John Tenniel's drawings of Tweedledum and Tweedledee for *Through the Looking Glass*.

"You took your time," the councillor said.

"Sorry, dear."

"And what seems to be the trouble?" asked O'Reilly civilly, looking the councillor in the eye.

"There's nothing wrong with me, so there's not. She's just not up to much. I want you to fix her, O'Reilly." He seemed to be unaware of his wife's presence. Barry noticed that Fingal's recent threat to "gut the councillor like a herring if he forgot it was *Doctor* O'Reilly," did not seem to be carrying much weight. Of course, O'Reilly's ace had been trumped now that it was no longer possible publicly to accuse the councillor of hanky-panky with Julie MacAteer. "And don't waste your time asking her what's wrong. She can't hardly get a sentence out of her."

Barry sat forwards. Something about the inability to do that rang a tiny bell. He listened intently.

"You'd think she was working on a trade union's go-slow. She can't finish a job about the house . . ."

"Sorry, dear . . ."

"And since that Julie MacAteeer, the wee tramp, quit, we've no maid, and there's no one but Flo to do the work."

"Sorry, dear . . ."

"Houl' your wheest, woman. I'm talking to the doctor."

Barry saw her flinch.

"Come the end of the day she's about as much use as a fart in a high wind. She gets as weak as water."

"I don't suppose you'd think of giving Mrs. Bishop a hand?" O'Reilly asked.

"Me? Away off. I'm far too busy."

Barry frowned. Weakness, inability to finish a task, or a sentence. Damn it, those symptoms were common in a rare neurological disorder, but he couldn't remember which one. There was another associated symptom and it was . . .

"I'm sorry to hear that, Florence," O'Reilly said gently. "I really am." He put a hand on her knee.

"She's been like that for the last six months. Never mind your sympathy. Do something." Bishop pulled out his fob watch, flipped open the lid, and scowled at the dial.

Barry felt like a villager waiting on the lower slopes of Mount Vesuvius for the inevitable eruption, but O'Reilly's virtually guaranteed seismic cataclysm failed to occur.

"I think," O'Reilly said, rising, "we'd better take a look at you, Florence."

"Get on with it then." Bishop made no effort to help his wife stand.

"I wonder if you shouldn't consult the vet next time, Mr. Bishop?" O'Reilly remarked.

"What are you on about?"

"Vets make diagnoses in patients who can't explain their symptoms by themselves."

"Just get on with it. I'm in a hurry. I'm going to be late."

"'For a very important date,' no doubt," said O'Reilly. Helping Mrs. Bishop to stand, he guided her to the examination couch.

Barry, hopping down from the table, had a vivid mental image of Councillor Bishop as the rabbit in Walt Disney's version of *Alice in Wonderland*, but he refused to let it distract him from watching O'Reilly carry out a rapid, yet thorough, examination.

O'Reilly frowned. "Come on down," he said, offering Florence an arm to lean on. With one eyebrow raised, he glanced at Barry and gave an almost imperceptible shrug, as if to say, "Buggered if I know."

Weakness, inability to finish a task or a sentence, no obvious physical findings? Barry screwed his eyes shut. Sometimes when he did, a remembered page of a textbook would appear. He vaguely saw something about demonstrating pathological fatigue. "Doctor O'Reilly?"

"Yes."

"May I ask Mrs. Bishop something?"

"Go right ahead."

"Is it hard to chew?"

"Aye," she said. "And I love my vittles, so I do."

Barry smiled at her. "This is going to sound a bit daft, Mrs. Bishop, but could you raise your arm above your head about thirty times?"

She glanced at O'Reilly, who nodded.

"Right," she said. She started to do as she was asked.

"How much longer is this going to take?" Bishop demanded. "I didn't come here to watch you put Flo through a bunch of physical jerks."

"Doctor Laverty?" O'Reilly asked.

"Only a bit longer."

Barry watched Mrs. Bishop start to sweat, and after twenty repetitions she heaved a deep breath and said, "I can do no more. My arm's banjaxed." It hung limply by her side.

"God almighty," Bishop said, "didn't I tell you she gets tired?"

"Indeed you did, Bertie," O'Reilly remarked. "I wonder why?"

Barry wasn't sure if O'Reilly was struggling to make a diagnosis or hinting that having to live with the councillor would tire an Amazon, never mind an overweight woman like his wife.

"Doctor Laverty," she said, "I think I can get my arm up again. Should I?"

"Please."

She lifted it.

"That's grand," he said. "Thank you." He noticed the damp stain in the armpit of her dress.

He was almost certain now. Her symptoms and how she tired rapidly but recovered equally rapidly were typical of—he knew, he knew—but damn it, he still couldn't quite remember what the disease was. Barry glanced at O'Reilly, who simply shook his head.

"Mrs. Bishop," Barry said, hating to have to admit defeat, "I think we've a pretty good idea what ails you."

"About bloody time," the councillor grunted. "What is it then?"

"I'm not exactly sure but—"

"No bloody wonder." The councillor stood. "A right waste of time this, O'Reilly, so it is."

"I think," said O'Reilly, "Doctor Laverty said he wasn't *sure.*"

"Aye. And we all know what *that* means. Laverty's a useless bugger."

Barry flinched but inwardly refused to let Bishop's scorn rattle him. He glanced at O'Reilly, who was taking a deep breath in preparation, no doubt, for giving Bishop the tongue lashing of his life. Barry shook his head and waited to see if O'Reilly would let him handle matters. O'Reilly clamped his lips shut.

Barry ignored Bishop and spoke directly to Mrs. Bishop. "Mrs. Bishop, I'm almost certain I know what ails you, but I'll need a day or two to talk to a colleague in Belfast. Could you come back on Friday?"

He saw her glance at Bishop, who shook his head and muttered under his breath.

"Or," said Barry, "we could send you up to the Royal for a second opinion from one of the consultants." This is what he and his contemporaries used to refer to scornfully as "kicking for touch," the safest tactic in a game of rugby football, and in medicine, to some degree, an admission of professional failure.

"Do both," snapped Bishop. "I want this sorted out as quick as possible, and them highheejins at the Royal have waiting lists as long as Bangor Pier."

Barry had to admit that the suggestion made sense. He saw O'Reilly nod in agreement.

"All right," he said. "Mrs. Bishop, please don't overtire yourself. Come back on Friday, and in the meantime I'll arrange things at the Royal."

"Is that it?" Bishop demanded, consulting his watch. "Are you done?"

"I am, Mr. Bishop."

"Come on then, Flo." Bishop grabbed his wife's arm and hustled her to the door. "I've to get things sorted out about the Black Swan."

"And a very good morning to you too, Councillor," O'Reilly said to the departing backs. "Do close the door after you."

The door swung shut.

"Gobshite," O'Reilly growled. "Unmitigated gobshite." He pulled his half-moon spectacles down his nose and looked over them at Barry. "I thought you handled him very well by the way."

Barry glanced down.

"So," O'Reilly asked, "what *do* you think's the matter?"

Barry hesitated. "I never was much of a hand at neurology."

"Nor me," said O'Reilly. "I always thought it was a race between the clinicians when the patients were alive and the pathologists after they'd died to see who got the diagnosis right."

Barry smiled. "When I spent my time on that service, we reckoned that the right diagnosis depended on who made it. The more senior the neurologist and the more sonorously he made his pronouncement, the more likely he was to be believed."

"Sure all of medicine's like that," O'Reilly said. "The way we were taught, a thing was so because the professor said it was." He stood and stretched. "Did you ever read a book called *The Cry and the Covenant*?

"By Morton Thompson?"

"The very fellah. It's about a nineteenth-century Viennese obstetrician called Semmelweis who made all his students wash their dirty hands in a solution of chloride of lime before they delivered a woman . . ."

"And he cut the mortality rate from childbirth fever from about one in ten to less than two percent . . ."

"And because he challenged the medical establishment of the time, they destroyed him. But he was right." O'Reilly parked himself in his chair. "Sometimes," he said, "sometimes I think we could use a few more like Semmelweiss to challenge the establishment." He scratched his head. "Enough philosophy. You haven't answered my question."

Being momentarily distracted by O'Reilly's observations had allowed the same mysterious meshing of Barry's mental gears that often helped him solve crossword puzzles.

"I have it," he said, grinning.

"And no doubt penicillin cures it. Would you mind letting me in on the secret?"

"She's almost certainly got Myasthenia gravis."

O'Reilly whistled. "I don't believe I've ever seen a case. It's rare as a hen's teeth."

It was all coming back. Barry rattled off what he had remembered. "A disease afflicting neuromuscular transmission. Characterized by fatigue of striped muscle and rapid recovery after a period of rest."

"You showed she's got that all right."

Barry carried on. "Hardly if ever fatal, but very debilitating. The symptoms may rarely be associated with thyrotoxicosis and with carcinomatous neuropathy."

"That's right . . . but I don't think a woman of that size could be riddled with cancer, do you?"

"I doubt it very much. And she's no other symptoms."

"So we can rule out a cancer somewhere?"

Barry hesitated. He'd made one mistake with Major Fotheringham by making assumptions that had turned out to be wrong. "Give me a minute, Fingal. Carcinomatous neuropathy doesn't usually show up until the cancer is really advanced, usually way past being treatable. Any patient that sick would be skin and bone by now . . ."

"Hardly Flo Bishop . . ."

"And if I'm wrong"—he swallowed—"she's beyond our help anyway."

"Some of them are," O'Reilly said quietly.

"I think we should concentrate on trying to find out if she has something we can help."

"Agreed . . . but we should have her thyroid hormone levels measured. Just to be sure about that."

"Right. And for primary Myasthenia there's a simple test we can do right here in the surgery, but I can't remember exactly what it is," he said. "I could go up to Belfast and have a word with Professor Faulkner at the Royal—"

"Why not just phone him?"

"Professor Faulkner *never* takes phone calls, at least not from very junior doctors, but I could catch him after he makes his ward rounds on Wednesday afternoon."

"You go right ahead. I'll look after the shop while you're away," O'Reilly said. He stood and shook Barry's hand. "If you're right, son, it'll be Laverty ten, Bishop nil . . . and it'll work wonders for your reputation. I'll see to that."

Barry refrained from asking how, but he relished the thought of discomfiting the arrogant little man. "I'd not mind putting one over the dear councillor." He laughed.

"You laugh away, son," said O'Reilly, "but remember, 'A man that studieth revenge keeps his own wounds green.' "

"You've lost me on that one, Fingal."

"It's from an essay by Francis Bacon called 'Of Revenge.' " There was a twinkle in O'Reilly's brown eyes. Barry knew that just because he had made the diagnosis first, the older man wasn't going to let him forget that "not all of us country GPs are entirely unlettered." It was all very well to be mentally patting himself on the back, but the question remained, was he right?

"You don't mind me taking over her management?"

O'Reilly laughed. "It's your case, Barry. You do as you see fit."

"Thanks, Fingal."

"Huh. Never mind thanks. Nip along . . ."

"I know, and see who's next." Barry headed for the door, somehow feeling less like a glorified receptionist, quite happy to do O'Reilly's bidding. As he walked out the door he heard O'Reilly musing, "I wonder what Bertie Bishop meant about getting things sorted out at the Black Swan?"

12

Her Rash Hand in Evil Hour

Barry ushered an elderly woman out through the surgery door. After the Bishops left, the morning had flown by. O'Reilly had let Barry handle the work, but his presence in the surgery must have been reassuring to the patients. It certainly had been to Barry as he steadily worked through the morning's caseload.

Boys with sniffles, sore muscles, seborrhoea, acne; men with arthritis, angina, haemorrhoids, upset stomachs. Mothers with fractious babies, difficulty breast-feeding; children with earaches; women with heavy periods, no periods, prolapse of the uterus. Most he could handle in the surgery, but he'd had to refer three people to specialists at the Royal Victoria: the man whose angina was worsening, the woman whose periods were so heavy she had developed anaemia, and the woman whose periods had stopped six months earlier, but who as far as Barry could determine, wasn't pregnant.

As each seemed to accept his advice—and most of them were gracious when they did so—Barry's confidence grew. Perhaps O'Reilly was right, that all Barry had to do was do his job to the best of his ability. He just wished that the results of Major Fotheringham's postmortem would arrive soon, but he knew that the Home Office pathologists could not be rushed, and all deaths for which the doctor could not sign a death certificate automatically fell under their jurisdiction.

He opened the waiting room door. One last patient, a young woman, sat on a bench in front of the hideous, rose-pattern wallpaper, flipping through the pages of a dog-eared *Woman's Own*. He guessed she was in her early twenties, a pretty, red-haired, freckled girl with emerald green eyes. She wore white cotton gloves, a short white raincoat, the cuffs of a long-sleeved blouse peeping out past the ends of the sleeves, and a tartan, ankle-length skirt.

Barry found that unusual. The short skirt, popularized by Courreges earlier in 1964, was all the rage with some young Ulsterwomen. Even so, the brief flirtation in June among London fashion circles with topless evening dresses had *not* caught on here. He smothered a smile.

"Morning," he said. "Will you come with me, please?"

She rose. "Doctor Laverty?"

"That's right."

"Oh," she said noncommittally, but followed him along the hall.

He let her precede him into the surgery.

"Come on in, Helen Hewitt," he heard O'Reilly say. "Have a pew."

She sat.

"Would you mind if I asked Doctor Laverty to take a look?"

Barry saw her blush and shake her head. His earlier hopes that perhaps he was gaining ground were rattled.

"Why?" he heard O'Reilly ask.

"I'm embarrassed, so I am." She stared at the carpet.

O'Reilly stood and put a hand under her chin, raising her head until she had to look into his eyes. "I know, Helen," he said, "but I'd guess what I've been giving you isn't working."

Barry saw her green eyes grow moist.

"That's right," she whispered.

O'Reilly glanced over his half-moons at Barry before saying, "Doctor Laverty may have some new ideas."

She half turned, stared at Barry, and glanced back to O'Reilly like a little girl seeking reassurance from her mother. Then she said quietly, "I suppose so." She took off her raincoat and gloves and rolled up one of her long sleeves. She stretched her arm to Barry and pointed at the hollow in front of her elbow. "It's that there," she said.

Barry bent forward. Her lower arm was, like her face, freckled. There was a rash in the antecubital fossa and on the skin of her palm. It was angry red, weeping, and scaly.

"It itches something ferocious," she said.

"And is it the same on the other side, and behind your knees?" he asked.

She nodded.

That would explain the gloves, the long sleeves, and the ankle-length dress. She'd be too ashamed to let people see her disfigurement. No wonder she'd not wanted to show it to Barry.

"You've got eczema," he said. He saw O'Reilly nod. Eczema, Barry thought, running through a mental checklist. "How long have you had it?"

"About two months."

So it wasn't infantile eczema, which appeared in babyhood and was often accompanied by asthma.

"Have you changed your diet recently?"

"I'm not fat," she said. "I've never been on a diet in my life."

Barry heard the hint of anger in her voice and cursed himself for forgetting how literal the Ulster patient could be.

"I'm sorry," he said. "I didn't mean to suggest you were overweight . . ." He hesitated, wondering if he dare compliment her, and decided that he should. "You've a wonderful figure."

"Aye. Well," she said, sounding mollified. Was that a flicker of a smile?

"I just meant, have you been eating anything different recently?" Eczema could be caused by some foods and cosmetics.

"Not at all."

"Helen and I have worked our way through her soaps, detergents, lipsticks, and nail varnishes," O'Reilly added. "And she doesn't use hair dye."

"You don't need to, you've beautiful hair," Barry said. That took care of another set of possible causes.

Her smile broadened. "And Doctor O'Reilly made me stop wearing stockings . . ." She looked to O'Reilly for further reassurance. O'Reilly nodded. "And my bra." She swallowed, clearly discomfited by having to reveal such personal details. "He said the nickel on the clips on it or on my suspender belt could be the cause."

Despite himself, despite seven years of training, Barry suddenly had a vividly erotic image of the young woman wearing nothing but scanty lingerie and, worse, of Patricia similarly dressed. He coughed, reminded himself that doctors were human but were obliged to deal with their own feelings. He banished the disturbing thoughts and tried to concentrate. "I see." He turned to O'Reilly. "Helen's not had any penicillin or streptomycin?" As a student he had been admonished against overexposure to those antibiotics. Contact dermatitis was particularly prevalent among nurses and doctors.

"No," said O'Reilly.

Barry hesitated. He'd been taught that some cases of eczema could be stress-related, but to raise the question, to suggest that someone might not be entirely in control, was fraught with risk. Any hint of mental illness was treated as the gravest insult by country folk. He recalled a woman who'd sworn blind that her husband was in jail rather than admit he was in a mental hospital. He tried to think of a tactful way to broach the subject, remembering how violently Maggie MacCorkle reacted when he first met her, suspected she was unhinged, and asked her if she had been hearing voices. He frowned, then said, "Has anything changed in your life in the last few months?" She couldn't possibly be offended by that—could she?

"Aye," Helen said. "I got a new job about three months ago."

Interesting. "Would you like to tell me about it?" Surely O'Reilly would have found this out or even known about it before she had consulted him. There were very few secrets in Ballybucklebo.

"I went to work for Miss Moloney. In her dress shop."

Hardly a stressful occupation. "How do you get along with her?" He saw fires burning in the depths of those green eyes.

"She's an oul' hoor, so she is. She has the personality of a bagful of hammers. She's a holy terror and she hates the young ones. She's a whey-faced oul' nag-bag . . ." She covered her mouth with her hand.

Barry waited. He knew he'd struck the mother lode. The young woman remained silent, staring at the floor. He coaxed her gently. "It's all right, Helen; whatever you say in here stays in here."

Helen looked at Barry. "She's driving me daft, so she is. Last week she caught me talking to Johnny Dougan. 'Helen,' say she, in her voice that would fillet a herring at ten fathoms, 'come away from that person.' She looked at Johnny as if he was something a boar'd thrown up in a pigsty. 'I'm not paying you to stand round blethering all day. The hats need rearranging.' They did not. Hadn't I spent all morning doing that?"

"It doesn't sound as if you're very happy there."

"Happy? I'd be happier hanging up by my thumbs."

Barry looked at O'Reilly. Surely he must have known this. Why hadn't he suggested she get another job?

"And don't bother saying I should get another job," she said. "Doctor O'Reilly's already told me he thinks working with the old witch has given me this." She pointed at the rash. "You said," she half smiled at O'Reilly, "working with Miss Moloney would make a saint take the rickets."

O'Reilly cleared his throat.

"So why not just leave?" It seemed simple to Barry.

"I wish I could, but I can't do it."

"Why not?"

"Wee Mary Dunleavy, Willy Dunleavy's girl."

Barry frowned. He recognized the name but didn't recall seeing a patient called Willy. Willy? He'd got it. The licensee and barman at the Black Swan. The Bible, he thought, had a book called Numbers that detailed the genealogy of the Israelites. He just wished there was a similar publication to help him keep track of the interrelationships of the local citizenry.

"What's Mary got to do with it?" he asked.

She sniffed. "Huh. Mary works part-time there. That Miss Moloney has a tongue on her like a drayman's whip, so she has. She never leaves the poor wee girl alone. She has her in tears half the day. Sure I couldn't leave wee Mary to face that by herself."

"Why not?"

"She's been looking for something else. She needs the money, but there's not that many part-time jobs here and she can't leave Ballybucklebo."

"She can't?"

"No, because her dad needs her to help out behind the bar, so he does. He can't afford to take on a full-time barman until he knows what's going to happen with the Duck."

It was all getting too complicated for Barry. What the hell had a pub got to do with a young woman's eczema?

"Oh." Barry looked to O'Reilly, who held out both hands, palms up. Barry guessed what the big man was thinking. It seemed poor Helen was stuck. He asked, "What have you tried, Doctor O'Reilly?"

O'Reilly consulted no records. He simply said, "Calamine lotion when the rash first blew up, then Lassar's paste—that's zinc oxide with salicylic acid—and when it didn't work, medical coal tar." He shook his head. "By the look of your arm, Helen, the tar's not doing a great deal either."

That left only the newer hydrocortisone ointment, and even that would not get at what Barry was sure was the root cause. He made one more try. "Are you sure you couldn't find work somewhere else?"

She shook her head vehemently. "Not as long as wee Mary's there. And she will be as long as her da needs her." She frowned. "Mind you, that might not be for much longer. She's main scared someone's trying to get ahold of the Duck and put her da out of a job, and that would be a calamity of the first magnitude. Then she'd have to ask Miss Moloney for a full-time job."

"Why would she think someone was after the pub, Helen?" O'Reilly asked. Barry heard the seriousness in O'Reilly's voice.

"Bedamned if I know, Doctor, but she told me her da was worried."

"Mmm," said O'Reilly. "Mmm." He pulled off his spectacles and put a hand on her shoulder. "Never you mind about the old Duck," he said. "You try not to let Miss Moloney upset you."

"Aye, and no harm to you, Doctor, but you try to stop the tide coming in."

"Fair enough." O'Reilly laughed. "Now," he said, "maybe Doctor Laverty here has a notion for a new ointment."

Barry watched as she stared at him; then to his surprise she said, "Back there a wee while, Doctor Laverty, you was trying to puzzle out how to ask me if I was astray in the head, weren't you?"

"Well, I—"

"And you were right tactful about it, so you were. So write you me the scrip, and I'll give it a wee try." She pulled down her sleeve and buttoned the cuff, rose, and waited until Barry filled in a prescription. "Thanks very much," she said when he handed her the slip. "I'd be right glad to get rid of this here itch." She rose.

"I can't promise it'll work," Barry said.

"Sure don't I know that? You're only a doctor . . . not the sainted Jesus Christ almighty."

Any feelings of pride Barry might have had for winning the young woman's confidence were stifled, but, he told himself, her attitude wasn't such a bad thing. At least her expectations were realistic. She'd be less disappointed if the results were poor—and less likely to blame him. "If I was, Helen, I'd chuck in my degree and go full-time into the laying-on-of-hands business."

"Aye," said O'Reilly, "and you could look forward to a bloody miserable Easter too."

Barry heard Helen join him as he laughed at the older man's irreverence. "Can you come back and see us in a month?" he asked.

"Aye, certainly, Doctor Laverty, but I'd better be running along now." She curled her lip. "The Wicked Witch of the West'll be having carniptions if I'm not back to give her a hand. She's a wheen of new hats coming in for the ladies. There'll be a brave few bought for Maggie MacCorkle's wedding."

"Right enough," said O'Reilly as she left, "and for Donal Donnelly's." He hauled out his briar and lit up. "So," he enquired, "how do you think the morning went?"

Barry shrugged. "Apart from the Bishops, well enough. And thanks for letting me do the work."

O'Reilly rose. "It should have you persuaded that not *all* the locals think you're Vlad the Impaler."

Barry laughed. "Who in God's name was he?"

"The inspiration for Bram Stoker's *Dracula*, and him a good Dublin man."

"Vlad the Impaler?"

"No, you goat, Stoker. The Vlad fellah. He was nearly as nasty a piece of work as Bertie Bishop. Mind you, fair play to Bertie, he hasn't started skewering peasants on spikes . . . at least, not yet."

Barry shuddered. "Nice subject just before lunch."

"You're right." O'Reilly clapped Barry on the shoulder. "Come on. Lunch. I'm famished. And we'll see what Kinky has in store for us for home visits this afternoon."

"We promised to call in on Mrs. McVeigh."

"We did indeed. Good on you for remembering." O'Reilly strode to the door. "And I think if there's not too many more calls to make, the pair of us should nip into the Duck on our way home."

"Why?" As if Barry didn't know. Fingal Flahertie O'Reilly never needed an excuse to drop in for a quick pint.

"Because . . . ," said O'Reilly, tapping the pipe mouthpiece against his lower teeth, "because Helen said Willy's worried that someone's after his place *and* Buggerlugs Bertie Bishop said something about sorting things out about the Black Swan."

"Ah," said Barry.

"Indeed," said O'Reilly. "I think 'something is rotten in the state of Denmark.'"

Before Barry could answer, "*Hamlet*," O'Reilly had gone through to the hall, and Barry could hear him yelling, "Lunch, please, Kinky."

13

The Place Had an
Ancient Permanence

"Here you are now, Doctors." Mrs. Kinkaid set a tureen in the centre of the table. She turned to leave. "I'll be back in a shmall little minute with the bread and cheese, so."

O'Reilly lifted the lid, and a rising cloud of steam momentarily blocked Barry's view of a rich red soup, a whorl of white cream and sprinkles of parsley on its surface.

"Gimme your plate," said O'Reilly. Then taking Barry's plate, he ladled the soup. The ladle made a clinking sound against the dish's bottom. "Here." He passed it to Barry, who lifted a spoonful to his lips. This was none of the Heinz canned stuff. The flavour of tomatoes was subtly complimented by a hint of ham and a soupçon of celery.

Kinky reappeared and placed a carving board bearing a loaf of wheaten bread, brown and nuggety, and a wedge of crumbly Cheshire cheese beside the tureen. She stood, arms folded, waiting. "Well?"

Barry didn't hesitate. "It's wonderful, Kinky." He glanced at O'Reilly, who seemed to be unimpressed. "Is it your own recipe?" Barry asked.

"It is, so. There was a great hambone left over from the party for the making of the stock, and Hughey's tomatoes have come on a treat. He gave me a wheen of them on Saturday."

"Hughey?" Barry had seen a Hughey recently. "The man with the riveters' deafness? Married to a Doreen?"

"The very fellah. Nice couple."

"Well, I'll tell you, Kinky," Barry said, carving a slice of wheaten bread for himself, "if there was an Olympic event for it, you could make soup for Ireland." He saw her smile.

He looked at O'Reilly, who was spooning soup into himself and taking great bites from a slice of bread, butter, and cheese, liberally scattering crumbs of Cheshire on the table. Barry expected him to have words of praise for Kinky, but O'Reilly said nothing. He didn't look at all content.

Mrs. Kincaid put a hand on her hip. "It's not your usual big lunch, Doctor O'Reilly dear, but . . ."—she glanced at his stomach—"a little moderation in all things is good for a man, and you're getting a belly on you like a poisoned pup."

O'Reilly sighed and said, "I suppose you're right, Kinky."

"I am," she said. "Now brush up those cheese crumbs, and don't you get your tie in the soup."

Before O'Reilly could answer, a white shape leapt onto the tabletop and made a beeline for the butter dish.

Mrs. Kinkaid stretched out one red hand, grabbed Lady Macbeth, tucked her under her arm like a rugby player carrying the ball, and tickled the cat under its chin. "Now, now, Your Ladyship. Keep your nose out of what doesn't concern you. Lord, Jesus," she said, "but she's a terrible divil for anything from the dairy. I'll take her away. Now you two enjoy your soup and bread and cheese." The last remark was directed at O'Reilly, who meekly said, "I will."

"Thanks, Kinky," Barry said, savouring the crunchiness of the crust of the bread, and smiling at how O'Reilly let his housekeeper mother him. The man needs a wife, Barry thought, but kept the idea very much to himself.

"I've nothing for you for after your lunch. Nobody phoned so you can have the afternoon off," she said. "A bit of quiet'll do you both a power of good."

O'Reilly shook his head. "We've to go see Myrtle MacVeigh," he said. "And it's a grand day for a drive, so when we're done there I think we'll run on down to Bangor and see how Sonny's getting along. We'll be a bit late for supper."

"Oh?" said Barry.

"Do you not remember? I want to drop in at the Duck."

Barry sat in the passenger seat. He was disappointed that Myrtle MacVeigh had not seemed to be very far along the road to recovery, although the burning when she urinated was gone and she'd been pleased about that. He'd had to agree with O'Reilly when he'd told Myrtle that Rome wasn't built in a day, and she'd have to be patient and wait for the new antibiotics to take effect. So, Barry realized, would he.

O'Reilly was driving at less than his usual frenetic pace because even he was cautious enough not to try to overtake the large private coach wending its way along the narrow back road to Bangor.

"Bloody American tourists," he grumbled. "Coming over here by the coach load to lil' ol' Ireland to find their roots, taking up half the bloody road and giving the local shopkeepers an excuse to jack up their prices."

There was some truth to what O'Reilly said. Ever since the fifties, as air travel became more accessible, increasing numbers of Americans had been coming to Ireland. No wonder. Half their eastern seaboard had been populated by the Irish. Barry knew only too well how masses of tenant farmers and their families, who'd been evicted during the Great Hunger, the potato famine of the 1840s, had fled on the coffin ships to a new life; what had started as a trickle had turned into a flood. Weren't Seamus and Maureen Galvin heading off soon to join her brother in California? Four of Barry's classmates had left for the States as soon as they had finished their houseman's year. The job prospects and the money were much better there.

Barry stared out the window at a field of ripening barley where the breeze sent ripples through the golden, bearded grain, making dull patches here and there. The bowed heads reflected less sunlight than their erect companions.

A single wood pigeon swooped low over the crop before climbing to land on top of one of the massive elms that grew behind the dry-stone walls flanking the road. The boughs touched the trees opposite, roofing the thoroughfare and filtering light through to the tarmac in dappled golden ponds and silent, dark pools.

Moss and jack-by-the-hedge clung to the chinks between the wall stones. Brambles, heavy with blackberries, thrust their thorny branches over the wall and scratched the car as it passed.

The car moved from the wood into full sunshine. Barry wound down his window and inhaled a mixture of the scents of mown hay, fertilizer, and exhaust fumes from the coach ahead. He could hear its engine note, deeper than the Rover's, along with the lowing of cattle from a nearby pasture, and the harsh voice of a cock pheasant in the wood now behind them.

Fair play to the Americans, he thought, for wanting to see the place where their forebears had come from. He knew he'd never have to make such a pilgrimage. Nothing would make him leave Ulster. Wasn't it half the reason he'd taken the job in Ballybucklebo in the first place? And yet—what if Patricia won that scholarship?

"Thank Christ for that." O'Reilly changed down and screeched past the coach, which had pulled into a convenient lay-by. The sudden acceleration interrupted Barry's thoughts, and bloody nearly broke his neck. He put a hand behind his head.

The fields gave way to where the fringes of the town of Bangor began to encroach on the farmland. Rows of semidetached chalet bungalows, their red brick walls too new to have been weathered by the rains, stood in serried ranks where Barry remembered fields. He and a boyhood friend had spent a dreamy evening in one of the pastures waiting for a family of badgers to leave their sett.

The new estates seemed to have been grafted uncomfortably onto the old Bangor he'd grown up in. But when O'Reilly was forced by the town traffic to slow down and the car wound its way past the old landmarks, Barry began to feel himself at home. Bangor Abbey, built on the sixth-century site of Saint Comgall's Monastery, sent its narrow spire towards heaven at the corner of Upper Main Street. The Bank of

Ireland building, built in 1934, still stood facing the junction between Hamilton Road and Lower Main Street, which ran down a hill past shops and three pubs to Quay Street. The dumpy McKee Clock, built of stolid sandstone blocks, stood where it always had, at the bottom of High Street, close to the three piers and the circular Customs House built in 1637 at the corner of Victoria Road.

He felt a deep sense of belonging here and could understand why the Americans came. Nothing in their bustling, striving, brand-new country could ever attain the permanence of a place like Bangor—or Ballybucklebo. If they were seeking their roots, they'd find them, deep and firmly anchored.

O'Reilly, fidgeting in his seat as the car crept along, finally turned into the drive of a large and graceful two-storey building. Barry recognized the dormer windows and high, tiled, catslide roofs, remembering when it had been an exclusive semidetached residence. A sign outside now read: Bangor Convalescent Home.

"Come on," said O'Reilly, getting out of the car.

Barry followed, up a broad flight of steps, through glass doors, and into a narrow linoleum-floored hall. The light was poor, his ears were assailed by a Mantovani waltz blaring from overhead speakers, and his nose was assaulted by the smell of boiled cabbage as it wrestled with the stink of disinfectant—and lost the bout.

O'Reilly stood in front of a semicircular desk. Behind it, a bored receptionist whose makeup, Barry thought, must have been applied with a bricklayer's trowel, filed her nails while indulging in a conversation with a young man in a grubby white uniform. He was probably some kind of orderly. A Harlequin romance lay open, spine up, on the desk.

"Ahem." O'Reilly leant over the desk.

The receptionist barely acknowledged his presence.

"Ahem." O'Reilly's throat clearing reminded Barry of the sound of a hungry bull mastiff.

The young woman turned her back.

Barry noticed a small bell on top of the counter, the kind with a button on top of a metal half sphere. O'Reilly's great fist smashed onto the button. The bell jangled so loudly Barry thought the members of the Bangor fire brigade would be sent rushing to their fire engine. He saw the orderly jump. Then the young woman turned slowly in her chair, looked at O'Reilly, and curled her lip. She pointed to a sign on the desktop. "Can youse not read? Visiting hours is over."

O'Reilly's voice was low, sinister. "I can read."

"So? It's after hours, so it is." She started to turn away.

"I can read the sign, and I can read your badge, Miss . . . Weir." His nose tip was alabaster.

"Aren't you the clever one?" she said over her shoulder.

"No." O'Reilly stood four square, both fists on the desktop. "Not really." His next words would have been audible on the foredeck of the old *Warspite* if they had been uttered on her bridge. "But I *am* Doctor O'Reilly. I *am* entitled to see *any* of my patients in this miserable apology for a nursing home at *any* hour, day or night . . ." Barry noticed a barometer hanging on a drab painted wall behind the reception desk and imagined it was recording a severe increase in atmospheric pressure. "And, I am quite willing to report to the matron what a miserable, impertinent, slatternly, idle apology for a human being you are, Miss Weir."

"Oh, Jesus," she said, standing. "Who's it you'd like to see, sir?"

"Sonny Houston . . ."

She started to flick through the pages of a ledger.

"Although as I suspect that not having the least interest in the inmates is part of your job description, you'll have some difficulty finding him."

The orderly interrupted. "He's the old recovering heart failure and pneumonia in Two-C."

"No," said O'Reilly, "he's not a couple of diseases lying in a bed. He's a real human being. He's the grey-haired gentleman with the Ph.D. who lives in Ballybucklebo and is temporarily making use of your premises." He turned to Barry. "Come on, Doctor Laverty." He began to stride towards a staircase, then stopped and faced the desk, letting his gaze shift from the orderly to the receptionist. His words now honeyed, he said, "I can find my way. Far be it from me to interrupt your conversation."

Miss Weir's face had gone paler than her makeup.

Barry followed in O'Reilly's wake, up a wooden-treaded staircase, along a corridor, and through the doorway of room 2C.

Four beds, two to each side, separated by the narrowest of aisles filled the room. Screens surrounded one of the beds, and from behind them came a man's reedy voice repeating a single word over and over: "*Nurse.*" There was an overpowering odour of faeces and stale urine. Elderly men occupied two of the other beds, one man wearing a cloth cap, the other flat out, his toothless mouth open wide, snoring as loudly as a ripsaw.

Barry recognized Sonny in the near bed to the left. O'Reilly had already perched himself on its foot. "How are you, Sonny?" he asked.

Barry saw the old man's face split into a smile. "Thank you for coming, Doctor O'Reilly. I'm very well, thank you."

"Are you?" said O'Reilly, taking the man's pulse.

From where he stood, Barry was pleased to note that Sonny's cheeks were no longer the slate blue colour they had been and the man's breathing was easy, not at all the way it had been two weeks ago when O'Reilly had him rushed into the Royal.

"And they're treating you well?"

"*Nuuurse.*" The thin voice came from behind the screens. The snores from the other bed intensified.

Sonny glanced down. "I mustn't complain."

"Mmm," growled O'Reilly. "You're too much of a gentleman to, aren't you?"

"Well, I—"

"*Nuuurse.*"

O'Reilly hauled a stethoscope from his jacket pocket. "Pull the screens, will you, Barry? Sonny, pull up your pyjamas."

Barry tugged the curtains along their overhead rails and slipped inside as O'Reilly listened to Sonny's chest.

"You're sound as a bell," O'Reilly said, pulling the stethoscope from his ears and helping Sonny adjust his jacket. "But you hate it here, don't you?"

"It could be better. It's noisy at night—"

Snooooore.

"*Nuuuurse.*"

"And in the daytime," O'Reilly remarked, wrinkling his nose, "the place stinks, the grub's rotten, you miss your dogs—"

"Maggie comes to see me every day, and she's looking after them—"

"And you want to go home."

Barry watched as the old man nodded and his eyes glistened. He looked sadly at O'Reilly.

"Right," said O'Reilly, "we'll see about that."

"*Nuuurse.*"

He rose. "I'll be back in a minute." He ripped the curtain back. Barry watched him depart and heard boots clattering down the stairs. He couldn't make out the exact words coming from below, but he could have sworn the floor under his feet shuddered.

Sonny swallowed, forced a weak smile, and said, "And how are you, Doctor Laverty?"

"I'm fine, and I've some good news for you. Councillor Bishop's started work on your roof."

"I'm glad." He leant towards Barry. "I don't suppose you'd know when it'll be finished?"

Barry was about to try to answer the question when O'Reilly, pursued by the orderly, came in.

"Get in there, see what he needs, and don't come out until you've fixed him up."

"Yes, sir." The orderly went behind the screens as Barry imagined a terrified mouse might scuttle from a cat. The calling stopped.

O'Reilly stood beside Sonny. "Right," he said. "You need to be out of here."

"I could go back and live in my car."

"Don't be daft. That's why you got pneumonia in the first place."

"Perhaps Maggie could take you in," Barry suggested.

"Oh, no, sir." Sonny shook his head. "We're not married yet. Tongues would wag. You know what they'd be saying about us. It wouldn't be proper."

"I do," Barry said, remembering the looks of distrust on the faces of some of the patients who had heard about Major Fotheringam. "Indeed I do."

O'Reilly scratched his head. "You can't go back to your house. It's not ready. You're right about not going to Maggie's . . . but I'm buggered if I want you to stay here." He paced into the narrow aisle. Then turning, he frowned and said. "Right. I'll have a word with the staff, persuade them to take better care of you . . ."

He'll persuade them, Barry thought, much as Torquemada and the Spanish Inquisition persuaded heretics to recant.

"Meanwhile I'll think of something."

"I'd appreciate that, Doctor O'Reilly." Sonny moved back on his pillows.

"Now," said O'Reilly, "you get a bit of rest. Doctor Laverty and I have to get back to Ballybucklebo. We've a bit of planning to do."

Barry didn't know whether to laugh or tremble. O'Reilly might have said "planning." Barry knew only too well that what he actually meant was plotting, and when O'Reilly set his mind to that activity the Lord above alone could predict the outcome.

14

Drink! For You Know Not Why You Go, Nor Where

"Out," said O'Reilly, stopping the Rover in the lane behind his house. "I'll shove the car in the garage. We'll walk to the Duck."

Barry stepped into the lane, massaging his knuckles. They were quite bloodless, so tightly had he clung to the sides of his seat as O'Reilly hurled the car along the main Bangor-to-Belfast road. He hadn't taken any comfort from the lines of a biblical verse painted on the side of a barn outside Bangor. It was a well-known landmark, but the promise that "whosoever believeth in Him should not perish, but have eternal life," had seemed hollow when O'Reilly took the well-named Devil's Elbow curve on two wheels. O'Reilly wanted to go to the Duck, and he wasn't going to waste any time getting there.

Now they'd arrived in Ballybucklebo, Barry reckoned he'd earned a drink too.

O'Reilly shut the garage doors, and Barry heard joyous barking as Arthur Guinness greeted the homecoming of his lord and master by slamming himself against O'Reilly's back gate.

"Hang on," said O'Reilly. "He wants his walk." He opened the gate only to be ignored by his canine devotee, who rushed at Barry.

"Sit!" yelled Barry, feeling as King Canute must have when he ordered the tide to forget about coming in.

Arthur for once neglected to hump Barry's leg. Instead he rose up, put both forepaws on Barry's chest, and licked his face.

"*Gerroff!*" O'Reilly yelled, yanking on Arthur's collar.

The dog obeyed. "I suppose, I should be grateful that this time he went in for a bit of foreplay before the main event," Barry said, using the back of his hand to brush the mud from the front of his sports jacket.

"Och, sure he's only an affectionate big lump, aren't you, Arthur?"

"*Aarow,*" said Arthur, looking adoringly at O'Reilly.

"He's about as affectionate as a cross between Casanova and Don Juan on testosterone. He's a bloody sex maniac."

"Not at all," said O'Reilly. "He's just full of the joys of spring and he's missing his exercise." He glanced at his watch. "Tell you what; we've plenty of time. You go on down to the Duck; I'll take Arthur for a walk, and meet you there later."

Barry hesitated. It was only last night on his way back from the O'Hagans' place that he'd thought about going in by himself for a quick one—but had decided against it. "Why don't I wait for you at the house?"

"Because," said O'Reilly, "I don't want to waste time coming back here. I'll be going past the pub on my way home from the shore. I'll be ready for my pint, and Arthur'll want his Smithwicks, won't you?"

"Aaargh," Arthur agreed, furiously wagging his tail.

Dear God, the bloody dog understands English, Barry thought, at least when it comes to beer. He just wished the big Labrador would comprehend "sit" and "gerroff."

"Come on," said O'Reilly. "Heel." He strode off.

Barry wasn't sure if the last remark was addressed to him or to Arthur, but the dog kept his nose exactly in line with O'Reilly's leg, and Barry trotted at O'Reilly's shoulder.

"Jesus," said O'Reilly, waiting for the traffic light to change. "It's hot."

Barry had to agree. The sun hung high above the village. The flowers in the municipal flower bed beside the Maypole were dusty, drooping, and dispirited. Even Arthur must be feeling the effects, he thought. The dog's pink tongue flopped and he panted heavily. Barry took off his jacket.

The light changed and O'Reilly strode across the road accompanied by the faithful hound. "Won't be long," he said, "but I've got to get this great lummox fit. Duck season starts next month."

Barry had to hurry to keep up. He remembered O'Reilly saying he and Arthur enjoyed a day's wildfowling as much as Barry enjoyed time on a trout stream.

O'Reilly stopped on the corner of Main Street and Shore Road. His next remark caught Barry off guard. "Arthur's not the only one. I have to get you fit too."

He frowned. "You mean I've to start exercising?"

"No, son." He clapped Barry on the shoulder. "I mean I've got to get you ready to run things on your own so Arthur and I can get away now and again. You trot on to the Duck and keep your ears open."

Before Barry could answer, O'Reilly had set off at a comfortable jog, yelling, "Hey on out, Arthur," sending the dog to lollop towards the shore.

Barry stood for a moment. Damn you, O'Reilly, he thought. You've done it to me again. It's the same as when you told me you'd not signed Major Fotheringham's death certificate. Was that for legal reasons, or was it because you wanted to force a postmortem? Did you really want to take Arthur for a run, or had you sensed I was a bit reticent about going into the Duck by myself? And what have I to keep my ears open about?

He turned left and walked the short distance to the Black Swan, took a deep breath, and feeling like the sheriff in a western about to face the baddies, pushed his way through the louvred, batwing doors.

After the brightness of the day, the dim light in the bar made it difficult for him to see. He could hear the low hum of conversation, and how it faded. Someone coughed. Someone clinked a glass on the marble bar. The air was tainted with tobacco smoke and the smell of beer. As his eyes adjusted he could make out the details of the single room, the black ceiling beams, the nicotine-stained and off-white plaster between the wooden joists, the tiled floor, the single bar with rows of spirits on the shelves behind it. O'Reilly had once told him the building dated back to 1648, when it had been part of a coaching inn, and that apart from there no longer being stables, it hadn't been altered since then.

Two men Barry did not know stood at the bar, one with his back turned, the other seemingly fascinated by a Guinness poster on the far wall, a poster Barry knew had been issued by the brewery some time in the forties and had probably been there ever since.

In the room itself, all but one of the few tables were empty. It was midafternoon and he knew most of the regulars would still be at their work. Three other men, all in collarless shirts and moleskin trousers, each wearing a duncher, the tweed cap that was the uniform of the workingman, occupied a table at the back of the room. One was smoking a dudeen, a short-stemmed clay pipe. All seemed to have developed a deep interest in the half-filled, straight pint glasses in front of them. None was known to Barry.

The publican, Willy Dunleavy, as ever sporting his floral-patterned waistcoat, stood behind the bar polishing a glass with a tea towel. Barry surmised that Willy's daughter, Mary, would be at work at Miss Moloney's dress shop.

Barry moved to the bar. "Afternoon, Willy."

"Aye," said Willy. "Hot out." He renewed his efforts to make the glass shine.

"Indeed it is," said Barry, waiting to be asked, "What'll it be?" Finally he said, "I'm expecting Doctor O'Reilly to join me."

"Is that a fact?"

The usual Ulster barman's response, "Will you have something while you're waiting?" was not forthcoming.

"Not too busy today, Willy," Barry said.

"No."

God, Barry thought, trying to drag any conversation out of the normally loquacious Willy Dunleavy today was like trying to pull teeth without an anaesthetic. And it seemed that as far as the customers at the bar were concerned, Barry might as well be a visiting wraith. When he glanced at the far table he could see the men there staring at him expectantly. Barry was hot and thirsty. Right, he thought, what had Frederick the Great said? *"L'audace l'audace, toujours l'audace."*

"I'll have a pint please, Willy."

The barman held the recently polished glass under the beer tap and silently started to pour.

Barry had to decide. Should he make one more effort to start a conversation or should he hold his tongue?

"Here." Willy set the glass on the bar top.

Barry rummaged in his pocket for change. He put a pound note on the counter. "Put one in the stable for Doctor O'Reilly and . . ."—why not?—"a Smithwicks for Arthur."

Willy seemed to brighten slightly at the mention of the dog's name. He nodded, took the money, made change, and gave it to Barry. Not a word was spoken, although Barry could hear snatches of conversation coming from the occupied table.

". . . your head's cut. That mare? Couldn't jump fences if her arse was on fire."

"I'm no' so sure about that. Have you seen the way she carries her tail?"

Barry heard a loud guffaw and the words, "No wonder. Your man that owns her feagues her, so he does."

Barry frowned. Feague? He'd not heard the word before and was tempted to wander over and ask the speaker exactly what it meant, but he realized that if he did he might be rebuffed. He'd wait and ask O'Reilly later.

He carried his pint to a vacant table and hung his jacket over the chair back. The first mouthful of the stout, even if it was bitter, was familiar and somehow comforting. Barry took a second pull and wiped the foam from his upper lip.

He'd been quite prepared to obey O'Reilly's admonition to keep his ears open, but as the only topic of conversation seemed to be about racehorses it hardly seemed worth the effort.

He leant back in his chair and considered his own situation. If his reception in here was anything to go by, his stock was not high in the village since the news had broken of Major Fotheringham's sudden death.

Someone had started the buzz. Barry wondered who? It wouldn't have been O'Reilly, and it was unlikely to have been Mrs. Fothering-ham. Probably one of the undertaker's men who had come to take the corpse to the mortuary at the Royal. If he got a chance he'd ask Mr. Coffin, the village mortician. Not that it really mattered. What was important was that since the word got out, many of O'Reilly's patients had treated Barry with suspicion.

Not all of them, but it was too early to know if the antibiotics he'd prescribed for Myrtle MacVeigh would work. They should. There was no reason to suspect Colin Brown's sutured hand wouldn't heal properly. The jockey Fergus Finnegan's acute conjunctivitis ought to be better by Friday.

Julie MacAteer and Helen from the dress shop had seemed to be grateful for his efforts. So were Kieran and Ethel O'Hagan. Donal Donnelly had been prepared to discuss his secret Arkle ploy.

Barry took a deeper swallow. On balance, perhaps his account was not as deeply in the red as he had feared. Perhaps O'Reilly was right about Barry keeping his head tucked in and simply getting on with his job, and damn it all, he didn't want to leave.

But then—but then there was Patricia. For her sake, he knew he really wanted her to win the scholarship. But for his? Barry drank, surprised to see that his glass was almost empty and noticing his head was a tiny bit fuzzy. What about for his sake? He could see clearly that deep in him he wanted Patricia to fail. To stay at Queens in Belfast. To stay close by him.

In vino veritas, he thought, wondering if he should order another pint.

He heard the doors creak open and slam shut, heard O'Reilly announcing, "Afternoon, all." Barry was surprised that there was virtually no response. "Christ," said O'Reilly, "it's like a bloody morgue in here."

Willy said quietly, "Good afternoon, Doctor O'Reilly. I've one on the pour for you."

"Good," roared O'Reilly. "My tongue's hanging out. It's hot as Hades out there."

Barry was aware of something bashing against his leg. Arthur, idiotic grin on his face, stood beside the table trying to beat Barry to death with his tail. "I've called a Smithwicks for Arthur."

"I should bloody well hope so, and your glass is empty."

"Right away, Doctor," Willy said, lining up another pint glass.

Barry waited for O'Reilly to join him, but instead he saw the big man lean across the bar. "You, Willy Dunleavy, have a face on you like a bulldog that's just licked piss off a nettle. What's up?"

Barry strained to hear, but Willy had lowered his voice and was muttering into O'Reilly's ear. He had no difficulty making out O'Reilly's side. He felt as if he were listening to a telephone conversation, trying to make sense of it while hearing only one participant's words.

"What? Can't be. The bangster was in here this morning?"

A bangster was a bully. Was O'Reilly referring to Councillor Bishop? He'd said he was going to the Duck after he left the surgery.

"Och, Willy, have a titter of wit. He can't do that. He's trying to bamboozle you . . . Jesus bloody Christ, I don't believe it." With that, O'Reilly grabbed his pint and Barry's second, headed for the table, and called over his shoulder, "Don't forget Arthur's." He smacked Barry's glass down so forcibly that some of the head slopped onto the tabletop. Then he sat in his chair and sank half his pint in one swallow. "Better," he said.

Willy appeared with a metal basin and shoved it under the table. Arthur flopped down, and Barry could hear the slurping noises. Like master, like dog, he thought.

"Welcome back." Barry wanted to ask him what that peculiar word "feague" meant. "Fingal, can I ask you something?"

"Later," said O'Reilly. "You said, 'Welcome back.' Some bloody welcome. No wonder the place is half empty and there's no *craic*," he said, looking Barry in the eye.

Still disappointed that no one had spoken to him, Barry swallowed and said, "You mean because I came in?"

O'Reilly guffawed. "Don't flatter yourself you're so important."

Barry bristled. "I didn't mean—"

"It's nothing to do with you." He finished his pint. "One more,

Willy." O'Reilly fished out his briar. "Willy and these poor buggers think Armageddon's just round the corner."

"Why?"

"You remember Helen said Mary was worried someone was trying to take over the pub?"

"Yes." Barry made a quick deduction. "Bishop?"

"None other than."

Willy appeared with O'Reilly's pint. "Thanks," he said. "How much?"

"We'll pretend it's your birthday, Doctor," Willy said. "On me." He walked away.

O'Reilly shook his head. "Willy's worried, and he's a bloody good reason to be." He lit his pipe. "What do you know about property ownership?"

"Not much," Barry said, thinking he'd not have to worry about things like that until he was making more than an assistant's salary.

"It's the land, you see."

"Fingal, what's 'the land'?"

O'Reilly emitted a mushroom cloud that would have done justice to the Americans' hydrogen bomb that destroyed the Bikini Atoll in 1954. "Land. It's the stuff places are built on. Unless you happen to be one of those peculiar people who live in a house built on stilts over water."

"Fingal, just get to the point."

"All right. In Ireland you can buy the lump of mud your house sits on. That's called freehold. But most premises pay rent to a landlord who actually owns the real estate. Leasehold. A lot of leases are long-standing." He started into his second pint. "The Duck's on a ninety-nine-year lease."

"Seems like a long time."

"Aye, it is except . . ." O'Reilly took another drink. "Willy took over a lease that started in eighteen sixty-five. It expires next month."

"Surely he can renew it?" Even in the dim light Barry could detect the pallor in O'Reilly's nose.

"You'd think so, but would you care to take a stagger at who holds the title to the property?"

"Bishop?"

"You've just won all the marbles. None other than himself, and do you know what he wants to do?"

"Take over the pub?" Barry looked round a room that went back nearly four hundred years.

"That's only the half of it. He wants to gut it and redo it with chrome, and plastic, and piped music . . . no more locals sitting round singing come-all-ye's. You'll never see the likes of Donal Donnelly, half stocious, bawling out, 'Come all ye dry-land sailors and listen to my song. It's only forty verses so I won't detain you long.' "

The thought saddened Barry. He'd heard Irish songs at his grandfather's knee, knew the words of many even if he couldn't carry a tune in a bucket. "It's like that Liam Clancy song, isn't it, Fingal? 'Winds of change are blowing—old ways are going . . . ' "

"And more's the pity. There'll be no more storytelling. No eejit up on his hind legs declaiming his party piece of poetry. Do you know what there'll be? Bloody top-of-the-pops rubbish from loudspeakers at ten million decibels whether the customers want to listen to it or not." O'Reilly banged his fist on the table. "We'll have to stop it or he'll lose all the local trade." He glanced at the men at the bar, then at the men at the other table. "He can't do that. The Duck's . . . God, Barry, it sounds trite, but it's the heart of Ballybucklebo."

"Nothing trite about it, Fingal. It's true. So why does he want to do it?"

"Remember the coach load of Yankees we saw?"

"Yes."

"Bishop wants to go after the tourist trade."

"No."

"Yes. Can't you just see it? A big neon sign in fake Celtic script outside saying, Mother Macree's Olde Irish Shebeen, and maybe Donal Donnelly outside the front door dressed like a leprechaun, silver buckles on his shoes, stovepipe hat, and a bloody great shillelagh in his fist, sitting on a stool, with his cap on the pavement and a big sign, Will Say Begorrah for a pound."

The image of Donal, despite Barry's concern, made him laugh.

"It's no bloody laughing matter," O'Reilly said. "Come on, finish up. It's time we were home."

Barry took another swallow. O'Reilly said nothing. Arthur peered out at O'Reilly, as if to ask, Where's my second pint? but O'Reilly ignored the dog. "Jesus Christ, Barry," he said. "As if looking after the sick and suffering wasn't enough, now we've to find a place for Sonny."

Barry had temporarily forgotten O'Reilly's promise in the Bangor Convalescent Home.

"And see if we can help Helen find a different job. *And* do something about Bishop and the Duck."

"And I suppose you'll have us both walking on water as an encore?"

It was O'Reilly's turn to laugh. "Hardly." He rose. "Now," he said, "before I started to get carried away, you said you wanted to ask me something."

"Yes. One of those chaps over there said someone feagues his horse. What the hell's 'feague'?"

O'Reilly's sides heaved. "Feague? You'd know it as a different expression, but it's a trick unscrupulous horse dealers use to make a horse look better than it is. You can judge a horse's spirit by the way it carries its tail."

"That's what he said."

"So," said O'Reilly, "just before the buyer comes to look at the beast, the dealer sticks a clove of ginger up its rectum. Feagues the poor creature."

The thought made Barry wince.

"If you'd a tail and something as hot as that in your behind, wouldn't you lift your tail up?"

"I would indeed."

"It would 'ginger you up' no end?"

"No doubt," said Barry. Right. That was the expression O'Reilly said he'd know.

"Now," said O'Reilly, heading for the door. "What we have to do is work out a way to feague Bertie Bishop." He stopped and called, "Heel, Arthur."

Barry let the dog pass. Having seen Bishop in action for more than a month, he thought perhaps O'Reilly was setting an impossible goal for them. But then, if anybody could feague Councillor Bertie Bishop, bring the man to heel as readily as Arthur obeying his master's command, it was Doctor Fingal Flahertie O'Reilly.

15

Respectable Professor of the Dismal Science

Barry stopped his elderly Volkswagen Beetle, waited for a gap in the heavy traffic, and turned left across the Grosvenor Road to enter the grounds of the Royal Victoria Hospital. He drove slowly past the Clinical Sciences Building and round a bend, and started hunting for somewhere to park. There seemed to be more cars in the lots than there were houses in Ballybucklebo, where at this moment O'Reilly was running the surgery.

It had been agreed the day before that he'd see to the patients, while Barry would come here to consult with Professor Faulkner about Mrs. Flo Bishop's suspected myasthenia gravis. Last night after supper, Barry had suggested to O'Reilly that he'd not only see the prof but would also take the opportunity to try to meet his old school friend Jack Mills. O'Reilly had a soft spot for Mills because they were both devotees of rugby football. O'Reilly had been capped for Ireland, Jack for Ulster.

It was odd, Barry thought, that in the politically divided country the only thing that represented the *whole* island was the national rugby team with players selected from the North and the South. It was a pity Ireland's citizens couldn't play together as well. He knew it was Jack's ambition to gain an Irish cap, but Barry doubted if the pressures of his friend's career would give him enough time.

It would be great to see Jack again and O'Reilly had made no demur; presumably he'd been in an expansive mood because Kinky had made up for the light lunch with poached Shimna River salmon for supper. Seizing the opportunity, Barry had also asked for the evening off. It had been granted.

He saw a Vauxhall start to back out of a place, so he pulled in nearby and waited.

He'd phoned Jack and he'd agreed to meet Barry for lunch in the hospital cafeteria. He'd also called Patricia. To his delight, although she had classes until five, she would be happy to meet him for a Chinese meal and then be driven back to the Kinnegar. She'd said it was economy of effort. The time she'd save not having to wait for a train would more than make up for the hour or so she'd lose by having dinner with him. She'd laughed when she said it, and he'd forgiven her at once.

The Vauxhall left and Barry pulled into the vacated spot, got out, and started to walk to the back entrance of the Royal, the teaching hospital where he had spent three and a half years as a student and one as a houseman.

He left the road and crossed the lawn separating the red brick Royal Maternity Hospital from the buildings of the Royal proper. After the quiet of Ballybucklebo, the constant noise of traffic on Grosvenor and Falls roads, which ran on two sides of the hospital complex, was loud and intrusive. Flocks of starlings and feral pigeons cluttered the grass.

He walked past the old concrete reservoir. Although it held water for firefighting, in the summer it served as a swimming pool for nurses and junior medical staff. He could picture Jack Mills, arms full of a squirming nurse, leaping into the pool with his burden and surfacing with her bikini bra held triumphantly aloft.

Barry crossed the cloisters beneath the ward units and went in by the basement entrance, past the door to the cafeteria, up a winding flight of stairs, and onto the main corridor.

He saw a crowd of blue-uniformed nurses, red-uniformed sisters, white-coated lab techs, chequer-uniformed floor cleaners, and brown-coated porters going about their business. Housemen and registrars in long white coats and medical students in short, white bum-freezer jackets strode purposefully. Lost-looking civilians, some carrying bunches of flowers, wandered nervously, peering at numbers outside wards or trying to read overhead signs giving directions. The precise place of everyone in the hospital caste system was identifiable by their clothes.

He heard the noise: an out-of-tune symphony of squeaking trolley wheels, the slapping of plastic ward doors closing, the clattering of shoe leather on the marble floor, the humming of electrical floor polishers, voices, beepers.

He inhaled the familiar hospital smells: floor polish, patients' meals, acrid disinfectant, vomit.

Barry stood for a moment getting his bearings. The staircase came out at Ward 3. There were twenty wards along the corridor; then a short passageway connected the main units to Wards 21 and 22. Ward 21 was neurosurgery, where—he swallowed—Major Fotheringham had been operated on. Barry's destination was Ward 22.

He started to walk, pausing to acknowledge greetings from staff members who recognized him. None it seemed had a moment to pass the time of day. He remembered it being the same last year. Barry had always been on some errand of mercy, always full of his own importance, failing to recognize that a junior house officer in the great hierarchy was probably less important than a bacterium. At least the specialists in microbiology spent a considerable amount of time with their microscopic charges.

Perhaps, he thought, as he passed Wards 17 and 18, the orthopaedic units, it was one of the attractions of general practice. People in the village took him seriously, even if it was only to wonder about his competence. Perhaps, he thought, one of the things that had made him study medicine in the first place, was the need to be taken seriously, to feel he was somebody, that he belonged somewhere.

He popped into Ward 19, urology, and had a quick word with the ward clerk. She promised she'd try to hurry up Kieran O'Hagan's prostatectomy, see if he could be moved up the waiting list.

Barry left the main corridor and quickly crossed the passageway. He let himself onto Ward 22. The nurses' desk was deserted except for the unit clerk, a petite brunette whose hair, lustrous as a piece of deeply polished mahogany, fell to her midback. She sat with her legs crossed, her skirt at midthigh. Barry remembered her great legs.

She looked up, smiled broadly, and said, "Look what the cat's dragged in. What brings you here, Barry?"

"How are you, Mandy?" He remembered her well. He should. He'd dated her a few times before he'd met the nurse with the green eyes. The one who was now going to marry a young surgeon.

"All the better for seeing yourself," she said, smiling. Clearly she bore no grudge about their parting.

"I need to see the prof."

She rolled her eyes. "Do you know about camels and needles?"

Barry laughed. "It's easier for a camel to go through the eye of a needle—"

"Than for anyone to see the great man." She gestured along the ward to where Barry could see a group of people clustered round the foot of a bed.

It was the classic "cast of thousands" that was regularly assembled to pay homage to a senior professor and, at least on the surface, hang on his every word.

The medical profession was represented by senior medical students and junior doctors whose ranks ascended from the lowly house officer, fresh from medical school, and on upwards through the grades of senior house officer, registrar, and senior registrar. These were the great man's myrmidons.

The nursing staff, equally sensitive to seniority, descended from the ward sister, junior sister, and staff nurse to the terrified-looking student nurse. Nurses in charge of a ward were called 'sister' as a throwback to the days when they had been in holy orders. These were the acolytes.

All the medical and nursing personnel danced attendance on the high priest, a diminutive man, bald as a billiard ball, sporting a polka-dot bow tie and wearing a long white coat, a patella hammer prominently sticking from one pocket, a tuning fork in the breast pocket. The high priest of neurology, Professor Malcolm Faulkner, M.D., F.R.C.P. (London), F.R.C.P. (Dublin), F.R.C.P. (Edinburgh). Regius Professor of Neurology at the Queens University of Belfast.

If a feeling of self-importance was vital to doctors, the prof's tank would be full to overflowing. How different from O'Reilly, Barry thought. That man doesn't give a hoot about those sorts of trivial embellishments. He gets his satisfaction from doing his job. And yet, Barry recognized that even O'Reilly relished his position at the top of the Ballybucklebo pecking order—and used it to his advantage.

"Don't worry," Mandy said. "He's in a good mood this morning. I'll grab him for you before he leaves."

"Thanks, Mandy. I'll only take a minute or two." He remembered the promise he'd made to Councillor Bishop. "I don't suppose you could speed up an appointment with the prof for one of my patients?"

"I could try. How urgent is it?"

Barry thought for a moment. "It's for the woman I want to ask Professor Faulkner about this morning. She may not need to be seen here if I'm right about her and can fix her up back at home. But if I'm wrong . . ."

"Tell you what," she said. "See how you get on with your patient. If she doesn't need an appointment, you'll not need to worry. If she does, give me a ring and I'll find her a cancellation."

"Thanks, Mandy."

"All part of the service. Now have a pew while you're waiting. Do you fancy a cup of coffee?"

"Still making that chicory stuff?" Barry remembered the countless cups of ersatz coffee he'd drunk.

She laughed. "The wondrous concoction made by the Camp Company? 'Fraid so."

He shook his head.

"Suit yourself. Go on into the ward office," she said. "I'll tell him you're waiting."

"Thanks, Mandy. I owe you."

He was ill prepared for the way she raised one eyebrow, pouted, and said, "Dinner some night would be nice."

He felt the blush start as he let himself into the small room and closed the door. Why was he always so clumsy around women? Jack Mills would have had an instant comeback, made her laugh, and probably taken her up on the offer even if he was dating someone else. But then Jack wasn't seeing Patricia.

Barry waited until the door opened. Professor Faulkner, accompanied by his senior registrar, Doctor Bereen, entered. "Laverty. Mandy says you're a GP somewhere in the bogs. You want a word." The prof's accents were clipped, very upper-class English. He'd come to Belfast from a senior position at Saint Bartholomew's in London.

"I'll . . . I'll . . . only take a minute, sir," Barry stammered. He was always uncomfortable in the presence of such an exalted figure.

"It's all you'll get. I've a very important meeting with the dean."

"Thank you, sir. It's about a patient."

"No doubt." The prof consulted his watch. "Get on with it."

Barry rapidly described Mrs. Bishop's symptoms and the physical findings. He felt like a student again, front and centre at the great man's ward rounds. "I think she's got myasthenia gravis."

"And you're sure it's not due to an underlying cancer or thyroid disease?"

"We've been able to exclude cancer pretty well, and we'll be measuring her thyroid hormone levels when she comes back to see us, sir."

"You seem to have remembered something I taught you." Professor Faulkner frowned, then drawled, "Mmmmm. Yes. Could be primary myasthenia, I suppose." He turned to the registrar. "Bereen?"

Bereen, standing ramrod stiff, began to pontificate, rattling off facts like the well-trained automaton Barry knew the prof would expect a junior member of his team to be. "Disease of the nervous system. Pathway still not fully understood. May be due to abnormal behaviour of acetylcholine at the neuromuscular junction. Symptoms and signs as Doctor Laverty has described and may include diplopia, dysphagia, dysarthria, and difficulty in chewing. On examination there is no wasting or fasciculation . . ."

He knew his stuff all right, but Barry wondered how Mrs. Bishop would respond to that mouthful of arcane medical mumbo jumbo.

"I think we know that, Bereen." The prof looked bored.

"Sorry, sir."

"Laverty?"

"Yes, sir?" Barry said.

"You'd a question? Ask."

For a moment Barry wondered if he should look for a large ring on the man's finger to kiss. "When I was a student you taught us about a simple test that would confirm the diagnosis, sir."

"Indeed. I'm glad something else I said got through." He spoke to Bereen. "One is forever casting pearls."

Barry almost gave up, but damn it, he wasn't here on his own behalf. Mrs. Bishop was in trouble. O'Reilly wouldn't have let himself be patronized. Why should he? "I'd appreciate it if you'd tell me about it." He deliberately neglected to add "sir."

"Forgotten, have you?" The prof's expression was closer to a sneer than a smile.

"Obviously or I'd not be wasting your time asking. And I've a sick woman to deal with."

"Tell him, Bereen."

"You give an intramuscular injection of neostigmine, two-point-five milligrams, along with atropine, one-point-oh milligrams, to prevent abdominal colic. The increase in power is quite striking in about twenty to thirty minutes."

"Thank you, Doctor Bereen," Barry said. "Thank you very much."

"Will that be all, Laverty?" The prof began to open the door.

"Yes. I can remember the treatment," he said formally.

"I should hope so." With that, the prof swept out, saying as he went, "I'll be busy with the dean, Bereen. Take care of my outpatients." He didn't wait for a reply.

"Christ," said Doctor Bereen, finally relaxing. "Thank God I've only another month to go on this service. I'd rather work for Adolf Hitler."

"You have my sympathy," Barry said. "My boss isn't a bit like that." Odd O'Reilly might be, unpredictable, given to storms and tempests, but never once had Barry seen him condescend to any living creature, and that included Arthur Guinness and Lady Macbeth. "I appreciate the help, and I'd appreciate it even more if you'd tell me how to treat myasthenia."

Bereen laughed. "I thought you said you knew."

"I did, but actually I don't. I'd had enough. He's not the Almighty."

"Christ, don't tell him that." Bereen flopped into a chair, pulled out a sheet of paper, and began to scribble. He handed the sheet to Barry. "There you are, mate. The details of the test and the treatment. Good luck with your patient."

"Thanks, and good luck to you with the prof."

Bereen stretched. "It's only another month, but I've been training for four years. Sometimes I envy you blokes who had the good sense to opt for general practice."

"You may be right," said Barry, thinking that perhaps applying for a training post in the Cambridge teaching hospital to be near Patricia might not be such a good idea. He knew he'd find it difficult to become some great chief's minion. "I've been enjoying general practice," he continued. It wasn't entirely true, not with the way things seemed to be in Ballybucklebo, but they were going to improve. Of course they were. And if the information he had now about how to deal with Mrs. Bishop did the trick. O'Reilly's promise to make sure the word of her cure got out would work wonders for Barry's reputation.

"Right," said Bereen rising, "I've to go and do the prof's clinic."

"Still in the basement?" Barry asked.

"The salt mines," said Bereen. "Yes."

"I'll walk down with you. I'm meeting an old pal for lunch in the cafeteria. Jack Mills."

"Good for you. Come on."

Barry followed Bereen out of the ward, and as they walked along the corridor a thought struck him. If he was successful in treating Mrs. Bishop, would O'Reilly be able to use that as a bargaining piece in the coming struggle with Councillor Bishop and his plans to take over the Duck?

16

Happy the Physician Who Is Called at the End of the Illness

The queue at the cafeteria counter was short. Barry had to wait for only a few minutes to pick up a cheese sandwich and a cup of coffee, and pay the cashier. "Hiya, Barry. How's about you?" she asked.

"I'm grand thanks, Connie."

Connie was, as ever, wearing enormous hoop earrings and sporting a beehive hairdo. She was as much a fixture in the underground cavern as the formica-topped tables scattered in the recesses between the arches supporting the roof. The place made Barry think of the catacombs under a mediaeval cathedral.

He carried his tray to a vacant table, wondering how often he'd eaten hurried meals in here. The facility was open twenty-four hours a day and catered to the junior staff: doctors, nurses, lab techs, radiographers, physiotherapists. Many of the tables were occupied, mostly by young women.

Barry washed down the white bread and processed cheese with a mouthful of lukewarm coffee. Kinky wouldn't approve of his repast. Nor would Patricia, he thought, and what she might say about the Chinese meal he was going to buy her this evening hardly bore thinking about.

He chewed slowly, listening to the buzz of conversation and the clink of utensils on crockery. He saw Jack Mills—tall, his broad shoulders stretching the seams of his long white coat—leave the counter and head over, pausing to stop and chat with a physiotherapist and then a student nurse, both blonde, both well endowed. The senior students and housemen called the place the "cattle market," filled as it was with women, many of them on the lookout for a marriageable young physician.

Jack came over, dumped his tray, and sat. "Doctor Livingstone, I presume?"

"Good to see you too, Jack." Barry noticed that Jack's normally ruddy, farmer's complexion looked pale under the artificial lighting, and the dark circles under his eyes seemed darker still.

Jack yawned and shovelled in a forkful of Irish stew. "How's life abusing you in darkest Ballybucklebo?"

Jack was the one man from whom Barry kept no secrets, hadn't needed to since they'd shared a study as schoolboys at Campbell College and then digs as medical students. "Could be better," he said.

Jack yawned. "Couldn't be any bloody worse than being a surgical registrar. Apparently sleep is only for the upper classes."

"Bad night?"

"Three in a row."

"My heart bleeds. You picked surgery."

"Next time, if there's any truth to this reincarnation business, I'm coming back as a galley slave. Should be easier. Three appendixes last night, and a perforated duodenal ulcer. I don't think the ulcer's going to make it." Jack did not seem unduly concerned.

"Doesn't that bother you?"

Jack shook his head. "Nah. We don't let ourselves get too close to the victims. Some of 'em pop their clogs. That's life." He gobbled more stew.

"One of mine did."

"Fell off the perch? So?"

Barry pushed his plate aside. He'd not eaten the crusts. They tasted too much like cardboard. "It's different in a village. You get to know the people, and they get to know you."

"Poor buggers. They'll survive. I've known you for eleven years. Hasn't done me a bit of harm." He grinned.

"Losing my patient hasn't done my reputation a damn bit of good . . . I may have to leave."

"And you like it there, don't you?" There was a hint of concern.

"Very much."

"So. Tell your Uncle Jack what happened."

Barry briefly went over the major's history. ". . . and we're still waiting for the postmortem results."

"And you're hoping something else helped your victim 'shuffle off this mortal coil'?"

"Yes, but it's taking forever to find out."

"Help," said Jack, "is at hand. Scuse me." He rose.

Barry watched his friend make his way past several tables, stop, say something, and then return accompanied by a short young man, whose pure white hair made him look older than his years.

"You remember Harry Sloan?" Jack said.

"Hi, Harry," Barry said, casting back for a memory of his classmate, a studious man, one who had tended to be private and was not often found at undergraduate parties. "How are you?"

"Nyeh . . ."

Barry remembered. Harry had a habit of prefacing many of his remarks with that peculiar "nyeh" sound.

". . . rightly, so I am."

"Harry's a budding pathologist, and purely by chance he's in the morgue this week assisting at the PMs."

"Pretty bloody gruesome, but you get used to it." He smiled. "At least you don't have to talk to the patients."

"I imagine you'd fill your pants if one of them spoke to you," Jack said.

"Nyeh. I'd run a bloody mile."

"Bet you couldn't beat Roger Bannister," Jack said.

"But you're enjoying pathology?" Barry asked, half thinking that at the moment not having to talk to the patients might hold some attraction.

"It's very interesting and the hours are good. Nobody's going to call you out at night."

"That," said Jack, "would have merit." He yawned. "Barry wants to know about one of your customers."

Barry stared at Harry Sloan. Could he possibly have the results already? Would there be something unusual, something for which Barry could not possibly have been responsible?

"Who?"

"A Major Fotheringham. He'd had a cerebral aneurysm clipped two weeks ago, then died suddenly on Sunday night last," Barry said.

Harry frowned. "Coroner's case?"

"That's right."

"We did the autopsy yesterday. Only one. I remember it . . ."

Barry held his breath.

"Didn't find nothing except for the brain surgery, and it looked good. No signs of any more bleeding."

Barry exhaled. "Nothing?" He felt his hopes rise. If the surgery results had been okay, then his misdiagnosis could not have been the immediate cause of the major's death. But that was only half the answer to his dilemma. He was hanging on to the belief that something, something for which he could not be held responsible, had been the reason for the man's regrettable demise. "And there was nothing else to see?"

"Nah." Harry shook his head. "Mind you," he said, "it's only the macroscopic findings."

Barry'd had to attend six postmortems during his training. The macroscopic examination came first, when all the organs were removed and scrutinized by the pathologist for any obvious disease. "Nothing?"

"Not a sausage," said Harry, "if you don't count the large intestine, which can look like one." He laughed at what Barry decided must be a pathology joke. "We'll have to wait for the histology."

Barry's shoulders slumped. All the vital organs—heart, lungs, kidneys, liver, brain, pancreas—would be preserved in formalin, and representative samples taken to be sliced more thinly than tissue paper, mounted on glass slides, stained, and examined under the microscope. "How long will that take?"

Harry knitted his brows, sucked in his breath, and produced a longer than usual "nyeh." Then he said, "Couple of weeks. The tech'll be making the slides today."

"Oh," Barry said. "Thanks." He'd have to steel himself to wait. "Harry, do you think you'll find anything?"

"Hard to say. It's a bit of a fishing expedition." He ran one hand through his white hair.

"Barry's worried," Jack said.

"I don't want to hold out false hopes," Harry said, "but once in a blue moon someone has a massive coronary—"

"But," Barry asked, "would that not show up with blood clots and damaged heart muscle you could see?"

"Aye, you'd think so, but it's not true. If the victim dies . . . nyeh . . . more or less at once, we can't see anything at all."

"But it would show up on the slides?"

"Oh, aye." Harry seemed to brighten up. "I've a notion," he said. "As soon as the slides are ready, I'll take a quick look-see myself, and if I think there's anything, I'll get one of the senior blokes to take a shufti."

"Would you?"

"Aye, certainly. Have you a phone number?"

"Here." Barry fished a small notebook from an inside pocket and scribbled down O'Reilly's number. "You'll probably get a Mrs. Kincaid."

"Nyeh. Mrs., indeed? Living in sin are you?" Harry Sloan grinned.

"She's the housekeeper."

"Fair enough. I'll remember. Anyway. Good to see you again, Laverty." Harry turned to leave. "I'll be in touch, but it could be next week."

"Decent lad," Jack remarked after Harry'd gone. "He'll see you right."

"I hope so."

Jack pushed back his chair. "You know, Laverty, sometimes you worry too much. All this fuss that's got your knickers in a twist will blow over. If this Ballybucklebo's what you want . . ."

"Professionally it is."

"O'Reilly'll see you right."

"I hope so, but there's something else."

"Not medical?"

"No."

"Not by any chance a certain black-haired, sloe-eyed damson called Patricia?"

Barry nodded. "And it's damsel, not damson. That's a kind of plum."

"I know, and you're right. Your Patricia's more of a peach." As he spoke, Jack's gaze followed a passing young nurse. His eyes ran over her from head to toe and probably saw through her clothes like an X-ray machine, Barry thought. "That one's more of a plum." He waved at her and she waved back, clearly unconcerned by the leer coming in her direction. "You could have your pick, you know."

"Maybe." Barry thought about the clerk on Ward 22. "Do you remember Mandy?"

"The bird you dated for a while. Dark hair. Great legs?"

"Yes. I saw her this morning. She wondered if I might take her to dinner."

"Christ. After you dumped her? She must be a glutton for punishment. Are you taking her?"

Barry shook his head. "I'm serious about Patricia . . . and I'm worried about her."

"Bad thing this serious, mate. What's got you worried?"

"She may be going to England. She's trying to get a scholarship to Cambridge. She'd be in with a bunch of very bright undergraduates there. Mostly men."

Jack whistled. "If she's that good at what she does, she's far too bright for the likes of you anyway."

"Do you think so?" Barry knew he sounded worried.

Jack frowned. "The truth? She may be. I've only met her once, but she didn't strike me as the kind of lass who'd be happy to sit at home getting the old man's tea, and pipe, and slippers ready."

"She's not. She wants to build dams and bridges."

"Probably wants to drive a bulldozer too. Not my type. Not one bit, but to each his own." He frowned. "What'll you do if she does go to England?"

Barry shrugged.

"I hesitate to suggest this, my old son, but if you're that serious about her, why not propose to her?"

"Do you mean it?"

"Why not?" He leant forward, elbows on the table. "This American sexual revolution thing is great for the likes of me, but there are still some rules."

"Like what?"

"If a bird's wearing an engagement ring, it's as good as saying, 'Private property. Hands off.'" Harry slipped into a Bombay Welsh singsong accent and wiggled his head from side to side like a Siamese temple dancer. "Oh, crikey. Not blooming cricket. All the sahibs is knowing about sacred cows, isn't it?"

He's doing Peter Sellers's Mr. Banerjee character again, Barry thought. "I hadn't really considered that . . . ," he said, wondering if he was ready to ask Patricia to marry him. "But I don't think she'd like you to suggest she was anyone's property—or a sacred cow."

"Just a figure of speech," Jack said, rising. "I have to run. Outpatients this afternoon."

Barry glanced at his watch, hoping his friend would stay a little longer. After all he had all afternoon to kill until he met Patricia. "You'll be too early," he said.

"Not if I go up to Ward Twenty-two first," said Jack, grinning. "You've no dibs on the wee brunette, have you?"

"No."

"You remember *White Christmas*?"

"Of course." The BBC showed it on television every Christmas, and the set was always crowded in the housemen's mess.

Jack was singing as he left, in a fair imitation of Bing Crosby's voice, "Oh-oh-oh, Mandy, I'm feeling quite randy. Let me buy you a brandy . . ."

17

I'll Love You till China and Africa Meet

Barry left the Ritz cinema on the corner of the Grosvenor Road and Great Victoria Street. To his left College Square ran past the buildings of the grandly titled Royal Belfast Academical Institution, known to the attendees and the citizenry as "Inst." Now it was a grammar school, but Barry knew that in the 1830s it had housed Belfast's first medical college.

The traffic was heavy and clamorous, and the air noisome with car exhaust fumes. Rush hour had started, and he had to wait to cross the road to the imposing granite-block towers of the General Assembly's building, the headquarters of the Presbyterian Church in Ireland.

He walked down Howard Street, humming, "I could have danced all night," off-key as usual. He'd really enjoyed the matinee of *My Fair Lady,* this year's Oscar winner for best film, which was still playing. He'd decided not to bother with the one showing next door, the Beatles in *A Hard Day's Night.*

He turned left onto Queen Street, where The Peacock, one of Belfast's first Chinese restaurants, had opened recently. The Peacock wasn't licensed, but permitted patrons to bring their own wine. He carried a bottle of Entre-Deux-Mers. He wasn't a connoisseur, but he knew that Patricia enjoyed a glass of wine, and the man in the off-licence had assured him it was a good white.

Brunhilde was still parked close by, where he'd left her earlier. Barry pushed through the door to the restaurant.

The single room was decorated with heavy, red-flock wallpaper,

Chinese dragons and pagodas embossed on the material. Tasselled paper lanterns hung from the ceiling. A picture of a giant panda done in fine stitch work on a silk background and framed in black bamboo decorated one wall. Oriental music filtered discordantly into the room. Barry could smell exotic spices coming from the kitchen at the back of the place.

A smiling Chinese hostess approached. She was wearing a green brocade, high-collared, floor-length, split-to-the-thigh cheongsam. The traditional Chinese fashion had been popularized in the fifties by the wives of British servicemen returning from Hong Kong, even though some older Ulsterwomen regarded it as pretty risqué. The hostess greeted Barry, took the wine to chill it, and ushered him to a table for two. "Would youse like a menu?"

"Please," Barry said.

"I'll only be a wee minute, so I will."

Barry smiled. The woman's features were classically Chinese, her accent pure Sandy Row. Thick as champ.

Three other tables were occupied. Five-thirty was early for the Belfast dining public. Barry heard the chimes over the door jangle, turned, and saw her. She wore low-heeled shoes, black pants, and a maroon sweater. Her hair was done up in a ponytail.

"Hi, Barry."

"Patricia." He rose and held her chair, waiting for her to dump an obviously heavy knapsack on the floor and take her seat. He shoved the chair under her. "Glad you could make it."

"So," she said, "am I."

Barry took his seat opposite her. "Busy day?"

"Nonstop. I hate architectural drawing."

Before he could say something sympathetic, the hostess reappeared. She poured green tea into two handleless porcelain cups. "Here youse are," she said, handing them menus. "I'll give youse a wee minute to think about what you'd like, and I'll bring the wine. I've it in the freezer."

Patricia sipped the tea. "Interesting." She opened her menu. "Good

Lord," she said, "this thing's about as big as the Domesday Book. How on earth are you meant to pick something?"

Barry watched her flip over the pages as she muttered, "Wontons? Moo goo gai pan? Glazed duck's webs?" She looked at him, one eyebrow raised. "What're glazed duck's webs?"

"I think they're a bit like our *cruibins*, except they're made of duck's paddles."

She wrinkled her nose. "Yeugh."

"I'm inclined to agree."

She reached across the table and took his hand. "Barry, do you come here often?"

The line from *The Goon Show* slipped out: "Only during air raids."

She laughed and he saw the sparkle in her dark eyes. "Be serious," she said, "because I've never been to a Chinese place before."

"Really? I thought you knew all about exotic cuisine. That lasagna the other night was lovely."

"Mum taught me how to make that, but Chinese restaurants are a bit thin on the ground in Newry and the Kinnegar. You'll have to help me order."

"All right." Barry squeezed her hand, surprised yet pleased that Patricia, normally so self-possessed, would ask for help. "Jack and I used to come here quite a bit." He neglected to tell her that so did he and Mandy and the green-eyed nurse. "We'd order two or three dishes and share."

"Let's do that. What would you suggest?"

"Do you like chicken?"

She nodded.

"Pork?"

"Please."

"Right. Leave it to me," he said, and he realized how much he enjoyed saying it.

"Wine, sir?" The hostess had come back from the kitchen. She showed Barry the bottle's label.

"Please ask the lady," he said.

Patricia looked at the bottle, nodded, and waited for the hostess to pull the cork and pour the wine into a glass. She sniffed, then sipped. "An amusing little wine . . . a bit cheeky," she said seriously. "Good nose. Just a hint of impudence. Probably from a south-facing slope."

Barry was impressed until he saw her shoulders shaking and her lips widen into a smile. He couldn't help himself, and in a moment his own laughter pealed out. Even the hostess was laughing.

"It's cold and dry," she said, "and just what I need after today."

The hostess poured for both. "Would youse care to order?"

"Please," Barry said. "Deep fried wontons, chicken fried rice, and sweet-and-sour pork."

"And would youse like chips?"

"No, thank you." He glanced at Patricia, and by her grin he knew she shared his thought. Only here in Belfast would the customers expect French fries with a Chinese meal.

The hostess left. Barry picked up his chopsticks. "Do you know how to use these?"

"No."

He leant across and took her hand, feeling its warmth, admiring her slim fingers. "Hold them like this." He positioned the two slim, tapered pieces of wood. "Then use them like tweezers."

"Easy for you to say," she said, but she soon seemed to get the hang of it.

A waiter arrived and set three dishes on the table.

"Those," said Barry, pointing at irregularly shaped thin wafers, each with a lump in the middle, "are wontons."

Patricia fiddled with her chopsticks.

"Pick one up with your fingers, and dip it in the plum sauce." He pushed a small bowl to her.

Patricia dunked a wonton in the sauce, popped it into her mouth, chewed, frowned, and swallowed. "That's rather good."

"Eat up."

Barry took her plate and filled it with chicken fried rice and sweet-and-sour pork. "The fried rice goes better with soy sauce," he said.

He watched her eat, enjoying her obvious pleasure as much as he was savouring his own meal. Finally she put her chopsticks down, took a sip of wine, and said, "I'm stuffed. And thank you, sir. It really was delicious."

"In China," he said, "you're meant to let go a dirty great burp to signify satisfaction. It's good manners."

"We're not in China." She hiccupped. "Excuse me." She dabbed her lips with a napkin. "Now," she said, "tell me about your day."

"I went up to the Royal, saw one of the profs, got some advice about a patient back home." Thinking of Ballybucklebo as home surprised him, but damn it, it was. "I had lunch with Jack and an old classmate." Should he tell her about the postmortem results? Why not? She already knew about his concerns. "He's a junior pathologist. He's trying to get me some quick answers about the patient I mentioned the other night."

"The one who died?"

"Yes."

Her hand covered his. "It's important to you, isn't it?"

"Very."

"It'll be all right. I'm sure."

"I hope you're right, but the preliminary results aren't very helpful. I'll have to wait for more tests."

"That makes two of us," she said.

He knew she was referring to her imminent examinations. Jack had suggested Barry propose, but . . . he couldn't. Not yet. He wondered if he could talk Patricia out of trying to go to Cambridge. "It seems like a very long way away," he said.

"What does?"

"Cambridge." He fiddled with his napkin. "Is going there really so important?"

He watched her face to see if she might bridle, but she pursed her lips and said, "Getting yourself reestablished in your practice is important to you."

"Very."

"Going to Cambridge is very important to me. Do you know they only started giving women the right to be awarded degrees in the

Senate House with the men in nineteen forty-eight? That's only sixteen years ago."

"No. I didn't."

"There are three women's colleges: Girton, Newnham, and New
Hall. New Hall was founded ten years ago, but half of the other colleges still won't admit us." She was warming to her theme, leaning forward over the table. "Until we get more women into Cambridge, ones
who'll do as well as or better than the men, those colleges will never
change. We're going to see that they do."

Barry saw how her eyes flashed. He wished she would seem to feel
as passionately about him. " 'To strive, to seek, to find, and not to
yield,' " he said quietly.

"What?"

"Tennyson. *Ulysses.*"

"I don't see what that's got to do with—"

"It's on a cross in Antarctica near Captain Robert Falcon Scott's
base camp. He didn't make it back from the South Pole."

"Barry, we're not talking about polar exploration."

"No," he said quietly, "but we are talking about pioneers." He
stared into her eyes and said as gently as he could, "Some of them
come to sticky ends."

She sat back. "Do you think *I* will?" Her eyes narrowed. She
snatched her hand from his. "Do you?"

Barry took a deep breath. "Patricia Spence, I reckon you can—and
you will—do whatever you set your mind to . . ."

He saw her shoulders relax.

"I'm being selfish. I don't want you to go. I . . ." He couldn't bring
himself to spit out, "I love you."

"I understand that," she said. "It'll be hard for both of us, but
surely you could get over to England for the odd weekend? I'll be
coming home for the holidays. It would only be for three years."

"Would it?"

She stared at the tablecloth, fiddled with one chopstick. "I'll not lie
to you, Barry. Three years is a long time. Either one of us could meet
someone else."

He wouldn't. He knew that. "I suppose," he said. The prospect of ending up like O'Reilly, still carrying a torch for one woman after twenty-three years, was daunting; he told himself, if you're not willing to risk everything by asking her to marry you, what other choice do you have? He sipped his green tea, the fluid only lukewarm and bitter to the taste. "I'm not going to persuade you to stay, am I?"

"I'm sorry, Barry."

The silence hung.

"Right," he said, beckoning the hostess and miming writing with a pen on the palm of his hand. "Time I got you home."

The hostess presented the bill, took Barry's money, and gave him change. "Thank you, sir."

He rose, left a tip, and stood behind Patricia's chair, waiting for her to pick up her knapsack and stand. "Here. Give me that," he said, holding out his hand for the bag.

She let him take it. He held the door for her as they left the restaurant.

"The car's down there," Barry said, pointing. He slowed his step to match hers.

He opened the passenger door and waited. She stood beside him but instead of getting in faced him. "Thank you for a lovely dinner."

"My pleasure." But Barry felt it had been more like the Last Supper.

She put her arms around his neck and kissed him, so hard that he had to take one step back. He was breathless when she pulled away. "Barry, please, *please* try to understand."

"I am trying," he said. "Honestly."

She kissed him again, and like a child who'd been taken to the circus to comfort it before a trip to the dentist, he let himself savour the moment and dismiss what the future might hold. He held her from him. "I do understand, Patricia, that anything you've ever really wanted to do, you've done."

She bowed her head.

"You're not going to stop now, are you?"

"No."

"All right. Hop in the car and I'll take you home." He shut the door after her, went round, and climbed in. Before he started the engine he turned to her. "One wee thing."

"What?"

He wasn't sure what imp was driving him, but her kisses had lifted his spirits. "This always doing what you set out to do?"

"What about it?"

"Don't ever try to put toothpaste back in the tube." As he started the engine he heard her gasp, heard her throaty chuckles, and felt her punch his arm lightly. "Right," he said. "Next stop the Kinnegar, then on to Ballybucklebo."

18

A Cat in Profound Meditation

The gentle light in the upstairs sitting room came from a lazy sun, still visible through the bay windows. It seemed to be taking its own sweet time deciding if it should slip beneath the distant Antrim Hills. O'Reilly sat in an armchair, briar belching, jacket off, tie unknotted, unlaced boots propped on a footstool. Barry saw he was reading a James Bond novel, *From Russia with Love.*

Lady Macbeth, fast asleep, lay on the hearthrug curled up with her nose beneath her tail, her white fur bright in a rectangle of sunlight. They made a picture of domestic tranquility, Barry thought. "Evening, Fingal."

"Welcome home." O'Reilly set his book on the side table, where Barry noticed for once there was no sign of a glass of whiskey. O'Reilly swung his feet off the footstool. "You're just in time. Kinky'll be up in a minute with a cup of tea."

Barry sat in the other big chair. "No nightcap tonight?"

"Later," said O'Reilly. "I've a confinement to attend. Miss Hagerty, the midwife, phoned half an hour ago. Jenny Murphy's in labour."

"Jenny Murphy?"

"Aye. You saw her with me last week for her thirty-seven week visit. She should have been in on Friday, but she's jumped the gun. I'm just going to have a quick cup of tea, then take a run-race over and have a look at her."

Barry waited to see if he'd be invited to join O'Reilly. He'd always enjoyed midwifery, but tonight would not be disappointed if he didn't have to go out. Despite his feeling momentarily elated when Patricia kissed him outside the restaurant, and when he'd made the inane remark about putting toothpaste back in the tube, the drive back to the Kinnegar had been subdued. He'd dropped Patricia off with a perfunctory good-night peck and had made no future arrangements, other than a vague promise to phone her.

He would be happy enough to stay here with his thoughts, but before his senior left he really should tell O'Reilly about the day's events at the Royal. "I saw Professor Faulkner," he said.

"A rare treat, no doubt. Arrogant little gobshite."

"You know him?"

"Indeed," said O'Reilly. "He went to some minor public school, picked up his plummy accent there. He sounds as if he has marbles in his mouth, but he's a country boy from Randalstown down in County Antrim. He was in my year at Trinity. Bald as a coot then. We called him Curly. Worst student in the class."

"Then how—"

"Did he rise to such dizzy heights? I'll tell you," said O'Reilly. "He brownnosed his way up. Ulstermen weren't conscripted in Hitler's war. There were too many of us killed in the first one. Your dad and I volunteered anyway, but Faulkner didn't. He took himself off to a London teaching hospital, Bart's or Guy's or some place like that. While we were off, Faulkner—he always had an eye for the main chance—was busy getting a training and sucking up to the bigwigs in London. Did him a power of good too."

Kinky had told Barry how, as a younger man, O'Reilly had had ambitions to specialize in obstetrics. But he had lost too many years when he'd volunteered and had no choice but to opt for general practice. Barry looked at the big man to see if there was a hint of bitterness in his last remark, but he was smiling. "Anyway. Did he give you any helpful hints about Flo Bishop?"

"His senior registrar did before he had to go do Faulkner's outpatients."

O'Reilly laughed. "It's always been the way. Juniors do all the work."

But not in your practice, Barry thought.

"You remember the first man in space?" O'Reilly asked.

"Yuri Gagarin. Three years ago."

"The very lad. Won't be long now 'til there's a real man on the moon." He scratched his belly. "Jesus, if they ever ask for a doctor to go, some bloody consultant like Faulkner from the Royal'll volunteer . . . for a fat fee, of course."

"You're daft."

"I'm not. You know how the higheejins work. He'll get the money . . . but his senior registrar'll actually make the trip." O'Reilly's face split into an enormous grin. He guffawed, and said as he laughed, "The junior'll go."

Barry burst out laughing.

He was still chuckling when he heard the door open. He turned and saw Kinky come in carrying a tea tray. "Is it music hall night at the Hippodrome?" she asked, setting the tray on the table. "The pair of you howling like a couple of hyenas, so."

"Just a silly joke, Kinky," Barry said.

"Huh." She poured. "I see you enjoyed it. Little amuses the innocent." She lifted the lid from a small cake stand. "I hope you'll enjoy my cherry cake."

"Of course we will and—"

Barry got no further. Lady Macbeth woke from her slumbers, gave one piercing yowl, sat bolt upright, leapt two feet vertically, hit the carpet, and took off running. Her tail was held like a horizontal question mark. She tore across the floor and out through the door, leaning sideways into the turn and travelling at a speed Barry thought would have given Donal Donnelly's greyhound, Bluebird, a run for her money. He heard the sounds of her paws hitting the staircase outside, a rapid loud *drumping* that faded as the cat ascended and grew louder as she made the return journey, and faded into a gentle padding as she recrossed the carpet, sought her patch of sunlight, glared at O'Reilly as if to say, "What are you staring at?" and then settled, curled, put her tail back over her nose—and promptly fell asleep.

"Mother of God," said Kinky, one hand raised to her mouth. "The poor wee dote must have got the wind in her tail. She'd me petrified, so."

"Perhaps something startled her," Barry said.

"I don't think so," said O'Reilly. "I heard a fellah say once he had a theory about why cats do that."

Barry anticipated that O'Reilly was going to pull his leg again. "Is it the same idea as sending a certain neurologist to the moon, Fingal?" he asked.

"No. I'm serious. This fellah's notion was that *we* think cats sleep a lot."

"Well, they do, Doctor O'Reilly dear," said Kinky.

"No," said O'Reilly. "That's what it looks like. Your man reckons cats are random-number generators. They lie about all day thinking up numbers until they hit the one they're looking for."

"I suppose," said Barry, "they pay attention to the stock market too?"

"Don't be daft," said O'Reilly, "but do think about this. According to your man, the magic number is twenty-six. When it comes up, the animal has no choice but to race about like a liltie."

"If you say so, Doctor dear," Kinky remarked, shaking her head as she might to a small boy who thought he'd made a clever remark. "Now drink up your tea before it gets cold." She turned to leave, then said, "And don't take too long over it. There's a baby coming."

"Away with you, Kinky," O'Reilly said through a mouthful of cherry cake. "It's like Sir Francis Drake and the armada. I've time for tea and cake and for a confinement too."

"I think," said Barry, "the old sea dog was playing bowls on Plymouth Ho."

O'Reilly chewed until Kinky left. "It's not just the tea and buns," he said, quietly. "I want to hear about what you learnt at the Royal."

Barry fished in his pocket for the note Doctor Bereen had scribbled, and gave it to O'Reilly, who read it, brows knitted, and handed it back. "Interesting," he said. "Certainly worth a try."

"I wonder," said Barry, "if we shouldn't ask Mrs. Bishop to come in tomorrow? The sooner we have an answer, the better."

O'Reilly raised one eyebrow. "Better for whom?"

"Well . . . ." Barry understood the question. O'Reilly was wondering if Barry was more interested in being proved right than in helping Flo Bishop. "The patient," Barry said firmly.

"Aye," said O'Reilly. "I hoped you'd say that."

"There's something else."

"Oh?"

"It occurred to me that if we do fix Mrs. Bishop, the councillor might feel he owed us, well . . . a bit of gratitude."

"And leave the Duck alone?" O'Reilly laughed. "And here I thought I was the only Scottish Italian in Ballybucklebo."

"Scottish Italian?"

"Aye. Mac. E. Avelli." He finished his tea. "You could be right," he said. "It's worth a try, but somehow I'd be hard to convince Bishop could spell 'gratitude,' never mind know the meaning of the word." He rose. "I'll think on it, but I suspect we'll need more strings to our bow than that. Once Bishop gets pound signs in front of his eyes—"

"I thought they were dollar signs."

O'Reilly laughed. "True. But never mind the currency. The bugger smells a profit. I think it'll take more to get him to change his mind, but I've no notion what that something else might be." He shrugged into his tweed jacket and tightened the knot of his tie. "Let's mull it over, see Flo on Friday, see what happens when you fill her full of neostigmine and atropine. There's no point going off half cocked. Patience," he said, "is a virtue."

Barry sighed. "All right. I'll wait." Wait. Barry was tired of waiting. Waiting to see if he was right about Mrs. Bishop. Waiting to hear from Harry Sloan. Waiting to see how Patricia fared in her examinations. "If you say so."

"I do," said O'Reilly. He bent and scratched the cat's head. "It's all very well for cats to hit twenty-six and gallop off in all directions, but—"

"I understand," Barry said.

"Good. Now nip down to the surgery and pick up the maternity bags. I'll go and get the car. Meet you at the front."

"You want me to come?"

"Of course I do. And get a move on. Time, tide, *and* women in their second labours wait for no man."

19

O Why Was I Born with a Different Face?

Barry set the two heavy maternity kits on the hall floor of a small, pebble-dashed bungalow. O'Reilly had gone ahead as soon as he parked the Rover, striding along a short driveway and in through a front door. He'd told Barry to bring the bags. At least he'd left the door open.

Barry was panting. So was someone else, and he could hear a voice he recognized as belonging to the district midwife, Miss Hagerty. "Good girl, Jenny. Huff. Huff. That's it."

"Get in here quick." O'Reilly shouted. "Bring the gear."

Barry lifted the bags and followed the noise along a carpeted hall where three plaster mallard climbed a white-painted wall beside an umbrella stand and a wall-hung, gilt-framed, oval mirror. He turned into a bedroom. Miss Hagerty and Doctor O'Reilly stood on opposite sides of a bed. O'Reilly, who had removed his jacket and rolled up his shirtsleeves, wore a pair of rubber gloves. Barry immediately recognized the patient, Jenny Murphy, remembered having seen her last week. Then she'd been calm, self-possessed, and apparently unconcerned about her impending second labour.

Now she lay on her back, eyes never leaving O'Reilly's, her face screwed into a rictus, upper teeth white against her bloodless lower lip, sweat glistening on her forehead. She was groaning. One hand clutched at her swollen belly, the silvery *striae gravidarum* on both flanks shining in the light.

Barry could smell the once-experienced-never-to-be-forgotten pungency of amniotic fluid and saw the puddles on a red rubber sheet Miss Hagerty must have spread on the bed earlier.

"Doctor Laverty," she said. Her face betrayed no hint of emotion, but then as O'Reilly once told Barry, Miss Hagerty had attended more than a thousand deliveries. Anyway, it was clear O'Reilly was in charge.

"Miss Hagerty," Barry said.

"Get the packs open, Barry," O'Reilly called, his back turned to Barry. "I'm going to examine you, Jenny."

Barry started to unpack the equipment as O'Reilly bent to his work. He straightened and turned to Barry. "Have a listen to the fetal heart." For the first time in his short few weeks working with the big man, Barry thought he could hear concern in O'Reilly's voice.

Barry moved up one side of the bed, smiled at Jenny, and palpated the uterus, searching for the baby's back. Listening over the back was the best place to find the sounds of the fetal heart. He could feel the uterus, firm, but not rock hard, now that the pain had passed, but . . . his hands moved more quickly . . . he couldn't make out any convexity in either flank. He took the Pinard fetal stethoscope from Miss Hagerty. "I'm going to listen in," he said, even though he knew that not being able to identify the lie of the baby would force him to try blindly to hear the faint, rapid tones.

Jenny nodded and tried to smile, but another labour pain hit. Her head tossed from side to side on the pillow. She screamed.

Barry knew he'd have to wait until the contraction passed. The short, aluminium trumpet was cold in his hand. Not being able to feel the baby's back was worrisome. It usually meant that the infant was lying with its spine in the middle of the uterus. If it was, the baby's head, which he knew was not a perfect sphere, would have the occiput, the back part of the skull, to the rear of the birth canal. Babies in this occipitoposterior position presented a broader diameter of the head and were more difficult to deliver.

"Get on with it," O'Reilly snapped, which surprised Barry. O'Reilly should know it was a waste of time trying to listen at the height of a contraction.

Jenny sat up. "I've to push," she screamed. "I have to push."

More evidence. A back-to-front baby's head often reached the pelvic floor muscles before the cervix was fully dilated, giving the labouring woman an overwhelming need to bear down. Pushing too early could hinder further dilatation. Barry felt Miss Hagerty sidle past.

"Puff out of this, Jenny." She held a face mask over the patient's nose and mouth. The plastic cone was connected to a small metal bottle, which Barry knew contained Entonox, a mixture of nitrous oxide and oxygen. It wasn't very effective, and judging by the way Jenny's eyes rolled above the mask's upper rim, the gas was not doing much to relieve her pain.

"Is she fully dilated, Fingal?" Barry glanced at O'Reilly. He'd never seen the big man sweat before.

"Don't bother to wash your hands," O'Reilly said. "Put on a pair of gloves and come and feel for yourself. Hurry."

Barry pulled off his coat, chucked it in a corner, ripped open the packet, and slipped on a pair of gloves. It bothered him that he didn't have time to scrub, but he was experienced enough to realize that sometimes in obstetric cases time was of the essence. Risks of infection, although small, must be taken.

O'Reilly nodded. "Well?" This time, Barry knew his opinion was not being sought because O'Reilly was trying to show a patient that he trusted his assistant. Fingal wanted Barry's advice either to confirm a diagnosis that he himself had already made or to give an answer that he could not find. It was a daunting thought.

"Sorry, Jenny," Barry said, moving past O'Reilly and sitting on the bed. He put his left hand on the abdomen just above the pubic symphysis and slipped the first two fingers of his right hand into the vagina. There was something solid just inside, but it didn't feel like the normal hard contours of the top of a baby's skull. He let his fingers explore, first to one side then the next. Could this be a breech presentation? He frowned and wished he were back in the Royal Maternity. A quick X-ray would give the answers.

He turned to O'Reilly. "Fingal, did you feel a head at the top of the uterus when you examined her abdomen?"

"I didn't examine it. Miss Hagerty was certain the head was in the pelvis."

Barry would have liked to have been sure, but he couldn't fault O'Reilly for not having examined the abdomen. The opinion of an experienced midwife was money in the bank. No head palpable at the top of the uterus meant that a breech presentation was unlikely, but even an experienced midwife could be wrong.

"Big breaths, Jenny. Big breaths," Miss Hagerty urged.

Barry's left hand felt the uterus beneath harden; it was becoming the great muscular piston that drove the baby deeper and deeper into the pelvic canal and in most cases out into the world. His right hand felt some advance. At the height of the contraction he forced his fingers higher. Normally it would hurt, but Jenny would be too preoccupied by the pain of the contraction—or so he hoped—because he had to know the condition of the cervix and try to ascertain exactly how the baby's head was lying.

His fingers told him that the cervix had vanished—it had thinned and opened. It would prove no barrier to delivery. But the shape of the baby's head was wrong. "She's fully, Fingal."

"Good."

Barry expected O'Reilly to ask about the presentation, but he said nothing more.

Barry groped and then his fingers stopped. Two tiny bony ridges ran laterally near the back of the birth canal, and above them he felt a rubbery protuberance, on each side of which was a dimple. His fingers retraced their steps. Yes. No question. He was feeling the baby's eye sockets and its nose and nostrils. It wasn't the top of the skull coming first. Somehow the head had become extended and was in the position a man might assume with his head thrown back, straining to look at a high-flying aircraft.

He heard Jenny grunting through what must be clenched teeth. Her belly muscles tightened as she bore down. His fingers felt the baby's head move further into the birth canal. "Face presentation," he said, trying to remember what he'd read about the condition. It occurred in one in five hundred births, was often associated with prematurity—and was frequently caused by some kind of fetal malformation. Was that why O'Reilly was tense? Had he already suspected that the baby would be abnormal, or had he simply not made the diagnosis?

As far as Barry could tell, the baby's chin was pointing at its mother's pubic symphysis. "Mento-anterior," he said. Thank God for that. If the chin had been to the rear, in the mento-posterior position delivery would be impossible. To attain the outside world, the wee one would have to tuck its chin against its chest. With the chin forwards, the back of the skull would have room to move against the soft tissue at the back of the birth canal. But facing the other way, the pubic symphysis would hold the skull back as effectively as a crossbeam bars a door. The only solution was a Caesarean section, and there wasn't time to transfer the patient to the Royal Maternity.

"You certain, Barry?"

Barry hesitated, then again palpated the landmarks—the nose, the nostrils, the eyebrows. He withdrew his hand and turned to O'Reilly. "Absolutely."

"That's what I thought too."

Barry glanced at O'Reilly. From the open look on the man's face, he was convinced his mentor had withheld the information, not to test Barry, but to let him bring an open mind to bear on the problem. Face presentation. Barry swallowed and said in a low voice, "Fingal, I've never delivered a face presentation."

He saw O'Reilly frown, purse his lips, glance at Miss Hagerty, then slowly say to the patient, "We'd no trouble delivering your first, had we, Jenny? And he was a big lad."

Jenny pulled the mask aside. "Connor was eight pound two and . . . uuunh . . ." She screwed up her face, clamped the mask over her nose, and inhaled deeply. "It's coming," she gasped.

Barry started to step aside to let his more experienced colleague take over, but O'Reilly shook his head, put one hand on Barry's shoulder, and said, "Get on with it. I'll assist. Here." He produced a red rubber apron, shoved the strap over Barry's head, and tied the waist string firmly. Barry was surprised that even at this moment, when he could feel his hands trembling, he had time to be grateful that his pants would be spared.

He heard clattering as O'Reilly finished opening the packs. "Here." O'Reilly nodded to a large syringe. Barry grabbed it and filled it with local anaesthetic. In face presentations there was no choice. He would have to make a large episiotomy.

Miss Hagerty would be able to see what he was doing. "Take a few really deep puffs, Jenny," she said.

Barry smiled his thanks to the district midwife. He drove the long needle in at the bottom of the vaginal opening and, at a sideways angle of forty-five degrees, advanced the tip beneath the skin between the vagina and the anus. The tissues bulged and blanched.

"Uuuuunh."

At the now distending opening of the vagina he could see the tip of the baby's eyelids, tightly shut and bulging; the nose; and above it, the lips, pouting, blue, and horribly distended. The pressure of the uterus ramming the head through the birth canal had trapped fluid in the baby's facial tissues, forcing them to swell.

"Sorry, Jenny," he said, praying the local had taken. Some of his older, more senior colleagues were certain that the distension of the perineum by a baby's head effectively deadened any pain sensation. But by the way most patients screamed when the incision was made, Barry remained unconvinced of the accuracy of that firmly held belief.

He slipped one blade of a pair of heavy scissors inside the vagina along the line of the local, narrowed his eyes, and cut hard. Blood ran from the incision, and its edges gaped. Ugly, he thought, but now there was room for the baby's head to swing without causing violent stretching and tearing of the flesh and, if too forceful, ripping right through the skin and muscle and into the rectum.

He glanced at O'Reilly, who nodded once and said, "Right, Jenny. Put one foot on my hip and one on Miss Hagerty's."

Barry waited until O'Reilly and the midwife, one on either side of the bed, had settled the patient's feet on their hips. In hospital, the more difficult deliveries were always facilitated by the use of stirrups. But in district midwifery a simpler method had to be used.

"Can you ask Jenny to push with the next contraction?"

O'Reilly and Miss Hagerty each put an arm behind Jenny's shoulders to help her half sit. "Ready, lass?" O'Reilly asked. "Deep breath, hold it, close your lips, and *puuush*."

Barry was surprised by how easily the baby's head advanced, and under the control of his hands, slipped into the world. As soon as the chin appeared, the head pivoted around the mother's pubic symphysis.

Even before Barry had delivered the shoulders, the wee one took its first breath, screwed up its puffy eyes, and expressed its discontent at having been pushed from the cosy womb, crammed down a constricted passage, and put out into a cold world. The baby cried, a long, harsh, wobbly little howl.

It was the most beautiful sound Barry had ever heard, but he did not let it distract him from easing out the child's arms, body, and legs. He held the baby in both hands to keep it from the pool of amniotic flood and blood on the rubber sheet. "Can you get the cord, Fingal?"

Both O'Reilly and Miss Hagerty lowered Jenny's feet to the bed and moved towards him. As O'Reilly clamped and cut the umbilical cord, Miss Hagerty handed him a thick warm towel.

"Is it a boy or a girl, Doctor?" he heard Jenny ask.

"It's a wee girl," he said, "and she's beautiful." Liar, he told himself. With the facial oedema and horribly pouting lips, she was grotesque. "We'll just clean her up a bit." He handed the towel-wrapped infant to Miss Hagerty, inclining his head towards the swollen face and raising a questioning eyebrow. He wasn't sure if the child should be shown to her mother.

"You wee dote," said Miss Hagerty to the baby. To Barry, she said, "Don't you worry, Doctor Laverty; sure a baby always brings its own welcome. As long as she's got all her bits and pieces, and we'll have Doctor make sure, mother'll be delighted, won't you, Jenny?"

The baby looked perfectly normal to Barry, apart from the facial swelling, which would, he knew, settle soon. He was concerned about how Jenny might respond when she saw her infant, but practical matters must take precedence. He still had to deliver the placenta and sew up the episiotomy.

He laid one hand on Jenny's belly to feel for the now empty uterus. It was shrunken and firm. The stump of cord hanging on the rubber sheet grew slightly longer, and there was a small gush of bright red blood. "Can you push again, Jenny?"

She did. The afterbirth came into view and flopped onto the sheet. Barry picked it up and made sure it was intact. A detached piece remaining in the uterus would lead to massive postpartum bleeding. It was complete.

"Well?" O'Reilly asked.

"Fine," Barry said. "Ergometrine."

"A wee jab, Jenny," O'Reilly said, driving a hypodermic into her thigh to inject the drug that would make the uterus contract firmly. "Well done, Barry."

Barry smiled at O'Reilly, who pushed over the suture pack. "I'll take a look at the wee one and have a chat with Mum. You do the embroidery."

Funny, Barry thought, when he'd been a student, repairing episiotomies was regarded as scut work by the senior staff. They always delegated the task to a junior so they could get home sooner. Now he was pleased to have the responsibility and bent happily to his work. As he put the third, deep, catgut stitch in the muscles, he could hear O'Reilly talking to the mother.

"My God," Jenny said, "what's wrong with the wee one's face?"

Barry flinched. Was she going to blame him?

"Not a thing," O'Reilly rumbled. "She was in such a hurry to see the world, she shoved her face out first and it's swollen with fluid. It'll all go away by tomorrow, and she'll be as beautiful as her mother."

"Are you sure, Doctor?" Jenny sounded uncertain.

Barry waited, knowing how O'Reilly disliked having his word challenged. "Don't believe me," he said. "Ask Miss Hagerty."

"Miss Hagerty?"

"The doctor's right, dear. She'll be right as rain tomorrow."

"If you say so, but what'll I tell my husband when he sees her?"

"That's easy," said O'Reilly. "Tell her she's the spitting image of him. But she has her health and that's all that matters."

Barry heard Jenny laugh, then say, "You're a terrible man, Doctor O'Reilly, but I do believe you. You'd not make jokes like that if you weren't telling me the truth."

O'Reilly grunted.

"Now, you'll be tired, dear. Would you like a cup of tea?" Miss Hagerty asked.

Barry smiled and knotted the last deep stitch. Tea. The universal Ulster cure-all. He heard Jenny say, "Yes, please." O'Reilly added, "And maybe Doctor Laverty would like one. He's earned it."

Barry smiled. He clipped the suture and started to repair the skin with one continuous, dissolvable suture, starting at one end of the wound and running it from side to side along the length. A subcuticular stitch would be less uncomfortable as the wound healed and wouldn't need to be taken out. He could hear Jenny making little cooing noises; then he heard a tiny burbling from the baby. He'd always known it. Nothing, nothing in his whole world was as satisfying as conducting a delivery and ending up with a healthy mother and a healthy baby.

He finished stitching and grabbed a handful of damp swabs. "Just going to clean you up a bit, Jenny. Don't be scared."

"Go ahead, Doctor," she said.

When he'd finished and had stripped out the soiled rubber sheet and his gloves, he stood and put a hand in the small of his back. Lord, he was stiff.

This was the second confinement he'd conducted in Ballybucklebo. Maureen Galvin's son, Barry Fingal, had been his first delivery.

For a moment he remembered that Addenbrooke's Hospital in Cambridge had an obstetrics department. But then he looked at O'Reilly, craggy-faced, beaming down at a smiling mother as she cradled her now sleeping newborn girl, rocked her gently, and crooned:

> "Bring no ill wind to hinder us,
> My helpless babe and me—
> Dread spirit of Blackwater banks,
> Clan Eoin's wild banshee,

And Holy Mary pitying us,
In heav'n for grace doth sue.
Sing hush-a-bye loo, la loo, lo lan.
Sing hush a bye loo, la lo."

As he watched O'Reilly and listened to Jenny's lullaby, Barry realized that pursuing a training position in obstetrics seemed less and less attractive and that even after only three days, it was getting much harder to consider going *from*.

20

To Spare Those Who Have Submitted
and Subdue the Arrogant

O'Reilly had gone straight into the surgery. Barry went to call the first of Friday morning's patients. Thursday's work had been light, which as far as he was concerned, was fine. He'd been sleepy when he got out of bed. Nighttime midwifery cases were always tiring, but the successful delivery of Jenny Murphy on Wednesday night had left him feeling just a little smug and, more importantly, able to face the Thursday patients with increased confidence.

Today would be different. He'd be seeing cases he'd treated earlier in the week, and he was eager, and a little anxious, to find out how his patients had fared.

He opened the waiting room door. Only nine or ten people were inside. Barry was surprised not to see Councillor and Mrs. Bishop. He frowned. Had they decided not to come back?

"Morning, Doc." Fergus Finnegan rose, snatched off his cap, and walked to the door. "Me first," he said.

"Go ahead, Fergus. Colin and me's in no rush." Mrs. Brown sat beside young Colin, who waved at Barry.

"Be with you in a minute, Mrs. Brown," Barry said, turning to follow Fergus. The little man's bowleggedness seemed to be accentuated this morning, yet he had a spring in his step. "Grand stuff that golden ointment," he said, as he turned into the surgery. "Morning, Doctor O'Reilly."

"Fergus, how are you?"

"Right as rain. Your man here, Doctor Laverty, has done me a power of good, so he has." He smiled.

So did Barry as he closed the door. "Eye's all better?" he asked. "Let's have a look." Barry led Fergus over to the bow window. "The light's not hurting?"

"Not at all."

Barry used one finger on the lower eyelid and one on the upper to pull them apart. The conjunctiva was clean and shining. The infection had been cleared up by the penicillin. "Looks like it's done the trick," he said.

"Och, aye."

O'Reilly coughed. "In that case I believe, Fergus, you owe me a quid."

"Right enough, sir." Still smiling, Fergus stuck his hand into his trouser pocket and pulled out a note. "Here y'are. Cheap at half the price to get my eye fixed."

Barry had quite forgotten about the bet. Now his pleasure at seeing the man's healthy eye was doubled by the realization that he'd promised to cover the ten pounds O'Reilly would have owed if the cure hadn't worked. Ten pounds out of his thirty-five pounds a week would have put a hole in his resources.

"Thank you, Fergus." O'Reilly took the pound.

Barry saw the little man wink. "I've more than that for you the pair of you, sirs," he said. "Are you for the races the morrow?"

"Indeed," said O'Reilly. "Wouldn't miss them."

"Pop you round to the paddock before the third. I'll give you the nod. I'm riding in that one myself, so I am."

"I'll see you then," said O'Reilly. "Now off you trot."

Fergus turned to Barry. "Thanks a lot, Doc. You done rightly for me, so you did. I'll not forget."

Barry opened the door. "My pleasure," he said, and he meant it.

He heard the front door close as the jockey left. He walked down the hall and came back with Mrs. Brown and Colin. The little lad wore a grey shirt, V-necked sweater, and a pair of shorts. His left sock was held up to just below his scabbed knee; his right lay in a crumpled tube round his ankle.

"Pull up your sock, son," Mrs. Brown said.

Barry was surprised to find O'Reilly was not in the surgery. He closed the door.

"So, Colin," he said, "how's your paw?"

"Show it to the nice doctor."

The little lad glanced down at his shoes and scuffed one on the carpet. He held out his right hand.

"Is it sore?"

The boy shook his head.

"He's shy, doctor, so he is."

And he's scared I'm going to hurt him, Barry thought. "Come on," he said, "hop up there." He lifted Colin and sat him on the wooden chair. He took the boy's hand in his own. The Elastoplast dressing was faded and grubby and a thin margin of black grime clung to its edges, but the rest of the palm was cool and not swollen. It was unlikely the wound had become infected. "Now," said Barry, walking over to get the instrument trolley, "I'm going to see if the stitches can come out." He poured Savlon into a metal basin. "Can you stick your hand in there, Colin?"

The child hesitated, glanced at his mother, and then slowly put his hand into the solution. He stared at Barry, who had laid out swabs, fine-nosed forceps, and a pair of scissors.

"Now," he said, "let's get the Elastoplast off." He lifted Colin's hand, and using the forceps started to tease the adhesive strip off. It came away cleanly. Colin didn't flinch. Barry dropped the soiled adhesive bandage into a Sani-Can and looked at the hand. Where the dressing had been, the skin was pallid and wrinkled, but the wound edges were clean and healing well. It was time to take out the four black silk sutures. Barry picked up the forceps, and Colin pulled his hand away. "No," he said. "Jimmy Hanrahan says it hurts like buggery."

"*Colin.*" Mrs. Brown held a hand in front of her mouth. "Where in God's name did you hear a word like that?"

"Jimmy Hanrahan says it. I told you." Colin said defiantly.

"Wait 'til I tell your da."

Barry had to work to keep his smile hidden. "It's all right, Mrs. Brown," he said. "Colin's just a bit frightened. Aren't you, son?"

The little lad nodded.

"Give me your hand," said Barry, "and if it hurts, I'll stop."

"Promise?"

"Promise."

The hand was slowly offered.

"Lay it on the towel there."

The boy did as he was told. Barry seized the end of one of the sutures with the forceps, lifted it gently so the loop gaped, slipped one blade of the scissors under the loop, snipped, and pulled. The stitch slid out. "That wasn't too bad. Was it?"

"No." The little boy's eyes were wide.

"Right," said Barry, "let's do the rest." The other three stitches slid out easily. "All done," he said. "You can take him home, Mrs. Brown."

"Thanks very much, Doctor Laverty." She grabbed Colin's left hand and started to pull him towards the door, but the little lad resisted, turned to Barry, and said, "That was wee buns, so it was. That Jimmy's full of shite . . ."

"*Colin.*" She hustled him to the door. "I'm sorry. God knows where he hears this stuff."

Barry knew he shouldn't, but this time he couldn't help laughing. "Don't be too hard on him, Mrs. Brown."

"Aye," said O'Reilly, who had appeared in the doorway. "Father, forgive them, for they know not what they do." He tousled Colin's hair.

"Luke twenty-three, thirty-four," Barry remarked. Then turning to Mrs. Brown, he said, "Kids learn from their friends, and all kids like to try to shock."

She looked doubtful, but said, "If you say so, Doctor." She glared at Colin, "But if I hear you using words like that again, you wee glipe . . . I'll wash your mouth out with soap, so I will."

Barry had no doubt she meant it.

"Feisty little tyke," said O'Reilly. "And there's another word for you like 'feague.'"

"Feisty? It's usually applied to something small and spirited, belligerent, like a Jack Russell terrier."

"Indeed," said O'Reilly, "but do you know its root?"

"No." Barry dumped the suture-removing kit into the little sterilizer, closed the lid, and turned on the steam. "But no doubt you're going to tell me."

"Either Anglo-Saxon or Middle English from the verb 'feis,' which being literally translated means 'to fart soundlessly.' " He grinned.

"I don't believe you."

"Suit yourself," said O'Reilly. "Sorry I had to nip out, but Kinky needed me to have a word on the phone with Bertie Bishop."

"Oh?"

"Seems he and the missus are much too busy to come in this morning . . ."

Barry was disappointed. He really wanted to run the test.

"I said it could wait until Monday."

"Damn." Barry was impatient to know if his diagnosis was right.

" 'Could I not see them after lunch?' demands Bishop, and him about as charming as a colour sergeant to a new recruit," said O'Reilly.

Barry waited. If O'Reilly had agreed, he'd have broken his first law of practice by letting Bishop get the upper hand.

"I told him to be here at one-thirty." O'Reilly slumped into his swivel chair. "And before you think I'm going soft in my old age, it suits me fine. I'm as curious as you are to see what happens."

Are you, Barry wondered, *or are you bending your own rules to give me a chance to be right?*

"But," said O'Reilly, "that's after lunch. Nip along . . ."

Barry came back with a stranger. He was tall and thin, with bushy but immaculately brushed silver hair, watery grey eyes, a sharp nose, a clipped silver moustache, and a receding chin. He wore highly polished black shoes, an expensive three-piece suit, handkerchief neatly folded in the breast pocket, and a striped tie Barry was pretty sure was that of a Guards regiment.

"O'Weilly?" the man asked. "I'm Captain O'Bwien-Kelly." His accent was rich, drawling. His replacement of the letter "r" with a "w" marked him as one of a group of upper-class Englishmen who still affected a pronunciation left over from Regency days.

"Indeed," said O'Reilly.

"M'yes. Gwenadier Guards ectually."

Barry had a mental picture of Elmer Fudd talking about a weally wascally wabbit.

"Guards, is it? Now there's a regiment. And a captain to boot?"

"Wather." The captain puffed out his chest.

O'Reilly didn't rise or offer to shake the newcomer's hand. "Doctor O'Reilly." He paused. "Surgeon commander, Her Majesty's Royal Navy . . . and I seem to remember, the Royal Navy's *senior* service."

O'Reilly fifteen. Captain O'Brien-Kelly love, Barry thought.

"Quite, but I didn't come to discuss the awmed fawces. I shall be here for some time. Guest of His Lawdship, the Mawquis. His son, the Honouwable, is a subaltewn with me."

"Comfy are you in the big house?" O'Reilly enquired.

"Living in his gate lodge, ectually. Quite cosy. I'm having a few days at his pheasants, on his wivver . . ."

Barry fondly remembered the afternoon he'd spent trout fishing on the Bucklebo.

"I may need medical attention duwing my sojourn. His Lordship assures me you're quite well qualified."

"Nothing special," said O'Reilly. "Just a country *gnáthdhochtúir*.

"A countwy what?"

"GP. Like my colleague Doctor Laverty here."

"Yes. Quite. *I* usually see a man on Hawley Street in London."

"This is Main Street," O'Reilly said. "Number one. In Ballybucklebo."

"On occasions, beggars can't be choosers."

"I've heard the rumour," O'Reilly said, a tiny hint of pallor appearing in his nose tip. He consulted his watch. "Now, Captain, far be it from me to rush you, but you may have noticed the waiting room's rather full."

"Local peasantwy, what?" He laughed shrilly. "Pwobably used to waiting."

"Some of them," said O'Reilly levelly, "are quite ill."

"Pity."

"I'd appreciate it if you start telling me what's bothering you."

"Not a sausage." The captain laughed again—or as Barry heard it, he whinnied. "Me? Fit as a flea."

"Mmm," said O'Reilly, pulling his half-moon spectacles down his nose.

"Just wanted to make contact. Just in case. One never knows."

"No, indeed," said O'Reilly, rising. "Will that be all?" He started to walk to the door.

"Indeed. Should be twotting along. Pleasant to meet you, young man," he said to Barry.

O'Reilly held the door open. Just before the captain left, O'Reilly asked, "Are you by any chance a sporting man?"

"The horses? Sport of kings? Yes, indeed. Woyal Ascot every year. Derby. Cheltenham Gold Cup. Wouldn't miss 'em. Your Iwish animal Awkle's doing vewy well."

"Himself? Oh, indeed," said O'Reilly. "It occurred to me that as a sporting man you might like to take a run-race down to the local meet here tomorrow."

"The gee-gees, by Jove? Imagine it could be wather fun . . . for a wustic affair."

O'Reilly nodded.

"Civil of you to tell me. Yes. I'll see if I can pop down."

Why, Barry wondered, was O'Reilly being so polite to this arrogant man?

"Do," said O'Reilly. "Maybe Doctor Laverty and me'll see you."

"Jolly good. See, O'Weilly, I knew I was wight to pop in and meet you for a sec. I can see we're going to get on swimmingly."

"Swimmingly," said O'Reilly, smiling.

Barry could see the infernal gleam deep in O'Reilly's brown eyes.

"Cheewio."

"Mmm. And pip-pip," said O'Reilly to the departing back. He glanced at his watch. "That fellah's a waste of good space," he said, "and of our time."

Before Barry could comment, O'Reilly said, "We're running late now, and we've still the surgery to finish, lunch, the Bishops, anything Kinky has for us for this afternoon, and Myrtle McVeigh to see."

"I'll go and get the next one," Barry said. "But a quick question. Why were you so polite to him? Inviting him to the races?"

"Ah," said O'Reilly, "I'm sure he'll have a lovely day there." The light deep in his eyes burned more fiercely. "And I'm positive he's just the kind of man who could benefit from meeting one of the local peasantry."

"You don't mean—"

"Indeed I do. The captain should get along famously with Donal Donnelly. After all, they're both great fans of Arkle."

21

You Have Got to Be a Queen to Get Away
with a Hat Like That

O'Reilly looked balefully at the bowl of salad Mrs. Kincaid set on the dining room table. "Is that it?" he asked.

"It is, so," she said. "It's full of vitamins, and it's very, very filling." Barry could see her eyeing O'Reilly's belly. "It'll do you a power of good, and it'll keep you regular."

"Mrs. Kincaid," O'Reilly growled. "I don't think my bowel habits are in your bailiwick."

Barry saw her purse her lips. But she ignored O'Reilly's remark. Turning to Barry, she said, "When you're done, Doctor Laverty, come out to the kitchen. I've your corduroy pants mended. That was a ferocious rip you'd in them."

"Thanks, Kinky."

"Say no more and eat up." She glared at him before turning to O'Reilly. "You've to see Myrtle this afternoon."

"And that's all?" O'Reilly asked.

"No," she said. "I was saving half a dozen more as a surprise, so."

"Come on, Kinky," O'Reilly said. "The salad's grand."

"Huh." She turned and left.

Barry was surprised that there were so few requests for home visits. Did it mean that, as he had feared, the practice was losing patients?

O'Reilly speared a piece of lettuce. "Bloody rabbit food," he grumbled. "I think, to quote P. G. Wodehouse, Kinky is showing a distinct lack of gruntle today."

Barry sliced into a hard-boiled egg. "I don't think she appreciated being told to mind her own business, Fingal. She worries about you, you know . . ."

"Mmmh."

"And I think she may be a little cross with me."

"Why?"

"Something I said on Sunday about the Beatles being more popular than Jesus."

"Oops. Kinky doesn't make a fuss, she's not one of the evangelical types, but she is devout."

"I know."

O'Reilly shoved another lettuce leaf round his plate, regarding it with the enthusiasm of an offending sailor for the cat-o'-nine-tails. "Maybe we should make a peace offering?"

Barry had had the notion on Sunday, but his concerns of the past few days had banished it. O'Reilly was right. "She'll be going to Maggie's wedding?"

"Indeed."

"I wonder if she'd like a new hat."

"Now there's a thought." O'Reilly shoved his hard-boiled egg in whole.

"We could pop in to Miss Moloney's, take a look at her stock . . . and see how Helen's getting on."

"Good idea. Maybe we could fit that in later. The Bishops'll take a while, but Myrtle should be quick." O'Reilly concentrated on finishing off his salad. He stared hopefully at the sideboard. "Nothing but bloody oranges," he said, rising, grabbing one, and peeling it. "I suppose this'll keep me regular too."

"Well, at least you'll not get scurvy," Barry said.

"No," said O'Reilly as the front doorbell jangled, "and hanging round here blethering won't get the baby a new coat." He glanced at his watch. "That'll be the Bishops." He strode to the door, held it open, and said. "Your patients. I'll watch."

"Right." Barry rose, left the dining room, crossed the hall, and went into the surgery to find Councillor and Mrs. Bishop firmly ensconced in the wooden chairs. "Afternoon," he said. "How are you, Florence?"

"How the hell would she be?" Bishop demanded. "You've not done nothing for her."

"Not quite true, Mr. Bishop. I have consulted with my colleague. He thinks I may be right."

"Maybe. Did you fix it up for us to see a proper doctor?"

"If necessary," Barry said, refusing to let himself get flustered. He sensed O'Reilly fidgeting on the examining table, where he had parked himself. "Could you stand up please, Florence?"

She rose heavily.

"Now," said Barry, "I'd like you to raise your arm as often as you can. Just like the last time."

"God," grumbled Bishop, "has she not done that before?"

"She has, Mr. Bishop, but I'd like Florence to do it again."

"Get on with it then." Bishop fumbled for his fob watch.

Barry had a little surprise in store for the councillor and enjoyed the thought.

Mrs. Bishop puffed and panted, and after a few attempts she conceded failure.

"That's fine," Barry said. "Just sit down for a minute." He helped her back into the chair. "I'm going to give you an injection, but get your breath back first."

Bishop stared at his watch. Barry prepared the neostigmine and atropine injections. "If you'd excuse us, Doctor O'Reilly?" Barry helped Mrs. Bishop to her feet and waited for O'Reilly to get off the couch. Then Barry led her there and closed the screens. "If you could just lift your skirt, pull the top of your knickers down, and bend over the couch?" Barry had adopted many of O'Reilly's tricks, but injecting patients through their clothes was *not* one of them. He swabbed a piece of white, dimpled flesh with methylated spirit, and rapidly gave the two injections.

"Ouch."

"Sorry. Get your clothes settled and maybe you'd like to rest on the couch?"

"Thank you, Doctor." She adjusted her clothing, and Barry helped her up. "Florence, it's possible the medicines might give you a bit of tummy cramp. Don't worry about it. It'll pass very quickly."

"All right."

Barry pushed back the screens, and although his words were meant for Mrs. Bishop, he spoke directly to the councillor. "Now," he said, "we have to wait thirty minutes for the medicine to work."

"*How long?*" Councillor Bishop shot to his feet and gobbled like an enraged turkey. "*How bloody long?*"

"Half an hour," said Barry pleasantly, relishing having the upper hand, which was after all O'Reilly's first law. "It'll not seem like long."

"Not at all," said O'Reilly. "Do make yourselves at home." He twitched his head to the door. "Doctor Laverty and I have an urgent case to deal with, but we'll be back in plenty of time."

Barry frowned. Urgent case? He really should stay in case Mrs. Bishop developed colic, but he followed O'Reilly through the door. When it closed, he asked, "What's urgent, Fingal?"

"I'd forgotten there's a rugby game on the telly tonight. If we walk round to Miss Moloney's now, we can come back for the Bishops, scoot out to see Myrtle, and be back in time for the game. And," he said wistfully, "supper."

"Fair enough."

Barry followed O'Reilly through the door onto Main Street, turned left, and headed to the centre of the village. The sun struggled to break through thin clouds that hung low over the lough. Barry noticed the first brown leaves among a stand of elms on the Ballybucklebo Hills. Autumn was coming.

The traffic was light. Women in head scarves went about their business, wicker shopping baskets over their arms. A youth with a cigarette stuck to his lower lip stood on a narrow, triangular ladder propped against the window of the greengrocer's, chamois leather grasped in one hand as he washed the glass.

Barry recognized a man in a striped apron coming towards them. The man managed to cross the road before the traffic light changed. But Barry and O'Reilly didn't, and they stood waiting as an Inglis bread van, a cyclist, and a horse and cart crossed Main Street. Barry noticed how the man on the bike glanced at O'Reilly, and he wondered how recently the cyclist had occupied a convenient ditch.

"Afternoon, Doctors," said Archibald Auchinleck, touching the peak of his bus conductor's cap. "Grand day."

"How's the back, Archie?" O'Reilly asked.

"I think it's on the mend. Them pills is great."

"Good. And the boy?"

The milkman's face split into a great grin. "I'd a letter yesterday. It's grand, so it is. Rory's getting leave next week, and he'll be coming home."

"That is good news, Archie," O'Reilly said, as the light changed to green. "And how's the fishing?"

Barry glanced at his watch. O'Reilly had said they'd make this outing to save time. The Bishops were waiting, and yet O'Reilly seemed to be perfectly happy to stand about and chat.

"I went out from Donaghadee last night," Archie said and smiled. "Got six mackerel and a gurnard off the Copeland Islands, so I did. Do you fancy a couple of mackerel, Doctor?"

O'Reilly shook his head. "They're a bit oily for me, but thanks, Archie."

The light changed, and Barry shifted from one foot to the other. Time was wasting. "Doctor O'Reilly . . ."

"Take your hurry in your hand, Barry," O'Reilly said. "We've to wait for the light." O'Reilly continued chatting with Archie until the next light change. "Come on, Barry," he announced, looking neither right nor left and stepping straight into the path of a cyclist who was trying to slow down. The woman just managed to jam on her brakes and stick one foot on the road.

Barry shook his head and followed past the shops until they came to a narrow red-painted door beside a window in which were two mannequins dressed in floral skirts and sweaters. Hats were displayed on glass shelves. A sign above the door read: Ballybucklebo Boutique. Hardly Carnaby Street, Barry thought. He heard the bell jingle when O'Reilly opened the door.

A gaunt, middle-aged woman, her pepper-and-salt hair pulled back in a severe bun, rushed out from behind a glass display case full of gloves, handkerchiefs, and handbags. Her thin lips were drawn up into a smile, but her hazel eyes were unsmiling,

She clasped her hands and made a little curtsey. Barry had a mental picture of a female Uriah Heep at her most 'umble.

"Doctor O'Reilly. What a pleasure. What a great pleasure, and this must be the young Doctor Laverty?" Her voice was indeed as Helen had described it—like cinders under a door. "How can I help you gentlemen today?"

"A hat," said O'Reilly. "For Mrs. Kincaid."

"I've just the thing." She fluttered, turned, and screeched in a voice that Barry felt could have opened a tin of sardines at ten paces: "Helen . . . bring the blue box." She turned her forced smile on O'Reilly. "My assistant's a simple girl. She's in the back." Then she yelled, "*Helennn.*"

Helen appeared through a bead curtain under an arch at the back of the store. She carried a blue hatbox.

"Not that one, you stupid girl. The navy blue one." She tutted. "So sorry to keep you waiting, Doctor."

Barry had already noticed that Helen was still wearing a long-sleeved blouse, a long skirt, and white cotton gloves. It didn't look as if the hydrocortisone ointment was working—not yet, anyway. She reappeared with a navy blue box.

"On the counter, girl. On the counter."

Helen glanced at Barry, rolled her eyes to heaven, and set the box on the glass.

"Don't just stand there. Open it."

"Yes, Miss Moloney." Helen lifted the lid, pulled out handfuls of tissue paper, and lifted a hat onto the countertop.

Barry stared at the confection. Emerald green, it was made of what looked like felt, shaped like a man's trilby with a wide brim, and turned down at the front and up at the back. The hatband was of darker green satin.

"Isn't it lovely?" Miss Moloney cooed.

"A thing of beauty," O'Reilly agreed, with a perfectly straight face. "Is it Mrs. Kincaid's size?"

"Yes, indeed."

"What do you think, Barry?"

It was like being back in the surgery, Barry thought, with O'Reilly automatically seeking a second opinion. "It's not what I think. It's what Kinky will think," Barry said.

"If you'll forgive me," Miss Moloney simpered, "I think Mrs. Kincaid will love it. Positively love it."

"Right," said O'Reilly. "We'll take it."

"Wonderful." She barely glanced at Helen. "Get it parcelled up. At once, girl. The doctors will be in a hurry." She moved behind the counter. "I'll just make out the bill."

Barry saw Helen sigh, reflexively scratch behind her left knee, and then start returning the hat to the box. "How are you, Helen?"

She shrugged. He was disappointed. He'd been right. The ointment couldn't be having much effect. No bloody wonder if the poor girl had to put up with being treated the way she was, day and daily. "I'm sorry." He was sorry too that although most of the other patients he'd treated since Monday had responded, Helen clearly had not. At least he knew she hadn't been expecting miracles. He wondered if O'Reilly was going to say anything to Miss Moloney about her treatment of her assistant, or whether perhaps he should mention it himself.

"Have you not finished yet?" Miss Moloney glared at Helen.

"Yes, Miss Moloney."

"Then don't stand around. Get into the back room and get those other hatboxes stacked."

Helen left, and Miss Moloney smiled again at O'Reilly. "You'd not believe the number of hats I've had to stock, with two weddings coming up." She wrung her hands, and this time her smile involved her eyes. Barry could picture the woman in her countinghouse, gloating over her profits. "Here you are, Doctor," she said, pushing the hatbox to O'Reilly. "And here's your bill."

"Give them both to Doctor Laverty," O'Reilly said, and before

Barry could protest, O'Reilly fixed him with a stare. "It was your idea, Laverty." He bade Miss Moloney a good day, turned and left.

The chimes over the door jingled as Barry sighed and pulled out his wallet. Bloody O'Reilly had just won a pound from Fergus Finnegan. Barry paid and took his change and the hatbox. He was still worried about Helen. "Excuse me, Miss Moloney . . ."

"Yes?" Her voice was cold; one eyebrow was arched.

"I wonder if you're not being a bit hard on Helen."

"I beg your pardon?"

It was as if the temperature in the shop had plummeted by a good ten degrees.

"What I mean is—"

"Young man, when I have the impertinence to come into your surgery and tell you how to practise, you may come in here and tell me how to run my business."

"I . . . that is . . ." He glimpsed Helen peering out from between the beads and had no difficulty understanding what she was silently mouthing: "Thanks, Doc."

"Good afternoon, Doctor Laverty," Miss Moloney said.

Barry clutched the hatbox, and as he left he heard Miss Moloney yell, "Helennn, get in here this instant."

He was glad O'Reilly had not been present to witness the little scene. Barry knew he'd not broken O'Reilly's first law. He'd left it in shards on the dress-shop floor. He quickened his pace to catch up with O'Reilly and tried to put that failure behind him. In the next five minutes he was going to find out what had happened to Mrs. Bishop.

22

The Cure for This Ill Is Not to Sit Still

O'Reilly was waiting in the hall. "Shove that in the dining room," he said, nodding at the hatbox. "We'll give it to Kinky later."

"We? I paid for it," Barry said, dumping the box on the nearest chair. "He who pays the piper—"

"Calls the tune." O'Reilly started to open the surgery door, then remarked, "Let's see if you've called *this* tune right." He went in.

Barry followed. He saw Councillor Bishop stumping up and down. "You said half an hour. It's been thirty-five whole minutes, so it has."

"Dear me," said O'Reilly. "How time flies." He took his usual chair.

"Would youse two get on with it?"

Barry went to the couch. "How are you feeling, Florence? No tummy cramps?"

"No, Doctor."

"Good." Barry remembered Bereen had advised giving atropine to avoid that possible complication, and praise be, it had worked. He still felt a tad guilty about leaving his patient alone while he went out with O'Reilly. "Let's get you up," he said. He helped her sit and get off the couch. "How many times can you work your arm now?" he asked.

"Och, Jesus. Not again," Bishop growled.

Barry ignored him and watched as Mrs. Bishop raised and lowered her arm, seemingly without any difficulty. "That's fine. You can stop now."

"It's a miracle." She looked at him wide-eyed. "I couldn't have done any better at Lourdes."

"You'd not be going to Lourdes," Bishop said. "You're a good Protestant, so you are. Lourdes is for Fenians."

O'Reilly coughed. "I think you mean Roman Catholics, Councillor."

"Aye, whatever. But I want to know now what is wrong with her and can you fix it? I'm fed up with her being useless."

"Your wife, Councillor," Barry said, looking directly at Mrs. Bishop, "is suffering from a disease called myasthenia gravis. Severe muscle weakness."

Bishop frowned, and Barry heard the suspicion in the man's voice when he asked, "You're not full of bullshite, like the time you and O'Reilly bamboozled me about that test?"

Barry wanted to smile, remembering how he and O'Reilly had completely flummoxed the councillor by making up detailed medical mumbo jumbo and swearing blind that they could prove he was the father of Julie MacAteer's unborn child. "No, Councillor. We are not."

"It's a very rare disease," O'Reilly rumbled. "I've never seen a case."

"There's likely a brave wheen of things you two haven't seen," Bishop said.

Barry was so pleased to have been proven right that he was able to put his failure with Miss Moloney behind him and to ignore the councillor's jibe. "Florence, you'll need to take some tablets. One as soon as you get up, and one or two every time you start to feel weak, but I promise you you'll be right as rain in no time."

"Honest to God?" she asked, eyes wide. "Honest?"

"I promise," he said, "and if Doctor O'Reilly would let me get at the prescription pad . . ."

"Right." O'Reilly stood and moved aside.

"I'll write you a scrip." Barry sat at the desk and filled in the blank form:

> *R Tabs neostigmine bromide. 15 mgms*
> *Mitte 100*
> *Sig 1h/m, 1 or 2 PRN. P.O.*

He wondered why it was necessary to scrawl in abbreviated Latin when a simple English order would have sufficed for one hundred tablets to be taken orally, one on rising, one or two as required. No wonder chemists constantly complained about trying to decipher prescriptions. "Here you are," he said.

"Thanks, Doctor Laverty. Thanks a lot. It'll be grand to get back on my feet." Barry saw the glistening of a tear on her left cheek and noticed how her hand trembled as she took the paper. He put a hand on her shoulder. "My pleasure," he said. "Come back and see me next week. I'd like to know how you're getting on."

"I will." She patted her tummy and smiled weakly. "Maybe I could get a few pounds off, too."

"It's a couple of stone you need to lose." Councillor Bishop strode to the door. "Come on, Flo," he said. "We've been here long enough, so we have."

"Just a minute," O'Reilly said levelly, but glanced at Barry as he spoke. "I want to ask you about the Black Swan, Councillor."

So, Barry thought, O'Reilly *was* going to try to play on Bishop's gratitude—if the man was capable of feeling thankful to anyone.

Bishop spun round. His eyes narrowed. "What about it?"

"A little bird told me you're not going to renew Willy Dunleavy's lease."

"That's none of your business, O'Reilly. Tell your wee bird to go and pluck itself."

Barry saw two simultaneous colour changes. Bishop's cheeks flushed bright red, and the tip of O'Reilly's nose blanched. They're like two gamecocks in the same barnyard, he thought, and he was surprised when O'Reilly said calmly, "A lot of folks in the village would like you to reconsider."

"They can 'like' away to their heart's content. Business is business, so it is."

"I see," said O'Reilly. He sighed. "Pity." It was the first time Barry had ever seen the big man accept defeat.

"Doctor O'Reilly," Mrs. Bishop interrupted, "Bertie doesn't—"

"Houl' your wheest, woman." The councillor rounded on his wife, the scarlet in his cheeks now puce. "Houl' . . . your . . . wheest."

"Sorry, dear," she said. She stared down at the carpet.

"I should bloody well think so." Bishop grabbed his wife's hand. "Come on to hell out of this now." The surgery door slammed as they left.

Barry stared at the departing backs, then turned to O'Reilly. "You gave it a shot, Fingal."

"Aye," said O'Reilly, "and missed . . . and Barry I'm stuck. Ever since we found out about the Duck, I've been racking my brains about how to get the wee bastard to change his mind. I can't think of a single thing."

"Don't worry, Fingal. I'm sure something will turn up." Barry wished he could believe it were true.

"Jesus," said O'Reilly, "you and Mr. Micawber." He shook his head. "Sometimes," he said, staring out the window, "I think I should stick to the doctoring but . . . this bloody place gets under your skin. You end up being part of it."

"I know," Barry said quietly.

O'Reilly grunted. "Anyway," he said, "I'm proud of you. You *were* right about Flo. She did have me foxed."

"Thanks, Fingal."

"The trouble is, I promised you if you were right I'd see to it that it worked wonders for your reputation, but without Flo or Bishop saying something, I can't tell anybody."

"Patient confidentiality. I know," Barry said. He was still glowing, thanks to his having been right and to O'Reilly's unconditional praise. He continued, "It's all right. I've had a couple of successes: the jockey and wee Colin Brown today, Jenny's delivery on Wednesday. Mrs. O'Hagan's happy about me fixing Kieran's retention. I think you were right, Fingal, about me just getting on with my job."

O'Reilly clapped Barry on the shoulder. "We'll see," he said. "And on the credit side, at least Bishop's getting on with *his* job at Sonny's. We should be grateful for small mercies."

Barry heard the hall telephone ringing, Kinky's voice, and the *ting* as she replaced the receiver. He watched as the surgery door opened.

"Yes, Kinky?" O'Reilly asked.

"It was Myrtle MacVeigh. She says she's up and running round like a bee on a hot brick, so. She's better, not to bother calling, and thank Doctor Laverty for them nighties-fer-aunties." She frowned. "Whatever in the name of the wee man they might be." She turned to Barry and tutted, "And you, Doctor Laverty, you forgot to collect your corduroys after lunch, so I've stuck them upstairs in your room."

"Sorry, Kinky." Barry smiled. "And thanks." He turned to O'Reilly. "Should we not maybe pop in on Myrtle anyway? Just to be sure?"

"And so you can revel in another of your triumphs in the healing arts?" O'Reilly asked, but he was grinning widely. "I don't think so," he said. "If we don't go, we'll have lots of time now before supper . . ." He glanced at Kinky.

"I've crab cakes on the go," she said, "and if you like I'll deep-fry some chips."

"That," said O'Reilly, as his stomach rumbled, "would hit the spot."

"And you'd have plenty of time to see your rugby, Fingal," Barry said, quite looking forward to a lazy afternoon.

"And," said O'Reilly, "for all the time it would take, we could pay that visit to Maggie you were talking about on Monday, Barry. See how the old girl's doing, and ask if she has any notions about where Sonny could go until his house is ready."

"Why not?" Barry had developed a soft spot for Maggie MacCorkle. He'd enjoy visiting her, and he was curious to see if she could help O'Reilly keep his promise about getting Sonny out of the convalescent home. It was hardly practising medicine but O'Reilly was right. Ballybucklebo did get under your skin, but then so did a certain civil engineering student. He started to the door. "Your car or mine, Fingal?"

Barry hesitated at the kitchen door. He'd let O'Reilly go first, so if Arthur made his usual sex-crazed charge perhaps his master could stop the animal. He heard O'Reilly yelling, "Come on, Barry. We've not got all day." He could not hear barking.

Barry stepped out into the back garden. An insistent sun was forcing its light through a thin layer of cirrus clouds, casting the back garden in dappled light and shade. The big chestnut tree, spiky conkers thick in its branches, threw a long shadow. The apple trees bent under the weight of their ripening fruit. Someone had mowed the lawn, and he could smell the subtle scent of grass clippings. No sign of Arthur. Good.

O'Reilly stood at the open back gate. "Arthur?" he yelled. "Arthur Guinness? Where the hell's that bloody dog?"

Barry looked into the kennel. Empty.

"I'll kill Donal Donnelly's brother, Turlough. Kill him dead."

"Why?"

"He's the one that cuts the grass. If I've told him once, I've told him a thousand times, 'Shut the bloody gate behind you.' Arthur's got out, and the Lord knows what he'll get up to."

Barry silently hoped that somewhere the big Labrador might find a bitch in heat and, for a change, have a go at her instead of his trouser leg.

"Can't be helped," said O'Reilly. "He'll be home when he gets hungry. Come on."

Barry waited until O'Reilly reversed out of the garage; then he climbed in and resigned himself to another kamikaze mission in the Rover. Something on the dashboard caught his eye. "Er, Fingal?"

"What?"

"Should the petrol gauge be reading empty?"

"Is it?" O'Reilly pulled onto Main Street and headed in the direction of Maggie's. "Pay it no heed. It's broken."

"Oh," said Barry, "do you have a reserve tank like Brunhilde?" His Volkswagen had a little lever that, if turned, allowed a gallon of petrol to run from a reserve tank.

"Not at all," said O'Reilly. "I never run out of petrol, and if I did I can fix it."

"Oh," said Barry, and he let the matter drop. He sat silently as

O'Reilly hurled the car along, finally screeching to a halt outside Maggie's cottage.

As Barry got out, he was greeted by five assorted dogs, yelping, wagging their tails, and vying for his attention. He saw Maggie sitting on her front porch in a canvas deck chair. He'd seen her hat before, a straw boater, but today she had sea pinks in the hatband. She rose, toothless mouth open in a wide grin, her weathered face creased by laugh lines.

"Can you call off the dogs, Maggie?"

"Och, sure they're only friendly beasts. Sonny wouldn't have them otherwise." Still, she called to the animals and shooed them through a gate into her fenced back garden. "And what brings you gentlemen here today?" She held her hand two inches above her hat. "Them— what do you muh call 'em—eccentric headaches is all gone."

"Glad to hear it, Maggie. We were just passing," said O'Reilly. "We wanted to be sure you were all right."

"As rain." She grinned her toothless grin and asked, "Would you like a wee cup of tea and a piece?"

"Not today, thanks, Maggie," said O'Reilly. "We're in a bit of a rush. Maybe next time."

Barry was heartily relieved. Maggie stewed her tea until it was strong enough to strip rust from a cast-iron boiler, and the last thing he wanted was a slice of bread and jam.

O'Reilly leant against the bonnet of the Rover and fired up his briar. "Actually, we came to ask your advice."

"Is it about that wee moggie Lady Macbeth again, Doctor?"

O'Reilly shook his head. "No. It's about Sonny."

Barry had not thought it possible, but her grin grew even wider. "Sonny? Sure he's grand. I saw him yesterday. He says to thank you. They're taking better care of him now."

Because O'Reilly asked them to, Barry thought. Asked with all the gentle persuasiveness of a battering ram against a castle's portcullis.

"Good," said O'Reilly. "He's making a grand recovery, but I think he'd get his strength back quicker if we could get him out of that place."

Maggie simpered like a girl. "He'd better. Buggerlugs Bertie Bishop's

fixing Sonny's roof, and him and me's getting wed next Saturday. You'll be there, Doctors?"

"Oh, indeed," said O'Reilly, "but the repairs won't be finished by then."

Maggie shook her head. "That doesn't matter. As long as they will be soon, that's all that matters. Sure he can move in here for a while, so he can. Even with his dogs and my pussycat, there's room enough for the pair of us."

"I know," said O'Reilly, "but I'd like to get him out even sooner."

Maggie frowned. "I'd take the old goat in tomorrow—haven't I got his dogs?—but what would people say?"

"Nothing too charitable," said O'Reilly. "That's why I was wondering if you had any suggestions?"

Maggie pushed back her straw hat and scratched her head. "Maybe Aggie? No. She's just taken in a lodger. Then there's Willy Mc-Coubrey, a bachelor man, him with the wooden leg. Farms out fornenst Paddy MacVeigh . . . I hear Myrtle's on the mend . . . but Willy's so contentious he could start a fight if he was the only one in a deserted house. Sonny'd go Harpic trying to live with that one."

Harpic, Barry smiled. It was a toilet cleanser with the slogan "Clean round the bend."

"Do you know, Doctor O'Reilly? I can't think of a single one." She frowned. "I hear Willy Dunleavy's wee girl Mary wants to go and work in Belfast. Get away from that Miss Moloney . . ."

"I doubt she could be out by Monday," said O'Reilly.

Maggie cackled. "I hear if Bishop has his way, Willy and Mary'll both be out very soon anyway."

Barry stood with his mouth slightly open. Were there no secrets in Ballybucklebo?

"So we're both stumped, Maggie?" O'Reilly knocked the dottle out of his pipe. "I'll just have to think some more on it. Are you seeing Sonny tomorrow?"

"In soul, I am." Maggie smiled. "Will I tell him you were asking for him?"

"Please, and Doctor Laverty too."

"I will, so I will," she said, "and I'll tell him you're doing your best for him. Sure you can do no more." She hugged herself. "And anyway next Saturday'll be here quicker than two shakes of a duck's tail, and then I'll be Mrs. Sonny, so I will, and you needn't worry your head anymore about where he'll be living."

O'Reilly opened the driver's door. "And Doctor Laverty and I will be there to dance at your wedding, Maggie, but we'll not make it if we don't get home now." He nodded at Barry. "Get in."

As Barry climbed in, he heard O'Reilly muttering to himself, "Bloody useless. I can't sway Bishop. I can't find a place for Sonny . . ."

"And I can't get Miss Moloney to let up on Helen," Barry said gently, and as he spoke, his own worries seemed to fade and he ached for the big man in the driver's seat.

23

All Beer and Skittles

The Rover's engine coughed, caught, spluttered, and expired. The car jerked spasmodically forward, and Barry was thrown back and forth in his seat.

"Holy thundering mother of Jesus Christ Al-bloody-mighty." O'Reilly wrestled the car into a convenient seaside lay-by.

Barry heard the tyres crunch over gravel and the squeak when O'Reilly put on the hand-brake. He tapped the petrol gauge and scowled at it. Barry could see it read Empty, and the needle refused to budge.

"Useless bloody thing," growled O'Reilly.

Barry decided it would be less than tactful to remind O'Reilly he'd been warned when they set out for Maggie's. The corollary to O'Reilly's first law for patients was equally applicable to junior doctors. "Out of petrol are we, Fingal?"

"Of course we're bloody well out. Get out yourself." O'Reilly dismounted.

Barry got out and waited. He'd seen O'Reilly in a hurry to see a rugby game before, but never a famished, craving his-dinner, wanting-to-see-a-rugby-game O'Reilly. "Oh, dear," Barry said. "Never mind. You said you could fix it."

He expected O'Reilly to pull a can of petrol from the boot, but instead he walked to the back of the car and unscrewed the cap of the filling port. "You watch this," he said, unbuttoning the fly of his tweed trousers and standing close to the car. "I'm in a rush."

"Be serious, Fingal. Even you can't change piddle into petrol."

"No," said O'Reilly, "but I'll let you in on the secret. I had to pull this stunt a year ago on my way to a delivery, and it worked like a charm."

"What does?"

"In this model of Rover the feed pipe to the engine is an inch above the bottom of the petrol tank, so any old muck lies at the bottom and can't get into the carburettor."

"I still don't . . . ," Barry gasped. After glancing up and down the road, O'Reilly moved even closer to the car. He grunted, and then Barry heard a hollow, metallic plashing as fluid from above hit the petrol below.

O'Reilly, one hand in front of him below waist level, said, "The petrol floats on the pish, and enough fuel gets into the engine to give me another ten miles. Plenty to get us to the nearest garage, and once I've filled her up, it's easy to bleed the petrol tank and get the widdle out."

Barry's laughter was drowned out by a rapidly approaching engine noise. He turned from O'Reilly to see a coach turn into the lay-by and stop. Several people piled out to admire the view across Belfast Lough. Over ceramic blue waters stippled with the white of distant sailboats, the lowering battlements of Carrickfergus Castle on the far shore crouched beneath the soft green roundness of the Antrim Hills.

Most of the tourists were looking out over the lough, some oohing and aaahing. But one, a large, older gentleman wearing a ten gallon hat, garishly checked sports jacket, and mustard-coloured pants, strolled over and stood beside O'Reilly. "Watcha doin', buddy?" His accent was definitely transatlantic.

Barry cringed for O'Reilly, who seemed not one whit abashed.

"Topping up the petrol."

"Petrol?"

"I believe in your country you call it gasoline."

"Sure do." He offered a large hand. "Bud Weismueller. I'm from Texas. That's oil country."

"Indeed," said O'Reilly, shoving himself back into his pants, doing up the buttons, and accepting the handshake. "Fingal O'Reilly. From Ireland . . . and this is Guinness country." He screwed the filler cap back in place. "Now if you'll excuse us . . . ?" He beckoned to Barry, who got in. O'Reilly turned the key, and the engine immediately caught.

Before O'Reilly could drive off, the Texan rapped on O'Reilly's window. O'Reilly wound it down. "Yes?"

"Shoot. I ain't never seen nothin' like that in all my born days. Wait 'til I tell Mamie." Barry thought Weismueller could not have looked more surprised if O'Reilly had simply stared at the Rover and by force of will made it levitate four feet above the ground. "Jeez Louise, you said it's Guinness, sir?"

"One of its many by-products," O'Reilly said with a straight face.

Bud Weismueller frowned and rubbed the web of one hand across his mouth. Barry thought that he was probably thinking of the money he could make taking bets. "Do you think Budweiser would work?" Weismueller asked.

"Oh, Indubitably," said O'Reilly, his face expressionless. "Now if you'll excuse us?" He put the car in gear and drove away.

"Work with Budweiser?" Barry snorted. "I doubt it. He should put it directly into the tank."

"Why?"

"Sure it's nothing but piss anyway."

Barry had the satisfaction of seeing O'Reilly wrestle with the steering wheel because he was laughing so hard. They were both still chuckling when O'Reilly filled the tank at the nearest garage and then drove on. Barry had managed to compose himself by the time O'Reilly stopped the Rover in the lane behind his house.

Barry climbed out and let himself into the back garden. Immediately he was greeted by Arthur Guinness, who, barking joyously, tried to cock a leg on Barry's trousers. Barry stepped aside. "You could have used your bloody dog back there, Fingal."

"Bloody's the right word. Where the hell have you been, sir?" O'Reilly glowered at Arthur, who instead of cowering, trotted proudly to his kennel and returned with a green Wellington boot. He sat and deposited it at O'Reilly's feet, the picture, Barry thought, of a gundog making the perfect retrieve.

"Christ," said O'Reilly, picking up the boot. "Where in the hell did you get this?"

"Arf," said a smiling Arthur, and wagged his tail.

"Idiot," said O'Reilly. "Now I'll have to go out after supper and drive around until I find the other one." He glowered at the dog. "Into your kennel, sir."

Looking suitably abashed, the dog slunk, tail dragging, into his doghouse. The animal had quite a list of distinctly uncanine character traits, Barry thought: satyriasis, dipsomania, and now kleptomania.

The last didn't seemed to bother O'Reilly. Grinning, he marched to the back door, calling over his shoulder, "Come on, Barry. I'm famished."

Mrs. Kincaid was on her hands and knees scrubbing the tiled kitchen floor, her ample backside higher than her head. She did not turn from her work but remarked, "We've had a little accident, so."

"Not my crab cakes?" O'Reilly asked.

"No." She straightened up and shoved a wisp of hair from her face with the back of her forearm. "But that cat . . ."

"What about her, Kinky?"

She blew out her cheeks. "I told you she loved anything from the dairy."

"Yes. The day she tried to get at the butter," Barry said.

"Well," said Mrs. Kincaid, "she didn't *try* this time. She ate a whole half pound off the kitchen counter, and then . . ." Kinky's black eyes narrowed. "Then she started to make a noise like a cement mixer, gave one almighty yowl, and sicked the whole lot up over my clean floor, so." She stood slowly, put one hand in the small of her back. "I didn't know whether to comfort her or kill her dead, the *gadaí*."

"Thief," said O'Reilly, for Barry's benefit. "Och, sure, Kinky, she's only wee."

"So," said Kinky, "are leprechauns, and look at the mischief the little people can get up to, souring milk, stealing babies. I yelled at her and off she ran like a liltie. I haven't seen her since."

Barry could see Kinky was serious about leprechauns. Despite having left her native Cork before the war, she still held on to her country superstitions.

"As long," said O'Reilly, "as she didn't steal the crab cakes."

Kinky shook her head. "No. They're in the oven. Run along now, and I'll have them and the chips along in no time. And if you see that wee creature, tell her, *dul chun an diabhail.*"

"Right, Kinky," O'Reilly said. "I'll do that."

As they walked along the hall, Barry asked, "What have you to tell Lady Macbeth, Fingal?"

O'Reilly laughed and turned into the dining room. "To go to the devil." He picked up the hatbox from where Barry had left it hours earlier. "I think," he said, handing the box to Barry, "what with you and your cracks about Jesus, me and my scowling at her salad, *and* Her Ladyship losing her lunch all over Kinky's floor, our timing in the peace-offering stakes couldn't be better."

"I hope so. I much prefer to see Kinky cheerful."

"Do you, so?" Kinky brought in two plates, each with four crab cakes and a pile of chips. "Here," she said, setting a plate before Barry and another in front of O'Reilly. Rather than dig straight in, Barry rose.

"And is there something the matter with your supper?" Mrs. Kincaid stood, arms folded.

"No, Kinky." Barry realized that by seeming to ignore her cooking, he had insulted her once more. He grabbed the hatbox and gave it to her. "I—that is, Doctor O'Reilly and I—have a wee something for you."

"Why? It's not my birthday or Christmas." She held the box in front of her.

"No," said O'Reilly, forkful of crab cake halfway to his mouth. "It's because we love you."

"Less of your soft soap, Doctor dear." But Barry could tell by the way she smiled that the gift and O'Reilly's words had pleased her. "Now eat up before it gets cold, and I'll run off and have a look in this."

"I will," said O'Reilly, and the better part of a crab cake vanished.

Barry tucked in. The cakes had a flavour of fresh Dungeness crab, what the locals simply called "eating crab." He couldn't identify the subtle spice, but it was delicious. The chips were golden, crisp, and firm. He didn't bother trying to start a conversation. He could see O'Reilly wolfing down his supper with the enthusiasm of a recently rescued, marooned mariner.

Barry was still eating when O'Reilly set his knife and fork on his now empty plate with a clatter, smiled at Barry, and said, "Just the job to set a fellah up for a lonesome wellie boot hunt." O'Reilly rose and headed for the door. "I'm off to see if I can find the brother to the one Arthur nicked. Keep an eye on the shop, and I'll be back as quick as I can. I still want to see that rugger game."

"Right." Barry was pleased to be left in charge. He pushed his empty plate aside and ran a finger round the inside of the tight waistband of his trousers.

"Excuse me, Doctor Laverty." Kinky stood in the doorway. "How do you like the look of that?"

He turned. The green felt trilby was set exactly on the centre of her silver hair.

"It suits you, Kinky," Barry said. "It really does."

"It's just what I needed for Maggie's wedding," she said.

"You'll be the belle of the ball." Barry thought of Rhett Butler giving Mammy a red petticoat. "Kinky, it's by way of saying I'm sorry for that crack on Sunday."

"What crack?"

"About Jesus and the Beatles . . . and Doctor O'Reilly's sorry too for turning his nose up at your lunches."

She shook her head. "Yerragh, Doctor dear, it's nice of the pair of you to worry about my feelings." She glanced down. "But then himself worries about everybody's feelings"—she looked back to Barry— "and I'm glad to see you're taking after him."

Barry blushed.

"Do you mind if I sit down?"

"Please."

She sat heavily on a dining room chair. "I have been a bit *cantalach* lately . . ."

"I'm sorry?"

"Grumpy, but it's nothing to do with you or himself, so don't you fret." She looked straight into Barry's eyes. "I told you a bit about myself and Paudeen."

Barry had been flattered last month when she'd confided in him about how she'd lost her husband, a Cork fisherman, years ago. "I do," he said quietly.

"It was August he was drowned. Sometimes it comes back to me, so."

"I'm sorry, Kinky." She still grieved after all these years. He couldn't help but wonder if he lost Patricia, would *he* still be yearning years later?

"What's done's done," she said. "I just wanted you to understand."

"Thanks, Kinky."

"Not at all. It's me to be thanking you for the hat. Imagine Sonny and Maggie. There's a thing."

Sonny. Barry wondered if Kinky could help. "Kinky," he said, "Sonny's stuck in that home in Bangor, and Doctor O'Reilly wants to get him out, but so far he can't find a place for Sonny to stay. You wouldn't happen to know of anybody with rooms to rent?"

She frowned. "I did. Brie Lannigan had a room but she let it to Julie MacAteer when the wee lass left the Bishops, but bedamned if I know of anywhere else. But I'll ask about."

If she could find somewhere, it would be one less thing for O'Reilly to worry about. And Bishop. Kinky might just be able to help there too. "There's another wee thing."

"Ask away."

"Have you heard about the councillor and the Duck?"

She snorted. "Who hasn't?"

"He and Mrs. Bishop were in here earlier, and Doctor O'Reilly asked the councillor to change his mind."

"Bertie Bishop? Change his mind? Did you ever try to pour molasses on a freezing cold day?"

"I know but it's all to do with the lease, and when Doctor O'Reilly broached the subject . . ." Mrs. Bishop's words and the councillor's violent hushing of his wife were as clear in Barry's mind as if they had just happened. "Mrs. Bishop started to say something—'Bertie doesn't . . .'—but that's as far as she got."

Mrs. Kincaid frowned. "He doesn't what?"

"I don't know, but could it be possible, just possible, that the councillor's claim to the title isn't sound?"

She laughed. "Anything's possible in Ballybucklebo, and that councillor's crooked as a corkscrew. It's a wonder when he walks over a parquet floor he doesn't drive himself into the woodwork, so." She wagged a finger at Barry. "Watch yourself, lad," she said. "It's one thing to care like himself, but don't you go getting as devious."

Barry knew it was meant as a friendly warning, but he found the suggestion flattering. "It's only a glimmer of an idea, but could you do a bit of sniffing around with Mrs. B?"

"I will, so. And now the dishes won't wash themselves." She rose. "And if you see that wee cat, tell her she's forgiven."

"It's Doctor Dolittle you want for that, Kinky. I can't talk to animals, but I know what you mean." He rose. "Off you go and get your work done. I'm just going to nip upstairs and take a peek at your fine needlework on my corduroys. Thanks for fixing them." He followed Kinky out and climbed the stairs. He knew he was clutching at straws asking Kinky to help solve O'Reilly's problems, but sometimes the Cork woman seemed to be able to find out things neither he nor O'Reilly could. She was like Della Street, that TV lawyer Perry Mason's secretary.

Barry hoped Kinky could take some load off the big man's shoulders, and as he started to climb the final flight of stairs he wished he could also get Kinky to help speed up Major Fotheringham's pathology report—and tell him what to do about Patricia as well.

He went into his bedroom and saw his pants neatly folded on the bed, the rent virtually invisible, so skillfully had Kinky mended it. He would have been very pleased had Lady Macbeth not been curled up sound asleep, half on the legs of the pants, half on the candlewick bedspread, her body well clear of the pool of cat puke smack in the centre of the seat of the trousers.

"Bloody cat!" he roared, and he could hear O'Reilly's voice in his.

He grabbed for the trousers. Lady Macbeth woke, leapt to her feet, arched her back, fluffed her fur, and spat at him. "Shoo!" Barry said, angrily. The cat sprang to the floor and vanished. Barry bundled up his trousers and took them downstairs. Mrs. Kincaid was drying the last of the dinner plates.

"Kinky?"

"What?"

"You won't believe this but—"

"Lord Jesus. Not again. Give them here," she said.

"Sorry about that."

"Och, it's not your fault." She took the pants. "Between him putting back the boot Arthur stole, and me cleaning up after the cat, the animals round here keep us busy enough."

Barry had expected Kinky to be irritated, but she seemed not the least bit put out. "I'd not have it else," she said. "Himself, the great *amadán*, needs the company."

It was a word Barry did recognize—it meant idiot. But he could hear the affection in her voice.

"Still," she said, "it's been better since you came, Doctor Laverty, so." She turned on the tap and started to run water over the stain. "It's not my place but . . . I told you last month and I'll tell you again . . . I hope you'll be staying."

Before Barry could reply, O'Reilly shoved his way in through the back door. "Found it," he said, beaming. "You'd never guess where. The back step of Donal Donnelly's mother's. He lives with her, you know. There was the other boot, all alone, just waiting for its opposite number. And do you know?" He lowered his voice. "Nobody saw me put it back."

"A good thing too," said Barry. "I can just see the headline . . . *Wellie Boot Snatcher Found: Eminent Physician on Bootnapping Charges*."

"Get away with you, Doctor Laverty," Kinky said, smiling. "Now go on, the pair of you, and watch your rugby match, and I'll be up later with a cup of tea and barmbrack."

"Great," said O'Reilly. "Come on, Barry."

The television set was in a small room on the first-floor landing, not in the upstairs lounge. O'Reilly had explained he couldn't stand the baleful eye of the blank screen staring at him if the set wasn't in use.

Barry took a small armchair.

"Sherry?" O'Reilly asked.

"Please."

Barry waited for O'Reilly to return, still thinking about what Kinky had said. He was twenty-four; O'Reilly, fifty-six. Damn it, the man was old enough to be his father. Perhaps that was why O'Reilly wanted Barry to stay. As a substitute for the son he'd never had. Barry wasn't entirely sure it was a role he wanted to play. Ulster fathers could be a bit overpowering, hesitant to give their sons the independence Barry wanted, and yet, at this very moment, when Barry was struggling to regain acceptance, it was a comfort to know that the older man was there.

"Here you are." O'Reilly, whiskey in one hand, gave Barry a glass, sat in the other armchair, and put his boots up on a footstool. "*Slainthe.*"

"Cheers," said Barry. He'd heard enough Irish spoken today. "What time's the kickoff?"

"Another ten minutes." O'Reilly stretched and yawned. "Well," he said, "the pair of us seem to have survived another week. I'd say it hasn't gone too badly."

Barry sipped his sherry. "True," he said, "but there's still a few matters outstanding." He thought again of the awaited pathology results, Sonny, Councillor Bishop—and Patricia Spence.

"Indeed," said O'Reilly, "but 'sufficient unto the day is the evil thereof.'"

"Matthew 6:34."

"True," said O'Reilly, "and don't forget, we've the horses to look forward to tomorrow. Do you know," he said, rising and switching on the set, "we're like a couple of fellows pushing wheelbarrows?"

"Pushing wheelbarrows?"

"Indeed." O'Reilly laughed. "Everything's in front of us."

24

There Were Multitudes Assembled

The Rover bounced over a rutted lane to a five-bar gate. Ahead Barry could see cars, estate wagons, Land Rovers, and horseboxes parked in ranks on a grassy hillside. A steward in a cloth cap, brown grocer's coat, and armband was directing traffic. O'Reilly stopped the car and gave the man a pound note.

O'Reilly paying . . . , Barry thought. Makes a change.

"Last row on your left, Doctor O'Reilly." The steward opened the gate.

"Right." O'Reilly drove slowly up a gentle hill, past six rows of parked vehicles, and along the aisle between the sixth and seventh row. He pulled in beside the last car and stopped. "Here we are," he said. "Out."

Barry stepped onto the springy turf and looked around. A black-thorn hedge surrounded the field. Two sycamores and a single rowan tree, its myriad berries scarlet harbingers of a hard winter—or so the locals believed—cast their shadows. A flock of jackdaws, flying as erratically as blown soot, circled one of the sycamores. Their bickering and gossiping nearly drowned out the noise of a tractor working somewhere in a valley.

Beyond the hedge the little Ulster fields, most bordered by dry-stone walls, rolled like gentle waves. These hillocks, he knew, were called drumlins, rounded hills left by the last ice age. Someone had once described County Down as looking like a basket of green eggs.

Cloud shadows hurried across fields where flocks of black-faced

Suffolk sheep and herds of Dexter cows went about their business. Both dual-purpose breeds—the sheep for their wool and mutton, the cattle for their milk and beef—were like the Ulstermen who kept them: hard-working, unspectacular, durable, and thrifty.

In the distance he could make out the tall, Georgian chimneys and slate roofs of Bucklebo House peeping over small beech woods. It was, he knew, home of the Marquis of Ballybucklebo in whose demesne lay these fields—and the all-important racetrack.

O'Reilly had walked round to Barry's side of the car. "There you are," he said, pointing down the hill. "The Ballybucklebo racecourse in all its glory."

Barry looked over the rows of parked vehicles, each surrounded by its passengers, some perched on shooting sticks, some on folding chairs, all tucking into picnics spread on the open boot doors. Men in jodhpurs, cavalry twill pants, hacking jackets, all wearing camel-hair caps, many with binoculars slung round their necks; women in slacks, tweed skirts, heavy woolen pullovers, blazers, most wearing gay silk headscarves that fluttered in the breeze. Their colours made Barry think there were hundreds of exotic butterflies on the hillside, but the noise of happy chattering was more like the sound of a flock of starlings. Labradors, springer spaniels, short-haired pointers, and Jack Russell terriers sat or lay on the grass. The breeds favoured by the hunting-shooting-fishing fraternity, who must have come from all over the Six Counties.

"Three miles and two furlongs," said O'Reilly. "That's the start there. They run on the track for half a mile, then out into the country, back round the other side of the track, round a curve, and finish back at the start line."

At the foot of the hill Barry could see a rope stretched between low white rail fences; further along the track the fences merged into dense hedges bordering a stretch of short-cut grass. He could see the first hurdle between the hedges, a barrier of woven withies mounted on larch poles. The track disappeared from his view where knots of spectators were gathering to watch the first race from behind the hedges.

"The jumps are four and a half feet high, and there's a tributary of the Bucklebo for a water jump." O'Reilly started to sing to himself:

"And it's there you'll see the jockeys and they mounted on
    so stately,
The pink, the blue, the orange and green, the emblem of
    our nation.
When the bell was rung for starting all the horses seemed
    impatient.
I thought they never stood on ground, their speed was so
    amazing."

"With me whack fol the do fol the diddlely idleay," Barry said. "I know the song, it's 'The Galway Races.'"

"Och," said O'Reilly, "the Galway folks give themselves all kinds of airs about their wee event, held on the seventeenth of August, but for a *real* race meeting nothing beats this one." He opened the Rover's boot. "Let's see what Kinky's put in for us." He wrestled a wicker hamper onto the boot's door. "None of your salad," he said with a grin as he opened the lid. "I think the hat worked wonders."

Barry waited as O'Reilly arranged a cold roast chicken, hard-boiled eggs, whole tomatoes, slices of baked ham, buttered wheaten bread, plates, knives and forks, salt and pepper, and two bottles of Bass ale on a chequered tablecloth. "Lunch alfresco," he said, tucking a napkin under his chin and opening a bottle of Bass. "Dig in. And there's more Bass where that came from." He handed the bottle to Barry.

Barry took it then and helped himself to ham, an egg, and a tomato. A single spaniel wandered over and stared hopefully at Barry's plate.

"Get away on home," said O'Reilly. The dog trotted off.

"You didn't bring Arthur, Fingal. I thought he enjoyed a day in the country."

"Jesus," said O'Reilly, ripping a drumstick from the bird. "With all these other dogs around? I'd be doing nothing but keeping an eye to him, and we've more important things to do today." He pointed to the space between the hedge bordering the track and the first row of parked cars. "We need to have a word or two with one of them fellahs."

There was a crowd milling around a series of raised daises. On each was a desk like something out of a Dickensian countinghouse. Above, mounted on two stout poles, was a signboard announcing the owner's name in garishly painted colours: "Honest Sammy Dolan— Best Odds," "William McCardle and Sons, Turf Accountants." Blackboards hung from the marquees, with the time of the race in chalk at the top and the horses' names and odds in a column beneath.

The bookies stood on their little platforms: big men, skinny men, men with florid faces; men in garish jackets; men in bowler hats and dunchers; bareheaded men; all with fixed smiles, all wearing leather satchels into which they stuffed pound notes in return for tickets recording the punters' wagers. The bookies were calling the odds, their competing voices making such a din that they drowned out the sound of the jackdaws. "Pride of Copelands, two to five on . . ."

"That'll be the favourite," O'Reilly explained. "You'd have to put five pounds down to win two."

"Breckonhill Brave the Third, evens . . ."

"I understand that," said Barry, sipping his Bass.

"Golden Boy, two to one."

"One pound wins you two," said O'Reilly.

"Ten to one the field. Ten to one the field."

"Those are the odds on all the other horses in the race."

"What's that lad doing?" Barry asked. He nodded to where a youth wearing white gloves stood slightly further up the hillside. His arms whirled up, down, sideways. He touched a finger to his nose, tugged his left earlobe.

"Tic-tac man," said O'Reilly. "He's signalling to his boss, telling him the odds offered by the competition, or any recent information from a jockey or trainer about a horse that might change its likelihood of winning. They each have their own private semaphore systems, and the gloves are so their hands are more visible. See?"

Barry saw one send a series of frantic gestures, and immediately Honest Sammy Dolan took a damp cloth and a piece of chalk and altered the numbers beside Breckonhill Brave's name from evens to one to two.

"Aha," said O'Reilly, "someone's got inside information about that horse. The odds have lengthened." He wiped his mouth with his napkin, finished his Bass, and immediately opened another bottle. "Have you had enough?"

Barry nodded.

"Right." O'Reilly shoved the wreckage of their lunch into the hamper and closed the boot. "Let's take a run-race down to the paddock and see if Fergus Finnegan's about the place."

Barry followed O'Reilly down the hill, their progress constantly interrupted by having to stop and exchange pleasantries with this one and that one. He was pleased to see how many strangers clearly knew who he was and by how they all seemed to treat him with good-humoured civility.

Vendors selling racing-form bills, soft drinks, ice cream, and sandwiches threaded their way through the crowd.

More words of the song O'Reilly had been singing ran in Barry's head.

> And it's there you'll see confectioners with sugarsticks
>   and dainties,
> The lozenges and oranges, the lemonade and raisins,
> Gingerbread and spices to accommodate the ladies,
> And a big *cruibin* for thruppence to be suckin' while
>   you're able.

The noise of voices grew as the two doctors approached the space in front of the bookies' stations. There queues of bettors, each studying his copy of the racing form from the sports pages of last night's *Belfast Telegraph,* waited to lay their wagers. Money and tickets changed hands with great rapidity.

Barry saw a familiar figure approaching. He'd not mistake the carrotty hair and buck teeth nor, he smiled, the green rubber boots the man was wearing.

"Donal," boomed O'Reilly, "how the hell are you?"

"Seamus and me got the day off from the roof job at Sonny's. It's coming on a treat, by the way. We finished putting up the frames and the rafters yesterday, and we'll start on the slates on Monday, so we will. I reckon another two weeks'll see us done."

"Good," said O'Reilly, with a glance at Barry, "but Sonny'll need somewhere to stay until it's ready."

"Like enough, but sure he's all right in that place in Bangor."

O'Reilly grunted.

"Anyway," said Donal, "great to see the pair of youse, but I'll have to run on. I'm powerful busy, so I am. I've a job as bookie's runner for Willie McCardle. I'm making a few more bob for Julie and me."

"How is she?" Barry enquired.

Donal frowned. "She'd a wee tummy upset this morning when I popped in to see her, but she says it's normal. Is it?" He looked at O'Reilly.

"Indeed."

Barry remembered that he'd had some concerns about the size and feel of Julie's uterus last week, but before he could ask Donal anything O'Reilly had grabbed the man by the arm and was asking, "Have you found any Englishmen yet, Donal?"

Donal put a hand in his pocket, and Barry heard a clinking noise. "Not yet, but if I do I'm ready." He winked at O'Reilly.

"Good. Doctor Laverty and I may just know the fellah you're looking for. Where can he find you?"

"At Willie's stand . . . unless I'm away off again on the phone to Ladbrokes laying off covering bets."

"I'll send him along if I see him," O'Reilly said.

"Great." Donal scurried away.

"Ladbrokes?" Barry was puzzled. All of this was new to him.

"Biggest bookmakers in the United Kingdom," O'Reilly explained. "The small bookies cover their bets if they're getting too many wagers on a horse by making counterbets. If the horse wins, their own winnings with the big company allow them to cover their debts to the punters."

"I see."

"And," O'Reilly rubbed his hands, "if Fergus sees us right, it is my sincere hope that a certain Honest Sammy Dolan won't remember taking my bet on Donal's Bluebird last month, but will have himself covered and be well prepared to shell out again later today."

"You made four hundred pounds on that, Fingal."

"Money well earned," said O'Reilly. "And if you remember, I gave the same tip to His Lordship. He won something too. That was the night I asked him if you could have a day's fishing on his trout stream." O'Reilly turned to walk on, but then stopped and said, "And speak of the devil and he's sure to turn up."

Barry saw two men approaching: Captain O'Brien-Kelly and an older gentleman with a mop of ill-trimmed grey hair sticking out from under a Paddy hat, yesterday's stubble on his cheeks. He looked like a gardener dressed as he was in a darned, red woollen cardigan, collarless shirt, corduroy pants—the knees of which Barry noticed were shiny with wear—and a pair of mud-splattered Wellington boots.

"Afternoon, O'Reilly," the older man said. "Grand day for the event, isn't it? There seems to be a very good turnout." Barry heard the gentle inflections of a public school–educated Ulsterman. Although the harsh edges of Ulster speech had been smoothed, there was no aping the accents of the English upper classes, no mistaking the man's origins. He stretched out his hand, which O'Reilly shook. "I think you've already met my guest, from my son's regiment." He indicated the captain, who smiled weakly at O'Reilly and ignored Barry. "And you must be Laverty?"

Barry frantically tried to remember the correct form of address for a Marquis and settled for "Yes, sir."

"I hope you'd a good day on my water last month."

"Yes, thank you, sir."

"Please feel free to take your rod up anytime . . . and you, Fingal, we'll be beating the outer coverts in a couple of weeks. The pheasants have done very well this year. Would you be able to get free and bring your gun and Arthur Guinness?"

O'Reilly's smile was bright enough to eclipse the sun that had just appeared from behind a small cloud. "I'd love to." He glanced at

Barry. "And I'm sure Doctor Laverty won't mind taking care of the practice for a day."

"If I'm—"

"Och, you'll be ready by then." He spoke with absolute certainty, and Barry smiled.

Before Barry could reply, he heard a high-pitched whinny coming from Captain O'Brien-Kelly. "I say, Bewtie," he addressed the Marquis. "Can't we twot on? I'd weally like to put something on that filly in the first."

Barry saw the marquis frown. Clearly he disapproved of bad manners, but he said, "You run along. I want to spend a little more time with the doctors."

"Wighty-ho."

"Captain," O'Reilly said softly, "the last time we met I told you there'd be a fellah here you should meet, another Arkle fancier. That's him there. Donal Donnelly." He pointed to where Donal was thrusting through the throng on his way back to the bookie's stand. "You really should have a word with him. Tell him I sent you, but you'll have to speak slowly." O'Reilly's tone became confidential. "He's a bit dim. One of the local peasantry."

"Slowly? Wather. I'd weally enjoy having a chat . . . after I've made my bet."

"Don't let me detain you," O'Reilly said, "and give my regards to Mr. Donnelly."

"Will do." The captain hurried off.

"Like a lamb . . ." O'Reilly let the rest hang.

"To the slaughter," Barry muttered under his breath, as his lips twitched into a smile.

"Getting on well with the young man?" O'Reilly asked.

The Marquis sighed. "He's my son's company commander. When Sean asked if I'd let the man come over for a few days, it was very difficult to refuse."

Typical, Barry thought. The man was too much of a gentleman to criticize his guest, but his evasive answer spoke volumes.

"He's staying in the gate lodge, I believe," O'Reilly said.

"That's right."

"Your Lordship, I've an odd kind of request."

Barry frowned. What was O'Reilly going to ask for?

"Please?"

"Have you met Sonny?"

"The recluse who lives in his car?"

"That's him."

The marquis smiled. "Yes, indeed. He's a most interesting man. Marvellous chess player, and he knows more about early Nabataean civilization than anyone else I've met. They're the chappies who built Petra."

"Ah," said O'Reilly, "the 'rose-red city half as old as time.'"

"Fascinating people," His Lordship went on, warming to his theme. "They've been an interest of mine ever since I was up at Caius."

Barry's shoulders slumped. Gonville and Caius College. The marquis had attended Cambridge University—now that was a place he did *not* want to think about today.

"That's Sonny," O'Reilly said. "He's stuck in a home in Bangor, and I'm looking for temporary accommodation for him."

"And you're wondering if I can help?"

O'Reilly nodded.

The Marquis frowned. "Ordinarily I'd be delighted, but we've a big house party this weekend—folks over for the races. But if any of them go home early, I'll let you know."

"That's very generous of you, sir."

"Nonsense," said the Marquis. "I'd much prefer Sonny's company to . . ." He inclined his head to where Barry could see the captain deep in conversation with a grinning Donal Donnelly.

Barry was so intent on watching the scene unfold he didn't notice the Marquis leaving. Soon Barry saw Donal give something to the captain and in exchange accepted what appeared to be a number of banknotes.

"Come on, Barry," O'Reilly said. "The one-thirty's just about ready to start. We'll watch it, and then . . ."—he rubbed his hands together and his eyes narrowed—"we'll go and see Fergus Finnegan. He said he'd have the word for us for the third."

25

Half a League, Half a League, Half a League Onward

O'Reilly gave what Barry thought was a splendid imitation of an ice-breaker in loose pack ice, shouldering his way through the throng milling round the near side of the start line. The spectators shoved and shouldered their way close to the fence, but a miraculously created sea-lane appeared in front of Fingal. Barry followed in his wake.

He heard snatches of conversation.

"Sorry, Doc . . ."

"You fancy Whinney Knowes at ten to one, Huey? Your head's a marley . . ."

"Jesus. Shove over, Paddy. You'd make a better door than a window. I can't see nothing."

"How's about you, Doctor Laverty?"

Barry smiled to acknowledge the greeting.

As far as he could tell, the people down here at trackside were mostly working-class. Their betters—their self-perceived betters—had vantage points higher up the hillside. The scrum that surrounded Barry was a far cry from the Cecil Beaton–dressed lords and ladies in the Ascot scene he'd watched in *My Fair Lady* a few days before.

"Tuck in there," said O'Reilly, indicating a space beside him at the white painted fence.

Barry leant on the wooden railing. He had a better view of the track from here. It was clear that the first couple of hundred yards were fenced; then the fairway ran between chest-high, boundary hedges and led to the first jump.

"That," said O'Reilly, pointing to the far side, "is the finishing post. If we wait here, we'll be able to see the start *and* the finish."

Barry had to strain to hear the words over the din. He wrinkled his nose. The turf of the track's grass had been mowed recently, and no one could mistake the odour of horse droppings.

A rope stretched between the starting post and a raised platform surrounded by low railings. He watched as a figure in a cloth cap and long coat climbed a ladder to the platform.

"Starter," said O'Reilly. "Won't be long. Here they come."

Barry saw a procession of eight horses approaching in single file. Each was led by a groom. The jockeys, all small men, sat upright in their saddles. All wore high leather boots, corduroy jodhpurs, and black velvet–covered, peaked hard hats. Every one carried a crop, but each rider sported a different coloured shirt, his racing silks. Every stable and every owner had their own pattern.

"See that fellah on the big gelding?" O'Reilly indicated a rider whose shirt was divided into four equal squares, two green, two scarlet. Barry nodded, but in truth he couldn't tell the difference between a gelding and cob if his life depended on it.

"Those are the marquis' colours."

"Oh."

The grooms led their charges to the starting rope, where the animals lined up shoulder to shoulder. The crowd was quieter now, and Barry could hear the jingling of tack, horses snorting, hooves stamping on the turf. The biggest animal, a chestnut, wrenched its head sideways and tried to bite its neighbour. The victim sidled away, the chestnut's jockey sawed at the reins, and both horses whinnied.

Barry was intrigued by the fierce intensity in all the animals' huge liquid brown eyes.

He saw the man on the platform raise a red flag.

"They're under starter's orders," O'Reilly said.

Every jockey, reins grasped in his hands, feet firmly in the stirrups, crouched forward, gaze fixed on the track ahead. The bent figures reminded Barry of the position a fetus assumes in the uterus.

He heard the jangling of a bell, saw the starter slash his flag down.

The rope was dropped and the horses flew forward. The sound of hooves thundering on the turf was as deafening as the row of a half battery of artillery using drumfire. Great divots flew from behind the animals. The earth where Barry stood shook underfoot. Already one had taken the lead.

Barry craned forward to watch the leader and then the pack hurl themselves at the first hurdle. The first horse flew over, pursued by several others. An unhorsed jockey cleared the jump with feet to spare, while his mount, reins trailing, had already started to nibble the grass on the near side. Barry involuntarily braced himself for the *thump* of a body hitting the ground, and hoped no limbs would be broken.

"Whinney Knowes at ten to one, Huey?" a voice from behind him remarked scornfully. "The only ten his jockey would get would be for artistic merit in a diving competition."

"Away off and fuck yourself."

Barry had to laugh. He'd just heard the classic Ulster rebuttal to any form of criticism.

The sound of hooves faded, but the rising and falling yells of encouragement from the spectators moved along the track like an ocean wave heading to and receding from a beach. The cheering died as the horses headed out into the countryside.

Barry could see across the track railings and over a ploughed field to a row of widely spaced larches. The trees marched along inside what must be the fence marking the far side of the track. In what seemed like no time, the field, now more spread out, charged past the larches, vanishing behind the trunks and reappearing like frames from a stop-action film.

Barry turned, stared back along the track, and waited. Already he could hear the distant hammering of hoof on grass, horses snorting, breakers of cheers rushing back to the finish-line shore. Above the perimeter fence he could see the tops of jockeys' and horses' heads pounding rhythmically as they rounded the final turn to gallop to the last fence. Up and over, up and over, up—and then, crashing, half the fence flattened, horse and rider struggling through the wreckage.

Two animals were neck and neck. Their jockeys crouched,

belabouring their mounts with their crops, straining forward in the saddles as if by sheer physical force they could urge their mounts ahead. The horses' nostrils flared, foam flew from their flanks, and the air stank of horse sweat. Barry half expected Eliza Doolittle to yell, "Come on, Dover! Move your bloomin' arse!"

From where he stood it appeared as if the larger horse had won, and its jockey wore the green and scarlet of the marquis.

The rest of the field straggled in, but there were fewer beasts than had started. The course had taken its toll.

" 'Then they rode back, but not, not the six hundred,' " said O'Reilly.

"Tennyson," said Barry. "Charge of the Light Brigade."

"True," said O'Reilly, grinning. "That's a very satisfactory result to the first. His Lordship should be pleased. Pity about the filly."

"What filly, Fingal?"

"Whinney Knowes. She refused at the first." His voice held a tiny hint of sadness that belied his grin.

"Do you know her owner?"

"Not at all," said O'Reilly, "but I do know someone who was in a hell of a hurry to put a bet on her. I hope his losses were nothing trivial." He guffawed. "Couldn't have happened to a nicer man."

And Barry remembered Captain O'Brien-Kelly.

"Come on," said O'Reilly, shoving his way away from the fence. "Let's go and find Fergus."

A field had been set aside to serve as a paddock. A steward stopped Barry and O'Reilly at the gate. "No admittance," he announced, squinting at them.

"Balls, Liam Loughridge," O'Reilly growled.

"Sorry, Doctor O'Reilly," the steward said, knuckling his forehead, "I didn't recognize yourself, sir."

"No bloody wonder. You've not been and got fixed up with those glasses I told you you needed, have you?"

"Not yet, sir."

"Get on with it. They'll not cost you a penny. Spectacles are free on the National Health."

"I will, sir, honest to God." He opened the gate. "Come on in."

Barry followed O'Reilly into a meadow. Already the entrants from the first race were returning. As the jockeys dismounted, the grooms took off the saddles, curried the horses' flanks, draped them with blankets, and led them to waiting horseboxes.

"There's Fergus," O'Reilly announced, striding across the grass. "Afternoon, Fergus. How's the eye today?"

Barry thought of his resolve not to enquire about a patient's health on his day off. O'Reilly, it seemed, did not subscribe to that opinion.

"Couldn't be better." Fergus winked at Barry. "You done good for me, sir, and you'll be busy on Monday. Three of the stable lads want to come in for to see you, so they do."

Barry was pleased.

"Never mind that," said O'Reilly. "What's the word for the third?"

Fergus Finnegan glanced around, dropped his voice, and said, "The favourite's a wee mare, Nancy's Fancy, but I'm riding a ringer. Come 'ere 'til you see him." He started to walk away, O'Reilly in hot pursuit and Barry bringing up the rear.

A groom stood holding a horse's bridle. Barry stopped dead. It was the biggest horse he'd ever seen. He stared up at the animal. The gentleness he'd come to expect in horses' eyes was sadly lacking, and instead fires burned in their brown depths, the same fires that flared in O'Reilly's when his nose tip turned white. The horse shook his head and snorted. Barry, fully expecting to see flames shoot from the flared nostrils, took a quick pace back.

"This here's Battlecruiser. His owner reckons he'll do better than that famous Yankee horse Man o' War. What do you think of him, Doc?" Barry could hear the pride in Fergus's voice.

"Jesus," said O'Reilly, moving to the animal and lifting its upper lip to inspect its teeth. "Was his sire an elephant?"

Fergus laughed. "You'd think so by the size of him. He's eighteen hands. The one elephant that could fly was Dumbo, so it was. I reckon Cruiser's dam must've seen the movie." He bent closer to O'Reilly.

Barry had to strain to hear the jockey whisper, "Show Battlecruiser a fence or a hedge, and he's over it like a liltie. It's like riding a lift. I had him out yesterday. Jesus, when we went up together I thought the pair of us was going to need oxygen." He held a finger alongside his nose. "He's never been out before so nobody's got a notion of his form, and the last time I looked the bookies have him at ten to one."

O'Reilly chuckled. "A wink is as good as a nod to a blind horse. Thanks, Fergus."

"Never worry your heads, Doctors. Now," he said, "I'll need to be going off to get dressed."

"Come on, Barry," said O'Reilly. "I think it's time for a wee word with Honest Sammy Dolan."

Barry had to hurry to keep up with a mission-bent O'Reilly as they made their way back to the bookies.

Honest Sammy Dolan was a short man, but made up for his lack of height by being very tall around. His cheeks were the colour of ripe plums; his eyes piggy and, Barry thought, mercenary. His voice, already overused from calling the odds, was hoarse.

Barry and O'Reilly waited in the queue. Barry read the odds blackboard. Sure enough, Battlecruiser was listed at ten to one. Barry scanned the names of the other horses. His eyes widened. At five to one was an animal called Patricia's Pleasure. He knew he would be stupid not to heed Fergus Finnegan's tip but still, despite his university education, once in a while Barry Laverty could be as superstitious as Kinky Kincaid.

O'Reilly stood in front of the desk. "Fifty pounds to win on Battlecruiser." After the proffered notes were grabbed and stuffed in a satchel, a ticket was issued.

"Good luck, sir. Next," Dolan said, with all the sincerity of a penny-in-the-slot scale that spoke the customer's weight.

O'Reilly stepped aside. "I'll see you at the start, Barry." He headed off.

"Sir?" Dolan asked.

Barry hesitated, handed over five pounds, and said, "Patricia's Pleasure to win."

By the time Barry forced his way through to the fence, O'Reilly was already there. The horses running in the third jostled behind the rope. Barry could see Battlecruiser and Fergus Finnegan. Not wishing to let O'Reilly know he'd disregarded the tip, Barry turned to a man standing beside him. "Excuse me. Which is Patricia's Pleasure?"

"That one there." The man pointed to a small roan. The jockey wore silks of vertical green and white stripes.

"Thanks," Barry said.

He heard the bell.

"They're off," O'Reilly roared. "Jesus Murphy, would you look at Battlecruiser?"

Barry did. The great horse was already two lengths ahead, his jockey moving him over to hug the inside rail. The animal pounded along the course, speeding past the white fence. Barry thought, if he takes fences the way Fergus said he would, he'll be unbeatable.

Battlecruiser neighed furiously and soared effortlessly over the hedge, clearing the top by what Barry reckoned was a good six feet. There was only one difficulty. Fergus had said all you had to do was show the horse an obstacle. Battlecruiser must have spotted the perimeter hedge the minute he left the white railing behind, accepted the challenge, and run halfway across the ploughed field in the middle of the course, determined it seemed to travel all the way to County Antrim.

"Holy thundering mother of Jesus," O'Reilly roared, ripping up his betting slip. "Fifty quid down the pipe. It would make the bloody angels weep."

Barry felt it wiser not to laugh.

"Right," said O'Reilly, turning. "Not much point staying to the end. I'm off back to the car for another Bass. Coming?"

Barry shook his head. "I'd like to see the finish anyway."

"Suit yourself." O'Reilly turned and started shoving. If, Barry thought, O'Reilly had come in like an icebreaker through the crowd, pushing people aside, he was leaving like a main battle tank, quite willing and able to crush anyone who dared to get underfoot.

Barry turned back to the track. The first horse over the final jump was ridden by a jockey wearing vertical green and white stripes. It was leading by a good four lengths, and it kept that lead as it passed the finishing post.

Barry made his way to the bookies and collected thirty pounds, his original stake plus his winnings from Honest Sammy, whose smile, he noticed, had slipped somewhat. Then he climbed slowly up the hill. He saw O'Reilly, open bottle of Bass clutched in one hand, in conversation with Captain O'Brien-Kelly. Barry stood and listened.

". . . it's all a bit awkwawd," the captain was saying. "I seem to have wather misjudged the form on a couple of waces."

"There's a thing," said O'Reilly. "It happens to the best of us. I'm down a bob or two myself."

"Weally? Pity. I was hoping you might be able to help me out."

"Oh?"

"Um . . . yes. You see, I can't find His Lowdship and I'm a bit stwetched."

"Oh?" Barry could see a flicker of a smile on O'Reilly's lips.

"I gave that chap . . ."—he turned and pointed down to Honest Sammy's stand—"a couple of IOUs. And I'm not pwecisely in a position to cover them. I . . . uh, don't suppose . . . as a bwother officer, Surgeon Commander . . . ?"

"Och," said O'Reilly, "do you know a fellah called Polonius?"

"Fwaid not. Betting chap, is he?"

"No," said O'Reilly, "more an advisor. He once said . . ."

Barry mouthed the words as O'Reilly intoned, "Neither a borrower nor a lender be."

"So you can't help me out?"

"I'd like to," said O'Reilly smoothly, "but my horse should be somewhere near the Holywood Arches by now, not in the winner's circle, so at the moment I'm skint."

"Pity." The captain's shoulders sagged. "Damn thing is, I'd be all wight if I hadn't spent one hundred pounds with that chap you wecommended."

"Mr. Donnelly."

"You were wight, O'Reilly, he is a bit dim." The captain's sneer offended Barry. He rummaged in his pocket and produced a silver coin. "Do you know what that is?" He shoved it under O'Reilly's nose.

O'Reilly must have noticed Barry's arrival. He glanced over and winked, then peered at the coin. "Begod, you'd swear it was the spit image of Arkle himself."

"It is, and I was able to get him to sell them to me for a pound apiece. He wanted two pounds, but the man hasn't a clue how to haggle. I took his entiwe stock."

"Och, sure," said O'Reilly, "and aren't you the astute one, Captain? But I doubt if you'll sell any here. Just about everybody'll have one or two in their pockets . . . just for luck."

"Oh."

"No market here," said O'Reilly, "but I'm sure you'll clean up with your regiment back in England."

The captain beamed. "I will, won't I?" His smile faded. "Twouble is I could use a bit of the weady. Wight now, in fact." He glanced nervously down the hill. Barry followed the direction of the man's gaze and saw a heavy-set man, shirt sleeves rolled up, the tattoos on his forearms clearly visible even from the hillside, leave Honest Sammy's stand and stride purposefully in their direction.

"Weally must be wunning," the captain said, departing rapidly.

O'Reilly laughed so much he had to bend over. "Wun, wabbit, wun," he gasped. "Oh, dear." When he stopped chuckling, he said to Barry. "So who won?"

Barry hesitated. O'Reilly could get a bit shirty when his advice was ignored, and he would have thought he was doing Barry a favour letting him in on Fergus Finnegan's tip. Damn it, he told himself, O'Reilly's my senior in the practice, not my father. "I did, Fingal. At least my horse did."

"What?" O'Reilly's eyebrows shot up. "Well, I'll be damned."

Barry waited for the inevitable storm, but O'Reilly threw an arm round Barry's shoulder. "Good for you, Laverty. You keep it up, standing on your own two feet. Here"—he rummaged in the picnic hamper—"have a Bass."

Barry took the bottle. "Thanks, Fingal. Sorry about your horse."

"Och," said O'Reilly, finishing his own bottle in one enormous swallow. "I'm still three hundred fifty pounds ahead with Honest Sammy, and you know what they say, 'Unlucky at cards . . . and the horses . . . lucky in love.' Maybe I'll meet a rich widow woman who's too proud to let her husband work."

Barry started to laugh but it struck him that as *he'd* been lucky with the horses, the logical conclusion to that was not something he wanted to consider.

"Aye," said O'Reilly, looking Barry straight in the eye, "there's the rub, isn't it?" He opened another beer. "Do you feel like running the shop on your own tonight?"

"Well, I—"

"Good, because I don't feel like it. I'd like to take a wander over to the Duck and have another word with Willy Dunleavy."

"If you think so, Fingal."

"Good. If you do that, I'll take care of things tomorrow and maybe . . ." He looked from under his brows at Barry. "Maybe you could see if that Miss Spence of yours is free."

26

Where the Mountains of Mourne Sweep
Down to the Sea

Brunhilde's near side tires scraped against the kerb of the Esplanade
as Barry parked opposite Number 9. When he'd phoned Patricia the
night before, she'd seemed pleased to hear from him. She sounded
tired, but agreed that a day away from her studies would be a good
idea. She said she'd make a picnic, and perhaps today, Sunday, they
could take a trip to the country.

He left the car and looked across the lough. Sunlight ricocheted
from the rippled surface. The distant Antrim Hills, purple and shimmering in the heat, were as indistinct as an out-of-focus photograph. A
solitary trawler shouldered its way east through the waters of the lough,
away from Belfast and the gaunt gantries of the shipyards. Barry supposed it was heading for its home harbour of Ardglass some thirty
miles further down the coast. Ardglass, famous for its herring.

He crossed the street and rang the doorbell to flat 4. His right hand
slipped unbidden to his crown to smooth the tuft of fair hair he knew
would be sticking up.

"Good morning, I . . . ," he blurted, but his breath caught in his
throat. Patricia stood in the doorway, her hair up in a ponytail. A dimple appeared in her left cheek when she smiled at him. Her blouse was
unbuttoned at her throat. He found it difficult not to keep staring at the
hint of cleavage between the bottle-green lapels. Her black stirrup
pants fitted closely, and their straps went under tiny, black low-heeled
shoes. She carried a picnic basket in one hand.

She kissed him lightly. "Good morning, yourself."

He tingled to her kiss.

"Now," she said, "before we go any further, I want to apologize for how I carried on last Wednesday night. Sometimes I get a bit carried away."

Barry smiled. "No apology needed."

"It's the work. I get so—"

"There'll be no more talk of work today. I'm off. You're off. So let's enjoy it."

She kissed him again.

"Come on." He took her hand and led her across the street, slowing his stride to accommodate her limp. "Give me the basket," he said. Then he took it, walked around to the driver's side, and put the picnic on the backseat. By the time he'd climbed in, she was sitting in the passenger's seat. Barry smiled. Patricia Spence wasn't a young woman to wait for any man to hold a door open for her.

He was so eager to drive off that he missed first gear. The old Volkswagen didn't have synchromesh in first. Brunhilde lurched on her springs.

"Did you fill the car with kangaroo petrol this morning?" Patricia asked, as the car shuddered to a stop and stalled.

"Sorry about that," he said, restarting the engine and pulling away from the kerb.

"Where are we going, Barry?"

"I thought we'd take a run-race down to Strangford."

"Lovely." She settled back in her seat. "You drive. I'm going to enjoy the ride. It'll be my last break before the big day."

"The exam?"

"Tuesday . . . then I'll have to wait for the results."

"It's tough," he said. He remembered having to hang around after his own finals were over until the dean appeared in the cloisters in the evening and read the list. "Atcheson, pass; Anderson, pass; Blenkinsop, fail"—poor Billy Blenkinsop had fainted—and on down the list until "Laverty, pass." "If you find it's getting to you, give me a call. I may not be able to see you, but at least we could have a bit of a blether."

"I may well take you up on that. It's like what I heard somebody say about the army. All hurry up . . . and wait."

And, Barry thought, you'll not be the only one waiting. He would be hearing soon from Harry Sloan about the histology report. Barry wished Harry would get a move on, because he wanted to put the uncertainty behind him. The way things had been going in the last week—how O'Reilly had quietly kept in the background, encouraging Barry, and the way the patients seemed more accepting of their new young doctor—all were helping him feel more at home in the practice. He still wanted to know what had killed Major Fotheringham, but perhaps whatever the young pathologist would have to say might not be as important in the long run as it had first seemed. Once the question was answered, he'd have only one more conundrum to sort out: Patricia and what to do if she was successful.

He glanced at her. She was staring out the window, frowning a little, perhaps preoccupied. Patricia wasn't one of those girls who felt it necessary to fill every moment with inane chatter. It was one of the things he liked about her. He swung the car onto the road that ran through Ballybucklebo, then onto the Six Road Ends. It would take them to Greyabbey and Kirkubbin. His destination lay halfway between Kirkubbin and Portaferry at the mouth of Strangford Lough.

Gransha Point was a narrow, lonely peninsula, bent like a dog's hind leg, stretching for three quarters of a mile into the shallow waters. It would take about half an hour to get there.

As he concentrated on his driving, he became aware of a low musical sound and glanced over. Patricia's lips were moving, and as he strained to hear he could make out the words of a song,

> "Where Lagan stream sings lullaby,
> There blows a lily fair.
> The twilight gleam is in her eye,
> The night is on her hair . . ."

He recognized the words of "My Lagan Love," one of the most beautiful of all the Irish love songs. He'd had no idea how rich a voice

Patricia had. He felt the hairs on the nape of his neck tingle as she sang on, and he listened enraptured until the last line.

> "And sings in sad, sweet undertone
>   The song of heart's desire."

"That was lovely," he said. I didn't know you could sing like that."

She smiled. "You know I like music."

"God," he said, "with a voice like that you should be on the stage."

She shook her head and laughed. "Nonsense. I just sing for the fun of it."

"You can sing for me any time you like." "The song of heart's desire," he thought. *My* heart's desire.

He saw that the turn to Gransha was coming up ahead, turned right onto it from the Portaferry Road, and drove slowly along a rutted lane. The old springs complained, and the gorse bushes bordering the lane made soft scratching noises on the car's sides.

He came to a broad, flat expanse of scutch grass in front of a lichen-encrusted, drystone wall. He stopped the car close to a stile where a rock step abutted a vertical slab of flat slate. He knew there was a similar step on the other side.

"Here we are," he said. "Hop out." He climbed out.

"Gosh," she said, "it's warm."

He was starting to sweat. "Hang on," he said. "I'll leave my jacket in the car." He dumped it in the backseat, collected the picnic basket and an old blanket, and joined Patricia in front of the vehicle. "We'll have to walk from here."

"Grand." She took his hand. "Let's go."

As he led her to the stile, he felt the sun hot on his back. Bees murmured in the gorse flowers. He heard the call of a wood pigeon—a burbling oboe's note, soft and low—coming from a copse on a low hill that tumbled to the shore on the far side of the bay between the point and the mainland. The grass was springy under his feet, and his step felt light as his heart.

Barry knew better than to ask Patricia if she needed help getting over the stile. He remembered how on the night he'd met her she'd bristled and told him that she didn't want his pity for her lame leg. "I'll go first," he said, climbing onto the step, clambering over the slate, and hopping onto the grass. He put the basket and blanket down and waited for her to steady herself. "Jump," he said, and when she did he caught her, held her, and kissed her. He was aching to tell her he loved her, but he shied away out of fear that she might not return the sentiment. "Nice," he said, and held her at arm's length. "Very nice." He turned and pointed ahead. "Do you see that collection of tumbled stones about halfway along the Point's shore?"

"Yes."

"That's where we're going. Come on." He guided her along the Point, past brackish pools of peat water the colour of stewed tea that were hidden among red benweed.

He jumped when a brace of small ducks exploded from beneath his feet, wings clattering as they strained for altitude, the leading bird making a hoarse *craaking* noise.

"Teal," said Patricia, and he remembered she was an amateur ornithologist. "The drake—he's the one with the brighter plumage—he's leading. They always do."

"You don't object to that, I hope?"

"*Barry.*" He could see she was laughing with him.

"There're lots of wildfowl down here," he said, as they crossed the grass to walk along the shingly shore.

"I know. I used to go to the wildfowl sanctuary at Castle Espie on the far shore of the lough. Greylag geese come from Spitsbergen to winter there. There used to be thousands of Brent geese, but they've been shot almost to extinction." He heard the sadness in her voice.

He squeezed her hand. "What a shame." Barry decided this was not the time to tell her that O'Reilly was a keen fowler.

A flock rose from the water's edge, wheeled, and jinked. Then it turned in unison and flew low over waves that heaped grey foam and yellow brown bladder wrack into a ragged tide line. The air was redolent of salt, and the scent of its sea tang pleased him.

"Those are dunlin," she said. "And that is a heron." She pointed up to where Barry could see a gangly bird that must have had a ptero-dactyl somewhere in its family tree. The big bird flapped its wings lan-gorously under fluff-ball clouds beneath a robin's-egg-blue sky.

He glanced back to watch the dunlin, moving like blown smoke, swing over a great, rusty oil drum. Barry heard the clangour as it moved with the tide, hitting the shingle and the rocks. "Not far now," he said.

"Thank you for bringing me here. It's lovely."

"Glad you like it, madam." Barry made a mock bow.

The wind blowing up to Newtownards at the lough's head fluttered the grass, and he watched her ponytail sway to the breeze's caress. Dear God, but she was beautiful.

"How's this?" Barry led her to the lee of the old sheepcote. "It's cosy here out of the wind." He bent and spread the blanket, setting the picnic basket at one edge. "Take the weight off your feet." She sat, arms clasped around her bent legs, chin resting on her knees.

He thought she looked like the statue of Hans Christian Andersen's *Little Mermaid.* "I used to come down here when I was a student," he said, "just to get away from Belfast for an hour or two."

"I've never been down on this side of the lough before, and it's re-ally no distance from Newry. Isn't that silly?"

"Not at all." Barry sat and put his arm around her shoulders. He felt her snuggle closer and rest her head on his shoulder. "I'll bring you here anytime you like." If you're still in Ulster, he thought.

"I'd like that, but . . ."

"No buts," he said. "Not today." He laid his hand on her cheek, feeling its smoothness, turned her face to him, saw fresh black coffee darkness in her eyes, and kissed her slowly, as softly as a man gentles a nervous colt.

She pulled her head back but kept her gaze fixed on his eyes. "I do like you very much, Barry," she whispered, "but . . ."

He tensed.

". . . be patient, be gentle, be slow."

He laughed. He couldn't help himself. She'd not said she wasn't ready to fall in love. She'd not. "I'll be gentle," he said, " 'as a cooing dove.'" Before he could tell her the quote was from Shakespeare, he heard again the notes of the wood pigeon, "just like that fellah." He stood and waited for his breathing to slow. Then he said, "It's too early for lunch. Would you like to walk out to the end of the Point?"

"In a minute." Patricia stood beside him and kissed him hard, the tip of her tongue finding his, but before he could hold her more tightly, she stepped back. "Thank you, Barry," she said. "Now show me the end of the Point." He was convinced if it hadn't been for her gammy leg she would have shouted, "Come on, I'll race you."

Together, hand in hand, they walked to where the strip of land narrowed and slipped into the waters. Barry was so full of her he felt no need to speak. He knew Patricia must sense his mood because she said nothing.

The wind was warm, the tide high. Occasionally a larger wave would toss spray right across the peninsula.

"Here we are," he said, halting at the water's edge. "Land's end."

"What a wonderful view."

"Isn't it? See all those islands directly across the lough, close to the far shore?"

"Yes."

"They're near Ringhaddy . . ."

"That's not far from Castle Espie . . ."

"That's right, and down there, off in the distance to our left . . ." He gazed across ranks of little whitecaps, green waters, and low islands to where mountain peaks stood sentinel over the southern part of County Down.

"Those're the Mountains of Mourne," she said.

"Slieve Nabrock, Slieve Nagarragh, and Slieve Donard." He named three because they were the only Mourne names he knew. He noticed clouds building above the highest, Slieve Donard, and hoped they weren't the harbingers of one of the sudden summer squalls that could sweep the lough. He sang gently:

> "Oh Mary this London's a wonderful sight,
> With people here workin' by day and by night . . ."

She laughed. "Do you play the tin whistle?"

"No. Why?"

"Because," she said, "you should. You've got a tin ear. You're about a semitone flat."

He grinned. "I know, and I don't care. I've just heard you singing, back in the car there. You could make it shine for both of us. It's a great song. Do you know the last line?"

She sang, "But I'd far rather be, where the Mountains of Mourne sweep down to the sea."

He stared at her, knowing those words were true for him, wishing they were true for her. "I hear you'll find Cambridgeshire's pretty flat," he said, and waited to see how she'd respond.

"If I get to go there." She stiffened. "I thought we weren't going to talk about that today."

"You're right. Sorry."

She tossed her head. "And anyway it is true. I'd far rather be here in Ulster, but even if things do work out for me, the Mournes'll still be here sweeping down to the sea when I come back."

And so will I, Barry thought. He pulled her to him and kissed her. "Right," he said, knowing he had to change the subject. "I'm famished." He knew it wasn't only the contents of her picnic basket he hungered for. "Let's go and have a bite of lunch."

Barry lowered the empty bottle of warm Harp Lager, wiped the back of his hand across his mouth, and burped. "Excuse me."

"I didn't know you were Chinese."

He frowned.

"You told me it was polite to burp in China."

That she'd remembered such a trivial thing pleased him. He put the bottle back in the hamper to lie among the crumpled greaseproof paper that earlier had held chicken sandwiches, buttered barmbrack, and a couple of apples. "Feast fit for a king." He left the lid open.

"I'm glad Your Majesty approves," Patricia said.

He moved across the blanket to sit by her side. "It was grand." Barry noticed that in the bay beyond the lee of the Point the waves were higher, steeper. The wind must be freshening, but it wasn't noticeable there in the shelter of the ruined sheepcote.

"It's been a lovely day," she said, running both hands across the top of her head and adjusting her ponytail holder.

"Hasn't it?" He bent, kissed her, and gradually, still kissing her, pushed her backwards until she lay on her side on the blanket. He moved his lips to her neck and felt hands behind his head holding him to her. He slipped one arm behind her, caressing her through the satiny material of her blouse. His hand stopped in the middle of her back. Good Lord. No bra strap. He'd heard about these feminists who refused to wear bras. Was Patricia making a statement or—he felt his pulse quicken as he realized nothing but a thin layer of material lay between him and her breasts—had she dressed deliberately this morning to make things easier for him?

He kissed her again, harder, tongue darting, meeting hers. Slowly and softly his hand slipped from her back, across her flank, and onto the flat of her belly. Her kiss, so powerful was it, forced his head back. His hand with dandelion-puff lightness cupped her right breast, and she stiffened, drew back, broke the kiss, and eyes shut, covered his hand with hers. He held very still, praying she wasn't going to thrust it away, rejoicing as she pressed it to her.

He closed his eyes and waited until her hand relaxed and moved his to the upper button of her blouse. He fumbled, footered—the bloody thing was stuck—but she didn't try to stop him. Finally the button sprang loose.

Barry knew they were going to make love here on the blanket on the soft grass.

He slipped his hand inside her blouse and felt the warmth of her.

She whimpered and nibbled his lip.

"Patricia, I . . ."

The lid of the picnic hamper slammed shut with a crash. He opened his eyes to see the edges of the blanket flapping as wind battered through the gaps in the stones. The dry dune grasses at the sides of the sheepcote were flattened. Waves pounded the shore.

He sat up and glanced at the sky. The clouds he'd noticed earlier over Slieve Donard had marched across the lough like companies of storm troopers. A single lightning bolt flared across the sky, and seconds later a roll of thunder like the drumming of a chorus of demented timpanists beat on his ears. He hated thunderstorms.

The rain started, heavy stinging drops, soaking his hair. He felt Patricia rise and he stood beside her. He put his arm round her. "Sit down close to the stones," he said. "Try to get a bit of shelter."

She shook her head, pulled away, ripped out her ponytail holder, raised both arms above her head, and turned her face up to the sky. The rain darkened her black hair to ebony, and it fluttered in the wind. She was backlit by another thunderbolt. She looked, he thought, like an Indian princess, worshipping the lightning god.

"I love storms," she shouted over the keening of the wind through the rocks.

Barry saw how the downpour had soaked her blouse; the wind plastered it against her, moulded it to her so her breasts were limned in bas-relief. "And I love *you,* Patricia," he shouted, but his words were drowned out by the thunder's crash.

He felt the raindrops, lighter now. The wind was easing. The grasses at the sides of the rock pile began to lift their heads, and out over the islands a single sunbeam burst through as the storm moved on its way, past Gransha Point.

She turned to him, her grin wide, dimple deep. "Whew," she said, "that was wonderful." She looked at his pants and started to laugh. "You're sodden," she said, "but it wouldn't be a day out with you if you could keep your trousers dry."

Barry was forced to agree. Almost every time he'd been with her, some disaster—from Arthur Guinness cocking his leg on him to Barry spilling a pint on himself—had left him with soaked britches. He laughed with her, but his gaze lingered on the sight of her breasts beneath her wet blouse. He feared the spell had been broken for her.

"We're both soaked," she said, glancing down at herself. "Would you look at me? I might as well be naked." She crossed her arms in front of her breasts. "I think we should be getting back."

No. But he swallowed, took a deep breath, and said, "All right." He stooped and began to fold the sodden blanket. "And don't worry about your wet blouse. I'll give you my coat to put round you when we get back to the car."

She knelt beside him to help, and she turned and kissed him quickly. "You are patient," she said, her voice low and husky. "Thank you."

"I love you, Patricia." He waited. He'd said it.

She stared down at the grass.

Why must he remember O'Reilly's words, "Lucky at cards . . . unlucky in love?"

She looked at him, unsmiling. A tiny crease appeared between her eyebrows.

"I do," he said.

She stood, slowly, and he closed his eyes. He couldn't bear to watch if she walked away, but instead she hugged him, kissed him, pulled back, and whispered, "And I love *you*, Barry Laverty, even though I know I shouldn't."

He didn't know what to say and knew he must look like a mooncalf standing there with an idiotic grin plastered on his face. "Oh, Jesus."

He took Patricia's hand and as he did the last of the clouds slipped from the face of the sun. The rays warmed him, and in their heat he saw tiny wraiths of vapour rise from her blouse. "I love you, darling," he said. "I love you."

27

Success and Miscarriage
Are Empty Sounds

Barry parked Brunhilde in the lane. He was relieved to see no sign of
Arthur Guinness in the back garden. Either O'Reilly had taken the
dog out, or the Labrador was off on another Wellie hunt.

Barry opened the gate, crossed the grass, and let himself into the
house. The smell of roasting duck filled the kitchen, and his taste
buds tingled. Kinky stood at the sink, peeling potatoes. He crossed the
tiled floor, grabbed her, and spun her round.

"Put me down, Doctor Laverty." Kinky laughed and her chins wobbled. "Put me down this instant, you *amaideach* man."

"I'm not idiotic," he said, letting her go. "I'm in love, Kinky." He
felt not a tad of the Ulster reticence that should have made him keep it
to himself.

"Huh," she said, still grinning. "For a learned doctor it's taken you
a brave while to catch on, so. Didn't I know that from the first time I
saw you and Miss Spence together?"

"It was that obvious?"

"Plain as the nose on your face," she said, "and I'm glad for the pair
of you . . . and for himself."

"Doctor O'Reilly? Why?"

"Sure, sometimes you're as easy to see through as a window.
Haven't I known you were thinking of leaving?"

Barry shook his head.

"Well, you have been, and I'd not like to see you go, nor would the
big fellah."

"The big fellah? Isn't that what they called Michael Collins back in the twenties?"

"Aye, but you know very well who I mean."

"I do."

"He's no spring chicken anymore, and he needs your help . . . and so do the buck eejits who live here, only some of them are too *cadránta* to see it."

"*Cad* what?"

"Bloody-minded. Never you mind them. You can't please everybody. Wasn't the sainted Jesus himself the greatest healer? But look what happened to him." She sniffed. "There's a brave clatter of folks who think you're doing just fine."

"Honestly?"

"Cross my heart, so."

"Thanks, Kinky."

"Don't thank me, and if your Miss Spence would make another good reason for you staying in Ballybucklebo, more power to her wheel."

Before Barry could tell her that Patricia and her plans could very well have the opposite effect, Kinky glanced down and shook her head. "Doctor dear, you've done it again. Your trousers . . ."

"Sorry, Kinky. I'll nip up and change." Barry turned to leave, feeling pleased by what Kinky had just said about his being needed, yet he was somehow unsettled. Since he'd recovered from his initial elation over Patricia saying she loved him, the thought of her going away kept gnawing at him like the throb of an infected finger. "Kinky?"

She was bent over the oven, wreathed in a gust of steam, scooping the melted fat off the duck. "What?"

He was going to tell her about Patricia, the exam, and Cambridge but decided not to. Instead he asked, "Is Doctor O'Reilly in?"

She closed the oven door. "He is not. His Lordship phoned a while back. God knows what he said, but Doctor O'Reilly went tearing off with a great big grin on his face. He said he was off to Bangor to get Sonny."

"Sonny?"

"That's what he said, but don't ask me what it's all about. Himself was in too great a rush to tell me more." She straightened her shoulders and put a hand in the small of her back. "When is he not? If it was his own funeral, he'd be going to it at the charge."

Barry laughed. "Don't worry. We'll find out about Sonny when Doctor O'Reilly gets back." He thought of the empty back garden. "Did he take Arthur?"

"He did not, and the eejit was in such a tearing rush he left the gate open behind him. Well, he'd better hurry back as quick. I'd not want this duck to spoil."

"I'll be ready on time, Kinky. I'll go and change right now."

Barry left and ran upstairs. He was short of breath by the time he got to his room, a combination of being too busy to take much exercise and Kinky's cooking. And judging by the smell of duck that had risen to the third storey, she was going to set another of her feasts on the table.

From below he heard the doorbell ring. He hesitated with one leg in his corduroys, and tried to hear what was being said. A man was talking to Kinky.

Barry finished putting on his pants, grabbed the damp pair, and hurried downstairs.

Kinky looked around as he arrived in the hall, where Donal Donnelly stood, cap in hands, just inside the front door. His usual grin had been replaced by a wide-eyed frown. "It's Julie, Doctor," his words tumbled out. "Can you come quick? She's bleeding something fierce."

"I'll get my bag." Barry shoved his wet trousers at Kinky, ran into the surgery, and grabbed his bag. "Where is she, Donal?"

"At Brie Lannigan's. I'd gone round to have my tea with her, like, and all of a sudden she grabbed her belly and let a howl out of her, so she did. I never heard nothing like it." Barry could see tears on Donal's cheeks. "And then there was this great big red stain on her dress . . . I got her up to bed as quick as I could. Brie's no phone, so I come round here as fast as I could pedal."

"Where does Brie live, Donal?"

Donal grabbed Barry's hand and tugged him to the open door. "Come on quick, Doctor. I'll show you."

He heard Kinky call, "I'll tell Doctor O'Reilly when he gets back." But he was so hard pressed to keep up with Donal, he hadn't time to reply. He saw Donal's multicoloured bike lying on its side in the rose-bushes where it had been abandoned in his rush to get to the door. "Round the back," Barry yelled. "My car's there."

Barry started the engine, waited for Donal to slam his door, and drove off. "Which way?"

"Turn left here on Main Street, right at the Maypole, along Station Road for about a mile." Donal hunched in his seat. "Can you not go any quicker?"

Barry ignored the question. Damn it, he'd been right to worry when he'd examined Julie last week and thought her uterus didn't feel quite right. He should have paid more attention yesterday when Donal sought reassurance about Julie's "wee tummy upset," but O'Reilly had been right too. Vague aches and pains were so common in early preg-nancy that such a complaint was usually brushed off by doctors with an offhand, "Oh, you get that sometimes." Mind you, he told himself, if a miscarriage is going to happen, there's not a damn thing can be done to stop it.

"I'm scared, so I am, Doctor." Donal lowered his voice. "She . . . she couldn't die, could she?"

"Of course not, Donal." Barry tried to sound confident. If Julie was miscarrying after what would now be eleven weeks since her last period—and he was pretty sure she was—well, the risk of death from haemorrhage, shock, or infection accounted for eighteen percent of all deaths due to pregnancy. *He* knew that, but what was the point of scaring an already terrified man?

"Oh, Jesus." Donal thumped a fist on the dashboard. "It's all my fault."

Barry was too busy trying to cross the oncoming traffic—the light for once was in his favour. He drove through a gap between a car and a lorry, changed down, and took the corner under the bridge onto Station Road. "How in the hell is it your fault, Donal?" Had the man had second thoughts about having to get married? Had he somehow persuaded Julie to go and see an abortionist? Barry shook his head.

Impossible. When the pregnancy had been first diagnosed, Julie had insisted that if necessary she would go to England, have the baby, and give it up for adoption. "I asked you—"

"I heard you. It's a judgment, so it is."

"For what, for God's sake?" Barry had to swerve to avoid a cyclist. At least, he thought, he hadn't adopted O'Reilly's habit of ploughing on regardless and letting the unfortunates fend for themselves.

"For putting wee Julie in the family way before we was married."

"I'd not worry about that now, Donal. Getting a girl pregnant could happen to anyone." Including me, he thought, if that thunderstorm hadn't come out of nowhere.

"If it wasn't for that, then it was for foxing the English gentleman. I took a hundred pounds off him, so I did, but it was for Julie and me, and the wean."

"A hundred?" No wonder the captain had confessed to being a little "stwetched." Was there any connection between Captain O'Brien-Kelly's impoverishment and O'Reilly having left to get Sonny? No time to worry about that now. Barry said, "I'd not get upset about that either, Donal. Nobody forced him to buy the half crowns."

"Aye, maybe so, but . . . do you think it would help if I gave it back?"

"I doubt it."

Donal looked crestfallen. "Pull in there, Doctor. At that red brick semi."

Barry parked, reached into the backseat for his bag, and followed Donal up a path to the right-hand house. Donal had opened the door. Barry followed into a narrow hall and up a flight of stairs. He was just in time to see Donal's back disappear through a doorway.

Julie lay on the bed. He could see that she was pale and sweating. A scarlet stain crept across the sheet that covered her lower half. He knew from experience that a little blood went a very long way, but to Julie and Donal it must look as if the bleeding was torrential.

He glanced under the bed to see if there were ropes of clots forming from blood that had soaked through the mattress. A woman would have to lose two or three pints before that happened. Good. No clots. She hadn't bled that much—yet.

Donal sat on a wicker-bottomed chair at the bedside, holding Julie's hand in his and stroking her blonde hair away from her forehead.

"Julie," Barry said, "can you tell me what happened?"

She tried to struggle up, but he sat on the bed beside her, careless of the bloodstain. "It's all right." He took her wrist between his thumb and first two fingers. The skin was clammy, her pulse rapid and very feeble. He didn't need a sphygmomanometer to tell him her blood pressure must have fallen. She was on the edge of going into shock.

She forced a weak smile. "It is now you're here, Doctor." She laid her head back on the pillow. "I started getting these wee cramps yesterday, and I thought they'd go away. But about an hour ago . . ." She bit her lower lip and screwed her eyes shut. "An hour ago they got to be fierce . . . just like that one, and then I started to bleed down below."

Barry glanced at Donal, who was looking up at him as a penitent might look at a priest, a longing for absolution in the man's eyes. Barry ignored him, opened the bag, and took out a paper packet of sterile gloves and a green-wrapped pack. He undid the outer covering of the pack and tore open the paper. "Where's the bathroom?"

"On the left," Donal said.

"I'll be right back." Barry left, washed his hands, and returned. "I have to examine you, Julie." He dried his hands on a sterile towel and slipped on the gloves. "Would you wait outside, Donal?" Barry was only vaguely aware of Donal leaving. He pulled back the bloody sheet. The stain on the undersheet had spread to both sides of the bed. "Can you open your legs?"

Julie did.

Bright red blood spurted from the vaginal opening. He was aware of its coppery smell. "Sorry," he said, slipping the first two fingers of his right hand inside. He could feel the cervix; it was partially open. Something spongy was stuck in it. This wasn't a difficult diagnosis. Julie was aborting, but she had not expelled the tiny fetus and placenta—and until she did, the bleeding would not stop. He tried to dislodge the tissues with his fingertip, but they wouldn't budge. His patient was going to need a dilatation and curettage—shortened in doctor talk to a D and C—and that had to be done in a hospital.

Barry removed his fingers, conscious of how the heat of the blood had warmed them, but inside he felt a chill. He tried to keep his face expressionless. "I'm sorry, Julie, but you're losing the baby. It's an . . ." He was going to use the medical term "incomplete abortion," but understood how the word could be misinterpreted. "You're having a miscarriage. We'll have to get you to the Royal."

"All right," she whispered. Then she moaned in pain.

It was all well and good for Barry to sound so damned confident. If he'd learned nothing else when he had studied gynaecology, it was that patients with an incomplete abortion, which was what Julie had, and who were in or close to being in shock, which she was, should not be moved until after they'd had a blood transfusion. To do so could kill the patient. Send for the "flying squad" had been drummed into him; send for the specially equipped ambulance staffed by doctors and nurses from the hospital, professionals who would bring blood with them and transfuse the patient before transport. And if necessary, they'd give her an anaesthetic and do what was required in her own home.

That was all well and good for those with the training and the instruments, but far beyond the capabilities of a country GP armed with only his bag. And sending for the squad would take time. Too much time.

Donal had said there was no telephone in the house. He glanced back at the bed. The bloodstain spread as he watched. By the time he found a phone, got through to the dispatcher, the team was assembled, and the ambulance came through the city traffic and covered the ten miles to Ballybucklebo, Julie could bleed to death.

He had to do something—and do it at once.

Barry stood, stripped off his gloves, and took a deep breath. He went to his bag and rummaged through it until he found what he needed: morphine to deaden the pain of the uterine contractions and ergometrine to make the uterus contract and to constrict the open blood vessels long enough, he hoped, for him to get Julie to the Royal before she bled again.

He charged two syringes. Morphine, fifteen milligrams; ergometrine, a half milligram. "I'm going to give you an injection, Julie." He didn't wait for a reply but in quick succession stabbed the needles into the muscle of her thigh.

Julie gasped with each stab, but within five minutes her breathing had gone from short sharp gasps to a steady rhythm, and thank God, the flow of blood had eased to a trickle. "Come in, Donal." He heard footsteps.

"Jesus Christ, is she dead?"

"No. I gave her morphine. It's knocked her out. And we don't have much time. I need a hand to get her to my car." Isn't that what O'Reilly would do?

"Doctor, has she lost . . . ?"

"I'll explain later," Barry snapped. While paying attention to the worries of patients and their relatives was an integral part of good medicine, on some occasions, and this was one of them, the practical took precedence over the emotional. He needed Donal now. It was no time for the man to crack up. "Get a clean blanket, and move yourself," Barry ordered.

Donal scurried away and returned with a bundle in his arms.

"Right. Help me get it under her."

"Doctor, should we not maybe give her a wee wash? She'd be powerful embarrassed if people saw her like that."

"Bugger it, Donal; just help me." Barry lifted Julie's head, thinking of a woman he'd seen last year who'd been too shy to ask her doctor about a lump in her breast until the cancer had turned into a festering, ulcerated sore, and the stink of it had so nauseated her family that they had insisted she seek medical advice. Rural inhibitions could kill patients. "Come on, man, move."

With Donal's help, Barry manoeuvered Julie onto the blanket. Together, using the blanket as a makeshift stretcher, they carried her downstairs and out along the path and into the backseat of the Volkswagen. "Get in with her and put her head on your lap. I'll be back in a minute." Barry had to collect his bag. If she started to bleed again, he would need the medications in it.

He was panting when he finally chucked the bag in the passenger seat, climbed in, and started the engine.

He could remember little about driving to Belfast, not even cursing the traffic slowing him down as he wound his way through the city and on up the Grosvenor Road. He'd stopped the car outside the entrance to the casualty department under the stony gaze of a life-size bronze statue of Queen Victoria, and he'd charged in through the swinging doors. A couple of uniformed ambulance drivers were sitting in the foyer having a smoke and cups of tea.

"Can you give me a hand?"

One of the men took a deep pull on his cigarette and slowly looked up. "We're on our break, so we are."

Christ. Barry pictured O'Reilly at the front desk of the convalescent home in Bangor. He steeled himself and said, "Listen, you. I'm Doctor Laverty. I've a woman outside bleeding to death. Get a bloody stretcher . . . and get it now."

The man jumped to his feet. "Sorry, Doctor. Right. Come on, Danny."

Barry waited until the men returned with a wheeled stretcher. "Out here." He stood and supervised as they loaded Julie onto the canvas sling, covered her with a blanket, and wheeled her straight into the nearest cubicle. He strode through the entry hall to the desk he remembered so well. Behind it, a red-uniformed nursing sister and a white-coated doctor were sitting chatting. He recognized the doctor. She'd been in his class. "Ruth, can you come see a patient of mine?"

She smiled at him. "Hello, Barry. Sure. What's up?"

"Incomplete abortion. She's lost a lot of blood. A lot."

Ruth was on her feet, issuing directions as she headed for the cubicle. "Right. Sister . . ."

Sister rose. "Nurse Corrigan, get the intravenous kit . . ." A blue-uniformed nurse hurried down the hall. Sister picked up the telephone. "I'll send for the blood technician, get the gynae registrar."

Barry let his shoulders sag. The efficiency of the hospital's senior nurses had always impressed him, and now that Julie was in good hands he could feel some of the strain slip away. But she wasn't out of the woods yet. He followed the young doctor and stood watching silently as she rapidly checked Julie's pulse and blood pressure. It seemed like only seconds after Sister appeared pushing a small, wheeled trolley that saline was dripping from an intravenous set into Julie's arm.

Ruth used the back of her wrist to brush a stray wisp of her auburn hair from her forehead. "Right," she said, "that'll hold her until gynaecology gets here. What's the history, Barry?"

He rapidly briefed his colleague, taking particular care to mention that he had given Julie morphine. As Barry spoke, a young blood technician arrived, took some samples, and vanished.

"Sounds to me as if you're spot on, Barry." Ruth slipped her stethoscope into her ears, inflated the blood pressure cuff, and listened. She smiled. "BP's coming up. The blood'll be cross-matched in no time, we'll get a couple of pints into her, quick D and C, and she'll be right as rain."

"Thanks, Ruth." He bent over Julie and saw her eyes flicker.

"Doctor Laverty?"

"It's all right, Julie. You're in the hospital. You're going to be fine."

She stretched out her hand, took his, and squeezed it. "Thanks, Doctor. Is Donal all right?"

"I'm going to see him now, Julie. Tell him what's happening." The staff here might be very efficient, but he knew only too well how relatives were routinely ignored. "I'll be saying cheerio, but I'll ask Donal to bring you in to see me in the surgery once you're discharged."

She didn't reply. She'd drifted off to sleep. He disengaged his hand and spoke to Ruth. "I'll go and have a word with . . . her husband." Donal would want to see Julie, perhaps stay so he could see her again when she came back from the operating room, but the visiting rules were very strict. Immediate family only. Boyfriends didn't count as family. No one would bother to check Barry's white lie. "Can I send him in when I've finished?"

"Fair enough."

"Then I'll be heading home."

Ruth smiled. "You ran her up here in your own car?"

Barry nodded.

"Jesus, it's the Victoria Cross for you, boy."

"What?"

" 'Devotion over and above the call of duty.' Isn't that what the citation says?"

"Away off." Barry blushed. He'd not seen it that way. "There wasn't time to do anything else."

"Huh," Ruth said, "there are plenty of GPs would have just phoned for the ambulance. I know. You should see some of the wreckage we get in here."

"Not Doctor O'Reilly," Barry said, without thinking. "Anyway, I'm off. I'm going to be late for my supper."

28

A Mysterious Way, His Wonders
to Perform

"Pity you missed the duck," O'Reilly remarked, pulling a napkin from under his open collar and setting the crumpled linen square on the dining room table. "The sherry trifle was good too. I left you some."

Barry looked longingly at the remains of the duck carcass and then at a tureen containing a few dried-up green peas. He saw a bowl with smears of colcannon clinging to the lip, and a nearly empty dish of apple sauce. A Waterford crystal bowl held half a sherry trifle. Its layers of whipped cream, Bird's custard, raspberries, and sponge cake were as clearly defined as the strata in a paleontological dig.

"Kinky says you dashed off with Donal Donnelly." O'Reilly looked vaguely apologetic. "It would have been a shame for me to wait for you and let dinner get cold." He did not meet Barry's look. "It would have upset Kinky."

That last remark came from a man who made it a point of principle never to make excuses, Barry thought. The bugger might have left me some dinner. He shrugged and said, "Julie aborted. She's in the Royal." He sat down. "I had to run her and Donal up there."

"Good for you," O'Reilly said. "Mind you, it's what I'd expect."

Barry made a tiny bow with his head.

"That's a shame about Julie," O'Reilly said, "but she's young yet. She'll have plenty more."

"I suppose so. Donal was pretty upset. He thinks it's divine retribution."

O'Reilly laughed. "For what?" He hauled out his briar and fired it up.

"In the first place, for getting her pregnant out of wedlock."

"I don't believe a word of it. Donal was worried about that? It's not so long ago in the country here a fellah wouldn't marry his chosen until after she'd proven her fertility in the most practical way. You need strong sons to run a farm."

"It's not so long ago that couples wouldn't get married until the lad's father died and left him the farm. Some of those 'lads' were in their forties and fifties," Barry said. "Times have changed, Fingal."

"Huh," said O'Reilly. "Don't I know it?" He didn't look very happy. He belched smoke, scratched his chin, and said, "About retribution . . . you said, 'in the first place.' Was there a second place?"

"Donal reckons he's being punished for gypping Captain O'Brien-Kelly with the Arkle medallions."

"Punished? Donal should get a medal of his own." O'Reilly's laughter rumbled.

"Why?" Barry leant across the table and started spooning trifle into a bowl. He was famished. It was hours since he'd eaten chicken sandwiches with Patricia on Gransha Point.

Before O'Reilly could answer, Mrs. Kincaid interrupted. Barry hadn't heard her come in carrying an empty tray. "Leave that trifle alone, Doctor Laverty dear. You shouldn't eat your pudding before your dinner, so." He saw her glance at the remains of the duck. "Pity greedy-guts here has eaten it all to himself and not even left you the pickings."

Barry expected O'Reilly to remonstrate. Despite Mrs. Kincaid's position as housekeeper, she was, after all, O'Reilly's employee.

"It was too bloody 'moreish,' Kinky," he muttered. "And it wasn't a very big duck."

"There's days, Doctor O'Reilly sir, a whole roast elephant wouldn't fill you, and now I've still Doctor Laverty to feed." She glanced at a clock on the sideboard. "I've time to make you an omelette," she said to Barry. "Would that do?"

"Lovely, Kinky. Thank you."

"Right." She loaded the tray with the dirty dishes and left. "I'll be back in a little minute."

"Jesus," said O'Reilly, rising and going to the sideboard to pour himself a large Bushmills, "they say a she-bear gets protective of her cubs. The way Kinky's looking after you, Barry, I think she's adopted you."

Barry smiled. He knew O'Reilly, for all his ability to understand the devious workings of human nature, had a blind spot about himself. If anyone in this house had adopted Barry, it was the big man. "I could do worse," he said. "You know my folks are in Australia for a year, and I'm kind of an orphan until they get back?"

"I do." O'Reilly took a pull of his Irish. "The Great South Land, *Terra Australis Incognita.* It's a country I'd not mind seeing myself." He looked over his whiskey glass and raised a bushy eyebrow. "I hear there are grand opportunities there for young doctors."

"There are, so Dad says." Ever since they'd first discussed the question of Barry's leaving or staying, O'Reilly hadn't mentioned the matter. "There're opportunities in Ulster too." Barry wished he could reassure the senior man that he'd made up his mind to stay, and if he was honest with himself he pretty much had—if it wasn't for Patricia.

"I'm glad to hear you say that."

Barry waited for what he assumed would be the next question—"So you've decided to stay on?"—but O'Reilly merely struck another match and relit his pipe.

If he didn't want to pursue matters, neither did Barry. "Fingal, you just said Donal should get a medal. Why?"

"God," said O'Reilly, "'moves in a mysterious way . . .'"

"'His wonders to perform . . .'"

"William Cowper," said O'Reilly. "Light Shining Out of Darkness." He refilled his glass. "You know we've not been much use trying to find digs for Sonny until his place is ready or until after he and Maggie are wed?"

"Kinky hasn't come up with anything?"

"Not a sausage. It was just a shot in the dark when I asked His Lordship for help. I didn't expect much then. Now I'd *like* to take the credit for what's happened since, but it has nothing to do with me."

"What *has* happened?"

"You remember when the captain tried to touch me up yesterday? He'd some minor financial obligations to Honest Sammy Dolan?"

"Yes."

"And you remember the gentleman from the tattooed fraternity who was heading our way? He looked like he was going to pull out O'Brien-Kelly's arm and beat him to death with the soggy end. At least that's what the good captain must have thought."

Barry could picture Sammy Dolan's enforcer. No forehead and almost trailing knuckles. "He was a big, angry-looking fellah, right enough." He said.

It was coming clearer, and Barry wasn't surprised when O'Reilly continued. "It seems that our yeoman of the guard eventually found the Marquis, who, and I'm sure this'll break your heart, didn't have more than a few quid on him."

"Are you saying the captain suddenly discovered he'd urgent business back in England?"

"In this part of the world there are venial sins, mortal sins . . . and welshing on a bet . . . and that's in ascending order of severity. He *could* have paid off the bookie himself if he hadn't blown his cash on Donal's Arkle medallions." O'Reilly's smile was broad, with a hint of satisfaction. "Apparently he was on the Belfast-to-Liverpool ferry last night. Purely a preventative measure you understand."

Barry laughed. "An ounce of prevention is worth a hundred pounds of cure."

"That captain was a living example of the old oxymoron 'military intelligence.' He was thick as two short planks," said O'Reilly. "Normally he would have been quite immune anyway."

"Immune?"

"Oh, aye. The Marquis would usually have settled any guest's gambling debts at once. Sorted it out with the offender later. The Chinese aren't the only ones who worry about loss of face. The old boy has a very finely tuned sense of honour."

"Then why didn't he do it?"

"Oh, he did, but not until after the captain had left. O'Brien-Kelly'll get a bill in the post from His Lordship," said O'Reilly, "but as the

Marquis told me on the phone this afternoon, he couldn't stand the little squirt and was happy to see the back of him. And he would be delighted to let Sonny have the gate lodge. He'll even send down Sonny's meals from the Big House."

"Wonderful, Fingal." Barry stared at his senior colleague, then said, "I have a half-notion that the Lord's not the only one round here to work in a mysterious way. If you hadn't encouraged Donal to go ahead with his crackpot scheme, and if you hadn't taken the trouble to ask the Marquis if he could help, Sonny would still be in the home."

O'Reilly grunted, let go a blast of smoke from his briar and smiled shyly. "Well . . ."

"No 'well' about it."

"Och, say no more, and anyway all's well that ends well. Sonny's pleased as Punch, and Maggie's like a cat with ten kittens."

"Did you drop in to tell her?"

"Not at all. I stopped and took Maggie down with me when I went to collect him."

"Decent of you."

"Rubbish. It was worth the price of admission just to eavesdrop on them when I had them in the back of the Rover. Maggie's been planning the wedding. She may call her cat the General, but the way she has things organized for next Saturday she could be Montgomery himself. She's arranged the battle as meticulously as he did before *El Alamein*."

"I hope," said Barry, who had read extensively about the campaign in the Western Desert, "she's not planning an artillery barrage for the kick off."

O'Reilly laughed. "I don't think so, but she was worried about where to hold the reception after. Half the village will be there on Saturday."

"You haven't offered your garden again like you did for Seamus Galvin?"

"No. The Marquis came down to the gate lodge to see Sonny settled in. He's taken a great shine to the old boy already. When I left to run Maggie home, the pair of them were blethering away about some new Nabataean dig in Jordan, early Egyptian papyri, and land titles in

Ireland under the Normans. I tell you, for once I was completely out of my depth."

"Not like you, Fingal."

"Jesus Christ, I'm not infallible," said O'Reilly. "I leave that up to the big fellah in the pointy hat in Vatican City."

Barry laughed. He wondered how often he'd seen Doctor Fingal Flaherty O'Reilly speak to his patients with all the sonorous authority of a pronouncement made ex cathedra by the pope. "I'm sure His Holiness will be relieved to hear it."

O'Reilly smiled. "Never mind that. The important thing is that His Lordship promised they can have the hooley in his grounds."

"That's great."

"It's just a pity there won't be the two weddings. I don't see Julie MacAteer being well enough to tie the knot with Donal for a week or two yet."

"I agree." Something occurred to Barry. "Poor Helen."

"Poor Helen?"

"Aye. If one of the weddings is delayed, her Miss Moloney could find herself overstocked with hats. I doubt if it'll improve her temper."

O'Reilly laughed. "We all have our crosses to bear. I'm sure Miss Moloney will survive until Julie and Donal do finally tie the knot."

"If they ever do." Barry mused aloud, "Do you think the pair of them will go ahead at all now that they don't 'have to'?"

"I don't know. I've wondered what a pretty girl like Julie sees in a bucktoothed, eejit like Donal, but then there's no accounting for love."

Barry could see the quizzical way O'Reilly was looking at him. "You're right, Fingal. There's not. I know that."

"Aha." O'Reilly walked around the table and dropped a hand on Barry's shoulder. "Bloody marvellous. She's a gem that Patricia Spence of yours. I'm delighted."

"Thanks, Fingal." Barry waited. Now was the time for O'Reilly to ask what Barry intended to do, but instead he went to the sideboard, topped up his own glass, poured a second whiskey, and handing the glass to Barry, said, "That news calls for a drink. *Slainte*."

Barry stood and raised his glass. "*Slainte mHath*." As he sipped the spirits he heard the door open.

Mrs. Kincaid wore her coat and an old hat, not the new confection—Barry guessed she was saving it to dazzle her friends at Maggie's wedding—and she carried her handbag slung over her right forearm. "Now," she said, setting a plate in front of Barry, "there's your omelette. Eat it up while it's warm." She glanced at his blood-stained pants. "Lord Jesus, not again. Leave them in the kitchen. I'll see to them later. I need to run on now or I'll be late for the Women's Union meeting at the church."

"Don't worry about them, Kinky—"

O'Reilly interrupted. "Will you be seeing Mrs. Bishop, Kinky?"

"Aye, so."

"I believe Doctor Laverty asked you to have a wee word with her?" Barry had mentioned his idea to Fingal.

"I will, so, and I've not forgotten. I'll see what she knows about Bertie and the lease for the Black Swan."

"Good."

"Get you sat down, Doctor Laverty, and tuck in like a good lad. And don't forget to leave them corduroys."

Barry sat. "I told you, don't worry about them, Kinky," he said. "They're going in the bin. I'll be buying some new ones."

"About time. Now will you do as you're bid? Eat up." She left.

"New pants? Have you fallen into a fortune?"

"No. But I won a few bob at the races," Barry said, through a mouthful of omelette so light and fluffy it was hardly there.

"I'd forgotten," said O'Reilly, "and I suppose it's burning a hole in your pocket. Pity that. You'll need to wait a day or two before you can spend it."

"Why?"

"Because," said O'Reilly, "in case you've forgotten tomorrow's Monday, and I think we're going to be busy as bejesus. I've a half-notion a few wee birds have been putting out the word you're not such a quack after all."

Barry started to smile, but Kinky stuck her head back round the door. "Busy tomorrow, is it? You'll be busy sooner than that, Doctor O'Reilly. Somebody's left something for you on the front doorstep."

"Not another kitten?" Barry asked, remembering how Lady Macbeth had arrived.

"It is not," said Kinky. "It's a single, solitary Wellington boot."

29

The Moving Finger Writes and,
Having Writ, Moves On

"If that bloody dog retrieves one more Wellie, I'll get him a muzzle,"
O'Reilly grumbled. "I was all over hell's high acre last night looking
for the other half of the pair. I didn't find it until I was away up in the
Ballybucklebo Hills." He opened the surgery door, then hesitated.
"Tell you what; I'm tired, so I'll go and get the victims this morning.
You do the work."

"Fine." Barry went in and sat on the swivel chair, pleased that
O'Reilly was letting him run the morning surgery. Damn it all, he'd
done his job to the best of his ability last week, things were improving,
and he was getting a good chance to become re-established.

O'Reilly came in, pursued by Donal Donnelly. Donal wore moleskin trousers and an old jeans jacket darkened by the rain that Barry
could hear rattling against the surgery windows. O'Reilly hopped up
on the couch.

"Morning, Donal," Barry said.

"Morning, sir."

Barry noticed how tired the man looked. He cradled his right hand
in his left.

"How's Julie?"

"They were great at the Royal after you left, so they were. She had
her operation, and she was sitting up with a wee cup of tea in her hand
when I went home last night. They're for letting her out on Thursday."

"I'm sorry about the baby."

"Aye, well. Can't be helped. The lady doctor there told me you done everything right, sir, and likely the baby wasn't forming properly. Maybe it was for the best. Maybe it's better to have an empty house than a bad tenant?" He managed a small smile.

Barry offered a silent thanks to Ruth, his classmate, who had taken care of Julie at the Royal. "Maybe it is, Donal."

"Aye, well," Donal said, "it's not Julie I've come about. I've buggered my finger."

"Sit down and let's have a look."

Donal sat in one of the straight chairs and stuck his right hand under Barry's nose. "I gave it a ferocious wrench lifting a load of slates working at Sonny's. I've left Seamus all on his own, but I'm no use. I can do nothing." He peered at his finger. "It's bloody sore, so it is."

Barry could see how the right middle finger was acutely bent forward at the first joint, bruised and swollen. A half-moon of dirt shone through the nail. "Can you move it at all?"

"No, sir."

Barry took hold of the tip and tried to extend it.

Donal snatched his hand away. "Holy thundering mother of Jesus. That hurts."

"Sorry, Donal." Barry glanced at O'Reilly, who seemed to have developed an abiding interest in his own fingernails. Barry was sure that the long tendon, which normally would pull the fingertip back, had been ripped right off its attachment to the bone. It had probably taken a small piece of the bone with it. An X-ray would tell, but bone chip or not, the treatment would be the same. "You've a mallet finger there, Donal."

Donal scowled at the digit. "Looks more like a bloody ball-peen hammer to me."

Barry smiled. "Some folks call it a baseball finger."

"Is that a fact? Baseball? Isn't that rounders for grown-ups?"

"Don't let an American hear you say that, Donal. They take the game very seriously," Barry said, "and I'm going to have to take your finger seriously. I'll have to splint it." He stood and went to fetch the instrument trolley.

"I'll get the water," said O'Reilly, slipping from the couch and taking a stainless-steel basin to the sink.

As Barry reached into a drawer in the trolley to pull out a roll of plaster of paris, he could hear water plashing into the bowl.

"How long's it going to take to get better, Doctor?"

"You'll be in the splint for six weeks." Barry pushed the trolley across to where Donal sat. "It could be quite a while after that before it recovers completely."

O'Reilly put the bowl of warm water on the trolley top.

"Six weeks?" Donal whistled. "And I'll not be able to work?"

"I'm sorry."

"It's going to hold up getting Sonny's roof done."

"Don't you fret about that, Donal," O'Reilly said. "Seamus and Mary and baby Fingal are off to California next week, so it'll get held up anyway."

Donal shook his head. "Poor ould Seamus. I tell you, that man doesn't want to leave Ulster. Not one bit."

Barry could understand how Seamus must feel.

"Don't you worry your head about Seamus," O'Reilly said. "He'll be gone. What *we* have to do is get the councillor to hire more men to finish the job."

Donal sneered. "Bertie Bishop? He's too bloody wrapped up making plans to get his hands on the Duck, so he is, to be bothered with a roof job."

Barry was busy fashioning a tube from the white plaster-of-paris bandage.

"We," said O'Reilly, "will see about that, and anyway, Sonny has a place to stay now, and then he can move in with Maggie after the wedding."

"Aye. But it's still not going to get the roof done." Barry watched Donal's brows knit. Clearly the man was concentrating, something Barry was sure was an unaccustomed exercise for Donal Donnelly. "I think," Donal said, "I'll maybe have a word with a few of the lads. I seen an American movie once, and a whole bunch of country folks all got together and they had a fellah's barn up in no time flat."

"You'd be saving Bishop money," O'Reilly said.

"Bugger Bertie Bishop. It'd be for Sonny and Maggie." He wagged his injured digit. "And I can't do nothing else to help, not with this thing wrecked."

"No, you can't," Barry said. "Right. Stick it out." He slipped the plaster tube over the finger from the tip to the base. "Now look." he pressed his own middle finger against his thumb, making a circle like an okay sign until the fingertip angled upwards. "Can you do that?"

"Ouch." Donal grimaced but did as he was told.

"Stick your hand in the bowl of water."

"That's brave and warm, so it is."

"Give it here, and keep the pressure on." Barry moulded the cast to the contours of the finger, feeling the warm water drip between his fingers as he squeezed. "There. Keep holding it against your thumb until the plaster dries." He went to the sink to wash his hands.

He could see Donal peering at the cast. "Thing of beauty that, sir."

"It's hardly a work of art, Donal, but it should do the trick." Barry came back from the sink and felt the cast. "It's drying nicely, so you trot along and come in and see me tomorrow. I'll need to make sure the cast's not too tight."

"All right, sir." Donal stood. "I think I'll take a run-race on my bike back to Sonny's, tell Seamus I'll not be back to work, and get him to come to the Duck with me tonight." He grinned. "I think Seamus could get most of the boys in the Ballybucklebo Highlanders pipe band to chip in for the roofing job."

"You do that," said O'Reilly, "and leave the door open when you go out."

"Right, sir, and thanks again, Doctor Laverty." Donal left.

O'Reilly shook his head. "I'm amazed. Who'd have thought Donal Donnelly would be the soul of Christian charity?"

"Could he really organize a work party, Fingal?"

"I don't doubt it for one minute." He walked to the door. "And speaking of work parties . . . do you think we might get on with the morning's business?"

"Sorry, Fingal. Yes, of course."

"Good," said O'Reilly. "I'll trot along and see who's next."

The telephone was ringing in the hall, and Barry heard Mrs. Kincaid answer. It had been another uneventful surgery. Lunch was over. O'Reilly was muttering under his breath about how if he had to eat one more salad, he'd be like the Johnny Cash song "Forty Shades of Green." Then he said, "You did a good job this morning, Barry. Many a young doctor would have rushed Donal off for an X-ray."

"Would it have made any difference to his treatment?" Barry already knew the answer.

"Not one whit." O'Reilly poked a finger behind a tooth and fished out a scrap of raw carrot. "But you'd have covered yourself from any accusations that you neglected the patient."

"Do you think I did?"

"Not at all, and you saved Donal having to go all the way to Belfast to hang about the radiology department for God alone knows how long, and even though it's not a matter I worry about too much, you saved the taxpayer a few bob. I told you," he said, rising, "you did well."

Before Barry had time to relish the older man's praise, Mrs. Kincaid came in. "Only one call again today, so. Mrs. Finnegan rang, worried that Declan's taken a turn for the worse."

"The man with Parkinson's disease and the French wife?" Barry asked.

"That's them," O'Reilly said. "Is that her on the phone now?"

"No, she called earlier. It's Mrs. Fotheringham, and she insists on speaking to you, Doctor O'Reilly."

"Oh, Lord," O'Reilly said. "Right. I'll see to it." He left.

Barry twisted in his chair and wondered what the woman could want. Certainly O'Reilly had gone out when her own doctor wasn't available last Sunday, but Doctor Bowman of the Kinnegar should be on duty today. And if Mrs. Fotheringham had been sufficiently distraught to leave the practice because Barry had misdiagnosed her husband's cerebral haemorrhage, she'd hardly be wanting anything to do with it now, not since his sudden death.

Barry heard O'Reilly return, and saw the way he was frowning. "What's up, Fingal?"

"Bloody woman," he said. "She demands to know what killed her husband. I can't budge her. She's adamant."

"But the results of the postmortem aren't in yet."

"I tried to explain that to her, but she's convinced you were responsible. I'm sorry, Barry."

Barry flinched.

O'Reilly laid a hand on his shoulder. "It's worse. She says if she doesn't get an answer soon, she'll have to have a word with her lawyer."

"What?" Barry heard his own voice rise sharply. "She's going to sue me?"

"She is if we don't get some answers."

"Christ almighty." Yesterday, with Patricia, he'd half decided he wasn't too concerned about the outcome of the autopsy. Now it was critical, because being sued was every doctor's nightmare. Until recently, malpractice actions had been virtually unheard of in Ulster. Litigation was a recent American import. It would utterly shatter the reputation he'd been trying so hard to rebuild. He looked up into O'Reilly's craggy face.

"I know what you're thinking, son. If it goes to court, it won't matter if they find in your favour. Just being sued puts the mark of Cain on a physician. We'll have to hope to hell the PM finds something."

Barry's head drooped. He'd not told O'Reilly what his old classmate Harry Sloan had said. He'd meant to when he'd come back from Belfast last Wednesday, but the conversation had been cut short by their having to rush out to deliver Jenny Murphy's baby. Barry had completely forgotten. "So far nothing's shown up," he said.

"What?"

"I had a word with a pathology registrar last week, an old acquaintance. He was at the initial examination, and he told me that everything looked pretty normal. He said we'd have to wait for the microscopic examination of the tissues."

"Bugger. That could take a couple of weeks."

"I know, but Harry, my friend, said he'd look at the slides himself. I'd hoped to hear from him by today or tomorrow."

O'Reilly paced to the far end of the dining room, then back again. "Right." He rubbed the web of his hand across his lower face. "Here's what we need to do . . ."

Barry waited, wondering what the hell anyone could do.

"You go and see Declan Finnegan. If he's worse, and he probably is, we'll have to get him up to see the neurosurgeons."

"I don't see what that's got to do with Mrs. Fotheringham—"

"Listen, will you? If you think it's what he needs, go on up to the Royal, get hold of the head of neurosurgery, Professor Greer, tell him I sent you—we played rugby together—ask him to see if he can get Declan in soon."

"All right."

"While you're doing that, I'll go see Mrs. Fotheringham and pour a bit of oil on her troubled waters, try to persuade her to hold hard before she goes trotting off to a lawyer."

"Would you?"

"Of course I bloody would," O'Reilly said. "One thing I've learned. If a patient's really angry—and Mrs. Fotheringham's madder than a wet hen—the longer you keep them waiting, the worse they get."

"But you already said you couldn't budge her."

"Aye, but you hadn't told me about the PM results then. Maybe I can get her to understand there was no more bleeding in the major's head, and so whatever killed him wasn't because you were slow off the mark making that diagnosis."

"I suppose it's worth a try, but why not just phone her?" .

"Because you can't see somebody's face over the phone. You can't judge what they're really thinking."

"God, Fingal, I hope you can get her to see reason."

"I don't know if I can, but I'll try." He put a hand on Barry's shoulder. "The best defence is attack."

"How?"

"Get some solid facts that prove it wasn't your fault."

"I could phone Harry."

"Yes," said O'Reilly, with a hint of disinterest. "I suppose you could."

"Jesus, Fingal, I can do better than that. It's what you just said. I could go and see him when I'm up at the Royal. Find out everything I can."

O'Reilly moved closer to Barry. "Son, you're like Saul on the road to Damascus. You've just seen the light."

Despite himself, Barry smiled.

"Right," said O'Reilly, heading for the door. "I'm off to beard the lioness in her den."

Barry turned back to the table and rested his head on his hands. God, but it was unfair. All that striving to get high enough marks at school so he could be admitted to the medical faculty, six years hard graft as a student, one year as a houseman, five weeks here developing, losing, but steadily rebuilding a reputation—and the whole bloody lot in jeopardy because of one stupid mistake.

He clenched his fists and asked himself, what would O'Reilly do? And the answer was perfectly clear. He'd *not* sit here feeling sorry for himself. He'd get on with things and hope for the best. Barry rose. Standing about with both legs the same length wouldn't get Declan Finnegan seen, or Barry Laverty up to the Royal Victoria Hospital.

30

A Lawyer Has No Business

Barry hurried along the Royal's main corridor, barely bothering to acknowledge the greetings of acquaintances, oblivious to the old familiar noises and smells. He headed straight for Ward 21, the neurosurgery unit.

He knew he must get hold of Harry Sloan, but his first priority was to arrange things for Declan Finnegan. Although Barry was desperate to find out if there were any results from Major Fotheringham's postmortem, and although they would be critical to Barry, the patient himself was beyond help. But Declan Finnegan wasn't—he hoped.

Barry had called at the Finnegan house earlier. It had been horribly apparent, even before he had examined Declan thoroughly, that the man's Parkinsonism had deteriorated badly. He'd lost control of his anal sphincter, and his wife was distressed by constantly having to clean him. But clearly she was more concerned about the assault on her husband's dignity. She was a French war bride who'd come to Ballybucklebo after the liberation of France in the 1940s. Fortunately she spoke English well; Barry did not have O'Reilly's fluency in her language.

Declan needed to be seen by a specialist soon, and to achieve that, O'Reilly had recommended Professor Greer.

Barry stopped at the front desk of Ward 21. He didn't know the strikingly handsome, fiftyish, red-uniformed nurse who sat there. "Good afternoon, Sister," he said.

Her pepper-and-salt hair peeped out from under her fall, the huge, starched triangular white headpiece worn in the Royal only by those of "staff nurse" rank or higher. It was a holdover, a symbol of nuns' wimples, although except in the Catholic Mater Infirmorum Hospital in Belfast, nuns were no longer seen on the wards.

She smiled at him, and he noticed the amber highlights in her grey eyes. "Can I help you?"

"Please. I'm Doctor Laverty. I was wondering how I could get hold of Professor Greer. I'd like to talk to him about a patient with Parkinson's disease. Doctor O'Reilly sent me."

"Doctor O'Reilly? Fingal Flahertie O'Reilly?"

"Yes. He's my boss."

"Good God. How is the oul' reprobate?" Her accent was pure Dublin.

"He's fine. You know him?"

"I used to," she said—rather sadly, Barry thought. "I knew him when I was a student nurse in Dublin before the war, and he was at Trinity College. He wasn't a half bad–looking lad when him and Professor Greer played rugby together." There was definitely something wistful in her voice. "And you want to see the prof?"

"Please."

She frowned and looked at the watch pinned to her apron. "Monday? Three o'clock? He'll be in his office dictating consultation notes." She rose. "Doctor Laverty, isn't it? With Doctor O'Reilly?"

"That's right."

"Hang on. I'll see if he can give you a few minutes."

Barry waited until she returned. "You're in luck. I'll show you the way." She led him past the desk, along a short corridor, and then stood holding open the door to a small office.

"Thank you, Sister," Barry said.

"Come in, Laverty." Professor Greer rose from in front of a paper-strewn desk. If anything, the man was even bigger than O'Reilly. His coppery eyebrows jutted over his eyes the way thatch overhangs an eave line, and they matched his shock of shaggy red hair. He offered his hand, with fingers that looked like sausages. His grip was firm but gentle. How, Barry wondered, did such ungainly hands perform the delicate manoeuvers necessary for the professor's work? "So," he said, "you're O'Reilly's pup?"

"No, I'm not. I'm his assistant."

Greer laughed. "Don't take on. When I was your age, learners were called pups . . . short for pupils . . . if you're working with Fingal, you'll still be learning."

"That's true." Barry relaxed. "Thanks for taking the time—"

"To see you? Why wouldn't I? You're one of us. Here," he pulled a chair closer to the desk. "Have a pew."

"Thank you, sir." Barry waited for the professor to take his seat, then sat himself.

"What can I do for you, Laverty?"

"Doctor O'Reilly wondered if you could help us with a patient?"

The professor laughed. "Another one? I did a cerebral artery aneurysm for the pair of you last month."

"I know," Barry said. "He died last Sunday." He knew his voice trembled as he spoke.

"Did he, by God?" Greer hunched forward and looked into Barry's face. "Another bleed?" He sounded concerned.

Barry shook his head. "The early PM results didn't show that. They haven't shown anything. We're waiting for the histology report."

"I'm glad it wasn't the surgery. I'd hate to have done a sloppy job." He sat back in his chair and steepled his big fingers. "Anyway, if he's dead there's not much I can do for him. It must be someone else you've come about."

Barry debated asking Greer if he had any idea what might have killed the major, decided it would be unlikely, and so came quickly to the point. "We've a man, Declan Finnegan, with very severe Parkinson's. He and his wife can't cope anymore. Doctor O'Reilly was wondering if you could see Finnegan with a view to surgery?"

"How old is he?"

"Sixty-four."

"No history of encephalitis?"

"Not that I know of, sir."

"Is he incontinent?"

"I'm afraid so."

"Probably due to hypertension or atherosclerosis."

"Does that mean you won't be able to operate?" While Barry was quite capable of diagnosing the condition, the finer points of its treatment fell within the specialist's field.

"I'll have to see him first." The professor frowned, turned to his desk, and consulted a large diary. "Give me his name and address."

Barry did and Greer scribbled in his ledger. "Can you get him up here on Wednesday at six? I'll fit him in as an extra after the clinic. Get things rolling. There might be something we can do."

"That's very kind of you, sir." Barry wondered if Greer would be willing to put himself out for any GP's patient, or whether he was doing this as a favour to his old friend.

"Rubbish." He turned back to Barry. "It goes with the job, but I'm sure being a GP, you know that? Out at all hours. Unless Fingal's changed, he'll be working the legs off you."

Barry had to smile. "He is."

The professor leaned forward. "You're enjoying it?"

"I am, but—"

"But you still get upset when you lose a patient? You saw people die when you were a student. We're meant to get used to it."

"I know, but it's still not easy, and this one's different."

"I'd guessed that."

"How?"

"I heard your voice, saw the look on your face when you said the man with the aneurysm had popped his clogs." He leant forward and put a hand on Barry's knee. "It's not your fault, lad."

Barry sighed, looked into the older man's eyes, and saw understanding. "This one might have been. I missed the diagnosis initially. Perhaps if we'd got him here sooner?"

"I doubt it. I remember the case. Small aneurysm. Small bleed. It was easy enough to repair, and the results were very good. He'd have had very little residual damage."

Barry took some comfort from the opinion. He wondered how O'Reilly was getting on with trying to persuade Mrs. Fotheringham not to go to her lawyer. Barry realized that if she did sue, he was going to need all the support he could find. He blurted out, "His wife's talking about suing me."

"Shite." The vehemence of Greer's obscenity startled Barry. "Bloody lawyers. They should stick to divorces and searching land titles. I suppose you've hardly slept since you heard?"

"I only heard a few hours ago. Doctor O'Reilly's gone to see the man's wife. See if he can get her to wait until we know for sure what killed her husband."

"Good. If anyone can talk her out of going ahead, it's Fingal O'Reilly." The professor frowned, his great eyebrows knitted. "And you said the histology results are still to come?"

"Yes, sir."

"Cheer up. With a bit of luck they'll let you off the hook."

"I hope so."

"So do I, but if they don't . . ."

Barry felt his fingernails digging into the palms of his hands.

"If they don't, you can call on me as an expert witness." He held out his hand, and Barry was comforted by the warmth in the man's clasp. "Jesus Christ, if you saw him very early and he just had a stiff neck . . ."

"I did, sir, and it was the only symptom."

"If that was all, I could have missed it too."

"Thank you, sir."

"Rubbish, and take my advice . . ." The man grinned. "God knows I've given it to enough patients. Hope for the best but be prepared for the worst . . . and if the worst does come, you'll have Fingal and me on your side." He walked to one wall and indicated a framed photograph of a group of young men in muddy boots, shorts, and green shirts with shamrocks on the right breast pockets. "Irish side, nineteen thirty-nine, at Landsdowne Road in Dublin. We beat Scotland twelve to three. Look." He pointed.

In the middle of the first rank, two youngsters stood smiling at the camera. One had flaming ginger hair; the other was obviously O'Reilly. Sister had been right. He'd not been a bad-looking lad.

"You'll have the backing of the two best second-row forwards ever to come out of Ireland."

Barry forced a smile.

"Good." Greer opened the door. "I'd like to chat longer, but . . ." He nodded to a Dictaphone. "Bloody paperwork."

"I understand, and thanks for seeing me, sir." Barry let himself out. He was pleased he'd been able to hurry things up for Declan Finnegan—or at least O'Reilly's friendship with Professor Greer had.

"Everything go all right?" Sister asked from behind her desk.

"Fine."

"Good and . . . Doctor Laverty?"

"Yes, Sister?"

"When you see Fingal Flahertie O'Reilly, tell him Caitlin O'Hallorhan said 'hello.' "

"I'll do that." Barry left the ward feeling a bit more cheerful after his chat with Professor Greer. He decided he might as well deal with a couple of other practice matters on his way to the pathology department. Ward 22 was next door. He'd not need to make an appointment for Mrs. Bishop now that he seemed to have her myasthenia under control. But it would be a courtesy to let Mandy know, and he was more than a little curious to discover how his friend Jack had fared.

She was sitting at her usual post, one leg crossed over the other. If anything, her skirt was shorter than the one she'd been wearing last week. He couldn't help notice a narrow strip of white thigh between the hem of her skirt and the top of her dark stocking. "Hi, Mandy."

"Not you again?" She smiled up at him. "What is it this time?"

"I just popped in to tell you not to worry about making that appointment I asked you about."

"For our dinner out?"

"No. For my patient with myasthenia."

"The one you wanted me to get Professor Faulkner to see in a hurry?"

"Mrs. Bishop. That's right."

She flipped the pages of a ledger. "I'd her pencilled in for next week. I can let somebody else have the spot. Thanks for letting me know." She narrowed her eyes, and her lips smiled. "And here's me all set to tell you to forget about taking me out." She patted one side of her hair with the palm of her right hand. "The strangest thing happened just after you left here on Wednesday. That old mate of yours, Jack Mills, popped in. I hadn't seen him for months."

"Did he?"

"Yes, he did. He took me out on Saturday night." She giggled. "He's a very generous lad is Jack. He brought me an orchid before we went out for dinner at the Causerie."

Barry remembered the Causerie, a smart, little, and quite expensive restaurant on Church Lane.

"And after dinner he bought me two brandies."

Despite his ever-present worry about Mrs. Fotheringham, Barry could barely suppress a smile as he remembered Jack's take on the old song from *White Christmas*. "Sounds like Jack," he said.

"He's dreamy, and I'm seeing him again this Saturday."

"I'm delighted," he said. "Give him my regards."

"I will." She pouted and narrowed her eyes. "I might give him more than that. If he brings me another orchid."

"I'm sure he will," Barry said, "but I have to be running along."

"See you, Barry." She dismissed him with a tiny wave.

Barry left the neurosciences department and went down the main corridor. He called into the urology ward, where he was delighted to discover that the unit clerk had been as good as her word. She had found a place for Kieran O'Hagan on her chief's surgical list. He'd have his prostatectomy next Monday and had already been notified.

He sighed as he left and carried on along the main corridor. Somehow he felt as if he were a patient, waiting for the results of investigations, hoping the results were favourable but unable to escape the nagging worry they were not. He knew his pulse rate was increasing as he neared the pathology department.

He tried to distract himself by thinking about what he had achieved today. He should be pleased. O'Reilly would be happy because matters had been speeded up for Declan, although it occurred to Barry that there probably had been no need for him to come to Belfast at all. O'Reilly, despite his reservations about the impersonality of telephone calls, *could* have called Professor Greer. Had he sent Barry so he'd have a chance to meet the professor himself?

Greer certainly had been most helpful and would be a very valuable ally—if he were needed. Barry could imagine the big, ginger-haired man towering over the sides of the witness box, and over the prosecuting lawyer. He could hear the authority in the professor's voice as he said, "The Good Lord himself couldn't have diagnosed a cerebral artery aneurysm if the only symptom to go on was a stiff neck."

The trouble was, it wasn't winning the case that mattered. It was keeping the whole sorry business out of court, and that wasn't going to happen unless Harry Sloan had some new findings.

Barry straightened his shoulders and lengthened his stride. He had to find Harry Sloan.

Why Didst Thou Promise Such?

The department of pathology was lodged in the Clinical Sciences Building. Barry was struck by how quiet the place was after the bustle of the clinical areas of the hospital. Of course there were no patients here, no visitors. The predominant smell was a mélange of floor polish and tissue preservatives, both almost overpowered by the peculiar animal scents coming from the vivarium where white mice and guinea pigs were housed.

The same smells had been there the first time he'd walked through the front doors of the place in June 1959, with the first two and a half years of his studentship at Queen's University behind him. He'd completed his studies of the basic sciences in the anatomy and physiology departments at the main campus on the far side of Belfast.

Once he'd passed the examinations in those and related subjects, it was time to move on to the Royal. There the daunting prospect of three and a half more years of studying pathology, microbiology, pharmacology, and forensic medicine had at least been softened by the knowledge that he and his classmates would finally be allowed to see real live patients.

He paused on the second-floor landing and walked across the tiles to peer, for old times' sake, through the windows of the double doors that led to the main lecture theatre. Just as in his day, the tiered seats were filled with students bent over their notebooks. They were the reverent congregation hanging on every word of their priest, the white-coated lecturer who stood behind a floor-mounted desk and pointed out the salient features of a slide projected onto a large screen.

Barry recognized the teacher, Doctor Lynette Fulton. She was what was known as a reader in haematological pathology. Blood diseases. She'd been regarded as something of a marvel by his class. The few women who graduated in medicine had usually chosen general practice or paediatrics, disciplines supposedly more suited to their gentler natures.

There was nothing gentle about Lynette Fulton. Just looking down at her reminded him of the god-awful bollocking she'd given him when he'd failed a test about myeloid leukaemia, her particular interest. Then he'd been mortified, but from his current perspective he felt gratitude for the way she'd offered to give him a crash course in the subject. Her efforts had saved his bacon when, of all things, leukaemia had been the main question on the final pathology examination.

He turned from the door and went up one more flight of marble-topped stairs. On the landing he stopped outside glass doors next to which a sign read DEPARTMENT OF PATHOLOGY. NO ADMITTANCE.

He pushed through the portals. On his right the doorway to an office stood open. Three secretaries, all busily typing, sat at three desks. They were preparing pathology reports, and unless matters had changed greatly since he'd been a houseman, the backlog would still frustrate the receiving clinicians. They constantly complained about how long it took to get the findings.

"Excuse me?" he said.

"Yes?" A small, bespectacled woman looked over her typewriter at him.

"I'm looking for Doctor Sloan."

He saw a frown starting.

"It's all right. I'm Doctor Laverty."

"Oh. Sorry. Harry's down the hall. Third on your left."

"Thank you." He left and walked along the linoleum, pursued by the staccato rattling of typewriter keys. Wooden doors, all closed, were marked with the name and rank of the occupants.

On the third door a sign simply announced: Pathology Registrar. Harry wasn't senior enough to justify the expense of a personal plate. Barry knocked and opened the door. The room stank of stale tobacco.

Harry Sloan sat on a swivel chair in front of a flat workbench. He had a half-smoked cigarette stuck to his upper lip, and when he lifted his white-haired head from the eyepieces of a binocular microscope, he rubbed his eyes and said, "Nyeh. Hiya, Barry. Come on in. You want that aneurysm's histology results, don't you?" He frowned. "Shut the door behind you and park yourself."

Barry did. The office was tiny, but at least there was a grimy window at the far end. Two walls held full floor-to-ceiling bookshelves. He recognized two of the tomes, *Muir's Textbook of Pathology* and *Boyd's Pathology,* each more than a thousand pages long. Remembering the countless hours he'd spent trying to slog through their dry contents, he could barely suppress a shudder. If he'd helped Jack Mills with his anatomy studies, Jack had saved Barry's professional life by discovering an abridged text, *Lecture Notes on Pathology,* that could be mastered in a fraction of the time it would have taken to digest Muir or Boyd.

Harry stubbed out his cigarette in a tin full of butts and ash. He coughed. "Bloody coffin nails are killing me. Nyeh."

"*Have* you had a chance to take a look at those PM slides yet?" Barry saw Harry Sloan blush, a deep beetroot red.

"Jesus, Barry, I'm dead sorry, so I am. I've not had a minute."

"Oh." Why, Barry wondered, did he feel like a small boy who had been promised a special treat, only to be told he wasn't getting it after all?

"I'm really sorry. I did try, but two of the technicians have flu. Everything's backed up. I don't even know if the aneurysm's slides are made yet. Everyone's up to their arses just reading the Pap smears the techs were supposed to screen."

Barry tried not to let his disappointment show.

"Aye. See, if there're no techs *somebody's* got to keep things moving. The women the smears come from are still alive." He looked straight at Barry. "Your patient's dead."

"I know." Barry must have failed to hide his chagrin.

"It's important, isn't it?"

"When I asked you about it last week, it was mostly for my own satisfaction. Maybe help repair my reputation in the practice." Barry hesitated. His fists tightened. "But I just heard at lunchtime today that if I can't explain why her husband died, the widow's going to sue me."

"What? She's what?" Harry jerked back so forcibly his chair rolled away from the desk. "I'm sorry, Barry. I really am."

"Thanks, Harry, but you see why I'm anxious to get the results?"

"Too bloody right. That's desperate. I'll see what I can do." Harry fumbled in a pocket for his packet of smokes. "Hold on." He picked up a telephone, dialed, and said to Barry, "It was one of the lads that got flu who was meant to prepare the PM slides. I'll have a wee word with the head tech. See what I can do."

Barry listened as Harry spoke.

"Hello? Hughey? It's me, Doctor Sloan. Right. You remember the coroner's PM? The one who'd had a subarachnoid? Aye. Look, I need the cardiac slides as quick as you can get 'em. Aye. I'll hang on." He shrugged at Barry. "Hello. Och, Jesus. What do you mean they're still not done?" He ground his teeth, but said in a placatory tone, "I understand. It's nobody's fault. Look, Hughey, I need a wee favour. Christ, I know you're busy, but a mate of mine could have a lawyer breathing down his neck unless I can get some answers for him . . . Right . . . Right . . . You're a sound man. I owe you a pint." Harry hung up and said to Barry. "That was Hughey McClements, the head tech. He says he'll get on it right away, but it'll take a day or two." Harry set his cigarette packet on the desk and consulted a notebook he'd taken from an inside pocket. "I've still your phone number. I'll give you a ring as soon as I've had a shufti."

"Thanks, Harry." Barry turned to leave. "I don't want to put you under more pressure but—"

"No bloody buts. I'm glad it's not me facing a lawyer." He gave a half-smile. "But then my customers don't have the get-up-and-go to sue anyone anymore." He rubbed his eyes and bent back to his microscope. "I'll be in touch the minute I have anything."

Barry left, glad to get away from the fug in Harry's office, but still smelling the lab animals locked in their cages in the basement. He tried to stifle his impatience, and wanted more than anything to breathe the clean air of Ballybucklebo. It would be a while before he got there. He'd done all O'Reilly had asked him to do at the Royal, but he still wanted to buy some new trousers, and he remembered he was supposed to give Patricia a call to wish her luck for the next day. Call be damned. The Kinnegar was on his way home. He'd drop in and see her.

A steady, chill drizzle blackened the seawall and the tarmac of the Esplanade. Barry heard the doleful moaning of a ship's foghorn out in the lough. The vessel was there somewhere, but quite invisible from where he stood. He turned up the collar of his sports jacket, hurried across to number 9, rang the bell to flat 4, and waited.

"Barry?" Patricia stood in the open doorway. "Come in out of that. You're soaking."

He followed her into her flat, hearing a tenor's voice soaring over the muted sounds of an orchestra. "Sorry to barge in like this. I just wanted to wish you good luck for tomorrow." Her table was strewn with open engineering texts.

"Sit down," she said, bending and switching on two bars of a small electric fire. "You must be foundered." She turned to her gramophone.

He sat on the sofa.

"I'll turn this off."

"No," he said. "Leave it on. It's . . ." Somehow 'lovely' would sound trite. "What is it?"

"*Turandot.* It's the aria 'Nessun Dorma.' It's a very old record my dad gave me. That's Enrico Caruso singing."

Barry held his finger to his lips, waiting in silence until the song was finished and Patricia had lifted the tonearm from the record. "You really love opera, don't you?"

She nodded. "It lifts your mind, and I could do with a bit of that today."

"I know. Big day tomorrow." He could see how she bit at her lower lip. "Have you got the pre-exam wobblies?"

She nodded. "I thought I could do some last-minute cramming today, but I can't concentrate."

He chuckled. "I shouldn't laugh," he said, "but it was exactly the same for me last year the day before finals started. I kept opening books, staring at the pages, and do you know, the bloody things might as well have been written in Sanskrit for all the sense the words made." He patted the sofa. "Come and sit down."

She sat beside him and took his hand.

He bent and kissed her, gently. "Do you know what 'fey' means?"

She nodded. "The gift. The second sight." She looked into his eyes. "Surely you don't believe in it? You're a scientist."

"I honestly don't know." He remembered how last month Kinky, who in absolutely seriousness had told him she was fey, had said he needn't worry because Patricia would come back into his life. And she had. "But I have the weirdest feeling that you're going to ace the thing."

"Honestly?"

"Honestly." Liar, he told himself. He had had no such feeling, but it was worth telling her to see the laugh lines deepen at the corners of her eyes. And if giving her a little extra confidence would help, it wasn't much to ask. He just wished she could lend him some comfort, but this was not the time to burden her with his troubles.

"I don't know whether to believe you or not." But she kissed him and he warmed to her kiss. "Thanks for saying it anyway." She rose. "Look. I'm not going to do any more work tonight. I can't concentrate. Would you like to stay for a while? I was going to make scrambled eggs."

He'd like nothing better, but he'd not arranged with O'Reilly to be away from the practice for any longer than it would take to run up to the Royal, try to sort things out, get back to Ballybucklebo, and tell O'Reilly what had happened. "I'd love to, but . . ."

He'd already stretched his time by stopping in Belfast to buy those two new pairs of pants and by calling in on her.

She sighed. "But duty calls . . . and your patients."

"I'm afraid so."

She bent and took his hand, looked up into his eyes, and said, her voice low, "It's one of the things I love about you, Barry Laverty. I think I'd be lucky to be one of your patients."

He felt himself blush. "Och . . ."

"I mean it."

Should he tell her he might be facing a lawsuit? That this and his concerns about losing her to Cambridge had given him a tight knot in his stomach? No. He'd already decided not to. "I love you, Patricia," he said. He held her and kissed her. Then he said, "And that's something we have to talk about—"

"I love you, and I know what you want to talk—"

"Not now. Later. Once the exam is over. Once you've won the scholarship." He said the words with all the conviction he could muster, hating them as he spoke, hating the thought of their being parted. "Now," he said, "I'll expect to hear from you tomorrow night. Hear how you got on."

"I'll phone."

"And I want to hear the minute you get the results."

She pursed her lips. "I promise."

"Good." He kissed her cheek and turned for the door. "One other thing."

"Yes?"

"Are you going home to Newry, or will you still be here on Saturday?"

"I'll be here."

"Good, because I'd like you to come with me to a wedding. Two lovely old folks."

"I'd like that."

"Great." He opened the door to see that the drizzle had turned into a steady downpour. "Do your very best tomorrow. I'll be thinking about you."

"I will."

"Now I have to run on and see what Doctor Fingal Flahertie O'Reilly has waiting for me." He ducked his head and ran to Brunhilde, hearing the door to Patricia's flat close behind him.

32

He Maketh the Storm to Cease

The kitchen was warm after the rawness of the day outside. During the short time Barry had been at Patricia's, the wind from the northeast had freshened and the rain kept coming in heavy squalls. Barry shifted the bag he was carrying and closed the door behind him.

The smell of brandy was overpowering. He wondered if Mrs. Kincaid was a secret tippler. She stood at the counter, vigorously stirring the contents of a bowl she held under one beefy arm. The bowl's contents were grey, glutinous looking, and studded with dark nuggets. He noticed a half-empty bottle of brandy close by.

"You're back, so," she said.

"I am." He moved closer and peered over her shoulder. The brandy fumes were stronger—much stronger. "What's that, Kinky?"

"It's this year's Christmas cake," she said. "I like to get it done a few months ahead so it's got time to mature. Here." She held out the bowl and gave him the wooden spoon. "Give it a stir for luck."

Barry knew better than to refuse, and heaven knew he could use a bit of luck. He plunged the spoon into the batter, but it was like stirring half-set cement. He marvelled at how easily Kinky had worked it. "There," he said, and he handed the bowl back.

Mrs. Kincaid decanted the mixture into a baking tin lined with greaseproof paper, set the full tin on a metal sheet, and popped it in the oven. "It'll not look like much when it's first done, but by Christmas when I've seasoned it with more brandy, put on a layer of marzipan, covered that with royal icing, and stuck on a few sprigs of holly, it'll be a thing of beauty, so."

"I don't doubt it." He wondered if he'd be here at Christmas to see it.

"Himself is very fond of my cakes." She closed the oven door.

Barry wasn't surprised, particularly because it was now clear to him where the brandy had been going. "Is Doctor O'Reilly back?"

"He is, and he's waiting for you. He asked me to send you up directly you came in, so."

Waiting to tell me what Mrs. Fotheringham said, Barry thought, and sighed. "Right." He went along the hall and upstairs. He could only hope that O'Reilly had been more successful this afternoon with Mrs. Fotheringham than he himself had been with Harry Sloan.

He paused on the landing and glanced at the photograph of HMS *Warspite*. Last week O'Reilly had used the ship's history of being battered at Jutland yet still recovering to fight again as a parable. It had seemed reasonable—then. Barry'd taken the older man's advice, and for a while it had been working. The patients *were* starting to trust him again. But now? If he landed up in court?

He shook his head, tucked his bag under one arm, and went into the lounge. The lights were on.

O'Reilly stood in front of the fireplace, holding a glass of whiskey in one hand, scratching the crown of his head with the other. He stared down at Lady Macbeth, who sat erectly on the carpet at his feet, front paws together, front legs stiff, tail swishing from side to side. She, in her turn, stared up at O'Reilly's moving hand.

The little white cat growled, and then as if propelled by a rocket booster, from a sitting start, she shot vertically and landed spread-eagled on the front of O'Reilly's waistcoat. Then she hauled herself onto his shoulder and crouched there, using her right forepaw to maul O'Reilly's fingers.

"I'll be damned," said O'Reilly, setting his glass on the mantel and enfolding her body with his now unencumbered hand. "That's bloody nearly six feet from a standing start." He set her gently on the floor. "What the hell's Kinky feeding you, Your Ladyship?"

"Your hand's bleeding, Fingal."

O'Reilly turned from the cat. "I didn't hear you come in." He pulled a hanky from his pants pocket and dabbed at his hand. "Only a scratch," he said and grinned. "Did you see the lepp of her? A thing of wonder. Maybe she has springs in her legs." He bent and scratched the cat's head. She rose, arched her back, and started to weave back and forth, thrusting her side against the back of O'Reilly's now motionless hand. He grinned at Barry. "I call this 'going on autostroke.' She seems to like it."

Barry could hear the animal purring.

O'Reilly waved at the sideboard. "Help yourself; then come and sit down." O'Reilly dumped himself in an armchair.

Barry tried to read any hint of an inflection in O'Reilly's voice, but it was flat. Matter-of-fact. He set his bag on the nearest chair, poured himself a sherry, and took the other armchair. He could hear the downpour battering against the bow windows, driven by what was now a fully fledged northeaster.

"Dirty night," said O'Reilly. "Heaven help the sailors." He picked up his glass from the mantel. " 'No man will be a sailor who has contrivance enough to get himself into a jail.' "

Barry thought O'Reilly was quoting Samuel Johnson, but he didn't feel like playing their now familiar game. He sat silently fidgeting, then took a sip of his sherry. He'd seen O'Reilly like this before—making small talk, refusing to come to the point—when he had something difficult to say. "I saw Harry Sloan," Barry said.

"Your pathologist friend?"

"Yes."

"And?"

Barry shrugged. "He still hasn't got any results."

"Bugger."

"He's going to try to hurry things up, but it'll still take a day or two. He'll phone me."

O'Reilly held his glass in one hand and tapped it with his index finger. He looked directly at Barry. "Will he deliver?"

"I think so."

"He'd better." O'Reilly rose, crossed the floor, and pulled the curtains. Their thick material muffled the sounds of the gale. "I saw the widow this afternoon," he said over his shoulder.

Barry felt his hand tighten round the stem of his glass.

"She's fit to be tied. I've not seen such naked anger for a very long time."

Barry swallowed. His palms had started to sweat.

O'Reilly stood and went to lean against the mantel. "It's normal, of course. When people lose somebody dear, they want to lash out." He fished out his briar. "And the widows who suffer worst are the ones who don't know why their husbands died. I saw it in the war. The folks at home could accept 'killed in action,' but 'missing' left them in ruins." He lit his pipe. "It's probably the most difficult thing people have to try to handle."

"What is?"

"Uncertainty."

"I know. Believe me. I do know."

Perhaps O'Reilly wasn't concerned for Barry's worries. He frowned and said, "You'd have to feel sorry for Mrs. Fotheringham. She's in a powerful state."

Barry tried to, but at that moment he felt a great deal sorrier for himself.

O'Reilly released a stream of blue smoke. "I spent an hour with her."

"So what's going to happen, Fingal?"

"Hard to be sure. I *think* I managed to calm her down a bit, get her to understand why she was so mad at you."

"Thank you."

"But I still couldn't make her understand that suing you won't bring the major back, won't make her feel any better if she wins the case."

"Could she? Win, I mean."

O'Reilly shrugged. "Who can predict what'll happen in a court of law? It's nothing to do with justice. Our legal colleagues seem to think a trial's some kind of sporting event, and the best lawyer gets the cup."

Barry hung his head. "I suppose I should get hold of my malpractice insurance company?"

"Maybe later, if you do hear from her lawyer," O'Reilly said, "but there's no need to cross your bridges 'til you come to them."

"It sounds like I'm going to." Barry put his glass of sherry to one side. "Doesn't it?"

O'Reilly tapped his pipe stem against his lower teeth. "Not necessarily. I did get her to agree that if we can give her a satisfactory explanation, borne out by hard facts from the pathologists, she'll drop it. But she's an appointment with her solicitor next Monday."

"Monday?" Barry stared up into O'Reilly's face.

O'Reilly nodded. "I'm pretty sure she'll wait until then, but I'm damn well sure of something else too."

"What?"

"I told you. The longer people don't know what's going on, the longer they have to stew over things, the madder they get. There'll be no stopping her if we haven't come up with some results by the weekend."

"I wish to God Harry would get a move on."

"You told him why there's such an all-fired rush?"

"Of course, but I didn't know she was seeing her solicitor on Monday."

"We've still until the weekend. Surely to God your friend'll have phoned by then? It can't take four whole days to look at a clatter of slides." O'Reilly let go a blast of tobacco smoke and said levelly, "I think we should sit tight and wait."

Barry heard the 'we'; it would have been so easy for O'Reilly to have said 'you.' "Harry's pretty reliable. He called the head technician the minute I explained about a possible lawsuit. I was there when Harry phoned. The tech said it would be a couple of days before the slides were ready."

"Couple of days? That's not too long. We could hear by Wednesday or Thursday." O'Reilly sank half his whiskey. "We'll let the hare sit." He moved to where Barry had set his sherry, handed the glass to Barry, and said, "Get that into you, son." He waited until Barry had taken a healthy swallow. "Now," said O'Reilly, "you'll get no sermons from me but you will get a bit of advice."

Barry looked up.

"There's not a bloody thing either one of us can do until your mate phones, so stewing over it'll do neither one of us a bit of good. We'll end up like a pot of Maggie's tea."

"Bitter as gall?" Barry tried to force a smile, not because he knew O'Reilly's advice was sound, not because he'd alluded to Maggie MacCorkle's brew, but because without ever saying it openly the man had shown his allegiance, and it was comforting to know he was on Barry's side. "Thanks, Fingal," he said quietly.

"What the hell for?"

"The advice, and for going to see Mrs. Fotheringham today."

"Bollocks." O'Reilly belched smoke. "Advice is cheap so you're welcome to it, and I had to see the widow. When she phoned it wasn't just to talk about lawyers. The woman was in tears."

"But she's not your patient anymore."

"And what the hell has that got to do with the price of corn?"

"I just thought . . . When we had our lectures on what to do if we were threatened legally, the law prof told us to say nothing to the claimant."

"Least said, soonest mended?"

"Yes."

O'Reilly went to the sideboard and recharged his glass. "I leave that kind of thing to the legal eagles."

He didn't need to say anymore. Barry already knew exactly where O'Reilly stood if he thought someone was in trouble, even if that someone was threatening to sue. He stared into his sherry.

When O'Reilly harrumphed, Barry looked up. "All right," O'Reilly said, "enough gloom and despondency. Seeing your pal wasn't the only reason you went up to the Royal, was it?"

"No."

"So, Doctor Laverty, despite all the foofaral with this current upheaval, you and I still have a practice to run. What else did you do?"

Barry finished his sherry and wondered, was O'Reilly asking because he really wanted to know, or was he trying to get Barry's mind off his worries?

"Well?" He glanced at Barry's empty glass. "Have another."

Barry rose and went to refill his glass. O'Reilly was right. They did have a practice to run. "I'd a bit of luck with a couple of other things," he said.

"And," said O'Reilly, "are we going to play twenty questions, or are you going to let me in on the secret?"

Despite himself, Barry smiled. "First off, the urology folks have a spot for Kieran O'Hagan. They'll do his prostatectomy on Monday."

"Good."

"And I saw your friend Professor Greer."

"Charley? How is the old fart?"

"He was very decent. He'll see Declan Finnegan on Wednesday at six, after his clinic is finished."

"That's Charley. Did you arrange for the ambulance to come and get Declan?"

"Not yet, but I will. Your friend Charley talked to me about Major Fotheringham." Barry saw one of O'Reilly's eyebrows rise. "I know," Barry said, "you wanted me to think about other things, but this is important. When I told Professor Greer what was happening—he did the major's surgery—he said if I needed an expert witness, he'd be happy to testify."

"With a bit of luck it won't come to that, but if it does it'll be good to have Charley in our corner." Barry glanced at O'Reilly's cauliflower ears and remembered that he'd been a naval boxing champion. "He's a bloody tough fighter," O'Reilly said. "He damn nearly beat me in the Irish University Championship in thirty-eight."

"He showed me your photograph . . . the Irish rugby team."

O'Reilly laughed. "Boxing, rugby . . . it's a bloody miracle I ever qualified from Trinity."

Trinity College, Dublin, the oldest university in Ireland. Barry remembered the odd look in the eyes of the neurosurgery ward sister when he'd mentioned he worked with a Doctor O'Reilly. "I met someone else from your university days, Fingal."

"And who would that be?"

"A ward sister. Caitlin O'Hallorhan." Barry watched to see how O'Reilly would take the news.

O'Reilly's glass stopped halfway to his lips. His eyes widened. "Who?"

"Caitlin O'Hallorhan. She said to give you her regards."

"I'll be damned. Kitty? I haven't seen her for years. Kitty O'Hallorhan? Mother of God." Barry heard a softness in O'Reilly's voice. "I wonder what she's been up to all these years," he said quietly.

"Why not give her a call?" Dear Lord. Was O'Reilly blushing?

O'Reilly harrumphed, took a great swallow of his whiskey and growled, "Because I'm much too busy. Never mind the practice, I've still to try to sort out Bertie Bishop and the Duck. Because, all your concerns notwithstanding, we still need to see Mrs. Bishop and make sure your treatment's working. Maybe you've forgotten, but Helen's eczema's not getting any better. We'll be running round like bees on a hot brick for the rest of the week, and the first chance we'll get for a bit of time off is next Saturday for Maggie and Sonny's wedding."

"Oh."

"I told you. This isn't a Butlins Holiday Camp."

"I know. It's just . . ."

"Just what?"

"Patricia writes her exams tomorrow."

"And you want time off to hold her hand?"

"I told her she could phone me if she was worried, but you were right about phone calls being impersonal. I'd rather go and see her if I can." Why was O'Reilly, who was usually so sympathetic when it came to Barry's love life, sounding so irritated? Was there a hint of pallor in his nose?

O'Reilly sighed. "All right. When you need time, ask." Barry'd been wrong about the man's schnozzle. It was its usual plum colour.

"Thanks, Fingal."

"Just don't ask for too much . . . because after all these years running this shop on my own, I've got used to having you about the place, Doctor Laverty."

Outside, the gale raged and howled against Number 1 Main Street like a wild beast tearing at the defences of a stockade. Inside, one of the curtains shuddered in the draught forced in through a crack in the window sash's caulking. Barry heard O'Reilly's words, looked up, and saw the affection in the big man's brown eyes. He felt a tiny inner warmth and knew it wasn't coming from his second glass of sherry.

33

Work On, My Medicine, Work

"Come on, Barry. Up." Someone was shaking his shoulder.

Barry muttered, "Go 'way."

"Get up, you idle skitter. Show a leg."

He recognized Surgeon Commander Fingal Flahertie O'Reilly's quarterdeck bellow, sat up, and rubbed his eyes. "Sorry, Fingal," he muttered. He could see O'Reilly standing by the bedside. "I'll be down in a minute,"

"I should bloody well hope so."

Barry blinked in the sunlight as O'Reilly threw the attic bedroom curtains open and then stamped out. Barry listened to boots clattering down the stairs. He yawned, climbed out of bed, stumbled along to the bathroom, completed his ablutions, and dressed hurriedly. If he'd learnt nothing else during his houseman's year, it was how to go from a deep sleep to full readiness in no time flat.

He trotted down to the dining room, still knotting his Queens University graduates' tie. Its diagonally blue and green stripes were separated by a thread of red.

O'Reilly was already seated, tucking into his breakfast. "Help yourself." He waved his fork to a silver chafing dish on the sideboard. "And get a move on."

The smell of kippers was overpowering. Barry lifted the lid, blinked through the cloud of steam, shoved a brace of kippers on a plate, and took his seat.

"Here." O'Reilly pushed a full cup of tea along the table. "Bad night?"

Barry, who normally slept like a baby, nodded. Then he accepted the tea, and put in some milk.

"Unh," said O'Reilly, spitting out a large bone. "I'm not surprised. You'd a lot to think about."

Barry swallowed his first mouthful, savouring the oak-shaving smoked herring. "I know." He remembered Professor Greer's remark: "I suppose you've hardly slept since you heard?" It had been three o'clock before he'd finally dropped off.

"Being sued hits doctors hellishly hard," O'Reilly observed, helping himself to a triangular piece of toast from the rack and buttering the slice. He peered under his eyebrows at Barry. "All of us—some more than others, and we may not ever have recognized it—all of us went into medicine because we need folks to think well of us. Even me. Some doctors want all their patients to love them. Not every patient will, but the daft buggers who want it kill themselves bending over backwards to try to satisfy the whole bloody world."

Barry stopped chewing and looked at O'Reilly. The big man never before had confessed any of his own feelings. "I suppose so."

"I bloody well *know* so, and when some patient we automatically assume should be grateful threatens to go to a lawyer, it's like a right, regal kick in the bollocks."

Crude, Barry thought, but he already knew only too well that what O'Reilly said was horribly true. "Have you ever been sued, Fingal?"

"Me?" O'Reilly reached for the marmalade. "Great stuff this. None of your Robertson's or Oxford brands." He spread it liberally on the toast. "Kinky makes her own."

"Fingal, I asked—"

"I heard you, and no, I haven't. Not yet anyway."

"Then how do you know—?"

"How do I know? Because you don't personally have to give birth to appreciate how much it hurts. You only need to see labour once. My best friend from Trinity, and he was a bloody fine surgeon, ended up in court. He won, but he was never the same man. I saw what he went through."

"Oh."

"And I'll be damned if I'll let it happen to you." To emphasize the point O'Reilly bit the slice of toast in half.

"I don't see how you can prevent it."

O'Reilly stopped chewing. "*I* bloody well do. One . . ." He stabbed at Barry with the toast. "Your mate may well come up with some answers."

It was suddenly clear to Barry that when O'Reilly had refused to sign the death certificate for Major Fotheringham, thus forcing the need for a postmortem, he had somehow foreseen what might happen. O'Reilly had immediately taken precautions to try to protect Barry— and of course the reputation of his own practice.

"Two . . ." O'Reilly took another bite. "If I have to, I'll go and see the widow again. She's all on her own, frightened, angry. Who knows? I sowed the seeds yesterday. Maybe when they've had time to germinate she'll have second thoughts about going to the law."

"Do you think that's likely?"

"I do not, but you like to fish, don't you?"

"Yes."

"I used to do a bit myself. I once asked an expert what kind of flies caught fish. Do you know what he said?"

Barry shook his head.

"He said, 'Only the ones you put in the river.'" O'Reilly grinned. "If you don't try, you'll never get anywhere."

"If you believe it would help with Mrs. Fotheringham." Barry knew he sounded doubtful.

"I'll think on it," said O'Reilly, swallowing and taking another bite. "Where was I? . . . Aye right. And three, I'll be buggered if I'll let you stew over this until we know for certain what's going to happen."

"It might be easier said than done."

"Oh," said O'Reilly, cocking his shaggy head to one side. "Is that a fact?"

"Fingal, it's all very well to try to be cold and analytical, but sometimes . . ."

"The heart rules the head?"

"That's right."

O'Reilly roared with laughter.

"It's not funny."

O'Reilly coughed and nodded. "You're right. It's not, but it is funny that you think there's not a way to stop that too."

"I don't see how."

"There's only one cure, and that's to keep so busy working at something you love . . ." He fixed Barry with a cold glare. "You do love your work, don't you?"

"Yes. I do."

"Q.E.D.," said O'Reilly. "I'm going to keep you so damn busy until we hear the histology results that you'll not have time to wonder what day of the week it is, never mind sit around getting your knickers in a twist about something that may not happen."

Barry could see the sense of the suggestion. "All right," he said. "I'll go along with that."

"Good," said O'Reilly, polishing off the last of his toast and rising. "And one other thing."

"What?"

"I know there's another love in your life."

Dear Lord. Today was the day of Patricia's examinations. He'd been so wrapped up in his own woes it had slipped his mind.

"I'll make sure you've time to attend to that too."

"Thanks, Fingal."

"Thanks, is it?" O'Reilly said, striding past the table. "The only thanks I want is for you to get that cup of tea and those kippers into you as quick as you can. In case you've forgotten, it's time to start morning surgery."

Barry tried to push his half-eaten breakfast away, but O'Reilly held the plate. "Finish your grub. Nobody should have to face the world on an empty stomach. We'll have a little division of labour. You eat. I'll start seeing the victims." He glanced at his watch. "But eat up quick. I want you in the trenches with me the minute you've finished."

A scowling woman he'd not seen before, dragging a snotty-nosed little boy behind her, stormed out of the surgery. Barry stood aside to let them pass. She ignored him. He went in.

"Who was that, Fingal?"

"Gertie Gilligan and her wee Tommy. He's only got a summer cold, but the way she goes on about it you'd swear she thought he'd got myxomatosis."

"What?"

"It's a disease of rabbits. The bunnies get runny noses. Most of them die. Gertie wanted the newest wonder drug. She can want. Antibiotics never cured a viral infection." O'Reilly rose from his swivel chair. "You have to do what's right, not what some eejit's read in *Reader's Digest* and thinks you're stealing their birthright if you don't give it to them."

"I'll remember that."

"Do. Now sit here. You're on the helm this morning." He strode out through the door.

Barry sat and idly read the boldfaced letters ranked in decreasing size on the Snellen eye-test chart that still hung askew on one wall.

"Guess who?" said O'Reilly.

He'd come back, pursued by Donal Donnelly, who sat in a chair and said, "Good morning, Doctor Laverty."

"Morning, Donal. Let's have a look."

Donal proffered his hand. Barry could see that the finger cast was already grubby, but the exposed fingertip was pink. He put the back of his hand against the exposed skin and was pleased not to feel any great sensation of heat. The cast wasn't too tight. "Looks grand to me, Donal."

"It's still bloody sore. There's more aches in it than in a small hospital."

"I warned you."

Donal nodded. "Aye, you did, sir. I'll just have to thole it, won't I?"

Barry had often wondered why a word, which ordinarily described a wooden rowlock, had come into the Ulster dialect to mean "put up with." " 'Fraid so. You might want to take the odd aspirin for your finger." Barry turned to the desk and scribbled on a form. "It'll need to come off in six weeks."

"My finger, sir?" Donal peered at the digit in question.

O'Reilly rumbled, "No, you goat. The cast."

"Oh."

Barry, for what seemed like the thousandth time since he'd come to Ballybucklebo, reminded himself of the literal-mindedness of the Ulster patient. He handed Donal the note. "There you are. That's a certificate for the unemployment people. I imagine you could use the money now you're not working."

"Thank you, sir, but I am working."

"What at?" O'Reilly asked.

"Well, not for any money, sir." Donal rapidly tucked the paper into a pocket. "But after I got back from seeing Julie in the Royal, I was in the Duck last night . . ."

"You do surprise me," said O'Reilly.

"And Seamus and me've got a bunch of the boys lined up to come round to Sonny's place in the evenings after their work. They want me to be gaffer, so they do. Supervise, like."

"Good for you, Donal," Barry said.

"Weeellll . . . Sonny's a decent oul' codger." Donal wouldn't meet Barry's gaze. "And all I have to do is sit on my backside and give orders. I reckon one more week and the place'll be as good as new." Barry saw the same look appear on Donal's face that had been there when he'd come to seek approval for the Arkle medallions scheme. "You'll not say nothing to Sonny, will you, Doctors? We'd like for it to be a surprise."

"You've our word on it, Donal," O'Reilly said, before turning to Barry. "Have you finished with the patient, Doctor Laverty? Because the waiting room's like Paddy's market."

"Scuse me, sir. There's just one other wee thing."

"Go ahead."

"Julie's on the mend. She's already got colour back in her cheeks . . ."

"I'm pleased," Barry said.

"She reckons if you hadn't been so quick off the mark she could've died."

"Not really." Barry felt warmth in his cheeks.

"And she's heard a wheen of rumours that you don't know your stuff . . ."

Barry's blush faded.

Donal stuck his cast under Barry's nose. "Her and me knows better, and she says for me to tell you now—and Julie'll tell you herself at the wedding if she's up to going—we're lucky to have the pair of youse here, so we are."

It was quite a speech for Donal. "Thank you," Barry said, "but it's my pleasure." Despite the niggling worry Barry knew how much Donal meant it.

"Right," said Donal. "I'll be off." He headed for the door. "See youse on Saturday." Barry looked at O'Reilly, who raised one eyebrow but said nothing as he too strode to the door to go summon the next patient. You were right again, Fingal, Barry thought. It's hard to dwell on what might be when you're fully occupied.

"Phew," said O'Reilly, when the last patient left what had been a crammed surgery. Barry could barely remember all the complaints he'd been asked to treat, but he was pleased that he'd seen the three stable boys Fergus Finnegan had said would be coming in. Like Fergus, one of them had been suffering from acute conjunctivitis, and nothing, absolutely nothing, would satisfy him until he'd been given a prescription for the magical "golden eye ointment."

O'Reilly stood and stretched. "There's not been as many customers looking for help since the Great Plague of London."

"Sixteen sixty-five," Barry said. "Cleaned out by the Great Fire in sixteen sixty-six . . ."

"That started in a baker's shop in Pudding Lane."

God, O'Reilly, you always have to have the last word, Barry thought. "And I suppose you were there to help put it out?"

O'Reilly chuckled. "You're so sharp, one of these days you'll cut yourself, Laverty."

Barry thought of the conventions of name use in Ulster. To call a man by his surname without any preceding title or Christian name was a subtle sign of either condescension or friendship, and he knew what O'Reilly had intended by calling him "Laverty." Not that Barry would have the temerity to call his senior "O'Reilly." He might think it, but it would be a long time before he'd feel comfortable using it to the man's face.

"Right," O'Reilly said, heading for the dining room. "Food."

Kinky was waiting for them. "You're late for your lunches, Doctors."

Barry wondered if Kinky was displeased. After all the years she'd worked for O'Reilly, she should be well aware that medical practices could not be run to a strict timetable. "Sorry," he said, "but we were up to our necks all morning."

"Well," she said, setting a plate in front of Barry and moving to give O'Reilly his, "it's only a cold quiche lorraine, so it's not spoiled."

Barry glanced at O'Reilly, who was regarding the yellow, pastry-crusted triangle on his plate with the enthusiasm of a dog fox for the Ballybucklebo hunt.

"Eat that up, Doctor O'Reilly. It didn't make itself." She stood, arms folded, and looked down on him.

He took a small mouthful and broke into a wide grin. "That's delicious, Kinky."

He was right, Barry thought, tucking into his own.

"Would it be otherwise?" she asked. Barry could see she was smiling.

It occurred to him that Kinky must take as much pride in her cooking and in quietly keeping the household running smoothly, as he did in his work, and the odd word of praise did not go amiss for either of them. "You're a marvel, Mrs. Kincaid."

"I'm no such thing, so." But her smile widened. "Well," she said, "maybe at the cooking . . ." Barry was about to agree when she added, "I've not done so well with Mrs. Bishop."

"Oh?" said O'Reilly in mid-chew.

"I did what you asked, Doctor, tried to find out about the lease of the Black Swan, but I don't think there's much that she really knows. I didn't get a chance to tell you before." Kinky frowned. "Now I shouldn't say this, for she's a nice woman, but I don't think Flo Bishop's the sharpest knife in the cutlery drawer."

Barry smiled.

"So we're no further on?" O'Reilly said.

"Well, maybe a toty-wee bit, but I can't make head nor tail of it. Maybe you can, sir? The one thing I *did* get her to say was that he's told her that he'll get the Duck as long as nobody finds out about the stream, and she's not to mention it to anybody. Between the jigs and the reels of all else we blethered about—getting Flo to finish a sentence is like pulling teeth without an anaesthetic—I almost forgot she'd said it."

"Stream?" Barry asked. "What stream?"

Kinky shook her head. "She didn't know. Besides, if the place was a water mill I could understand, but what a stream's got to do with a pub, I'm blessed if I know."

"Nor me," said O'Reilly, "but I've a half-notion who might."

Barry listened attentively, but as was often the way O'Reilly did not expand on his thoughts. "Leave it with me" was all he said before asking, "Do you have the afternoon's list?"

"I do." Kinky pulled a sheet of paper from her apron pocket. "Here."

O'Reilly scanned it rapidly. "Not too bad," he said. "A couple of calls in the housing estate. We'll need to nip in and tell Declan Finnegan about his appointment, and I'd like to finish up in the gate lodge."

"To make sure Sonny's all right?"

"Something like that," O'Reilly said noncommittally. Before Barry could ask if there was another reason, O'Reilly added, "And we need to get back here by teatime."

"Another rugby game on the telly?"

"No, you eejit. You've to phone your Miss Spence."

34

Life's Too Short for Chess

The bright colours of the doors of the terrace houses were the only variations in a row of otherwise identical, grey stucco facades. It was as if in the painting each tenant had tried to hang on to a shred of individuality. The Finnegans' door was green. When Mrs. Declan Finnegan opened to O'Reilly's knocking, Barry saw she looked even more haggard than she had the day before when he'd called to examine her husband.

"*Bonjour, Madame. Comment allez-vous aujourd'hui?*" O'Reilly's French, as far as Barry could tell, was accentless. "*Et votre mari, comment va-t-il?*"

She shrugged. "*Moi, je suis très fatiguée. N'importe.*" She held her hand, palm down, and rocked it from side to side. "*Mais mon pauvre, petit Declan . . .*"

Barry could see how she pursed her lips, saw the moisture in her eyes, a single tear trickling down her cheek. He stood back as O'Reilly used one finger to wipe away the tear, then enfolded the woman in a bear hug. "*C'est dur. C'est dur. Je comprends,*" O'Reilly said gently. He translated for Barry's benefit. "She says she's very tired, but it doesn't matter . . . it's Declan."

"And you told her it's hard, but you understand." Barry heard Mrs. Finnegan sniffle. He waited while O'Reilly produced a polka-dotted handkerchief and gave it to her.

"*Merci, Docteur O'Reilly.*" She blew her nose and returned the hanky. *"Entrez, s'il vous plait."* She stepped aside and indicated that they should go into the house.

O'Reilly shook his head. *"Merci, Mélanie, mais nous vous apportons simplement des bonnes nouvelles concernant Declan."*

Barry saw the immediate interest in her gaze, which flickered from O'Reilly's face to his own and then back to O'Reilly. *"Des bonnes nouvelles? Dites-moi, la vérité, est-ce que vous pouvez faire quelque chose pour Declan?"*

"Can we help Declan? Barry?"

Barry stumbled, trying to formulate the words before he spoke. *"Hier j'ai visité . . ."*

"It's all right, Doctor Laverty; I do understand Henglish." She managed a weak smile. "But it is *plaisant* for me to speak my own language with Doctor O'Reilly."

"I had to give up French at school to concentrate on science so I could get into medical school."

"I think it is better you did, because you understand about Declan. Doctor O'Reilly said you have news?"

He nodded. "I was trying to say that yesterday I went up to the Royal and saw the best nerve specialist in Ireland. Professor Greer."

"And what did he say, please?"

Barry glanced at O'Reilly and saw how he had one eyebrow raised. "He couldn't make any promises . . ."

O'Reilly nodded. Once.

"But he'll see Declan tomorrow. At six o'clock. I've arranged for the ambulance to come and collect you both to take you up to town."

"So quick? *Ce n'est pas possible.*"

"It is, when the professor's a friend of Doctor O'Reilly."

Barry heard a torrent of incomprehensible French. By her tone and inflection Mrs. Finnegan was thanking O'Reilly profusely. O'Reilly cleared his throat, and Barry was convinced that if O'Reilly's complexion wasn't already florid, there would be a hint of a blush on the man's cheeks. "Now, now," he said. "Doctor Laverty did all the work."

She turned to Barry and lowered her head. "Thank you, Doctor. Thank you very much."

"Mrs. Finnegan, I told you, Professor Greer didn't make any promises."

"*Je comprends*, but we will be trying." He saw her eyes shining, but she rubbed them with the back of one hand and stood erectly, shoulders back. "Now it is in the hands of *le bon Dieu*."

"It is," said O'Reilly, "but the good Lord will be getting a little help from Professor Greer."

Mrs. Finnegan managed a tiny smile. *"Vous êtes un homme très mauvais, Docteur O'Reilly."*

"Och, sure, wicked's not the half of it, and we promise you, don't we, Doctor Laverty? If anyone can help Declan, it's the Professor."

"It is," said Barry, "and they told me you should take Mr. Finnegan's pyjamas and sponge bag. He may have to stay in for a day or two."

"D'accord."

Barry watched the emotions warring on Mrs. Finnegan's face: anxiety, sadness that she and her husband would have to be parted, relief that if he were admitted she'd have some respite from constantly nursing him.

O'Reilly laid a big hand on her shoulder. "And don't you go blaming yourself, Mélanie, because you're feeling relieved that you may not have to look after Declan for a day or two. A break'll do you a power of good. You've nothing to feel guilty about."

How had O'Reilly known she'd be feeling guilty as well as relieved? Barry hadn't considered that aspect.

"I'll try not to," she said.

"Good," said O'Reilly. "Professor Greer will give us a call to tell us what he thinks, and one of us'll pop round to explain it to you."

"Merci."

"Now Doctor Laverty and I have to be going." His face cracked into a grin. "You said I was *mauvais*?"

She nodded.

"You're right. Wicked it is." He spoke directly to Barry. "And there's no rest for the wicked, is there, Doctor Laverty?"

Barry sat in the passenger's seat as O'Reilly hurled the Rover along the Bangor-to-Belfast road. He wound open the window so the fumes of O'Reilly's pipe could escape.

Barry thought about the visits they had completed in the housing estate. Both had been straightforward.

One, a wheezing little boy, was known to O'Reilly. When Kinky had mentioned his name, O'Reilly knew that the mother was well enough used to her son's asthma to know when to ask for the doctor to rush round straightaway to deal with a serious attack. And more importantly, she knew when not to panic.

Barry had taken a quick history and listened to the child's chest. Then he pulled his stethoscope from his ears. He could not have improved on the treatment regime his senior colleague had arranged. Once Barry had given the lad an injection of 1:1000 adrenaline, the wheezing as he inhaled had eased. By the time O'Reilly had explained to the mother that the tablets of isoprenaline sulphate, which she had been told to administer when an attack started, were *not* to be swallowed but put under the child's tongue, the patient was out in the street kicking a soccer ball with his friends.

The other visit had been what O'Reilly called a comfort call. As soon as Barry had met the octagenarian grandmother, he'd realised she was beyond medical help. The old soul was happily living in a world of her own. Convinced she was back at her convent school, she insisted on calling O'Reilly "Father," and wouldn't let them leave until Fingal had made the sign of the cross and chanted a benediction.

Her daughter, Bridget, a woman in her sixties, had thanked him, but she had adamantly refused any suggestion that it might be time for Granny to be admitted to a long-term care unit. "Family's family," she'd stated.

O'Reilly had nodded and told her that she should feel free to call anytime.

"Sometimes," he'd explained to Barry as they'd driven away, "it's all we can do. Simply be available when they need us."

"She should be in a home, Fingal."

"Aye, indeed, but you heard her daughter, and as long as Bridget's prepared to go on taking care of her mother, the least we can do is pop in when she asks us to. I like to think it helps a little." It wasn't the sentiments that had impressed Barry. It was the way O'Reilly accepted his obligations without the least suggestion that it was other than perfectly natural for him to do so.

Just as natural as was O'Reilly's ignoring yet another cyclist and slamming the big car around a sharp curve with two wheels on the grass verge.

"Right," said O'Reilly, slowing down. "Here we are." He parked outside the red-brick, single-storey gate lodge of the marquis' estate.

Barry stepped onto the gravel. The high ornate wrought-iron gates were open, and at the head of a long drive he could see the Georgian portico of the Big House. A half-timbered shooting brake was parked outside the lodge. He assumed it would belong to the groundskeeper.

O'Reilly hammered on the door. "Anybody home?"

To Barry's surprise the door was opened by the marquis himself. "Ah, O'Reilly and young Laverty." Dark brown eyes smiled from under a thatch of ill-trimmed iron-grey hair. "You've come to see Sonny?"

"Aye," said O'Reilly. "How is he, sir?"

"Come in and see for yourselves."

Barry followed the two men along a short, parquet-floored hall, where the heads of two stuffed and mounted roe deer gazed balefully down from an oak-panelled wall. He went in through an open doorway into a small, tidy sitting room. Mullioned windows gave a view past huge elms to a manicured sweep of lawn where several evergreens had been shaped and tonsured by the topiarist's art.

Sonny, dressed in a woollen cardigan over a white shirt, and neatly creased black pants that fell to a pair of tartan carpet slippers, had been sitting on an overstuffed armchair but was in the act of rising to greet O'Reilly. A brass-topped table, the metal intricately filigreed in the Indian style, stood in front of the chair. The chessboard on the table bore the irregularly placed chessmen of a game in progress. "Doctor O'Reilly," Sonny said. "What a pleasant surprise."

"Should I leave you alone with your patient, Doctors?" the marquis enquired.

"Not at all," said O'Reilly. "And sit you down, Sonny." He moved beside Sonny's chair, and as soon as the old man was seated he took his pulse.

From where he stood beside the marquis, Barry could see that Sonny's eyes were bright and he had no difficulty breathing, although there was a hint of grey above his cheekbones. That wasn't surprising. Even before he'd been taken seriously ill, the man had suffered from a minor degree of chronic heart failure but O'Reilly had it well controlled with digitalis and a diuretic.

"Your ticker's going away like a well-tuned steam engine, Sonny," O'Reilly said, releasing his wrist. "Do you still have the heart pills we gave you?"

"Yes, Doctor."

"Keep on taking them. You've a big day coming on Saturday." He turned to the marquis. "Will you be arranging for Sonny to get to the church, sir?"

The marquis smiled. "I'm the best man. I'll run him there in the Rolls."

Sonny coughed, but Barry's concern that the noise might be a symptom vanished when he realized Sonny was only trying to attract O'Reilly's attention. "Could I ask you for a favour, Doctor O'Reilly?"

"Fire away."

"Maggie's too shy to ask you herself."

Barry had some difficulty imagining that Maggie MacCorkle could be shy.

"Her da's dead a long time and she wants everything done properly. She wanted me to ask you . . . would you walk her up the aisle and give her away?"

"Me?" O'Reilly's grin was vast. "I'd be delighted." He glanced sideways at Barry, who heard the wicked edge to his senior colleague's voice when he asked, "Would she like Doctor Laverty here to be her page boy?"

Sonny, and the marquis joined O'Reilly's laughter. Barry felt a smile start and realized that laughing at himself wasn't such a bad thing. "I will . . . if that's what she wants."

"Good lad," said O'Reilly.

Sonny shook his head. "That won't be necessary, sir, but thank you for offering."

"I think," said the marquis, "all this talk of weddings calls for a glass of sherry." He moved to a sideboard. "Please be seated, gentlemen."

"I don't suppose you'd have a drop of John Jameson's, Your Lordship?" O'Reilly asked, moving the table and the chess set aside and lowering himself onto a small sofa.

"Naturally, Fingal, and . . . I suppose it's all right for Sonny to have something?"

"Indeed," said O'Reilly, accepting his glass but refusing the marquis' offer of water.

Barry sat beside O'Reilly and took his sherry.

The marquis remained standing. "To the happy couple." He raised his drink.

"That's a grand drop," said O'Reilly, swallowing half the whiskey in the glass. "Better than the stuff Willy pours at the Duck."

As Barry sipped he heard the marquis say, "The Duck? I've been hearing rumours about the Black Swan. Something about a takeover bid by that man Bishop."

O'Reilly nodded. "The lease runs out soon, and Bertie Bishop is the landlord. He's refusing to renew and wants to turn the ould Duck into a tourist trap. Rip out the old stuff and stick in tons of chrome and plastic."

"Good Lord. That's horrible." Barry saw the marquis frown. "Can't we stop him?"

"I've tried," O'Reilly said, "but the man has a skin as thick as a rhinoceros. He'll not listen to reason. He owns the property the Duck's built on. The only thing that would stop Bertie Bishop would be some hurdle he can't jump."

For a second Barry had a picture of a jockey, *sans* horse, vanishing over the first jump at the Ballybucklebo races—and O'Reilly's horse soaring over a fence—the wrong fence. He heard Sonny cough again.

"Excuse me, Your Lordship . . ."

"Yes, Sonny?"

"You remember, sir, we were discussing Norman land titles in Ireland?"

"I do indeed."

Sonny nodded. "If I recall correctly, you told me that when John de Courcy conquered Ulster for Henry the Second in eleven seventy-seven, one of his knights, your ancestor, was granted all the rights to the townland of Ballybucklebo."

"True. But we've had to sell off a great deal. It costs rather a lot to keep the estate running. That's how the land the Duck was built on was lost ninety-nine years ago." He frowned. "I'd have to consult the family papers, but I've no doubt what Doctor O'Reilly says is true. Somehow Bishop's been able to buy the title from the descendants of the original purchasers. He can do what he likes when it comes to renewing or not renewing Willy Dunleavy's lease."

Barry saw O'Reilly fiddling with one of the chess pieces. "Mrs. Kincaid says Mrs. Bishop told her that Bertie's keeping mum about something to do with a stream."

"Is he, by Jove?" The marquis began to smile. "A stream?"

Sonny stood, almost spilling his sherry. "I'll bet your family didn't sell the salmon rights, sir."

Barry listened attentively. Salmon rights?

"Indeed not. That would have been unthinkable."

"And I know," said Sonny, "because I found out about it when I was looking into the history of the village, that a small branch of the Bucklebo River had to be roofed over in a culvert because it flowed, indeed still flows, under the crossroads and . . ."

"Under the Duck? Hah." O'Reilly sank the rest of his whiskey in one swallow. "Ha, bloody ha." He was grinning. "And the fish still use it to come inland and spawn?"

"Oh, yes," said Sonny.

"I'm sorry," Barry said, "but I don't understand."

"It means, Doctor Laverty," the marquis said levelly, "that when my forebears sold the property, the property Bishop now owns, the deed would carry a codicil that no structural alterations could be made to any buildings there if they might interfere with the salmon run. At least not without our family's permission. The Normans were very particular about fishing rights."

"So Councillor Bishop can't go ahead with his plans for the Duck unless you allow him to, Your Lordship?"

"I'm sure gutting the place would qualify as structural alterations." The marquis frowned. "I suppose he could get his lawyer to challenge me on that point, but it would be tied up in the courts for years."

Barry shuddered. He didn't like to be reminded of lawyers.

"Would you fight him, Your Lordship?" O'Reilly asked.

"Bishop? He's a horrid man. Of course I'd *like* to fight him, but the legal costs would be enormous."

Barry saw O'Reilly bend to the chessboard, examine the pieces, and glance back at the marquis. "But legally, *legally,* if he tries to bugger about with the old Duck, you could threaten to stop him?" O'Reilly moved a white castle. "And if he insists on going to court . . ."—he moved a black bishop to counter the castle—"Bishop's astute enough to work out for himself how much it would cost him to fight. He'd be crippled financially."

"You're right. All I need to do is *threaten* to go to court." The marquis' grin was almost as broad as O'Reilly's, who lifted a white knight and knocked the black bishop off the board.

"And that, I think is checkmate," said O'Reilly, pointing at the black king.

"I do believe you're right, Fingal," the marquis said. "Here," he said, stretching out his hand, "your glass is empty. Let me refill it."

O'Reilly shook his head. "No, thank you, sir. Doctor Laverty and I have to drop in at the Duck on our way home . . . have a word with Willy . . . and I'd not be surprised if he'll want us to have a wee half-un to help him celebrate. And then . . ." He looked straight at Barry. "And then the pair of us will have to be getting on home. We've a few phone calls to make."

35

The World Turned Upside Down

The Duck's batwing doors creaked shut behind Barry. He had to wait until his eyes became accustomed to the dim light. There was none of the usual hum of conversation. The place sounded deserted. He saw two figures standing at the bar: Archie Auchinleck and a tall, suntanned young man in a khaki uniform with a corporal's double stripes on the sleeves. Barry guessed the soldier was Archie's son.

"Evening, Doctors," Willy said from behind the bar. "What'll it . . . ?"

"Whiskey," O'Reilly called. "And Barry?"

"Sherry, please." He'd already had one with Sonny and the marquis.

"Good lad. Never mix the grape and the grain. Go and have a seat."

Barry went to the nearest table and waited as O'Reilly strode to the bar, turned sideways, and leant on one elbow. "Evening, Archie. Evening, Rory. Home on leave? Nice to see you."

"I got home last night. It's great to be back, Doc," Rory said. He smiled and lifted his straight pint glass of Guinness. "You can't get a drop like this in Cyprus."

"Nor in the whole bloody Med. At least you couldn't when I was there," said O'Reilly. "How long are you home for?"

"Two weeks, sir."

"Make sure your son makes the most of it," O'Reilly said to Archie. "Willy, give young Rory and his da a pint on me."

"Thanks a lot, Doctor O'Reilly," Archie said.

O'Reilly ignored the thanks. "How's the back, Archie?"

Barry saw the milkman's face split into a great smile. "Right as rain. Them pills was cracker, so they were."

"Good," said O'Reilly, with a glance at Barry. "And I'm sure it doesn't hurt to have your young fellah home for a while either."

He's at it again, Barry thought. The man's never really off duty. Not even in the pub.

O'Reilly clapped the soldier on the back. "Have you no mufti, Rory? I would've thought you'd want to get out of uniform and into civvies."

"I will, sir, but . . ." Barry saw the look of affection pass between son and father. "Da asked me to wear it tonight. I think he wants to show me off, like."

"Just right," said O'Reilly. "I'd be proud of you too. Pity there's only me and Doctor Laverty and Willy to see." O'Reilly turned back to the bar. "Jesus, Willy, are you distilling that whiskey?"

"Sorry, Doctor." Two glasses were set on the bar. O'Reilly paid and took his change. "Business still slack, Willy?"

"It picked up a wee bit in the last day or so," Willy said, "and come nine o'clock the place'll be bustin'. The Rooftop Rangers Regiment'll be in, so it will."

"Who?"

Willy smiled. "That's what I call all the lads from the Highlanders who go straight to Sonny's after work. They don't even go home for their supper. Donal Donnelly has them hard at it, and not just the bandsmen. Just about every able-bodied man in the village wanted to help when the word got out. And the womenfolk take them out loads of tea and pieces so they can eat on the job."

Barry had never understood why a sandwich would be called a piece—but in Ulster it was.

"Aye, and with all the work they're quare nor thirsty when they come in here."

"Good for them," said O'Reilly, picking up his glass.

Willy lowered his voice, and Barry had to strain to hear. "And that's not the half of it. They even have Constable Mulligan giving a hand." Willy's grin was huge. "He comes in with them, and if the place stays

open after ten o'clock closing time, him being still here and all, he'd
have to arrest himself before he arrests me."

"Och," said O'Reilly, "what the eye doesn't see, the heart doesn't
grieve over."

"Aye," said Willy, "and do you know something else, sir?"

O'Reilly took a mouthful of whiskey. "No, but you're going to tell
me."

"Right enough. Donal says it's the village's wedding present to Sonny
and Maggie, and he wants for it to be a surprise. He has everyone sworn
to secrecy. It's all right to ask somebody new to help, but they have to
promise to keep their mouths shut even if they can't turn up on the site.
And *you* know how rumours usually fly round this place."

"Och," said O'Reilly, "it's one of the miracles of modern commu-
nication. Telegraph, telephone . . . and tell a Ballybucklebo resident."
He drank again, as Willy laughed.

Barry had to smile. O'Reilly was certainly spot on with *that* diagnosis.

"Right enough," said Willy, "but nobody's let the cat out of the bag
yet. Nobody's said a dicky bird and . . ." He lowered his voice, and
although Barry strained he couldn't make out what was being said.
Whatever it was it took some time, and O'Reilly finished his drink as
Willy rattled on.

Barry immediately assumed Willy didn't want him to hear, and he
wondered if that was a not-too-subtle indication that he still wasn't
fully trusted. He told himself to stop being paranoid.

"Bloody marvellous!" O'Reilly roared. "That beats Banagher." He
hauled out his briar, lit up, and glanced at his glass. "Jesus, Willy.
There's a hole in this glass. It's empty."

"Sorry, Doc. Will I . . . ?"

"Of course you will; then bring it over to the table . . ." O'Reilly
picked up Barry's glass. "And seeing as how you're not too busy, pour
one for yourself . . . I'm pretending it's your birthday, the way you
did for me last week . . . and you come over and sit with us. Doctor
Laverty and I have something to tell you."

He ambled over to the table and gave Barry his sherry. "Here. Get
that into you." O'Reilly hauled out a chair and sat.

"Cheers." Barry sipped. "I must say you're being very generous tonight, Fingal. Drinks for Archie and his son. One for Willy."

"Och," said O'Reilly, "Rory was the first baby I delivered here when I took over the practice, and after what we've heard about the lease for this place, are you not in better spirits too?"

"Yes. A bit."

"Aye, good," said O'Reilly, turning sideways and stretching out his legs. "And if Arthur Guinness was here I'd buy him a couple of Smithwicks, but he's on probation."

"For wellie-napping?"

"Indeed," O'Reilly said. He hunched forward. "You'll never believe what Willy just told me."

"Go on."

"It's the greatest project since Moses parted the Red Sea. Not only are the lads doing their damnedest to finish the repairs at Sonny's by Saturday night, but Sonny's got no furniture . . ."

"A man who lived in his car hardly would have, would he?"

"Not so much as a footstool, so the boys have got their heads together. Seamus and Maureen Galvin have a table and a clatter of cutlery they're not taking to America. Mr. Coffin, the undertaker, has half a dozen chairs. This one has sheets, that one has a bed, the other one has pots and pans. The list goes on. I don't know what Donal said to get them all fired up, but according to Willy they're as enthusiastic about the whole thing as a bunch of Richard the Lionheart's crusaders were to take Jerusalem. The plan is to have Sonny's place ready to live in by the time the wedding's over."

"Good God. That's fantastic. What a lovely thing to do for Sonny and Maggie." Barry knew he should be grinning, but for some reason he felt a prickling in his eyes and realized he was on the verge of crying. He was grateful for the dim lighting and hoped O'Reilly hadn't noticed.

"Aye," said O'Reilly. "Everyone knows that the pair of them *could* squeeze into Maggie's cottage at a pinch, but it's really far too small for two people, five dogs, and Maggie's cat. When Sonny proposed to Maggie years ago, they planned to move into his place, and they would have but for the row with Bertie Bishop about the roof."

"And the roof's getting fixed now. It's wonderful for the two old folks."

"It's more than that," O'Reilly said seriously. "The whole place's boiling about Bishop's takeover plans for the Duck, and they know he wasn't overexerting himself to get the roof job done in any great hurry. I think it's the village's way of telling Bertie Bishop that they don't need him. That they can manage perfectly well without him. He can, in a word, or rather a few words, stick it in his ear and—"

"Sorry to interrupt, sirs." Willy handed O'Reilly a full glass. "You said I was to join you?"

"Sit down, Willy." O'Reilly pulled his legs out of the way.

Barry shifted in his chair as Willy sat.

"It's a wee drop of port, sir," Willy said, nodding at his own glass. "*Sláinte.*"

"*Sláinte mHath.*" O'Reilly sipped and then said, "Jesus Murphy, Willy, that's Black Bush . . ."

Barry knew it was the best whiskey produced by the Bushmills distillery in County Antrim.

"That's none of your cooking whiskey." O'Reilly smacked his lips. "That's what my old father, God rest his soul, would have called a *real* drop of the craythur."

"I'll not charge you extra for it, sir. I'm finishing up my stock," Willy said, and Barry could see the sadness in the man's eyes. "I'm pleased Sonny and Maggie are going to have a place, right enough, but I still have to be out of here when the lease is up."

"Do you now?" said O'Reilly, leaning back in his chair and letting go a vast cloud of smoke. "That's what Doctor Laverty and I wanted to talk to you about, Willy."

Willy sat rigidly. "Have you got Bishop to change his mind?"

"No," said O'Reilly, "not yet . . ."

Willy's shoulders sagged.

"But by Jesus, we're going to, aren't we, Barry?"

He said it so forcibly that Barry had no choice but to nod. He waited as O'Reilly explained the details of the stream under the pub, the fact that the marquis owned the salmon rights, and most importantly, that His Lordship felt strongly that the Duck shouldn't be mucked about with by Bertie Bishop—and would make damn sure it wasn't. How he'd do that wasn't explained.

All very well, but the marquis hadn't actually promised to go to court. O'Reilly was gambling on Bishop's being frightened off by the threat. But what if Bishop wasn't? Barry knew O'Reilly liked to bet on greyhounds and horses, but here he was wagering with Willy Dunleavy's future. Barry hoped to God O'Reilly was right in his judgment of Bertie Bishop.

"You're having me on, Doctor O'Reilly." Willy's eyes were wide. "It's the truth? About the stream business and His Lordship. Honest to God?"

"Honest to God, Willy. Cross my heart."

Barry hoped O'Reilly had his fingers crossed too. In Ulster, a promise made with crossed fingers wasn't binding.

"I don't know what to say."

"Ah," said O'Reilly, "that's exactly what I want you to do. Say nothing to *anybody*."

Willy nodded.

"You see," O'Reilly continued, "if you don't mind, I think I should be the bearer of the glad tidings to the worthy councillor, and I don't want him to get a whisper of what's in store."

Right, Fingal, Barry thought, and you'd better make bloody sure he caves in.

"I'll houl' my tongue, Doctor, but there is one wee thing."

"What?"

"Can I tell my Mary?"

"She'll keep it to herself?"

"Don't be bloody silly . . . sorry, sir . . . but bartenders hear as many secrets as you doctors. We'd not last long if we couldn't keep our traps shut."

"No need to apologize, Willy," O'Reilly said. "It was silly of me to have asked."

"You see, Mary's having a god-awful time with that Miss Moloney over at the dress shop. If I can be sure . . . You are absolutely certain, sir, that we'll be able to stay on?"

Barry waited to see how O'Reilly would answer.

"Willy, nothing's *sure* in this life except death and taxes, but the marquis says he'll fight Bishop to the extent of his resources."

True, Barry thought, but those resources weren't as limitless as Willy must believe, because Willy said, "Then I can give her a full-time job and she can get away to hell out of that place. Jesus, the number of times the wee girl's come home in tears. She says Miss Moloney gets so angry she goes up and down like a hoor on hinges."

"I know what you mean," Barry said, thinking of how she'd taken him to task when he'd tried to ask her to go a bit easier on Helen. "She went up one side of me and down the other last week."

O'Reilly glanced at Barry. "Willy, you go right ahead and tell Mary."

Willy stood, sank his glass of port in one swallow, and said, "Get those into you, Doctors. There's more coming." He turned and spoke to Archie and his son. "Are youse two on for another pint . . . on me?"

"Aye, certainly," Archie said. "What's the occasion?"

Willy beamed down on O'Reilly. "Doctor O'Reilly here says he's pretending it's my birthday." He winked broadly. "What he doesn't know is that thanks to him and Doctor Laverty . . . it bloody well is." He headed for the bar.

"We shouldn't really be doing this, Fingal," Barry said. It wasn't having another drink he was thinking about.

"I," said O'Reilly, who by his scowl had followed Barry's line of reasoning perfectly, "could not disagree with your diagnosis more, Doctor Laverty. We bloody well should. And we're going to drink to it and to you know what else?"

"No."

"To the good ship Ballybucklebo and all who sail in her. She's a grand wee place." He finished his drink. "I for one wouldn't want to be anywhere else on God's green earth."

Barry hesitated. Then he said, very seriously, "You know, Fingal, I could drink to that myself."

"Right," said O'Reilly, "but it will be the last one." He glanced over to a circular clock hanging behind the bar. "Quarter to six. One's all we've time for before we head home. Kinky'll read us the riot act if we're late. And you," he said, stabbing at Barry with the stem of the briar, "have to phone your Patricia."

"I don't bloody well believe it." O'Reilly opened the back gate. "Where are you, Arthur Guinness?"

It was a question Barry would be happy to be answered. He was wearing one of his new pairs of pants, and he did not want to have them muddied by the Labrador's amorous advances.

"Jesus, Barry, would you look at that?" O'Reilly pointed to a heap of freshly excavated earth beside the back fence. "Either we've got the biggest mole in Ulster, or Arthur Guinness has been watching that film *The Great Escape,* with him cast as Charles Bronson, 'The Tunnel King.'" He bellowed, "Arthur?"

The dog did not appear.

"Damnation." He strode off towards the kitchen door, calling over his shoulder, "Come on, Barry. Arthur had better pretend he's one of Bo Peep's sheep and make bloody sure when he comes home he's dragging his tail behind him."

Barry followed O'Reilly through the door and into the kitchen where Kinky stood wiping flour from a pastry board. O'Reilly was nowhere to be seen.

"Doctor Laverty," she said.

Barry sniffed. "What's that you're cooking, Kinky?"

She smiled. "'Tis a beef stew with suet dumplings, and it'll be ready in twenty minutes, so."

"Lovely," Barry said. Then he asked, "Kinky, have there been any phone calls for me?"

"Not the one."

"Damn." It was six fifteen now so he could forget about hearing from Harry Sloan. If Harry didn't have results by now, he'd not be calling first thing in the morning. Barry'd have another day of uncertainty to face, another day to try to simply get on with his job, as if the bloody thing wasn't in jeopardy.

"Were you expecting to hear from somebody?" Kinky asked.

"Not really."

"I think," she said, "if you don't mind me saying, you *were*." She stopped and looked him straight in the eye. "You will hear," she said, "and you'll hear exactly what you want to. I don't know what that is . . . but it'll not be for a day or two yet."

"How do you know, Kinky?"

She smiled. "I can't tell you that. I just do. You mark my words, so." She crossed the kitchen and stood on tiptoe to return the pastry board to its place on a top shelf. "Now, I've work to do so trot along and get ready for your supper like a good lad."

Barry wondered as he climbed the stairs what the blazes Kinky had meant by "you'll hear exactly what you want to"? How did she know what he wanted to hear? That Major Fotheringham's postmortem had turned up the needle in the haystack? That his future was assured in Ballybucklebo? He sighed. But then, he banged his hands off the banister, would he stay if Patricia had won the scholarship?

He went into the bathroom. As if those questions weren't enough to gnaw at, could O'Reilly really coerce Bertie Bishop into giving up his notion of taking over the Black Swan? Perhaps, Barry thought, he himself had enough on his plate. He'd leave that one to O'Reilly.

He washed his hands, was troubled by a fleeting image of Pontius Pilate, realized he must support his older colleague, and headed downstairs into the hall.

O'Reilly was talking on the telephone. ". . . right. I'll pick you up at ten thirty on Saturday. Bye." He replaced the receiver with a loud *ting*, rubbed his hands, smiled broadly, turned, and saw Barry. "None of your business," he said.

Barry held up both hands. "I wasn't going to ask."

"Good," said O'Reilly. "Now. I'm off for a widdle—"

"Into the Rover's petrol tank?"

"Ha bloody ha. " But O'Reilly was grinning. "No. Upstairs." He nodded at the receiver. "Your turn." O'Reilly started to climb.

"Thanks, Fingal." Barry lifted the receiver, dialled Kinnegar 657334, and waited. "Hello. Patricia?"

"Barry?"

He thought she sounded tired. "How did it go?"

She sighed, then said, "It was bloody awful. I told you in the Chinese place that I hate architectural drawing. Two of the six questions involved drawing up plans. They were horrid. I made a complete mess of both of them. I can't have won. I can't."

He thought she sounded close to tears. He knew he must say something, but what? "Patricia, listen. I'm an expert in sitting exams . . ."

"Not in civil engineering."

"It doesn't matter. I took them for six years. An exam's an exam, and I'll bet you're going through exactly what I did, and what all my friends did."

"What's that?"

"If we hadn't learnt much about the subject, we were always sure we'd passed. We were too ignorant to know how much we *didn't* know." She'd not appreciate being reminded that failure was always a possibility, but he ploughed on. "Those were the exams some of us failed."

"That's a great comfort."

"Now just hang on. There's the other side. Once in a while some of us really did have a firm grip on the subject." He had to smile. In his own case and in Jack Mills's, that hadn't been too often. "Immediately after those tests we were convinced we'd failed because we were acutely aware that no matter how much we knew, there was always a hell of a lot more we should have known. But that didn't mean we hadn't done well."

"Honestly?"

"Of course. I'll bet you're doing the selfsame thing; indeed I'll bet you've aced it."

He heard her sigh. "I'm not so sure."

"Come on. Cheer up. Even if you're right"—he glanced around to be sure he couldn't be overheard—"I'll still love you . . . darling."

"I know and . . . I love you, Barry."

He pursed his lips, grinned, and made an okay sign with his finger and thumb.

"Barry . . . ?" He heard the hesitation. "I'd like to see you soon, but I can't."

"Why not?"

"Dad and Mum think I should be home in Newry now to wait for the results."

Damnation, he thought. But he said, "It's maybe not such a bad thing to head home." At that moment he'd not mind being able to have a few words with his folks about his own troubles, but they were in Australia. Although what his dad would say if Barry ended up in court was not something he wanted to think about.

"I knew you'd understand."

"There are times families come in handy, and this is one of them."

"Dad's picking me up here at seven, but I'll be back on Saturday morning, and I promise if I get any results before that, I'll phone you at once."

"I'll never speak to you again if you don't."

"Barry!"

"I'm as anxious as you to hear." Even, he thought, if my reasons for anxiety are a bit different from yours. "Listen," he said, "you go home. Try not to worry too much. Worrying won't change anything . . ." A fine one you are, Barry Laverty, he thought, to be giving *that* advice. "And I'll see you on Saturday. I'll pick you up at one. The wedding's at two."

"All right," she said, "and I'll try not to worry. I promise."

"Good lass." He blew her a kiss. "I'll be thinking of you."

"I love you, Barry. I'll see you on Saturday." But before he could speak he heard the line go dead. He hung up and wondered what was keeping O'Reilly. Unless the man had serious prostatic trouble like Kieran O'Hagan, he shouldn't be spending such a long time in the bathroom. Barry realized his senior colleague was being tactful.

Barry went into the dining room and sat at the table. He jumped when Lady Macbeth, apparently arriving from thin air, landed on his lap, butted at his tummy, and started to turn circles in his lap, lifting each paw high and putting it back down with considerable force, a series of actions O'Reilly called "twiddle and stamp."

Barry idly fondled the cat's head and was rewarded with a continuous, rumbling purr.

"There you are, Your Ladyship," O'Reilly announced on his way to his seat at the head of the table. He sat. "Buggered if I understand it, Barry," he said.

"Understand what?"

"Cats are meant to roam around, but Her Ladyship never leaves the place. Dogs are meant to be homebodies, but Arthur has wanderlust. The world's turned upside down. Lord Cornwallis's band played that," said O'Reilly.

"Who?"

"General Cornwallis. "The World Turned Upside Down." That's the tune his regimental bands played when they marched to surrender to the American revolutionaries after Yorktown, the battle that lost George III the American colonies."

"I didn't know that, but I know some of the words of the song:

"If buttercups buzzed after the bee,
    If boats were on land, churches on sea . . .""

"That's it," said O'Reilly, picking up a bread roll. "I wonder does Bertie Bishop know the tune?"

"Why?"

"Because tomorrow you're seeing Flo Bishop to find out if your treatment's working. No doubt the great panjandrum will be with her, and Yorktown be damned, that battle was really only a skirmish. Bertie Bishop has a date with a real donnybrook . . . his Waterloo."

36

Yet I Shall Temper So
Justice with Mercy

"God," said O'Reilly, taking his place at the head of the dining room table, "a surgery like this morning's would give a man an appetite."

Barry sat. There was some truth to his senior colleague's words, but Wednesday morning had flown by for him, patient by patient. He'd had no time to dwell on anything else. He'd certainly not given any thought to his stomach.

"Any calls for this afternoon, Kinky?" O'Reilly asked, when Mrs. Kincaid came in.

"Two," she said, "but neither's urgent." She handed the list to O'Reilly and set a willow-pattern tureen in the middle of the table.

"Just soup again?" O'Reilly was pouting.

"With all the dumplings you put inside you at dinner last night, you need something lighter for your lunch," she said. "But there's hot-buttered barmbrack for after. I've to run along and toast it." She hesitated at the dining room doorway. "Maybe the raisins in the brack'll sweeten you up, Doctor dear."

Barry hid his smile as he lifted the tureen's lid. "Fingal?"

"I suppose so." O'Reilly sighed and passed his plate. "What's Kinky given us this time?"

Barry inhaled a mixture of the scents of garlic, cloves, onion, and rich meat. "Smells like mock turtle to me." Barry returned the full plate to O'Reilly, then helped himself.

"Huh." O'Reilly sniffed, filled his spoon, and shoved it in his mouth. "It is," he said, smiling. "And it's bloody good." He eyed the tureen. "Just a pity there's not more of it. Galloping about half the night looking for Arthur Guinness, then having the surgery as full as it was, would make anybody ravenous." He shovelled in another mouthful. "Now, hold your wheest," he said, "and let me eat up. My grandfather used to say, 'Eating time's eating time, and talking time's talking time' . . . and he was right."

Barry was happy to say nothing because he didn't trust himself not to giggle. He'd conjured up a picture of a vole he'd learnt about in his first-year biology classes, an animal that ate twice its own weight every day. In his imagination, the little rodent had bushy eyebrows, cauliflower ears, and a bent nose, and it was ladling soup into itself as if it hadn't eaten for weeks. Barry emptied his plate, glanced at the tureen, saw that it held about half a serving, and decided discretion was the better part of valour. "Do you want to eat that up, Fingal?"

"Shame to waste it."

Barry heard the ladle scrape so hard against the tureen's bottom that he feared O'Reilly had removed the blue pagodas and weeping willows fired into the china.

Someone rang the front doorbell, and Barry heard Kinky open the door. He was happy to let her deal with whoever it was. A month ago he'd have been out of his chair and into the hall to see what the patient was complaining of. Now he had complete faith in Kinky's ability to tell emergencies from routine cases. O'Reilly had called her his Cerberus, the dog that guarded the entrance to the underworld. It was a fair description.

Barry thought he could hear Bertie Bishop's voice. O'Reilly had arranged for the Bishops to be seen at one o'clock so he and Barry could take as much time as the consultation required. They'd not have to worry about the waiting room being full, and other patients unreasonably delayed.

"That was great, if a little on the stingy side," said O'Reilly, pushing his plate away. The remnants had disappeared down O'Reilly's throat in three swallows. He sat back, rubbed his waistcoat's belly button, and announced, "To paraphrase the Reverend Dodgson, better known as Lewis Carroll, 'Soup of the noontime, beau-ootiful soo-oop!'"

"*Alice's Adventures in Wonderland?* Or *Through the Looking-Glass?*" Barry asked. "I can't remember."

"Neither," said O'Reilly, "can I."

"It was *Wonderland,*" said Kinky, coming in with a plate of barmbrack and a pot of tea. "I read it when I was a little girl. And it was the Mock Turtle said it, so." She put the plate and teapot on the table and lifted the empty tureen. "I've often wondered what real turtle soup tastes like, but those creatures are hard to come by in County Down."

"Actually, it's quite delicious," O'Reilly remarked, "but it's a bit hard on the poor old turtle. Stick to the mock stuff, Kinky. It's grand."

"Glad you enjoyed it," she said. "Now don't take too long over your tea. I've just let Bertie and Flo Bishop into the surgery. He's as irritable as a dog with fleas, pacing up and down like a bullock in a gelding pen."

"Och, sure, the exercise'll do him good," said O'Reilly, helping himself to a slice of barmbrack. He grinned at Kinky. "Doctor Laverty and I have a little surprise for him."

Barry cleared his throat. It was all very well for O'Reilly to sound confident. His plan to discomfit the councillor was far from foolproof.

"Aye, so?" She cocked her head to one side.

Barry poured himself a cup of tea and lifted a piece of the speckled toast.

"Yes," said O'Reilly, "and we've you to thank for it."

"Me?"

"Indeed. You found out from Flo about the stream that runs under the Duck."

"A stream under the Duck? Now there's a thing."

"Yes. And that stream, small as it is, is going to be Bertie Bishop's downfall. He'll not be able to do anything with the Duck."

You *hope* it's going to be his downfall, Barry thought. He expected Kinky to ask why the little waterway was so important, but she simply nodded and said, "If you say so, Doctor O'Reilly. I'll take your word for it. Just don't let him know who told me. He's a vindictive little bashtoon, and I'd not want him to go after Flo."

"Don't worry about that, Kinky," O'Reilly said. "Flo and her secret are safe with us." He grinned at Barry. "But Bertie Bishop isn't, is he?"

"I hope not, Fingal."

"That," said Kinky, "is the best news I've had all week. You're going to scuttle him, aren't you?"

"We are," said O'Reilly, with the confidence of a man placing a bet after the race was over and the results were known to him, but not to the bookie.

She smiled and bobbed her head slightly. "Sometimes Doctor O'Reilly, the pair of you are the great ones for the quoting, but if you sort out Bertie I've a thought for you."

"Go on."

"Do you know what King David said after Saul and Jonathan were killed?"

"I do," said O'Reilly. " 'How are the mighty fallen'?"

" 'Tell it not in Gath,' " she said, chuckling, her chins wobbling, " '. . . lest the daughters of the Philistines rejoice.' "

"Good for you, Kinky," O'Reilly said, "but this isn't Gath, it's Ballybucklebo, and the word'll be out like a flash."

And what will you say to Willy if Bishop calls your bluff? Barry thought.

O'Reilly rose and dusted barmbrack crumbs off his waistcoat. "Let's wait until we've had a word with Bertie. I've a notion that with the right encouragement he might be persuaded to spread the word himself *and* do my young colleague a bit of good while he's at it."

Barry wondered what O'Reilly meant, but O'Reilly was out of the dining room and heading for the surgery before he had time to ask. "Come on, Doctor Laverty," he called from the hall. "It's a terrible shame to keep the Bishops waiting, and they're your cases. Both of them. I want you to bring the tidings of comfort and joy to Bertie, but I'll be there to help out if you need me to. Lead on, Macduff."

Barry rose, eager to see how Mrs. Bishop was doing, but uncertain about how he should handle the councillor. This was O'Reilly's scheme. He should see it through.

The councillor had stopped his pacing, and he and Mrs. Bishop were seated on the wooden chairs. Barry knew O'Reilly had shortened the chairs' front legs years ago so that the patients would be uncomfortable and would not be tempted to stay too long. By the look on both the Bishops' faces, the strategy was working.

Bertie Bishop was dressed in his black suit, holding his bowler hat by the brim, turning it between his fingers. Mrs. Bishop wore a simple blue dress and a little hat with a half-veil. Barry thought she looked brighter, less lethargic. The councillor half turned when Barry said, "Good afternoon."

"About time, Laverty," the councillor grumbled. "Where the hell's O'Reilly?"

"And a very good afternoon to you too, Bertie," O'Reilly said pleasantly, entering the room with a nod of his head to Barry. He hoisted himself on the examining couch out of Bishop's line of sight.

Barry took the swivel chair. "Hello, Mrs. Bishop. How are you today?"

"Doctor Laverty." She positively beamed at him. "It's a miracle, so it is. I've been taking them wee pills . . . just like you said, and I'm running round like a bee on a hot brick, and sure wasn't I telling Cissie Sloan this morning how grand I am? and I've all my energy back . . ."

"Too much if you ask me," the councillor said. "A week ago she couldn't finish a sentence. Now she never stops craking on . . ."

"And I can do all my housework, and I'm not one wee bit tired, and my bowels is great, and I've my appetite back, but I haven't put on an ounce, and . . ."

"See what I mean? I can't get a bloody word in edgewise."

Barry glanced at O'Reilly and immediately had to look away. His senior colleague was grinning from ear to ear. It would *not* be appropriate for Barry to laugh. "I'm very glad to hear you're feeling better. Very glad," he said. "Now Flo, you remember the last time you were in I asked you to lift and lower your arm?"

She stood. "Like this?" Her arm went up and down effortlessly. "I could keep this up all day, and . . ."

"You . . . you can stop," Barry said quickly. "That's excellent, Flo. You can sit down." He looked at O'Reilly, who held up one thumb. Barry nearly held up one of his own he was so delighted that his diagnosis and prescribed treatment had both been right. "You're on the mend. I'm very pleased."

"Not near as pleased as I am, Doctor Laverty, and . . ." She turned to her husband. "You said these two doctors were nothing but a couple of quacks, and I'd be better off seeing a vet, and that there was nothing wrong with me, and I was just bone idle, and . . ."

"Yes, dear," the councillor said. He raised his eyes to the heavens, then looked at Barry. "I don't suppose you could maybe cut the dose down a bit, Doctor?"

"I'm sorry," Barry said, "but I don't think so."

"I don't want you to," she said, "and I want to ask you, Doctor, if you've any other pills?" She glanced shyly down at her ample girth. "I'd like to lose a bit of weight, and as far as I'm concerned I hardly eat enough to feed a sparrow, and Cissie Sloan says when she was all slowed down and her bowels bound up you give her tablets that fixed her thyroid, and she lost weight, and . . ."

"Hold on a minute, Flo," Barry interrupted, glad that O'Reilly had had her come in the afternoon with lots of time to spare. He was beginning to feel a tiny tad of sympathy for the councillor. "I can't discuss another patient with you." He remembered Cissie Sloan very well. Pity she shared a surname with a pathologist about whom he'd rather not be reminded. Last month Barry'd diagnosed Cissie's hypothyroidism, a diagnosis O'Reilly had missed. "The pills I gave her won't do for you unless there's something wrong with your thyroid gland."

"Oh." Mrs. Bishop looked crestfallen.

"Perhaps," Barry said, "we should get it checked just in case." That was a slice of luck. He'd forgotten to order the test last week even though he knew myasthenia gravis could be a sign of a thyroid disorder. Now he could send her off for the necessary testing without having to confess his sin of omission. A bit dishonest perhaps, but certainly the kind of opportunity O'Reilly would have seized, judging by the way he was holding up his thumb again. "I'll write the forms," Barry said, swivelling to the rolltop desk and scribbling a requisition.

"I suppose," Mrs. Bishop said, "if my thyroid's okay I'll just have to go on a diet."

"That's right."

"Have a word with Kinky about that," said O'Reilly a little testily. "She's very big on soups and salads."

Barry smiled and handed the form to Mrs. Bishop. "They'll do the blood tests down in Bangor. It'll save you a trip up to Belfast."

"Great. Bertie, you can run me down this afternoon, and I could do a bit of shopping, and I need a new hat for the wedding, and the hats in Bangor is far better than them ones in Miss Moloney's, and . . ."

"I can do no such thing," Councillor Bishop snapped. "I've to see Willy Dunleavy at two and get this thing with the Duck wrapped up."

Barry hesitated.

O'Reilly leant his head to one side and offered both hands, palms up, arms outstretched to Barry, saying in mime, "It's all yours, son."

Barry clenched his right fist. If he was going to bluff Bertie Bishop, this would have to be handled with as much confidence and authority as he could muster. "That would be the matter of the lease, Mr. Bishop?"

"It's none of your bloody business, Laverty, but yes. It is."

"Mr. Bishop, when you were in here last, Doctor O'Reilly said a little bird had told him you were going to chuck Willy Dunleavy and Mary out, and you told us the little bird could go and pluck itself."

"I did and I meant it, so I did."

Barry took a deep breath. "Mr. Bishop, Doctor O'Reilly and I have been having a word with a much bigger bird. Much bigger."

"What are you on about?" Bishop's little eyes narrowed.

Barry fixed Bishop with a glare and said levelly, "The marquis of Ballybucklebo owns the salmon rights to the stream that runs under the Black Swan."

Bishop's eyes widened. He sat back in his chair, then leapt to his feet. The colour drained from his face. He gobbled. The wattles of his neck quivered. His face turned puce.

Barry felt his clenched fist relax. "The salmon rights, Councillor."

"Who the hell told you about the stream? Who the hell told you?"

He turned on his wife. "Jesus, Flo, have you been flapping your jaw when I told you not to?" His grip on his bowler tightened. His knuckles turned white. "Have you?"

She was reduced to silence, which Barry, although he knew he shouldn't, found refreshing. "Mrs. Bishop, did you say anything to me or Doctor O'Reilly about this?"

"No, but . . ."

"There, Councillor. You can't blame your wife." Barry looked at her and rapidly shook his head. He had no intention of letting her say another word. They'd promised Kinky they'd protect her. "In fact, it came out in a conversation when His Lordship and Sonny were discussing Norman land titles. Sonny knew all about the stream." He was bending the truth again, but it was in a very good cause. "His Lordship told us you can do nothing to the Duck without his permission."

"We'll see about that, so we will. I'm going to lose a fortune if I can't go ahead."

"But," Barry said, "the marquis was very clear about the conditions of the deeds."

"Deeds, is it? Deeds, by God? I'll take him to court." Bishop stood, eyes narrowing again. "I'll get those bloody rights, so I will."

The man's response was exactly as O'Reilly had predicted. If Barry was going to checkmate him, he'd have to force Bishop to believe that a lawsuit wasn't going to work.

"The marquis is quite prepared for you."

"Prepared? How's he prepared? I know for a fact all his money's tied up in running the estate." There was a more confident tone to the man's voice.

Barry's fingers curled. He glanced at O'Reilly, but the big man's face was impassive, a poker face. And poker hands could be won if a bluff was courageous enough.

"Councillor Bishop, I was there, and so was Doctor O'Reilly when His Lordship said he'd fight you to the limit of his resources. The very limit."

Bishop's brow wrinkled. He looked at O'Reilly and back to Barry. "Did he say that? Honest to God?"

Barry nodded. He watched the play of emotions on Bishop's face. The man must be calculating how much potential profit he'd be losing against the costs of a lawsuit. His mind must be working, Barry thought, with the speed of one of those new IBM computers.

"You're not having me on?" There was a catch in his voice. "The limit?"

"Mr. Bishop," Barry said, with all the dignity he could muster. "I'm a doctor. What the hell would I have to gain by lying to you?" This victory, the Duck, Willy's and Mary's futures, and the preservation of O'Reilly's reputation, that's what. Barry held his breath.

The rotund little man flopped back down onto his chair. "Jesus. That buggers it." He scowled at Barry. "I'd go bust." His head drooped.

Barry exhaled. He'd won and the feeling was grand.

"It's all that ould goat Sonny's fault. I should never have let you two talk me into fixing his bloody roof."

"Actually," Barry said, "you're not."

"*Now* what are you on about? I've had Seamus and Donal out there working for the last ten days."

Barry shook his head. "Since last night Donal has had a work crew from the village hard at it . . ."

"And," O'Reilly added, "apart from the materials it's not costing you a penny, Bertie."

"You mean . . ."

"That's right. You're getting the labour for free now."

"Free? Nobody does nothing for free. What are they after?"

"I think," Barry said, "the whole village would like you to leave the Duck as it is."

"I don't have much choice about that, do I?" Barry thought the fat little man was going to spit.

"No," said O'Reilly, slipping down from the examining table, "you don't, but you could turn it to your advantage."

Barry watched Bishop's eyes narrow and a furrow appear between his eyebrows. "My advantage?"

"Well," said O'Reilly, "your stock went up last month when you agreed to fix Sonny's roof."

"I'd not have if you two hadn't . . ." He bit off the rest of the sentence. "But nobody knows about that except us, do they?"

O'Reilly nodded. "And nobody need know about the deeds. You just tell the village you've changed your mind. It's your civic duty as a councillor."

Mrs. Bishop chipped in, "I think you should, Bertie. I really do, and everybody would be all pleased, and . . ."

"Jesus, Flo, when I want your opinion I'll tell you what it is. I'm talking to the doctors. Now houl' your wheest. Go on, Doctor O'Reilly."

The use of his senior colleague's title was not lost on Barry.

"I think, Bertie . . . you and Flo'll be at the wedding, won't you?"

"Aye."

"And there'll be lots of speechifying?"

"Aye."

"You're an important man round here. You could say a word or two."

"I suppose."

"And," said O'Reilly, "far be it from me to put the words in your mouth, but it would be a grand time to make the announcement."

"It would, wouldn't it?"

"You could say something else too, Bertie." Mrs. Bishop wagged her finger at her husband.

"I told you to houl'—"

"I won't. I've something important to say." She turned to Barry. "I'm sorry, Doctor Laverty, but some folks round here have been saying you don't know your job."

"Don't let the gossip worry you, Flo." At that moment, still savouring his defeat of the councillor and knowing that O'Reilly would be delighted, Barry could afford not to be upset by her comment.

"But I think you done a miracle for me."

"Hardly a miracle," he said.

"Well, *I* think it was, and I know . . . didn't you just tell me you couldn't discuss Cissie Sloan with anybody?" The words rattled out. "So you can't go round blowing your own trumpet about fixing me up. Can you?"

"No, I can't."

"But *you* could, Bertie. When you're up on your hind legs, blowing on about what a Christian you are, it wouldn't hurt to say a word or two about Doctor Laverty and me, and . . ."

"All right, Flo. All right." The councillor sighed and set his bowler on his head. "I'll say the words on Saturday, but youse doctors won't say nothing about the deeds?"

"Not a word," said O'Reilly. "We know it's important for you to look like the white knight."

"In that case," said Bishop, turning towards the door, "come on, Flo. I'll take you to Bangor."

"There's only one more thing, Bertie," O'Reilly said.

"What?" Bishop swung back.

"I think . . . now I could be wrong . . . it would be appreciated by the lads working at Sonny's if somebody went round to the Duck and bought a couple of barrels of stout and took them out to Sonny's. Fixing roofs is thirsty work."

Bishop clenched his teeth. "Jesus, between you and Laverty you'll have me ruined. I won't. They can buy their own booze."

"If you don't, it's just possible the word could slip out about the marquis and the lease, and what an opportunist you really are." Barry heard the steel in O'Reilly's voice.

"All right, O'Reilly."

"No," O'Reilly said. "No. No. To you, Bertie, it's *Doctor* O'Reilly and *Doctor* Laverty. Do try to remember."

Bishop took a deep breath, used both hands to pull on the brim of his bowler, and muttered, "All right, *Doctor* O'Reilly." He grabbed his wife by the hand. "Come on, Flo."

"No," she said, standing her ground, "not until you've said thank-you to Doctor Laverty."

Barry could see and hear Mrs. Brown telling her son Colin to say thank-you to the nice doctor for stitching up his hand.

"Thank you, Doctor Laverty," said Councillor Bishop.

"Now," said Mrs. Bishop, pulling the councillor's hand, "you can take me to Bangor and . . ." The couple left. The last thing Barry heard as the front door was closing behind the couple was, "and . . ."

O'Reilly leant against the couch, pulled out his briar, lit up, and chuckled. "Well done, Barry." He belched smoke.

"It is nice to be right once in a while," Barry said.

"It is, and you've been right more than once in the last couple of weeks."

Barry inclined his head. "Thank you for rowing into the discussion, Fingal."

"I hardly needed to. You did just what I expected. I was watching your face. I know you don't like bending the truth, but the way you told Bishop about the marquis going to the limit . . ."

"That was your line to Willy, Fingal."

"And what's wrong with using one of my lines?"

"Nothing."

"It's just like when I was boxing. Nothing beats the old one-two punch."

Barry grinned. "You fixed the councillor again, Fingal."

"No." O'Reilly jabbed his pipe stem at Barry. "You fixed him, Barry. I just gave the last nail in his coffin lid a wee tap. We're a good team." He shoved the pipe back in his mouth. "Right. Willy knows, and Sonny and the marquis, and Kinky, of course, but we should say no more about this. We can let Bertie's moment of glory come as a surprise to the locals."

"Fair enough."

O'Reilly's grin was wide. "And once he's made the public announcement . . ."

"He'll not be able to retract."

"Game, set, and match," said O'Reilly. He started to the door. "Right. We've two home visits to make, a quick trip into the Duck to tell Willy that he's really safe, then home . . ."—his stomach rumbled—"home for tea."

37

How Glorious He Has Restored the Roof

"It'll be easier when the kiddies go back to school next month," O'Reilly remarked from where he sat on the couch. Thursday morning's surgery had seemed to Barry like a paediatric outpatients clinic. Summer colds, hay fever, one case of severe sunburn, and one little boy with a glass marble stuck in his left nostril. The case had reminded Barry of his old professor of otorhynolaryngology's dictum: "Never stick anything in your nose or your ear smaller than your elbow."

O'Reilly had let Barry do the consulting, barely offering a word or a nod of encouragement, never questioning Barry's judgment. Just as well he made me work, Barry thought, while O'Reilly went to fetch the next patient. His prescription for keeping me too busy to dwell on unpleasant matters was working—up to a point.

O'Reilly held the surgery door wider. "Go on in, Helen," he said. "I'll be back in a minute." He closed the door.

Barry rose. "Hello, Helen. Have a seat." He noticed she wasn't wearing gloves or a long-sleeved blouse. The sun's rays soaring in through the bow window put highlights in her chestnut hair. She used both hands to arrange her ankle-length skirt underneath her. Then she sat and crossed her legs.

"How are you this morning?"

He saw the laughter in her eyes. "Better," she said, "much better." She held out her arms to him. "See?"

The angry, red, scaly rashes in the folds of her wrists and elbows had faded to a barely noticeable pink. "That's very good," he said. "How about behind your knees?"

Helen stood, turned, and hitched up her skirt.

Damn. The skin behind her knees was no better. "That's not so good."

She dropped her skirt. "It's not as bad as it was." She sat. "It's not nearly as itchy, and it'll really start to improve by tonight."

Barry was puzzled. He parked himself in the swivel chair, leant forward, and steepled his fingers. He realized he needed only half-moon glasses to be a living replica of his mentor. "Why this evening, Helen?"

She crossed her legs. "I'll be handing in my cards after work today."

Barry heard the door open, looked up, and saw O'Reilly enter. "It's only me. Pay no heed," he said.

Barry turned his attention back to the patient. "You'll be giving your notice, Helen?"

"Oh, aye. Now that wee Mary's going to be all right, so she is."

Barry glanced at O'Reilly, who stood in the background, arms folded, one eyebrow raised.

"Mary's da's able to find more work for her," Helen said. "Don't ask me how, with that man Bishop going to take over the Duck." Her lip curled.

"I'm not sure . . ." Barry bit off the words, "how Mr. Dunleavy can do that, under the circumstances." They hadn't taught him at medical school just how important hiding the truth could be in the day-to-day running of a practice. "I'm sure Willy knows what he's doing."

"He's a sound man, Willy Dunleavy," O'Reilly added, with a wink to Barry.

"Anyhow," Helen said, "Mary'll be all done tonight. She's only part-time so she can go any time. I'll be gone then too."

"I thought you'd have to give at least a week's notice, and Miss Moloney's going to need help. In the next couple of days she'll be selling all those hats for the wedding." He saw a light, deep in Helen's emerald eyes, a light that burned fiercely—and it wasn't simply reflected sunlight.

"Maybe she will and maybe she won't," said Helen. "We'll just have to see."

"I'm not sure I understand."

She tossed her hair. "Do you know, Doctor Laverty? Least said, soonest mended."

He was being told to mind his own business. "Fair enough." He took one of her hands, turned it over, and inspected the healing rash. "More to the point, it really does look as if the eczema's clearing up."

"It is."

"To be honest, Helen, I don't know if it's the treatment or the fact you'll be leaving Miss Moloney's that's doing the trick, but I think you should keep on using the ointment for a while longer." He released her hand.

"I'll do that, Doctor Laverty. I just thought I'd pop in today to let you know I was getting better. It never hurts for anyone to be told they're doing their job right. If only that ould heifer Moloney knew that."

"Thanks, Helen." Barry rose. "I think you're a better psychologist than me."

"Divil the bit of that," she said, with a shake of her head. "And you're a good doctor." She rose. "Only once in a while, the Lord helps those that help themselves. And leaving Miss Moloney is up to me. Not you."

"True."

"So," she said, "I'll maybe see you both on Saturday?"

"You will that," O'Reilly said.

"Good, and I'll let you know then how I got on with Miss Moloney."

"Good," said Barry, showing her to the door. "I'll be interested to hear."

"You'll hear all right. I've a wee going-away present for her."

Once more he saw the fires burning in her eyes. Even though he hadn't the faintest idea what she was talking about, he was somehow grateful, that the going-away present was meant for someone other than him.

Barry closed the surgery door and faced O'Reilly. "I wonder what she means by that?"

"Did you see the look in her eyes?"

"I did."

"'Nor hell a fury like a woman scorn'd,'" O'Reilly said.

"Congreve. *The Old Bachelor*," Barry said, without thinking. Then he looked at O'Reilly, himself a fifty-six-year-old widower thanks to Hitler's *Luftwaffe* in 1941. O'Reilly was grinning, clearly not one bit upset to be reminded of his loss, a loss Barry knew had come after only six months of marriage.

"Well done, Barry. A couple of days ago you wouldn't have bothered even trying to give me the source, but you're right. It was William Congreve. Sixteen ninety-three, and if memory serves that was only three years after the Battle of the Boyne."

"Of glorious and immortal memory," said Barry. He went over to the desk, asking as he did, "Who's next?"

O'Reilly's answer was the scraping of a match against the sandpaper side of a matchbox, followed by a gout of tobacco smoke. "Helen was the last for the morning. But I've a bit of news for you."

"Oh?"

"Aye. I went out a minute ago to make a call."

Barry tensed. Could O'Reilly somehow have contacted Harry Sloan?

"I had a wee word with Charley Greer."

Barry's shoulders slumped.

"He saw Declan last night. He's sorry he didn't phone us then, but there was a car crash and he was in the operating theatre half the night, sorting out a depressed skull fracture. Anyway he was waiting until he had the results of some tests before he phoned."

"What did he say?"

"Charley reckons Declan's a good candidate for surgery. His cerebral angiogram's just finished, and Charley's had a look at the plates. He says the X-rays of the arteries show only a tad of atherosclerosis. He can't cure that, but at least he's pretty sure he can give the old boy a bit of relief from his Parkinson's symptoms."

"I'm glad to hear that. His wife will be pleased."

"She's not the only one. I've known Declan and Mélanie since I came here. They're a lovely couple. It's been miserable watching the poor old fellah go downhill." O'Reilly tapped his pipe mouthpiece against his lower teeth and said, almost to himself, "I wonder should I have sent him up to see Charley sooner?"

Barry wasn't sure what to say. Ever since the major's cerebral bleed last month, Barry had found himself in quiet moments asking, What if? What if he'd been more thorough in his examination? What if the guardian angel of doctors had been on duty that night and had nudged Barry to wonder whether there might be something more at stake than a simple stiff neck? He knew he was young and inexperienced, was bound to have doubts, but he had never suspected that O'Reilly was troubled by those kinds of questions.

"It's always a bugger," O'Reilly said quietly, "trying to decide when to hold back and when to act. Declan and Mélanie won't have that many years left together. Maybe if I'd sent Declan for surgery sooner, the years would have been better." O'Reilly shoved his briar back into his mouth, shrugged, and said, "I did ask Charley and he didn't think he would have done anything back then. He isn't too keen to operate unless the symptoms are seriously advanced."

"And they are now. Declan's tremors are much more pronounced. He can hardly take more than a few steps, and the poor man's incontinent. He wasn't as bad the first time I saw him with you, and that was only a few weeks ago."

"You're right." O'Reilly stared out through the surgery window before turning back to Barry. "What Charley's doing is pretty new, and it's very much a last-ditch effort. To tell you the truth I'm not entirely sure what the nutcrackers do now. Back when I was a student, if only one side of the patient's body was affected they cut nerve tracts in the spinal cord in the neck. The tremors stopped but the patient could be left paralysed down that side."

"I had to scrub for a case last year," Barry said. "It's pretty eerie. It's all done under local anaesthesia."

"Really?"

Barry nodded. "The idea is to destroy the diseased part of the brain, either the globus pallidus or the thalamus, that causes the trembling. The surgeons freeze the scalp, make tiny holes in the skull, and use a device clamped to the skull to guide a needle down through the brain into the target."

"And the patient's awake?"

"They have to be. I'll never forget the surgeon watching the man's hand. As the tissue was destroyed the trembling got less and less. It was quite remarkable. Every once in a while the surgeon would ask the patient to wiggle his fingers. As soon as he had the slightest difficulty the needle was removed. It's a pretty narrow margin between improvement and making things worse."

"I can understand why Charley's in no tearing rush to operate."

"So can I. A cure's not guaranteed, and some of the patients are much worse off than before they had the surgery."

"That's what makes Charley Greer such a damn fine surgeon."

"What is?"

"He doesn't just know how to operate . . . he knows *when* to operate and that's important. Some of the younger surgeons are far too quick off the mark." O'Reilly headed for the door. "He's not sure what day he'll do it, but he's agreed to keep Declan in. Mélanie needs the rest. That's one call we've to make this afternoon." He opened the door. "We'll go round and let her know, deal with whatever's on Kinky's list, and finish up out at Sonny's. I'd not mind seeing how Donal and his merry men are getting on."

As O'Reilly had promised, they'd visited a grateful Mélanie Finnegan to explain about Declan, then made three other calls at houses in the estate. Myrtle MacVeigh, fully recovered from her pyelonephritis, had asked for Barry to have a look at young Peter, who'd twisted his ankle jumping down from Paddy's tractor. Barry had assured her that no bones were broken—it was only a minor sprain that would heal with a few days' rest.

By the time O'Reilly had driven to Sonny's house, the mid-August sun was casting long shadows.

O'Reilly had to leave the Rover some distance from the house.

Parked cars, vans, and a milk float straggled along the verges of the narrow road.

"Come on," O'Reilly said, striding off.

As Barry followed he heard the squabbling of a flock of jackdaws. They wheeled and tumbled over three ivy-covered elms that grew behind the wall on the opposite side of the road from where O'Reilly had parked. He noticed how dull the trees' spearhead-shaped leaves looked. Several at the top of the centre elm were already turning. It was early for that, he knew, but it had been a drier than usual summer.

The evening air was buttermilk warm, scented with mown hay and musk mallow. Swallows dived and soared, wings flickering, forked tails never still, feeding on early evening moths. A cloud of midges swirled beneath one of the elms, each insect a tiny stitch in the gossamer fabric of the dancing swarm.

A pied wagtail bobbed along the top of the roadside drystone wall, his black-and-white evening dress bright in the sunlight. The bird scolded Barry: "*Tchizzick, tchizzick.*"

"Come on," O'Reilly yelled, holding the creaky old cast-iron gate open.

Donal's Abstract Expressionist bicycle was propped against the gatepost. Barry hesitated and stared at the scene ahead. "What did Willy call them?"

"The Rooftop Rangers Regiment," O'Reilly said. "But I think he underestimated. It's more like the whole bloody army's in there."

Men worked in the garden, shifting Sonny's collection of junk to one end beside his dogs' caravan. Shouts and sounds of hammering rattled down from above where Barry could see five men lying flat on ladders with special flanges hooked to the ridge line of the roof. They called to each other and whaled away, driving nails through holes in the grey-blue slates. Among them he recognized Archie Auchinleck and his son Rory. Most of the roof was finished.

Seamus Galvin was climbing a ladder with a hodful of slates over his shoulder.

As Barry and O'Reilly walked along the path, Barry noticed the weeds that had been growing in feral splendour the week before had been trampled flat by the comings and goings of the workers. He wondered if the crew would have time to work on the garden as well as the house.

A group of women, clearly being directed by Maureen Galvin, who had baby Barry Fingal slung in a tartan shawl on her left hip, clustered round a makeshift table set up outside the front door. Planks had been laid across two sawhorses. The boards were covered with damp tea towel–draped plates of sandwiches. Rows of thermos flasks, bottles of milk, and saucerless teacups were arranged in ranks.

"Hello, Doctors," Maureen said, hitching the baby higher. "Grand evening for the job."

"How are you, Maureen?" O'Reilly asked, chucking the bairn under his chin and being rewarded by a crow of laughter.

"Grand," she said. "Would you like a sandwich?"

"Now there's an idea," said O'Reilly. "It's well past my teatime." He helped himself.

"Doctor Laverty?"

"No, thank you, Maureen. If I don't eat up all my supper when we get home, Kinky'll not be too impressed."

"Maybe a cup of tea?"

"Now there's a notion," a voice said. Barry turned to see a smiling Donal Donnelly stretch out his left hand and accept a cup from Maureen. His right arm was bent across his chest, the plaster cast on his finger grey-white against the blue of his collarless shirt. "Evening, Doctor Laverty," he said, "the roof's coming on a treat."

"I can see that . . ."

"Scuse me. *Jesus Murphy, Andy,*" Seamus yelled up to a young man Barry didn't know. "If you were laying sod, I'd have to tell you to put it down green side up. Them joists go the other way round."

"Sorry" came drifting down from the roof.

"Reminds me," said O'Reilly, swallowing the last of his sandwich and eyeing the plate, "of the English builder who told Paddy he was so bloody ignorant he couldn't tell the difference between a joist and a girder."

Donal grinned. "Doctor O'Reilly, that one has whiskers, so it has.

'Ignorant is it?' says Paddy. 'Joist and a girder?' says he. 'I can so tell the difference . . . Joyce wrote *Ulysses* and Göethe wrote *Faust*. There's the odd scholar in Ireland, you know.' "

Barry, who hadn't heard the old chestnut, laughed.

"Scholars?" O'Reilly helped himself to another sandwich. "I don't remember who called Ireland the land of saints and scholars . . ."

"Neither do I," Barry said.

"And I'm not so sure about the scholarship," O'Reilly said, "but you've put together a right saintly bunch out here, Donal. I'm proud of you."

"Thanks, Doctor," Donal said shyly. "Maybe it'll make up a wee bit for what I did to that Captain Kelly fellah?"

"Your sins are forgiven, Donal," O'Reilly said, grinning and eating half his second sandwich in one bite. "How's Julie?"

Donal ran a hand through his carroty hair. His smile was so wide his buckteeth shone whitely. "I got her out of the Royal this morning, so I did. She's a wee bit peaked, but"—he turned to Barry—"your lady doctor friend said that's to be expected. She's back home having a wee rest. I wanted to stay with her, like, but she told me to come on out and get on with the job. You'll get to see her on Saturday, Doctor Laverty."

"I'll look forward to it."

"Scuse me," Donal said, frowning, setting his now empty cup on the table and pointing with his injured finger to the path. "Here comes trouble."

Barry turned to see Councillor Bishop stamping towards the house. Willy Dunleavy and an out-of-uniform Constable Mulligan followed in Bishop's wake, pushing a wheeled trolley, perched on which were two large kegs. He could hear the trolley's wheels bumping over the paving stones and a clinking of glass that must be coming from a crate beside one of the kegs.

The councillor wheezed to a halt in front of the table. There were beads of sweat on his forehead. "Who's in charge here?" the tubby man demanded.

Donal swallowed. His Adam's apple bobbed in his scrawny neck. "I'm the Hat, sir, so I am."

The Hat, Barry knew, was the term used in Harland and Wolff's shipyard for the foreman.

"Are you?" said the councillor. "Well, tell these men where to put the kegs."

"Right, sir." Donal turned and shouted, "Mickey, grab a couple of the lads and get another table made. I want it done in two shakes of a duck's tail." He glanced at Bishop. "You'd know all about ducks, wouldn't you, Councillor?"

Bishop growled.

Barry watched as a second trestle was jury-rigged. As soon as it was done, Bishop clambered on top and held up his hand for silence. "All youse men," he roared, "pay attention, now."

Heads turned. Men on the roof stared down.

"I never give no permission for any of youse to be working here, so I'm not paying youse nothing, so I'm not . . ."

Barry heard a dull muttering.

"But I was having a wee word with Doctor O'Reilly, and he come up with the notion . . ."

Barry's mouth opened. Bishop wasn't going to take all the credit?

"The doctor reckons a couple of pints on the Bishop Building Company Limited wouldn't hurt. Willy here will pour as soon as the kegs is ready."

The cheer sent the distant jackdaws clattering into the blue sky.

"And don't none of youse forget it when the council elections come round." Bishop jumped to the ground. He spoke quietly to O'Reilly. "I've told Dunleavy on the q.t. he can stay, but I'm saving the announcement for the wedding." Bishop turned to Barry. "And I've not forgotten you did fix Flo, Doctor Laverty, and I should be grateful." He sighed. "I just wish you could fit her with a silencer."

"She's better, so be thankful for small mercies, Bertie," O'Reilly said, "and remember you married her for better or for worse."

Any further discussion was cut short by Willy shouting, "Who's for the first pint?"

"Now, Willy," said O'Reilly, hauling Barry along and moving to the head of a queue that was forming in front of the keg-laden trestle. "Who else would it be?"

The sun had gone behind the Antrim Hills when O'Reilly put his car in the garage. Barry opened the back gate and was almost bowled over by a happy Arthur Guinness.

He stood his ground and roared, "Sit, you bloody lummox!" as O'Reilly would have. To his surprise the dog's backside hit the grass, and Arthur grinned up at him.

"No boots today, Arthur?" O'Reilly asked, peering round the garden. " 'Bout time you saw the error of your ways." He patted the dog's head. "Go to bed now. I'll maybe take you for a walk after supper."

The dog obeyed.

"Supper," said O'Reilly, rubbing his hands and heading for the kitchen door.

Barry hurried to keep up. He couldn't identify the aroma filling the room, and there was no sign of Kinky. O'Reilly was holding a sheet of paper. "She says dinner's in the oven, but there's no rest for the wicked. Kinky's had to go out—don't ask me why—but one of us is going to have to forgo his supper for now and nip round and take a look at a kid with the croup."

"Do you want me to go?"

O'Reilly shook his head. "Nah. Maureen's sandwiches'll hold me for a while, and it'll only take half an hour or so. It's Eimear Fleming's wee lad, and they live on Main Street. I can walk over and give Arthur a run while I'm at it."

"Fair enough."

O'Reilly handed Barry the note. "There's a message for you too."

Barry took the sheet of paper and was reading it as O'Reilly left.

"Doctor Laverty," he read in Kinky's copperplate handwriting, "a Doctor Sloan called. Wouldn't leave a message or a phone number, says he'll be busy tomorrow, but he'll be in touch."

38

Your Hat Has Got a Hole In't

The sudden ringing of the hall telephone stopped Barry's spoonful of breakfast porridge halfway to his mouth. Eight o'clock? Too early for Harry Sloan to be calling. Pathologists rarely started work before nine. Barry glanced across the table at O'Reilly, who merely shrugged and said, "Kinky'll see to it."

Barry heard Kinky's voice as only a murmur, the *ting* as she replaced the receiver; then the door flew open. He turned in his chair. Kinky burst in. The last time she'd moved so fast had been when a batch of her scones had nearly burnt in the oven.

"It's Agnes Arbuthnot . . ." Kinky's eyes were wide. "She says you've to come . . . to come at once. To the dress shop. I've never heard Aggie so het up. You'd think all the divils in hell were after her."

"Good God. What's the trouble?" O'Reilly asked.

"Aggie'd gone to have a word with Miss Moloney. The door was shut and the curtains were drawn, but she says she was able to peep in through the side window . . . she was tripping over her words . . . and she saw Miss Moloney lying on the floor."

O'Reilly leapt to his feet. "Hold the fort 'til we get back, Kinky. Come on, Barry. Get your bag."

Barry was already halfway to the surgery.

"We'll walk," O'Reilly yelled, opening the front door. "It'll be quicker than getting the car."

Barry grabbed his bag and rushed to catch O'Reilly. As they strode along Main Street, Barry nearly running to keep up, he had to shout to make himself heard over the row of the heavy morning traffic of the commuters from Bangor to Belfast. "Has she a history of anything, Fingal?"

"She'd a bad case of piles a couple of years back, but for a spinster woman of fifty-one who lives on her own she's been remarkably healthy," O'Reilly roared back. "The worst thing I know about her is that she's bitter enough to have sufficient acid in her veins to recharge the batteries of a submarine."

A heavy diesel lorry, slowed by the congestion, grumbled and roared and strangled any further conversation. It belched exhaust fumes that made Barry's eyes water.

Could she have fallen, he wondered? Off a stool perhaps, if she'd being trying to reach an upper shelf. Fainting could happen in early pregnancy, particularly with a tubal pregnancy, but she was too old for that. She *was* the right age to have a heart attack or, perish the thought, a cerebral bleed. O'Reilly was right about her acidic personality—was she the type to have a duodenal ulcer that had perforated?

He was still trying to sort out the diagnostic possibilities when they arrived at the dress shop.

"Thank the Lord Jesus you've come, sirs." A scrawny woman, red hair twisted on plastic curlers half-hidden by a headscarf, stood on the footpath. "Miss Moloney's lying on the floor looking like a stunned mullet." She wrung her hands in the hem of her apron and jigged from sandaled foot to sandaled foot.

"Calm yourself, Agnes," O'Reilly said. "See if you can get in, Barry."

The red door of the dress shop was shut. Barry put his face close to the glass of a small side window and held his hand alongside his cheek to allow him to peer into the dim interior. He could make out Miss Moloney lying sprawled on the floor. "She's out flat, Fingal."

"Then open the door, you eejit."

Barry tried. It was locked. He turned for help and was in time to see O'Reilly shooing Agnes Arbuthnot. "Get you on home now, Aggie," O'Reilly admonished. Thanks for the call. You did well, but there's no need for you to hang about rubbernecking."

"It's locked, Fingal," Barry said.

"Out of my way." O'Reilly looked like a rugby forward trying to smash his way through the opposition. He took a pace back, lowered one shoulder, and hurled himself against the door.

Barry heard the wood of the frame splinter as the lock was ripped free. The door swung open.

O'Reilly's momentum carried him inside, and Barry followed.

"Push the door closed, Barry," O'Reilly called over his shoulder. "We don't need half the village in here gawking over our shoulders."

By the time Barry had shoved the door back into the splintered frame, Miss Moloney was starting to sit up. Her eyes were wide. She supported herself on one hand while the other flew to her head. Her usually tight bun was untangled. Strands of pepper-and-salt hair straggled down the nape of her neck, and a few wisps hung over her face. She made a keening noise through clenched teeth, then asked, "Where am I?"

"In your shop," said O'Reilly. "You took a wee turn."

She stared at the doctor, clearly recognizing him. "A wee turn was it?"

"You must have fainted," O'Reilly said, looking closely into her face and starting to take her pulse.

"And it's no wonder," she said, beating her free fist against her thigh. "I'm ruined. Ruined." She grabbed O'Reilly's arm. "That Helen. I'll kill her. The ungrateful wee bitch. I'll kill her dead." Her voice was more grating than Barry remembered. A string of spittle hung from her lower lip.

"Indeed," said O'Reilly. "Do you know what day it is?"

"Of course I do. It's Friday." She folded her arms across her chest and rocked back and forth. "It's the day I was going to sell all my hats. Now I can't."

"Why not?"

"Would you look at what she's done to me?" Miss Moloney groaned and pulled herself to her feet. She wobbled and sat down heavily on a chair. "Just look." She pointed at a hat stand and then across to the counter.

Hatboxes were stacked untidily on the glass countertop among crumpled heaps of tissue paper. The tallest pile leant sideways, defying gravity and looking like a miniature Tower of Pisa.

"There's not a hat left." Miss Moloney stared up at O'Reilly. "Not the one."

Actually, Barry thought, there's a great number of hats left, if they could still be described as hats. Every stand had its occupant, but every piece of the milliner's art was battered beyond recognition.

"Never mind that now, Miss Moloney," O'Reilly said. "You passed out and someone sent for us. What made you faint, do you think?"

"Me heart," she said dramatically, "it's broken in me." She screwed her eyes half shut. Her downturned lips quivered. Barry noticed that she shed not a single tear. "Broken like the tablets Moses smashed when he came down from the mountain."

"Are you short of breath, having any pains in your chest? In your jaw? Down your arm?" O'Reilly pulled his stethoscope from his pocket. "Your pulse is nice and regular, and it's only a wee bit fast. About one hundred." This last remark was addressed to Barry.

No sign of cardiac irregularity, not a symptom, and Miss Moloney didn't have the pale clammy look of someone experiencing a myocardial infarction. If anything, her face was flushed.

"Pain? Pain? Only in my poor heart. It's broken in me. I near took the rickets when I came in to open up this morning." She held her right wrist against her forehead. "I was so upset my breath rushed in and out of me like I'd been running a marathon; everything went grey, and the next thing I knew was that you were here, Doctor."

By the look of her, Barry thought, she wasn't seriously ill. She'd almost certainly got herself so worked up that she'd hyperventilated, and that could certainly cause syncope. Judging by the smile on O'Reilly's face, he'd arrived at the same conclusion.

"Now," O'Reilly said in a soothing voice, "just you sit there, get ahold of yourself, and tell us what happened."

"Tell you? I'll show you." She rummaged in a pocket of her skirt and pulled out a folded sheet of paper that she thrust at O'Reilly. "Read that." Her voice climbed the register. "*Read it.*"

O'Reilly read aloud,

> *Dear Miss Moloney,*
> *I write you this by way of giving my notice. I'll not be in*
>   *ever again. As a going-away present I've rearranged*
>   *your hats.*
> *Your humble and obedient servant,*
>
> *Helen Hewitt.*

Barry remembered the blaze in those green eyes yesterday. So that's what she'd meant by a going-away present. He liked her use of the classic valediction of a formal business letter. The sarcasm was certainly not lost on him. Had Miss Moloney seen it too? He smiled not only because he was relieved to see that Miss Moloney was not having a real heart attack, but because Helen's revenge tickled his funny bone.

Judging by the wreckage, she must have taken every hat in turn from its box and stamped on it. He could imagine her gleefully satisfied look every time her shoe squashed a hat.

Miss Moloney sat up more rigidly, then bent forward and grabbed the nearest hat. She cradled it to her and tried to smooth it with one hand. "You poor wee thing," she said, "you poor wee dote."

And in her voice Barry heard the care of a mother for an injured child. O'Reilly had said she was single. Perhaps, he thought, perhaps her hats *were* her children.

O'Reilly tucked his unused stethoscope back in his jacket pocket. "Well," he said, "it looks as though it was a false alarm." He smiled at her. "I think you're going to survive."

"Survive, is it? *Survive?* I've stocked up on hats for *two* weddings, and first of all that ungrateful wee hussy Julie MacAteer goes and cancels hers."

"I hardly think Julie did that on purpose," said O'Reilly. Barry heard the chill in O'Reilly's voice.

"And then . . . then just before I have a toty chance to make up my losses, Mary Dunleavy up and quits, and now . . ." She thrust the ruined hat she'd been cradling at O'Reilly. Barry surmised it had been a weird creation of cream and red felt, with a yellow veil and with half a cock pheasant's wing stuck in the band; "Now Helen goes and does this? To me?" She jabbed her finger against her bony chest. "*To me?*"

"Indeed," said O'Reilly, "I can see why you'd be a bit upset."

"A bit? *A bit?* I'm fit to be tied. I'll have the law on her. The police. I want the police. I want her in the Crumlin Road Jail. *Jail.* Do you hear me?"

Where no doubt, Barry thought, you hope there'll be a rack and red-hot branding irons. But there was no doubt that if Miss Moloney did press charges, Helen could get into a great deal of trouble. He waited to see how O'Reilly would react.

"Ah," said O'Reilly, "would you like me to phone them? I'm sure Constable Mulligan would be glad to drop by."

"That eejit? He couldn't catch a cold on a wet day. Not at all. I want the CID, the Special Branch."

"Special Branch, is it?" said O'Reilly. "I hardly think busting a few hats would interest the antiterrorist squad."

"It ought to," she screeched. "That's what she is. A terrorist. *A hat terrorist.*"

Barry knew he should be concerned for Helen. But the poetry of the justice she had brought down on Miss Moloney—and his image of Ballybucklebo as the crime centre of County Down, populated as it was with wellie-nappers and now hat terrorists—forced him to hide his smile behind his hand.

O'Reilly paced to the door, turned, walked back, and stood over Miss Moloney. "No," he said, "I don't think Helen is a terrorist."

"Then what is she? You tell me that!" Miss Moloney's eyes blazed. She sat, arms akimbo, staring into O'Reilly's face. "She's a hellion. A harpy."

"I'll tell you, all right." His voice was calm and measured. "She's a high-spirited girl who tried hard to please you—"

"*Please me?* She'd enough trouble pleasing herself. Even before this . . . this outrage."

"She's a girl who was getting sick because of the way you were treating her."

"Me? *Me?*" Miss Moloney's voice rose in pitch. "I looked after her and Mary as if they were my own flesh and blood."

Barry said, "I did try to tell you, Miss—"

"Tell me what? *What?*" She turned on him, eyes narrowed.

"That maybe you could have gone a bit easier on Helen."

" 'Spare the rod and spoil the child.' Did you ever hear that, Doctor Laverty? Discipline, that's what that girl needed." Her breath started coming in short gasps.

Lord, Barry thought, she's starting to hyperventilate again.

O'Reilly put both hands on her shoulders. "Miss Moloney," he said sternly, "take a very deep breath and hold it."

She did as she was told.

"Now breathe as slowly as you can, and when you're ready and calm we'll have a wee chat about this state of affairs." He looked directly at Barry as Miss Moloney followed his instructions.

"Are you ready to discuss this now?" O'Reilly eventually asked.

"There's nothing to discuss. Helen did this. Helen's going to have to pay for it, and that's an end to it."

"How long have you lived here, Miss Moloney?" O'Reilly asked.

"All my life, and what's that got to do with the price of corn?"

O'Reilly shook his big head. "You should know how Ballybucklebo folks enjoy a good joke."

"There's nothing funny about my poor hats."

"But the folks here would think there was." His left eyelid made the tiniest wink in Barry's direction. "The minute they found out about this you'd hear the laughs and the roars of them all the way to Donaghadee."

Barry saw her frown. Her tone was more controlled when she asked, "And they'd be laughing at me, wouldn't they?"

"I fear so, Miss Moloney," O'Reilly said gently. "I do indeed fear so. Helen's a popular girl."

"And you mean I'm not?"

"Och," said O'Reilly, "that's not for me to say."

Barry saw her shoulders shake. He heard the tiniest sniffle and saw her eyes moisten. "Nobody really likes me," she whispered, "and I don't know why. And I know they already snigger about me behind their hands. They call me one of nature's unclaimed treasures. It's not my fault." Miss Moloney started to wring her hands, looked into O'Reilly's face questioningly, and asked quietly, "What am I to do?"

O'Reilly put his thumb under his jaw and crooked his index finger over his lower lip. He frowned; then removing his hand, he said, "Well, for starters, if nobody knows what actually happened here there'll be nothing to laugh at."

She looked at him.

"The three of us know. Helen knows, and that's all."

"Did Agnes Arbuthnot not see anything?" Barry enquired.

O'Reilly shook his head. "She told me all she saw was Miss Moloney lying here on the floor. What did you see, Doctor Laverty, when you looked through the window?"

"Miss Moloney."

"And when did you notice the hats?"

"Not until I was in the shop."

"Ah," said O'Reilly, "in the words the Great Detective never actually uttered, then it's elementary, my dear Laverty. Aggie didn't see a thing."

"I don't understand," Miss Moloney said, as a tear ran down her cheek.

"Here," said O'Reilly, handing her a hanky. "Blow your nose."

She obeyed like a little child.

"You'll not tell anyone, will you, Miss Moloney?"

She shook her head.

"And doctors aren't allowed to divulge any information, so that just leaves Helen."

Barry understood, if he hadn't before, how much of the life of Ballybucklebo, and the smooth social turning of its wheels, depended on lubrication by charitable half truths and secrecy. He supposed all small communities were the same. He wondered how many other secrets O'Reilly knew, and if some of his influence over the inhabitants lay in that knowledge? "Mum's the word," Barry said.

"But what'll we do about Helen?" Miss Moloney asked.

"Be nice to her," O'Reilly said.

Barry watched the battle of emotions on Miss Moloney's face. She clearly didn't want to be the laughingstock of the village, and yet being nice to Helen must be the last thing on her mind. "How can I be nice to her when she's cost me all this money?"

"I know a rag-and-bone man who'd give you a good price for the damaged hats," O'Reilly said.

"A good price?" Her eyes narrowed. "It would need to be close to a hundred pounds."

O'Reilly whistled. "A hundred? I think that could be arranged. If you like . . . you don't have a car, do you?"

"No, Doctor O'Reilly."

"I could nip round after surgery and pick up the wreckage. Take it to the fellah."

"Would you?"

"Och, aye," said O'Reilly, "but there'd be a couple of conditions."

Her eyes narrowed. "Conditions?"

He nodded. "One. You close the shop today. Stick a notice in the window: Closed Due to Illness. That won't be hard to substantiate. Aggie Arbuthnot'll have the word out you're dead and buried by the time Doctor Laverty and I get back to the surgery."

"She's got a wicked tongue, that Aggie." Miss Moloney sniffed. "If I have to close, and I might as well . . . I've no stock left . . . I think I'll go away down to Millisle and spend a few days with my sister."

"I think that would be for the best," O'Reilly said. "Don't you, Doctor Laverty?"

"Yes, indeed."

"You might even be surprised when you come back to Ballybucklebo to find the folks here are feeling sorry for you because they know you've been sick," O'Reilly said. "They're always quick to take a wounded soul under their wings."

She managed to smile weakly at him. "They might, mightn't they?"

"No question about it, unless Helen lets the cat out of the bag, but I'm sure she won't . . . if you treat her right."

Barry saw Miss Moloney's jaw tighten.

O'Reilly's words were gentle, his enquiry guileless. "How many weeks' wages do you owe Helen?"

"How many . . . ? One. Twelve pounds ten shillings."

"So, plus a week's severance comes to . . . twenty-five pounds. From a hundred? That leaves you seventy-five pounds." He glanced at the door. "Less what it costs to have the lock fixed. I'm sorry about that, but you were looking pretty sick when we arrived."

"I don't care about the stupid lock," she said. "I know you two doctors were doing what you had to." She glanced round at the wreckage of her hats. "And you've done a whole lot more for me too. I could've been ruined. But if you *can* get the money . . ."

"Never fear," said O'Reilly, "and I'll make sure Helen gets her money too."

"But . . . but—"

"But what?" said O'Reilly as if ordering an ordinary seaman to some menial task on the *Warspite*. "If you want Helen to keep quiet, you'll pay her off." He fixed her with a glare.

"All right," she said, "I will."

"Good. Now the sooner Doctor Laverty and I get the morning's work done, the sooner I can come and get the old hats. So, if we're not going to keep the other patients waiting, it's time we were back in the surgery."

"Right."

Barry went out of the door, and as he left he heard O'Reilly say, "I'm glad you're feeling better, Miss Moloney. I'll pop round about twelve thirty. Good morning."

He caught up with Barry, and together they walked side by side back to Number 1.

Barry was feeling relieved in a purely professional sense that there had been nothing more seriously wrong with Miss Moloney than a hyperventilation-induced attack of what an earlier generation would have called the vapours.

He was also once again in awe of the speed of O'Reilly's mind. He'd understood the real threat to Helen. Because he knew nobody likes to be laughed at, and had grasped the financial implications of the situation, he'd been able to play on his patient's emotions. He'd manipulated Miss Moloney's fear of being mocked and her greed. Helen was to be spared, and she might well have been prosecuted if O'Reilly hadn't intervened.

Barry *was* wondering where O'Reilly was going to get the one hundred pounds, but his train of thought was interrupted when O'Reilly said, "She's a sorry old duck, Miss Moloney. She had a fellah once, but he jilted her about a week before they were to be wed and she started to dry up inside. Apart from the sister, she's no family; lives above the shop, goes to church on Sundays, and that's about the height of her life."

"That's sad, Fingal."

"Aye," he said, "it'll be a good thing for her to get away for a few days." He smiled. "It might not be a bad thing either for Helen to look for a job in Belfast. Then she'll not be running into Miss Moloney. I think she'll be carrying quite the grudge."

"You're right, and Helen's a bright girl. She shouldn't have much trouble finding work."

"She's bright all right." He smiled. "Helen Hewitt. Do you know where that name comes from?"

"No."

"The original Hewitts came to Ireland in the thirteenth century. The name actually means 'a clearing,' and by God, Helen certainly cleared Miss Moloney's stock."

And that, Barry thought, raises the question of who was going to pay for the damage. "Do you really know a rag-and-bone man, Fingal?" he asked.

O'Reilly shook his head.

"Then where's the—"

"Money coming from?"

"Yes."

O'Reilly blew out his cheeks. "I won four hundred pounds on Donal's Bluebird last month. I lost fifty quid on that great lummox of a horse, Battlecruiser, at the point-to-point . . ."

Surely O'Reilly, the man who'd forced Barry to pay for Kinky's new hat, Barry thought, wasn't going to . . .

"I'll still be two hundred and fifty pounds ahead."

"But it's your own money."

"Och, sure," said O'Reilly, opening the door of Number 1. "When it comes to money won on wagers, 'the Lord giveth and the Lord taketh away.' Would you have had any better ideas on how to keep the ould witch quiet? Would you like to see Helen go short? God knows the girl hardly has two brass stivers to rub together."

Barry shook his head as he followed O'Reilly into the hall.

O'Reilly closed the door and laughed so hard he started to cough. It wasn't until he'd stopped coughing that he managed to say, "And wasn't it worth the price of admission just to see the battered bonnets of Ballybucklebo and the look on Miss Moloney's face?"

"A hundred pounds?" It was taking Barry three weeks to earn that much money.

"Aye." O'Reilly suddenly became very serious. "And if you as much as breathe a word about it to anyone—anyone—what I'll do to you would make what Miss Moloney wanted to do to Helen look like a pleasant day in the park."

"I understand. I'll say nothing." But Barry knew he didn't understand. He wondered when, if ever, he'd fully comprehend the workings of the mind of Doctor Fingal Flahertie O'Reilly.

"I'm glad to hear it," said O'Reilly, walking into the surgery. "And now be a good lad and nip along and see who's first."

39

Experience Is the Name Everyone Gives to Their Mistakes

"Our American cousins," said O'Reilly, "have an expression, TGIF. Thank God it's Friday." He stood at the sideboard, pouring predinner drinks. "I, for one, agree. I've had enough of Hippocratic endeavours for one week."

Barry stared through the windows of the upstairs sitting room, barely listening to O'Reilly, hardly taking in any details of the view past the mizzle-dampened, lopsided steeple of the church where the next day Maggie MacCorkle would become Mrs. Sonny.

Not another word had been spoken about Miss Moloney's hats, but true to his promise, O'Reilly's first stop after lunch had been at the dress shop, where the battered bonnets, concealed in paper shopping bags, had been loaded into the boot of the Rover.

When they'd returned from making their afternoon rounds, O'Reilly had vanished for half an hour to dispose, Barry presumed, of the hats and to find Helen Hewitt and give her her money. He'd only been back for five minutes.

It was all very well for O'Reilly to be talking about celebrating the end of another routine working week, Barry thought. There was still no word from Harry Sloan, and Mrs. Fotheringham's deadline of Sunday evening was rapidly approaching. He fidgeted in the armchair.

"Sherry?" said O'Reilly, reaching for the decanter.

Barry shook his head. He felt like having something stronger. "No, thanks. I'll have an Irish."

"Good man ma da," said O'Reilly pouring. "The ould *uisce beatha*, or if you prefer Latin, *aqua vitae,* the water of life. Here." He handed Barry the glass. "Do you want water with it?"

Barry shook his head. "No, thanks."

"Jesus," said O'Reilly with a grin. "Drinking it neat like a real Irishman. Good for you, son. None of your drowning it or, heaven help us, sticking ice in it the way the Yankees do. Do you know," he said, "I think they like the ice for the same reason we tell mothers to put bad-tasting medicine in the fridge."

"Because chilling it numbs the taste buds?"

"Exactly." O'Reilly took a healthy swallow. "And why in the name of the wee man would you want to spoil the flavour, when Mr. John Jameson has gone to all that trouble to distill the stuff right in the first place?" He took another drink. "It's about time you got off that sherry anyway. Fortified wine? It's neither fish, fowl, nor good red meat."

"I happen to like sherry."

"So did I when I was your age, but I grew out of it." He raised one bushy eyebrow.

Is he telling me it's time for me to grow up? Barry wondered. He held his glass in one hand and stared at the amber liquid, noting the tiny transparent curtains where some had flowed down the inside of the glass.

"Pardon?" O'Reilly asked.

"I didn't say anything."

O'Reilly nursed his glass of whiskey and looked down. "I thought I heard you say, 'Cheers' or '*Sláinte.*'"

"Sorry," Barry said. Lifting his glass, he muttered, "*Sláinte,*" and took a swallow.

"Aye," said O'Reilly. "*Is fearr an tsláinte ná na táinte.* Health is better than riches."

"I'm sure you're right," Barry said. He drank again.

O'Reilly growled something and lowered himself into the other armchair. "All right, Barry. You've had a face on you like a Lurgan spade all afternoon. Cheer up, for God's sake."

"I'm sorry."

"So am I. You know, son, I've been proud of you for the last few days . . ."

Barry looked into O'Reilly's face. There was gentleness in the man's expression.

"You've done well not letting this PM business get the better of you, carrying on with your work. It's a lesson all doctors have to learn. You have to keep your own troubles to yourself because, trite as it may sound, the customers come first." He frowned, took a deep drink, and said, as if to himself, "Sometimes they come first a bit too much, and you can have a bugger of a job closing your mind to them. It doesn't hurt to get away once in a while."

Barry wondered if he meant that doctors should get away physically. O'Reilly never seemed to take more than a few hours off. Did the whiskey help him to blot out his concerns? Maybe, but it wasn't helping Barry.

He forced a weak smile. "Perhaps *I* need to get away. I could've done better today. I missed the diagnosis of that wee lad's measles this afternoon."

"Why?" O'Reilly held his head tilted to one side. "Why did you miss it? It's not a difficult one to make."

Barry flinched and tried to explain. "Because measles usually occur in *late* autumn. The boy had a runny nose; his eyes were inflamed and sensitive to light. Given the number of cases of hay fever we've seen recently, I thought . . ."

"Aye," said O'Reilly. "Sparrows are more common than canaries sitting on Irish telegraph wires. One of my old profs used to say that."

"So did one of ours. Common diseases occur more commonly . . . but it's our job to keep an eye out for the unusual. I didn't bother looking in his mouth. I should have." And damn it all, the same thing, rushing an examination, was the reason he found himself in his current predicament. "You found the Koplik's spots inside his cheeks."

"I did, and any eejit could have made the diagnosis once he'd seen them."

It was a simple statement. O'Reilly's nose tip was its usual plum colour, and his eyes did not hold any suggestion of disappointment.

"I'm sorry."

O'Reilly swirled the whiskey in his glass. "And how long have you been in practice, son?"

"You know bloody well. Six weeks."

O'Reilly nodded, seemingly unruffled by the edge in Barry's voice. "And how many cases of measles have you seen?"

"Two or three when I was a student." He didn't like to be reminded of his lack of experience. "Christ Almighty, I only graduated last year."

"Did you ever have them yourself?"

Barry shook his head.

"You must have been a lucky lad. I'd a terrible dose when I was nine." O'Reilly had a faraway look in his brown eyes. "I'll never forget old Doctor O'Malley. He used to come and see me every day. Funny old bird. He had muttonchop whiskers and always wore a morning suit. He was a damn good doctor *and* he'd played a ferocious game of hurley as a youngster. He played in the All-Ireland finals for County Cork."

Just like a certain colleague of mine, Barry thought. Old-fashioned in many ways; no muttonchops, of course; a damn fine physician; and at one time a very good rugby player. Barry could remember having chicken pox at age ten, being very impressed by his parents' GP, and knowing it was then that he had decided he wanted to be a doctor. "Fingal," he asked, "when did you decide to go into medicine?"

O'Reilly guffawed. "I don't think I actually know, but I do remember being fond of old O'Malley. In my last year at Clongoes Wood School it was time to think of a career, some of the lads I played rugby with were going to Trinity, and I thought medicine seemed as good a choice as any."

"And it has been?"

"For me?" He frowned. "For a while there, when I was in the navy, I used to wonder if I'd have been happier as a sailor, but that notion passed. It passed the same way it does for all the youngsters who want to be firemen or engine drivers." He rose and looked out the window. "It's suited me fine, Barry. Just fine . . ." He turned and stared at him.

Barry looked into O'Reilly's face. His lips were curved in a small smile, and there was brightness in his deep eyes when he said, "And it's going to suit you fine too, son, because, Laverty, for a young man, you've all the makings of a good doctor . . ."

Barry looked into O'Reilly's face. The smile had gone.

"And like all youngsters you want everything at once. You want to be Sir William Osler, Louis Pasteur, and Alexander Fleming all rolled into one . . . and you want it now. Today."

"I suppose—"

"Jesus Christ, there's no supposing. It's the truth, and do you know how I know? Do you?" Now there was a bite in O'Reilly's voice. "Because, and I've told you this before, I wasn't always fifty-six. How the hell do you think I felt a couple of years out of medical school, stuck on HMS *Warspite* with a thousand men to look after?"

"Scared?"

"Bloody well petrified." O'Reilly lifted his hand. "It's different in a war. You have to learn quickly, and you get to be experienced by making mistakes." He took a deep pull of his whiskey. His smile was starting again, and it broadened as he spoke. "Experience is a wonderful thing. It lets you recognize the same mistake when you make it again . . . and again until one day you stop making that bloomer."

O'Reilly's words, and his assurance that he thought Barry was going to make a good doctor, made Barry smile.

"That's better," O'Reilly said. "Now, while I'm in the mood for preaching a sermon, I'm going to tell you something else. When I asked you why you missed the diagnosis of measles, I thought you might have had a different answer." O'Reilly's voice was level. "I thought you were going to tell me your mind was on other things."

"Well . . ." There was no point dissembling. He looked O'Reilly in the eye. "I wanted to get home in case Harry had phoned. He said he'd be in touch. We're awfully out of touch when we're making home visits."

O'Reilly nodded. "The thought's occurred to me too. Wouldn't a telephone that you could keep in your car be a wonderful thing?"

"You'd need an awfully long telephone wire."

O'Reilly laughed. "Och, I'm sure one day some genius'll invent a short-range wireless telephone like the Talk Between Ships we had in the navy." He stretched, then looked at Barry. "We do have a phone in the house. Any point trying to get hold of your mate now?"

Barry shook his head. "He'll have gone home and I don't have his number. I don't even know where he lives so there's no point asking directory enquiries for help. The phone book's full of Sloans."

"Pity," said O'Reilly, swallowing the last of his whiskey and striding to the sideboard to refill his glass. "I was certain we'd have heard. I was wrong. I could have been wrong about something else too."

"What?"

"I said that if I thought it was necessary, I'd go and see Mrs. Fotheringham again. I haven't."

"Do you think it would help?"

"Honestly, Barry? I don't know." O'Reilly parked himself in the chair and stuck his booted feet on the footstool.

"Then why bother?"

"Because you don't give up a fight in the middle of the tenth round." He looked enquiringly at Barry. "There's another thing. I've known her for years. Yes, she's all airs and graces. Yes, she's a born-again hypochondriac. Yes, she's the most demanding bloody woman in God's creation, but—and it's a big but—she and her late husband were remnants of the Raj. They had all of those values, good and bad, but they included a deeply felt sense of fair play and an absolute belief that if one's word had been given it must be honoured." He crossed his legs. "She's promised me she'll drop the suit if we have evidence it wasn't your fault."

"But we don't have the evidence."

"Yet," O'Reilly said. "Not yet—"

He was interrupted by something tiny scuttling across the carpet, Lady Macbeth in hot pursuit. A mouse. The little creature ran up the side of the footstool, along O'Reilly's trouser leg, and was now trying to burrow inside his waistcoat. He grabbed it and held it firmly in one hand; then he set his glass on the coffee table, and stood. Barry could see the sharp nose and whiffling whiskers peeping out above the top of O'Reilly's index finger.

Lady Macbeth stood on her hind legs, front claws firmly stuck halfway up O'Reilly's trouser leg. She made an eldritch growling, and Barry felt the hairs rise on the nape of his neck. He could only imagine how the mouse must feel.

"Get to hell down, cat," O'Reilly said.

She paid no attention. Her tail thrashed, and her growling went up at least an octave.

"Grab Her Ladyship, Barry."

Barry rose and tried to catch the animal. She ripped her claws free, dragging ragged loops of tweed from the fabric of O'Reilly's trouser leg. Barry managed to hold on to her. "Got her," he said.

"Good," said O'Reilly. "Hang onto her until I get this 'wee, sleekit, cow'ring, tim'rous beastie' out of the house." He left the room, closing the door behind him.

Barry set the cat on the carpet.

She fixed him with a steely glare, spat, and then sat and hoisted one hind leg so the knee was behind her ear, and began to wash her bottom. Barry had read some author who said cats engaged in such an ungainly pursuit looked as if they were playing the cello. It was an apt description.

If Her Ladyship could sit, so could he. He went back to his chair and sipped his Irish. It was a damn sight harsher on the throat than his usual sherry, but it was certainly producing more of an inner glow.

What the hell was it about O'Reilly that any creature, mouse or man, instinctively knew it could run to him if it was in trouble? Barry shook his head. He was damned if he knew, but it was true—and it was a great comfort. Maybe someday people would feel that way about him. One day, after he'd served his time like his mentor.

The cat had finished her washing and was curled up in a ball by the time O'Reilly returned. "I put it out in the back garden," he said. "Arthur won't bother it. That mite really did have a 'panic in his breastie.' You should have felt the rate its wee heart was going." He smiled shyly. "I couldn't resist it. I was curious. I listened in with my stethoscope. You never heard the like." He sounded astonished.

Barry could picture the big man, gently holding the bell of his stethoscope over the mouse's tiny chest, and the look of innocent wonderment that would have come into his eyes. "They say the Greeks prized the enquiring mind," Barry said.

"And you're more yourself if you can be bothered to make a remark like that." O'Reilly smiled, picked up his whiskey, and sat. "You've had a minute or two to think about what I was saying, Barry, when we were so rudely interrupted . . . what do you think about my idea? Should I keep up the good fight? Go and see the widow?"

Barry wasn't sure how to answer. He noticed his glass was empty. He went to the sideboard, helped himself, turned, and said, "It won't be easy."

"For who? Me? For Mrs. Fotheringham?"

Barry shook his head. "No. For me."

"You?" O'Reilly stood holding his glass. He frowned. "Why you?"

"Because I've no choice. If anyone has to talk to her, it's me. It's my responsibility."

O'Reilly clapped Barry on the shoulder. "I knew you'd say that. I just bloody well knew it."

O'Reilly had never even hinted that Barry should go, nor had he made any effort to help Barry arrive at the decision. He felt as if he had been submitted to some crucial test and had unwittingly passed.

"I'm proud of you, Barry," O'Reilly said, raising his glass. "And you'll not be going alone. If we haven't heard by Saturday, we'll drop in on her on Sunday."

"Thanks, Fingal. I appreciate . . ."

Barry heard Kinky's voice, and then her footsteps coming upstairs. He saw O'Reilly's eyebrow lift in a question and knew they were both thinking the same thing. Barry's palms grew damp.

She stuck her head round the door. "Doctor Laverty. There's a call for you, so."

Barry's pulse quickened.

"It's your Miss Spence. You'd best run along and speak to her. She sounded all excited."

As he ran to the door, he heard Kinky scolding O'Reilly. "Lord Jesus, Doctor O'Reilly. If it wasn't bad enough having to keep an eye on the young man's trousers. Would you look at the state of your tweeds?"

Barry took the stairs two at a time and grabbed the receiver. "Hello. Patricia. Where are you?"

"In my flat." She did sound excited.

"But I thought you weren't coming up to the Kinnegar until tomorrow." He heard her laugh. His hand tightened on the plastic. "You've won, haven't you?" He tried to sound enthusiastic.

"Yes. I have. You were right. Isn't it wonderful?"

"Amazing." He swallowed. "Well done. Congratulations." He'd no trouble knowing exactly how she would be feeling. He'd gone through the same thing himself just over a year ago. "Laverty, pass," the dean had read from the list of finals results. At first there was numbness, disbelief, understanding, and then an overwhelming urge to cheer and caper about.

"Are you there, Barry?"

"Yes. Sorry."

"Can you come over? I wanted to see you so much I got Dad to run me up tonight."

Barry hesitated. "I don't know. I'll ask O'Reilly. Hang on." He set the receiver on the hall table and turned to the stairs but heard O'Reilly bellow from the landing.

"Well? Has she won? Kinky said she was excited."

"Yes. She has. She's back and she's in her flat."

"Bloody marvellous." O'Reilly held his hands clasped above his head like a prizefighter who had scored a KO. "Well, don't just stand there, both legs the same length, you great glipe. Go and see her and give her a big hug from me."

40

Good News from a Far Country

The Volkswagen's wipers struggled back and forth, trying and failing to clear the windscreen of drizzle. It wasn't heavy enough to let the blades move freely, and their rhythmic scraping on the glass was as grating as fingernails on a blackboard. Barry hunched forward and concentrated on where he was going, along the winding road to the Kinnegar.

It was difficult to see ahead, and not only through the streaked windscreen.

He knew he loved her. Had known since the first night he'd kissed her. You were meant to rejoice when someone you loved won a victory, and he did—for the success itself—but the thought of Patricia's going away tore at him.

Jack had urged him to propose, give her a ring, mark her as his property, but he couldn't. Was it because he was scared of the idea of marriage, because he thought he was too young at twenty-four? Or was it because one of the things he loved about her was her spirit, which like a wild pony, should be tamed only when the animal was ready? Damned if he knew.

But the fact was she'd won and she'd be going to Cambridge. The question was, did she love him enough to save herself for him? Christ, it sounded like something from a cheap romance novel. Time, he supposed, would tell, but he already knew how much he hated uncertainty and waiting for answers to questions over which he had no control. And time, in this case, was going to be three long years. It would seem like forever, just as trying to get to the Kinnegar was taking much longer than he'd anticipated.

He accelerated along a straight stretch, then slowed for a corner. Christ. There were brake lights up ahead, and the bulk of a lorry loomed out of the rain. He slammed on the brakes and wrestled with the steering wheel as Brunhilde slewed to the left. Then, tyres squealing, she juddered to a halt a few feet from the lorry. The soles of his feet tingled.

He peered around the vehicle ahead to where a line of cars formed a tailback from something. Barry closed the door and sat hammering his fist on the steering wheel, and as the line crawled forward, he followed. He was almost abreast of the holdup before he could see what it was.

A sports car had slammed head-on into an army lorry. The lorry was probably from the nearby Palace Barracks. A group of uniformed soldiers stood, huddled like a flock of frightened sheep, beside their lorry. He could see several of the troops bending over two of their number who lay on the grass. There was no sign of an ambulance, but a police car, roof lights flashing, was parked on the verge where two bottle-green uniformed Royal Ulster Constabulary officers stood, directing traffic.

Barry hesitated, stopped, and wound down his window, hoping he'd not be needed, but knowing he would be. "I'm a doctor," he yelled to the nearest officer. "Do you need a hand?"

"Pull over behind the police car, please, sir."

Blast, Barry thought. But he did as he was asked, left Brunhilde, and collar turned to the damp, trotted back to the accident.

"Thanks, Doc." One constable, a heavyset man, pushed his cap back on his head, and said, "Christ, it's a right bollocks, so it is. Could you have a wee look at the driver of the sports car first?"

"Right." Barry followed the officer.

The little red two-seater was barely recognizable. Shattered glass crunched underfoot as he walked round to the driver's side. A young man had been slammed halfway through the windscreen. Barry shuddered. The man's face was covered in blood, and his head lolled at an impossible angle. Barry closed his eyes. That lad was dead as mutton. Death always bothered him, but he mustn't let it. He had his job to do.

Barry put his fingers under the jaw and felt for the carotid artery. The man's skin was clammy, and there was no pulse. Barry slid his hand inside a blood-soaked shirt. He could find no heartbeat. "How long ago did this happen?"

"We got the call on the radio twenty minutes ago, sir, but we just got here ourselves."

Barry stood. "I'm sorry, but it's far too late to try cardiac massage. I'm afraid there's nothing I can do for him." Steam from the broken radiator slid wraithlike into the drizzle.

"Aye. That's what I thought myself, but you never know. Pity about that. He was only twenty. I had a look at his driver's licence."

In the distance Barry heard the *nee-naw* of an ambulance's siren.

"Is there anyone else you'd like me to see?" He hoped the answer would be no, but he knew two other men were down.

"Could you maybe just take a wee look at the squaddies over there? See if any of them need to go straight to the hospital, like?"

"Of course."

"I've put a call in to the barracks. There'll be an army ambulance here to take the ones that aren't too bad back to the medical officers, but that ambulance there"—he pointed to the newly arrived, yellow-painted vehicle—"is down from the Royal. Whoever got here first, and went and dialled 999, had enough wit to send for us *and* ask for an ambulance."

"Fine." Barry sighed, as together they walked over to the soldiers.

"This here gentleman's a doctor, so he is. Who does he need to see?"

A sergeant stepped forward and stood at attention. "Lots of bumps and bruises, sir; they'll keep, but could you take a gander at the lads that're down?"

"Right." Barry knelt on the wet grass beside a pale, sweating private. He was conscious, his breath coming in short gasps. "I'm Doctor Laverty."

"Private Jenkins, sir." The man's English accent was obvious. He groaned, then whimpered, "It's me fuckin' leg."

"Are you sore anywhere else?"

"Nah." The soldier gritted his teeth.

"What day is it?"

"Christ, I don't give a bugger. It's me leg."

Barry decided it was unlikely the man was concussed. He could always ask about that later, and the leg certainly needed to be examined. "Let's have a look."

Barry didn't consciously think of the checklist he'd have to run through for a trauma case. He took the man's pulse. A bit rapid, that was to be expected, but not dangerously so. When Barry peered into the soldier's eyes, he saw at once that both pupils were the same size, so it was unlikely he'd sustained a head injury. "Come on, soldier. What day is it?"

"Bloody Friday."

Barry ran his hands swiftly but firmly over both sides of the chest. "That hurt?"

"Nah."

The soldier didn't yell, so he'd probably not had any ribs broken. There was no need to be concerned that a jagged rib end would puncture a lung. There were no complaints, no sudden in-drawing of breath as Barry pressed on the abdomen. No internal bleeding.

He turned to examine the man's legs. The left shin was bent at an angle, and through the ripped and blood-spattered khaki trousers nacreous bone stuck out, jagged and ugly. Compound fracture of the tibia and fibula.

He felt a hand tugging on his shoulder and heard a voice saying, "Out of my way, sir. We're trained in first aid."

Barry turned to see an ambulance attendant bending over and looking at him.

"Jesus, Doc. It's yourself? You're the fellah that brung in the abortion the other night, so you are."

He recognized the man, Larry—no, Danny—who'd been having his break when Barry took Julie MacAteer to the Royal.

"Doctor Laverty," Barry said. Dispensing with any more formalities, he added, "You'll need splints and a stretcher. Have you any morphine in the ambulance? I've left my bag at home."

"Aye. Morphine? Right, sir. I'll get it." The ambulance man went back to his vehicle.

Barry turned to the injured soldier. "Sorry about this, but your leg's broken. I'll make you more comfortable in a minute."

The soldier groaned and said, "I'll not be playing soccer . . . ah, Jesus . . . tomorrow."

"No, Private. You'll not. You'll be on a long paid leave courtesy of Her Royal Majesty." Barry smiled.

The soldier managed a weak grin. "I've bloody well earned it, ain't I?"

"Here you are, sir." The ambulance man handed Barry a stainless-steel box. He pulled out the hypodermic, charged it with the narcotic, and rolled back the soldier's sleeve. Seconds later a quarter grain of morphine sulphate was in the private's bloodstream. "Give that a few minutes to work; then dress and splint his leg," Barry said.

"Right, sir."

Barry got to his feet and stepped over to the other casualty, who was sitting up, clutching his head. Blood trickled between his fingers and made twin rivulets along both sides of his nose.

"I'm a doctor," Barry said.

"Aye. Right." The soldier took his hands away. His scalp was split across the crown.

"Look into my eyes," Barry said to the injured man. This one did have a head injury; he could be bleeding inside his skull. But his pupils were equal in size, and when Barry covered each eye in turn with his hand and then rapidly withdrew it, the pupil constricted. "What day is it?" he asked.

"Friday, sir. I'd know that. The lorry was taking us up to Belfast for a night off, so it was. I was going to the Crown Liquor Saloon on Great Victoria Street." His accent was pure Belfast. The man knew time and place so he wasn't disorientated, another good sign.

Barry examined the gash closely. It would need sutures. For a moment he considered running him back to the surgery and attending to the job, but he realized the soldier would get to the Royal more quickly in the ambulance. He turned and called, "Danny, can you or your mate bring a dressing pack?"

"Soon as we've this splint on. Don't worry about it, Doc. If it just needs a bandage, me and him'll take care of it."

Doctors were not expert bandagers, and Barry knew the ambulance personnel would do an excellent job, so he said to the soldier, "The ambulance lads'll get that dressed for you in no time; then they'll take you up to the Royal."

"Thanks, Doc." The soldier lay back and clutched his head. "Jesus, I'd rather be going to the pub. I'd go a pint right now. Maybe two or three."

Barry returned to the first casualty. The two ambulance men had splinted the shattered bone and were lifting the patient onto a stretcher. Barry followed them back to the ambulance and waited until they had loaded the man aboard.

It wouldn't hurt to be able to speak to the casualty officer on duty at the Royal and tell him what to expect. "Is your radio working?" he asked.

"Aye, certainly. Do you know how to use it?"

Barry shook his head.

"Never worry." Danny made sure the soldier's head was well settled on a pillow, then spoke to his mate. "Away you on and clap a dressing on that lad's nut. I've to give Doctor Laverty a wee hand, so I have. Come on, Doc."

Barry followed him to the ambulance's cab, where Danny climbed in and reappeared moments later holding a microphone on a flexible extension cable.

"Who'd you like to talk to?"

"Surgical registrar."

"Right. Hang on." He started talking into the mike. "Here." He handed the mike to Barry. "You're in luck. He's in the casualty department. They've gone to get him. Now you see that there button?"

Barry nodded.

"Hold it down when you want to speak. Say 'over' when you've done, and let it go when you want to listen. Have you got that?"

"Thanks, Danny."

Barry was listening to a crackle of static when a voice said, "Welcome to the Royal Victoria Hospital Mortuary and Chinese Take-out. Over."

Barry smiled. He recognized the Cullybackey accent and the hopeless irreverence of Jack Mills. He pressed the button. "Jack, it's Barry. I'm at a traffic accident on the Bangor-to-Belfast road. I've a compound tib-fib. I've given him morphine, and there's a head injury that'll need a few sutures. Over." He let the button go.

"Jesus, you get around, don't you, mate? He's had morphine? Okay. I'll make a note. And there's a suturing? All grist to the mill. When'll they be here? Over."

"Half an hour. Forty-five minutes. Over."

"Fair enough. How the hell are you anyway, Barry? Over."

Barry knew he shouldn't tie up the emergency frequency with chitchat, but an idea struck him. "Have you seen anything of Harry Sloan, Jack? Over."

"Saw him yesterday. He looked like shite. There's flu all over the pathology department. He's probably at home with an ice pack on his head and a couple of hot Irish whiskeys in him—"

Barry was so eager he depressed the button and started speaking over his friend.

"Do you have his phone number?"

"Sorry, mate. Not here. Over."

"Christ. Do you know where Harry lives? Over."

"Camden Street. You still sweating over that path report you wanted? Over."

"Damn right I am. It's important. Over."

"I'm working all night, but I'm off tomorrow. I'll nip over and see if he's home. Where can I get hold of you? Over."

"Try phoning O'Reilly's practice. The number's in the book." Barry remembered the wedding. "Jack, I'll be out all afternoon at a wedding reception. If you can't get me on the phone, would you be able to nip down to Ballybucklebo? It's not far. Over."

"For you, Laverty? I'd climb the highest mountain. Swim the deepest ocean . . . and even crash a Ballybucklebo wedding . . . especially if there's a pint in it for me. How do I get there? Over."

Barry told Jack how to get to the marquis' estate.

Jack said he'd better free up the channel; then he continued, "But one way or the other I'll be in touch. Sorry we can't deliver the chop suey, sir. Royal Mortuary and Chinese Take-out. Ying tong iddle I po, and out."

Barry remembered the pair of them in his digs listening to Spike Milligan, Peter Sellers, and the rest of the cast of BBC's *Goon Show* belting out "The Ying Tong Song." He was smiling as he handed the mike back. "Thanks, Danny."

"Excuse me, sir." The constable reappeared. "The army ambulance is on its way. They'll take care of the others, but thanks for seeing to the two lads."

"You don't need me for anything else?"

"Just the paperwork."

"Damn."

"Aye, I know," said the constable with a grin. "It's like the fellah in the lavatory said, No job's over 'til the paperwork's done."

Barry found himself laughing loudly. It wasn't much of a wisecrack, but after the intensity of working with the casualties he found it hilarious. "That's awful," he said, still chuckling.

"I know that, sir, but sure if you didn't laugh sometimes you'd have to cry, so you would. I've been a peeler for nine years and . . ." He nodded at the wrecked sports car. "I still get the heebie-jeebies when there's a dead one."

"I know what you mean," Barry said, but he thought, perhaps it was easier for a doctor. He didn't like to recall the number of bodies he'd seen, starting with the cadaver they'd dissected in his second year. Yet the finality of death was never easy to accept. If nothing else, his own troubles be damned, it made him grateful to be alive and able to laugh at the constable's joke. "All right," he said. "What do you need to know?" He glanced at his watch. "But get a move on. I'm already late for something." He pictured Patricia's flat and hoped she'd have a fire burning. He'd not noticed the rawness of the evening while he'd been working, but now the damp was seeping into his bones.

"This'll only take a wee minute." The policeman produced a spiral notebook and a pencil. "I need your name, and address, and telephone number."

Barry gave them.

"Thank you, sir. See, because there's been a death we may have to call you to the inquest as a witness, so we might."

Christ Almighty, another possible day in court. Shakespeare had been right when he'd said, "Let's kill all the lawyers."

"I understand, Constable," Barry said.

"And this here . . ." The constable produced a long form. "If you'd just write a brief report about what you seen and sign at the bottom . . . there . . . I'll fill in the details about the time and place later."

Barry pulled out his pen, dashed off a brief but accurate statement, and signed his name. He handed the form back.

"Thanks, sir. Run you away on, and thanks again."

Barry walked to Brunhilde. The policeman held up the traffic to let him drive away. At least the drizzle had stopped. He was soaked, bloodstained, and hardly in a condition to visit Patricia, but he was going to, even if he was a mess and his hands were trembling. Was he shaking because he was chilled or because of the carnage he had witnessed? Now he was no longer working by instinct, he had time to think about what had happened. He should be inured to death by now, but that poor wee lad had only been twenty. What a bloody awful waste.

"Barry. Barry." Patricia flung open the front door. "Barry, I . . ." Her hand flew to her mouth. "Dear God. Look at you. Are you all right? What happened?"

"Sorry I'm late. I'm fine, but there was a road accident. I had to help out."

"You poor soul. Come in. Lord, but you're soaked through. Go on into the bathroom." She held a door open. "You're covered in blood. We can talk when you've got yourself washed. There's a clean towel on the rail."

"Thanks." Barry went in, cleaned himself up, and dried his hair. In the mirror he saw the stupid tuft sticking up on his crown and automatically smoothed it down with one hand. He saw his lips were turned down in a scowl. He told himself, "Smile, you daft bugger. She's won."

Since leaving the crash he'd been getting his thoughts about Patricia in order. He'd decided not to dwell tonight on the implications of her win, but to celebrate with her. Why not? He'd enough of gloom and despondency in his life. O'Reilly had said doctors needed to get away. Why shouldn't he try to lose himself in her happiness, if only for one evening?

He'd wondered about stopping to buy her a bunch of flowers, but he'd have had to drive well out of his way to the nearest florist's, and the accident had already delayed him. He had had time during his drive to prepare a little speech of congratulations.

He rehearsed the words, then went into the living room where Patricia stood holding a bottle of Chianti and a corkscrew. Two glasses sat on the table. "Now you're looking better," she said. "Tell me what happened?"

He'd tell her what he was going to say about her scholarship later. "There was a traffic accident on my way here. I stopped and helped out a bit. One lad had a broken leg and another one a cut head. That's where the blood came from. Scalp wounds bleed like the bejesus." And one man was dead, but telling her wouldn't bring him back to life. Why pour cold water on her big moment?

She shuddered. "I don't think I want to know the details."

"No. You don't . . ." He glanced down, his speech banished by the image of the young man's corpse. At least his hands had stopped trembling. "But I want to hear yours. It's not every night you win a scholarship—or the football pools."

"I don't do the pools." She laughed and twisted the corkscrew home, and then pulled the cork. As if trying not to let pride fill her voice, she said, "But I did the exam, and I won."

Barry moved to Patricia and took the bottle from her. Then he grabbed her, hugged her, and kissed her hard. "I'm delighted," he managed to say at last. "Congratulations."

"You don't mind that I'll have to go away?" she asked shyly.

Of course he bloody well minded, but his concern was selfish, and this was not the time for selfishness. "I told you, I'm delighted and very, very proud of you."

"I love you, Barry."

"I know, and I love you." He pecked her cheek. Then, not wanting her to dwell on their forthcoming separation, he said, "Come on, I want to hear all about it." He took the glasses from her and set them on a coffee table.

She clapped her hands, like a little girl, he thought, who has been given the dolly she so much wanted. "I got the letter in the afternoon post. It had a Cambridge postmark and a Cambridge crest on the envelope." She smiled shyly. "I had to ask Mum to help me. My hands were shaking so much I couldn't open it."

"I'll bet they shook more when your mum told you the results."

She nodded. "I was gobsmacked. I couldn't believe it. I had to read it for myself. Dear God, Barry . . ." He heard awe in her voice. "I've done it. I've actually done it."

"It's wonderful." Barry took the bottle and poured two glasses. "I'm proud of you. Here." He handed her one. "Come and sit down." He waited for her to join him on the sofa, raised his glass, and said, "To your success."

Together they drank.

She lowered her glass. "And I'd promised to tell you as soon as I heard. I'm sorry I blurted it out over the phone, but I couldn't keep it to myself, and telling you on the phone wasn't good enough." She hugged him and kissed him so hard he almost spilled his wine. "I had to see you. Dad understood. He ran me up . . ."

"I'm glad of that," he said, seeing the joy in her dark eyes, loving their brightness.

"I still can't believe it. The award covers all my fees, books, equipment, and board and lodge for three years. I'll be living at Girton. That's one of the all-women colleges . . ."

He let her prattle on, understanding how unlike her it was to be so loquacious, how the excitement had built up inside her like steam in a whistling kettle.

"I'll have to pay, or at least Dad and Mum'll have to pay my travel expenses."

"I suppose that means you'll only be coming home for the long holidays?"

"That's right. I'll be off to England in the first week of September, but I will be home for Christmas. . . ."

"I'll be looking forward to it." He wanted to sigh, but instead forced a smile.

"And Easter, and I'll have two months off in the summer . . . if I'm not doing some kind of practical course." She took another drink. "Isn't it wonderful, darling? Isn't it?" She kissed him, and he tasted her through the wine.

The "darling," spoken with such naturalness, should have warmed him, but he felt a chill, already imagining her whispering it to some intense, long-haired undergraduate or, worse, to some junior don. Last year, a nurse, then so important, but now a fading memory, had dumped him for a young surgeon with better prospects than his own. He imagined Cambridge professors were paid a lot more than country GPs.

He tilted his head back and stared into her eyes. "It *is* wonderful," he said, "and I love you."

She didn't answer but kissed him once more, as lightly as butterfly wings on his lips; her perfume filled his senses. She sat back, took his hand, and said quietly, "Thank you."

"For what? For loving you? That's easy."

"Yes, but for more." She frowned. "I've been terrified about how I was going to tell you. I know what you're thinking. I know you think we'll drift apart . . ."

Barry lowered his gaze.

"But we won't. We won't. How could I not love, and go on loving, a man who's been dreading my winning, but who has not said a word about it and has celebrated with me? Hasn't let his worries show? You have a gift, Barry Laverty. It's no wonder O'Reilly thinks you're one of the finest young doctors he's met in years."

"O'Reilly said that?" O'Reilly said *that*?

"He did. When I was chatting to him a couple of weeks ago at the big party in his garden. He said your gift is to be able to feel what other people are feeling. And it's more than that. You don't just feel. You act on those feelings, just as you did when you learnt I'd won the bloody scholarship. You put yourself second."

"Well, I . . ." He could feel the heat of pleasure in his cheeks. "If it's true about feeling things and O'Reilly said it, then all I can say is, 'It takes one to know one.' I swear Fingal's telepathic."

Her smile had faded when she said, "And you admire him for it, don't you?"

He nodded.

"And you'd not mind being the kind of doctor Fingal O'Reilly is, would you?"

"No. I'd not." This was getting a bit too serious. "Warts and all. He's not perfect, you know."

"Neither," she said, "are you." She picked up her wine and sipped. "If you can read minds like O'Reilly, what am I thinking now?" She smiled and cocked one eyebrow at him. "Go on. What's on my mind?"

"Right now? I haven't the foggiest notion." Somehow he felt awkward. She'd always been confident, but now she seemed to be more than confident. The word "cocky" came to mind. Had success gone to her head? He wasn't sure if he liked the new Patricia.

"Huh," she said, "some mind reader." Suddenly her arms were round his neck, and she was pulling him to her, kissing him, her tongue flickering. She took his hand and held it to her left breast, and he felt the pressure of her hand and the warmth beneath it. She put her lips to his ear and whispered, "You think the man has to be the pursuer, don't you? 'Me Tarzan, you Jane.' Well, times are changing, and because they are you can't possibly read my mind."

He cupped her breast, feeling his whole body tingle; he screwed his eyes tightly shut and then felt the loss of her as she gently stood up and moved away, still holding his hand.

"Bring your wine," she said, and he opened his eyes and looked up at her smile.

"If you *had* known what I was thinking, you'd have beaten me along to the bedroom. It's the first door on the left."

41

She and I Were Long Acquainted

"I know it's only ten thirty. I'm sorry I'm so early, but it's such a lovely day." Barry followed Patricia through the front door of Number 9, The Esplanade, and into her flat. He closed the door behind him, took her in his arms, and kissed her, wanting her even more than he'd wanted her so few hours ago.

She pulled back and said slightly breathlessly, "I don't mind that you're early, but look at me. I'm a mess. I'm just out of the bath."

"You're beautiful," he said, even though her hair was damp and hung limply, and she wore no makeup. She was in an old, tatty dressing gown and pink, fluffy slippers.

"And you're nuts if you think that right now." She shook her head.

"Ah," he said with a grin, "vanity, thy name is woman."

"There's coffee in the pot," she said, moving away from him. "Would you like a cup?"

"Please."

She poured his coffee and put in some milk. She knew how he liked it. It was as if they were a long-married couple, comfortable in their morning ordinariness.

"I love you," he said.

"And I love you, Barry. I really do." She handed him a cup.

He took it, set it on the table, and held her to him. "Last night was wonderful. Thank you."

She kissed him, then smiled into his eyes. "Mmm."

He strangled the urge to untie the gown's belt and slip his hands beneath. God, he wanted her, but he sensed that now was not the time. He moved back, sat on the sofa, and gulped a mouthful of coffee. It was too hot. He burnt his lip, spluttered, and almost spilled the cup. "That's bloody scalding," he said.

She laughed. "So take your time, silly."

And he knew by the way she looked at him she wasn't talking about the hot drink.

"You sit there quietly," she said, "and I'll go and get ready."

"Fine." He made himself comfortable as she went along to the bathroom and closed the door. He heard the humming of a hair dryer and knew she'd be holding both hands above her head, as she had last night while he'd kissed her breasts. Stop thinking about it, he told himself. Stop it.

He stood up, then walked to the window to gaze past the tiny front garden where the rough, sea salt–burned grass straggled in brown tufts. He looked across the narrow road, and the seawall to where a fleet of racing yachts tacked close-hauled to the upwind mark. They'd be the Fairy class from Royal North of Ireland Yacht Club in Cultra.

The white sails were taut, straining against the wind, as the boats heeled to lee, spray from their bow waves shimmering and making tiny, ephemeral rainbows in the bright sunlight. It seemed to be a very long time since he'd had a chance to race, and he'd loved his sailing.

He heard the bathroom door open and close, turned, and glimpsed Patricia slipping across to her bedroom. Carrying her dressing gown over one arm, she was quite naked.

Perhaps it was watching the yachts that made him think of a passage from one of C. S. Forester's *Hornblower* books where the sailor hero and his new wife, Lady Barbara, are dressing, and she is wearing a transparent shift: "Women, once the barriers were down, really had no sense of decency." He smiled at the thought, and at the knowledge that Forester was wrong. It wasn't a matter of decency, but rather an indication of comfort and trust.

"I'll not be much longer" came from the bedroom. "Just putting on my face."

"Take your time," he called back. He was happy to wait. He sat on the sofa. "I came early because O'Reilly's gone off to pick up someone in Belfast, and Kinky's holding the fort until the service. She'll arrange an ambulance for anyone she thinks is really sick, and tell everyone else to come back tomorrow. There were no early calls, and I got bored sitting there waiting for the phone to ring."

"You mean waiting for calls from patients?"

"Yes." And perhaps from Jack Mills. But if Jack did phone, Kinky would take a message, and if he didn't, he'd promised to come to the reception this afternoon. Sitting playing with Lady Macbeth had not kept Barry from stewing. O'Reilly was right; doing something you loved, and he'd meant practising, could keep your mind off your worries, but so could being with someone you loved. "I reckon everyone's too busy getting ready to see Sonny and Maggie get hitched to be bothered to get sick," he said.

"It's going to be quite the do, isn't it?"

"The whole village is buzzing. Has been for the last week. If the rest of the folks are as excited as Kinky, it'll be standing room only in the church. She's had her new hat on and off half a dozen times." He remembered the song she'd been singing to herself as she admired her hat in front of the mirror above the hall table, and did his best to mimic her:

> "I have often heard it said by me father and me mother,
> That going to a wedding has the makings of another."

"That," she said, coming from her room, "is an interesting thought, but God, Barry, you couldn't carry a tune in a bucket." She turned her back to him and said, "Do me up please, darling."

She wore a high-collared, bottle-green blouse with a row of buttons down the back. The material gaped and he noticed her bra strap, black against her white skin. He stood and started to work, but his fingers were clumsy as he fastened the buttons. She'd left her hair down, and it fell in an ebony cascade to her shoulders. He pushed it aside and dropped a kiss on the nape of her neck. "There," he said, as he closed the final button.

"Ta." She spun round to face him. "How do I look?"

He eyed her up and down from her half-heeled patent pumps, past her calves—she clearly was not one bit concerned by the small amount of wasting from the polio in the left one—over her knee-length tartan kilt, and past her blouse to her almond eyes. "Stunning," he said, "absolutely stunning."

"Thank you, kind sir." She dropped a little curtsey. "Dad bought me the blouse yesterday."

"As a 'well done for winning the scholarship' present?"

"Sort of. He is proud of me."

"I'm not surprised. So am I." He hugged her.

"Don't mess up my hair."

He let her go, knowing he had to get out of the flat or he'd soon be trying to make a mess of more than her hair. "Look," he said, "we've plenty of time before the ceremony. I thought we might go for a drive."

"Where to?"

"Sonny's house. It's been derelict for years. But Donal Donnelly, he's one of our patients, and a bunch of the boys have been fixing it up. It's the village's wedding present to the happy couple, and it's to be a big surprise. I'd really like to see how they've finished the job."

"How absolutely lovely of them." A little frown creased her forehead. "There is something extra special about wee villages. I can see why you'd want to settle down here."

He nodded, knowing that she still did not understood that he might have reasons to leave too, and that she was one of those reasons.

"I'd like to see the place," she said. "I really would. Hang on. I'll get my handbag."

Barry parked close to Sonny's gate.

"What on earth is that?" she asked, pointing to Donal Donnelly's bike of many colours where it lay propped against the gatepost.

"Donal must be here," Barry said. "That's his machine."

"I hope," she said with a grin, "he has better taste in interior design."

Barry laughed. "Donal's all right. He may be a bit odd, but he has a heart of corn." He took her hand. "Come on, let's go and inspect the great project."

He paused at the gate. He barely recognized Sonny's house. The scaffolding had vanished. The new slate roof glowed darkly in sunlight that brightened the green-painted front door and window sashes, and flashed from the washed and polished glass. He was pleased to see window boxes on the lower sills. Maggie would like that.

Tarpaulins in one corner of the garden covered what must be the huge heap of Sonny's belongings. Years of sitting unsheltered from the elements would have ruined them. Two of his old motorcars were parked beside the caravan, which waited patiently for the return of Sonny's five dogs. Barry noticed that the vegetable garden had been weeded.

When he pushed the gate open, the hinges no longer creaked.

Patricia's heels clicked on the paving stones as he led her to the front door. The lawn had been newly cut, and the air smelled of grass clippings. A single goat's-beard weed had survived between a crack in the stones, and Barry's foot scattered its ball of downy seeds to float like miniature parachutes along the breeze. There was less wind inland here than he'd noticed earlier out on the lough.

He could hear a combine harvester working in the distance and the lowing of a cow. Two birds, black-caped and white-flanked, with long, broad tails, swooped erratically overhead, their cries harsh giggles.

"Magpies," Patricia said. "Two of them. That's lucky."

"I know." He squeezed her hand. "One for sorrow . . ." He repeated the country belief: "But there won't be sorrow if you salute the bird . . . two for joy . . ."

She continued the rhyme, "Three for a girl. Four for a boy. Five for silver. Six for gold . . ."

He finished it. "And seven for a secret never to be told . . . but I'll tell you a secret, Patricia Spence." He kissed her. "I love you."

He'd have kissed her for longer, but a loud cough interrupted. "Pardon me, Doctor Laverty sir." Donal Donnelly stood in the open doorway, his shock of ginger hair untidy, his buckteeth white in the middle of his grin. They really would be the envy of every hare in the Six Counties, Barry thought. He remembered thinking the selfsame thing the first time he'd met Donal, on the day last month when he'd been lost at the Six Road Ends. He'd been on his way to his job interview with Doctor Fingal Flahertie O'Reilly, M.B., B.Ch., B.A.O.

"Morning, Donal." Good Lord, the man was blushing. "Grand day."

"Oh, aye. Grand indeed."

"Donal, this is Miss Spence," Barry said. "Patricia. Donal Donnelly."

"Pleased to meet you, Miss," Donal said, knuckling his forehead. He shifted from foot to foot. "If youse'll excuse me, I'll be running along. I've to get into my uniform. Me and the rest of the Highlanders are going to be a guard of honour after the wedding, so we are. There's been nothing like it since Her Majesty the Queen came to Bangor a wheen of years ago." Donal stopped fidgeting. "Honest to God, I know you've been busy, Doctor, so maybe you'll not have heard, but all the ladies are fit to be tied, so they are."

"Because Sonny and Maggie are getting wed?"

"Not at all, sir; they're tickled pink about that, they've been talking about nothing else all week. All the best dresses is out and ready, so they are. The smell of mothballs would gag a maggot, but all women-folk wanted new hats for the big day . . . and do you know what?"

Barry made an effort to hide his smile. "What, Donal?"

"The dress shop was closed on Friday, and the silly besoms had all waited 'til the last minute. There wasn't a hat to be had for love nor money."

"Oh, dear."

"Dear's not the half of it," Donal said. "You'd've thought half the plagues of Egypt had come to Ballybucklebo."

Barry choked back a remark he was going to make, that at least the firstborn children had been spared. Under the circumstances it would have been less than tactful.

Donal plucked a long grass stem from a flowerbed, started to chew the end, and said seriously, "I heard that it was only the one plague, and it hit poor ould Miss Moloney hard. But then you'd know about that, Doc."

"Perhaps."

"Aye," said Donal, inspecting the now flattened piece of grass. "Aggie Arbuthnot told her cousin Cissie Sloan, and she told Finnoula Robinson, and she told my Julie, and Julie told me, and what do you think?"

Knowing how a rumour could become distorted as it passed from mouth to mouth, Barry was able to say quite honestly, "I haven't the faintest idea."

"Aggie seen her lying on the floor and she sent for youse doctors and she never saw Miss Moloney again." He lowered his voice to a half whisper. "Aggie thinks youse had her shipped off to Purdysburn, like."

Purdysburn was the Belfast mental hospital. Barry could tell by the expectant way Donal was looking at him that he was fishing for information, and given Donal's interest in thoroughbreds like Arkle, it was typical of the man to try to get it straight from the horse's mouth. "You know very well, Donal, I can't discuss patients."

Donal's hopeful look fled.

"But I can tell you Miss Moloney *was* unwell, and she's gone off to spend a few days with her sister."

Donal visibly brightened. "Right enough? Aye, well, I'm glad to hear that. I was never that fond of the ould biddy, but I'd not want her to go to the airport."

"The airport?"

"Maybe you don't remember, sir, but before they changed the name to Aldergrove, the Belfast Airport was called Nutts Corner, so it was. Anybody went crackers we used to say—"

"They'd gone to the airport. I understand, Donal." Barry had to laugh before he could continue. "Don't worry about that. She'll be right as rain in a day or two."

"I'm pleased," said Donal. He started to close the door, obviously impatient to get home to pass on this fresh bit in the ongoing saga of Miss Moloney. "I'm away on," Donal said, closing the door.

"Donal?"

"Aye?"

"Would it be all right if Miss Spence and I had a look round inside?"

"Aye, certainly. Help yourself; just don't bother to snib the front-door lock when you leave."

"Fine." When Barry had first come to the village after living in Belfast, the country habit of never locking doors had seemed strange. Now he found it reassuring.

"Right," said Donal. "I'm off . . . and if I don't see you through the window . . . I'll see you through the week, so I will." He cackled at his own witticism.

"Aye, and if *I* fall through the mattress . . . I'll see you in the spring. Go on with you, Donal, and make sure the Highlanders do a good job."

"Right, Doctor." Donal trotted off.

Barry led Patricia into the hall. There was an overpowering smell of fresh paint. The walls were cream, and bare of any decorations. A rug covered most of the floorboards. The door to his left stood ajar. "What's in here?" He pushed the door open.

"The dining room," Patricia said.

Sun's rays coming through the front windows made dust motes twinkle between a cut-glass chandelier and a pine table surrounded by four, wooden, hard-backed chairs. Two places were set on a chequered tablecloth. A vase of freshly cut flowers, their perfume rich and heavy, sat flanked by two brass candlesticks in the middle of the table. A hand-drawn card read, "Welcome home, Maggie and Sonny. Your dinner's in the fridge."

Patricia stood wide-eyed. "It's lovely. You told me the place was derelict."

"It was two weeks ago."

"If the rest of the place is like this, your friends must have worked like Trojans. It's as if . . . as if the fairy godmother from *Cinderella* had waved her magic wand."

"Somehow," he said, "I've a bit of difficulty casting Donal as the fairy godmother, but you're right. And I'll bet the rest of the place is—"

He recognized a deep voice that came booming into the room. "Helloo. Anyone home?"

What on earth was Fingal doing here? Probably, Barry thought, just as curious as I am to see the place. "Just us, Fingal. Come on in."

He heard boots clumping on the floorboards and then muffled by the rug. There were lighter footsteps. Someone was with O'Reilly.

O'Reilly stood in the doorway, dressed ready for the wedding. He seemed uncomfortable in his morning suit, Barry thought, looking like a ploughman fresh from the fields, scrubbed, and shoved into formal attire. A tiny piece of tissue paper clung to O'Reilly's jaw. He must have shaved more closely than usual this morning.

"Morning, Fingal," Barry said. "You've met Patricia Spence."

O'Reilly nodded in her direction. "And what the hell are you doing here, Laverty?" He didn't seem pleased to see Barry.

"Just having a look around." Was O'Reilly disappointed because Barry wasn't still back at Number 1 in case a patient needed him? "Kinky's looking after the shop."

O'Reilly cleared his throat, shook his head, turned, and said, "It's all right. It's just young Laverty. Come on in, Kitty."

Caitlin O'Hallorhan walked through the doorway.

Barry's mouth opened. So *that* was who O'Reilly had been talking to on the phone the other evening. He'd told Barry it was none of his business who he'd gone up to Belfast to collect this morning. Well, well.

"Sister," Barry said with a small bow, "nice to see you again. I hardly recognized you—" He was about to say "without your uniform on," but cut off the sentence. "This is Patricia Spence. Patricia, Sister O'Hallorhan."

As the two women were exchanging the to-be-expected noises— "Please call me Kitty" and "It's Patricia"—Barry had a good look at the ward sister, who'd known O'Reilly when he'd been a student at Trinity College.

The first time Barry'd met her, he'd thought her a handsome woman. But out of uniform she was striking. She carried herself erectly. Her well-tailored, two-piece, maroon suit complemented her trim figure, and even if the skirt seemed a little short for most women in their fifties, her stiletto-heeled pumps and dark stockings accented a pair of legs that Barry reckoned were not bad at all. Not at all.

Kitty's hair, now freed from the confines of her starched uniform headress, was shining silver. Barry wondered if the darker patches had had a little help from a bottle of tinting. In the sunshine, the amber flecks in her grey eyes seemed golden, and the laugh lines in the corners of her eyes deepened as she smiled and said to Barry, "I see you're a man of your word, Doctor Laverty."

"I'm sorry?"

"You did give Fingal here my regards."

O'Reilly's collar must be too tight, Barry thought, watching him tug at it with one finger. If anything, the big man's florid complexion was a darker hue. "Well," he said, "old *friends* from student days should keep in touch."

"Och, indeed, Fingal," she said, with a wicked grin, "to be sure. What's twenty-five years to old friends?"

O'Reilly made another harrumphing noise, hauled out his briar, struck a match, hesitated, and then asked meekly, "Do you ladies mind if I smoke?"

Patricia shook her head.

"Go right ahead," Kitty said. "I've always liked the smell of pipe tobacco."

O'Reilly busied himself, making sure the pipe was drawing well, puffing and belching streams of smoke.

You don't fool me, Fingal Flahertie O'Reilly, Barry thought. You're at a loss for words, and I've seen you use that trick, just like your old *Warspite* laid a smokescreen. "We've only just got here and as far as we can tell, Donal and his merry men have done a superb job," Barry said.

"Have they, by God?" O'Reilly asked, with a look at Barry. "Is this all you've seen?"

"So far," Barry said.

"Then lead on, Macduff," he said to Patricia. "You show Kitty the rest." He grabbed Kitty O'Hallorhan's hand and pulled her aside. "You go with Miss Spence, please. I need to have a word with my young colleague."

O'Reilly had said "please"? Barry refrained from correcting O'Reilly's misquotation from *Macbeth*. He didn't want to embarrass the man in front of Kitty. He waited for the women to leave, and said, "Yes, Fingal?"

But O'Reilly didn't seem to be paying attention. He was staring at Kitty O'Hallorhan's retreating back, saying quietly, "I haven't seen that girl for years, and she hasn't changed one scrap. Not one scrap."

Barry waited as O'Reilly tapped the mouthpiece of his pipe against his teeth. Then the big man remarked, "She's one powerful woman." His pipe had gone out, but he didn't seem to have noticed.

Barry coughed. "You said you wanted a word, Fingal?"

"What?" He turned to face Barry. "Right. Yes. I'm glad I ran into you. I need a bit of a hand."

"What with?"

"After the service."

"How?"

"I should've asked you earlier, but it slipped my mind. Someone has to drive Kitty to the reception."

Did it slip your mind, Fingal? Barry wondered. Or did you not want to tell me who you were bringing?

"You see, Sonny's still pining for his dogs. They're at Maggie's. I want to nip over and bring them to His Lordship's . . ."

"And you want me to bring Kitty?"

O'Reilly nodded. "Aye, and I'd like you to pick up Arthur Guinness too."

"I can do that."

"Good lad." O'Reilly clapped Barry on the shoulder. "I knew I could count on you."

"My pleasure."

Faint giggles came from above, along with the sound of women's voices. Both men looked up and waited as heels clicked down the stairs. Kitty and Patricia came in. Patricia was holding on to Kitty O'Hallorhan's arm, as if the pair of them were old friends. Both were smiling broadly.

"Well?" O'Reilly asked.

"It's wonderful," said Patricia. "The kitchen's all set up. Two of the bedrooms are unfurnished, but the third has a huge brass bed, chintz curtains, and a lovely view down over the fields to the lough away in the distance. Sonny and Maggie're going to get a great start."

"Good," said O'Reilly, avoiding looking directly at Kitty O'Hallorhan. "It's bloody well time the pair of them finally got together." He struck another match, then fixed Barry with a glare. "Now," he said, "plans." He sounded more like the old O'Reilly. "I'm sure, Barry, you and Miss Spence would like to have a bit of time on your own . . ."

And even if we didn't, we're going to get it, Barry thought.

"I'm going to take Kitty to the Old Inn in Crawfordsburn for lunch." His stomach growled.

"That's fine," Barry said, looking at Patricia with a tiny shake of his head. "I'm not hungry, are you?"

"Not a bit." She smiled back at him. "There's sure to be enough to eat at the reception."

"Good," said O'Reilly, "that's settled then. We'll be off. We'll see you in the church." He held the door wide open, bowed slightly to Kitty, and waited for her to precede him through the door.

Barry took Patricia's hand and led her to the front door. He held his finger to his lips. He was dying to ask Patricia what she thought of Kitty, but he wanted to wait until O'Reilly was out of earshot.

He watched O'Reilly hold the car door open and saw Kitty climb in. Then he distinctly heard her saying, "Now you will drive carefully, won't you, Fingal? You know you nearly hit a cyclist on the way down here."

42

Brightly Dawns Our Wedding Day

Sonny and Maggie were now man and wife 'til death did them part. Sonny kissed the bride; the minister, his right hand raised, gave the benediction; and the bridal procession headed past the congregation and down the aisle to the thunderous organ chords of the "Wedding March."

Barry glanced up to the roof beams of the old church, where octagonal lanterns hung on chains and multihued sunlight, tinted by its passage through a stained-glass window, sparkled from the lanterns' glass and made the spiderwebs in the ceiling's corners shine. He wondered how many weddings the church had seen. It had been built in 1743.

He let Kitty and Patricia precede him as they left their front pew to head for the porch. By the time they were outside, much of the rest of the congregation had already vanished. They would be hurrying to the reception at the marquis' estate.

Barry was blinded by the sunlight and deafened by the roaring of the great Highland bagpipes. Two columns of Highlanders, distended bags under their arms, drones on their shoulders, flanked the pavement. Donal Donnelly stood at what he probably considered to be attention. His kilt drooped to midcalf, his sporran was askew, and his caubeen was pushed to the back of his head. He held a silver-headed mace aloft, clearly not discomfited by the cast on his index finger. He was revelling in the exalted position of drum major.

Barry stepped in front of the two women and beckoned. It was useless trying to make himself heard over the racket. He skirted the ranks and headed for the back lane where Brunhilde was parked. At least behind Number 1 the sounds of the pipes were muted, but in the back garden Arthur Guinness sat, head thrown back, yodelling horribly out of tune with the band.

"I'm sorry," he said to Kitty, "but Fingal told me to bring the beast. I'm afraid one of you is going to have to share the backseat with the Hound of the Baskervilles."

"I'll do it," Patricia said. Barry held the seat forward and helped her climb in, unable to keep his eyes off the length of thigh exposed as she scrambled aboard. He remembered last night and wished they could have the car to themselves for the drive.

"Come on, Arthur," he called, holding the gate open. "Heel."

The dog glanced at Barry's new pants, shook his head as if deciding that having a go at Barry wasn't worth the effort, and climbed in beside Patricia.

He flipped the seat upright. "You're next, Sister O'Hallorhan."

"It's Kitty," she told him, getting in.

He ran round the car, got in, and started the engine. "Next stop, the reception."

Well-wishers, those perhaps in less of a hurry to get to the reception, stood cheering on both sides of Main Street. Up ahead Barry saw a small jaunting car. Maggie, Sonny, and the marquis, as best man, were perched on its benches. A becapped Fergus Finnegan sat in the driver's seat, urging a small donkey to plod along. A sign on the back of the vehicle said, Just Married.

Barry passed them. As he did, he saw the cross of black hair on the donkey's back, reminding him of the Irish belief that all donkeys were so marked to remind their kind forever of the part one of them had played in bringing the Virgin Mary to Bethlehem.

There was a distinct attar of dog coming from the backseat. Barry wound down his window.

He heard Patricia say, "Who's a good boy then?" and a glance in the rearview mirror showed the big black Labrador curled up in the seat, head on Patricia's lap and a look of besotted adoration in his brown eyes. Barry knew how the dog felt.

Soon he came upon a cyclist retrieving his bicycle from the ditch. He was not one bit surprised. O'Reilly may well have succumbed to Kitty O'Hallorhan's request to drive more carefully, but Fingal himself was fond of referring to the inability of leopards to change their spots.

He wondered if the wedding reception would be a match for the party in O'Reilly's back garden two weeks ago. He'd find out soon. It would certainly be of a different tenor to the solemnity of the just-concluded wedding ceremony. Barry was not a religious man, but the words, going back to the time of James I, were familiar and their cadences a comforting reminder of the permanence of a place like Ballybucklebo.

The gates of the estate were wide open, and Barry could hear the distant noises of a crowd. He drove slowly along the gravelled drive, past the topiary animals, smiling at the one that looked to him like a deformed duck, the one he'd first seen when he'd come here to go fishing on the Bucklebo River.

He found a place to park, got out, and then opened the passenger door. He yelled over the racket, "Let's go and see if we can find Fingal." As soon as Patricia climbed out, Arthur followed and galloped off, ignoring Barry's cries of "Sit, sir."

He took Patricia's hand and nodded to Kitty. "Come on. It's not going to be easy finding him in this mob."

Half of the lawn was occupied by a head table that ran at right angles to several other long tables. Some of the dining area was in bright sunlight, while some was dappled by the shadows of the old elms that grew inside the wall of the demesne.

The rest of the lawn was packed with a milling scrum. Never mind the whole village—the entire townland must be here. Everybody seemed to be yelling at the top of their voices. Dogs barked, children screamed and laughed, and snippets of conversation assailed Barry's ears.

A huge monkey puzzle tree, its downward pointing branches dark green and prickly, was surrounded by a ring of children, circling it and loudly singing,

"Ring around the rosies,
   A pocketful of posies . . ."

Something nudged Barry's leg. He glanced down to see Arthur Guinness, looking up as if to say, "I've found the boss. What's keeping you?" Arthur was, after all, a gundog. He turned and started to weave through the legs of the revellers.

Barry looked ahead in the direction of the dog's progress and spotted O'Reilly chatting to the marquis' gamekeeper.

"There he is," he said, and lengthened his stride.

"Take your time, Barry," Patricia called. "Heels and grass are not the best combination."

Barry took her hand and slowed his pace. He heard snippets of conversation as he passed groups of neighbours.

"And wee Colin's hand's healed up a treat, and he never felt the stitches . . ."

He smiled at Mrs. Brown as he moved forward, holding onto Patricia's hand and hoping Kitty was able to keep up.

"Not at all, Myrtle . . ." He overheard Finnoula Robinson speaking to Myrtle MacVeigh. "Aggie seen Miss Moloney lying on the floor until the doctors come. She was white as a sheet. No one's seen hide nor hair of her since."

Barry smiled. The information he'd given to Donal earlier this morning didn't seem to have percolated too far. As he moved past, he enquired, "Feeling better, Myrtle?"

"Och, aye. Them nighties-fer-aunties was cracker." She grinned broadly and turned back to Finnoula. "Go on. I want to hear more. What do you think happened to the ould biddy?"

Barry could smell meat cooking. He craned over the throng until he could see that a curl of smoke wafting past the Georgian facade of the Big House was coming from a whole pig being roasted on a spit. Kinky was keeping a watchful eye on the proceedings. He could make out the bright green of her new hat. He waved at her, but she mustn't have seen him. Oh, well, she was here, and he'd catch up with her soon enough to ask if Jack Mills had called.

Barry had been so busy trying to attract Kinky's attention that he bumped into Archie Auchinleck, who was talking to Constable Mulligan. "See you that Bertie Bishop? Him and he's going to close the Duck? He's a miserable wee gobshite, so he is. A born-again fuck . . ." Archie must have caught sight of Patricia. "Scuse me, Miss. Youse weren't meant to hear that."

"I didn't hear a thing, Mr.—?"

"Auchinleck."

Patricia stopped, Kitty beside her, to chat with Archie. He was blushing to the roots of his hair.

Barry finally managed to reach the edge of the crowd, where he waited for the women. He felt someone tugging his jacket, turned, and saw Helen Hewitt. She was wearing a short-sleeved blouse and a very short skirt.

Barry had to put his ear close to her mouth to hear over the din.

"I hear that ould targe Miss Moloney's not too happy," she said, with a wicked grin. "Serves her right. She's a personality like a bagful of hammers, so she has." He saw the fire in her green eyes. "But maybe I was a *bit* hard on her. I nearly fainted, so I did, when Doctor O'Reilly came to see me yesterday with my wages and a week's severance. I never thought I'd see a brass farthing. He told me she'd gone away for a few days."

"What else did he tell you, Helen?"

"Not to say nothing to no one about what I done."

"Have you?"

"Not at all." She shook her head defiantly. "What was between her and me stays between her and me. Anyhow, I'll not be staying here long. I've got a job in a Belfast linen mill, and I start on Monday."

"I'll be sorry to see you go."

"Aye. Well, it's for the best, and . . ." She beckoned and Barry bent lower. "My rash is nearly all gone, so it is, since I quit that bloody shop."

He nodded and mouthed, "Good."

"I hope to God I never need a doctor again, but if I do, I'll be coming back here to see yourself, so I will. I'm right glad you come to work here with the ould fellah. He works himself far too hard."

Before he could reply, the crowd all cheered at once. When the noise died to a more subdued level, he heard Helen say, "See you, and stay on in the practice here." She squeezed his arm. "Now, run away on with your lady friend. She's lovely, so she is."

Helen left as Patricia drew level. "And who was that?" There was just a tiny edge in her voice.

"One of my patients."

"Oh," she said, "that's all right then."

Gosh. Was she becoming possessive? If she was, Barry didn't mind one bit.

O'Reilly was moving away from where, close to the house, Willy and Mary Dunleavy stood behind a drink-laden table. Queues meandered away from the makeshift bar. It seemed a bit quieter at the edges of the crowd, and Barry heard faint bells merrily pealing somewhere in the distance. There weren't any in the Presbyterian church, so it must be coming from the steeple of the Catholic chapel. A generous gesture, he thought. Maybe this ecumenical business he'd read about could get a head start in Ballybucklebo.

Ethel and Kieran O'Hagan moved to his side. "Doctor Laverty," she said, "it's great you've got Kieran fixed up for Monday. He'll be admitted tomorrow night." Her wrinkled old face reddened, and she whispered, "I'd not have fancied trying that plumber's trick again."

"My pleasure. I'm sure you'll be fine, Kieran."

He thought how two weeks ago he'd made a mental note not to ask patients how they were when he was having his day off. Now he understood why O'Reilly had enquired about a man's eye troubles at the races, had been happy to answer medical questions even in the Mucky Duck. The truth was, a country GP in a place like Ballybucklebo was never off-duty—and it wasn't such a bad thing.

He saw Patricia point, and it was his turn to follow as she and Kitty headed to where O'Reilly was now parked at the head table. Further along, the Presbyterian minister and his wife were sitting.

O'Reilly rose as the women arrived, pulled out Kitty's chair, and waited until she was seated.

"Come and sit down, Barry," O'Reilly roared. He held a large glass of whiskey in one hand. "The bride and groom should be here in a few minutes, so if anyone wants a drink before the formalities start—and that includes you, Reverend—it's speak now or forever hold your peace."

"Glass of white wine for Patricia," Barry said, seeing her nod of approval. "And . . ." He almost ordered a sherry, but he remembered O'Reilly's remark about "growing out" of sherry drinking. "A small Bushmills, please."

O'Reilly held up one thumb and took the other orders.

"And two glasses of orange juice," the minister said, smiling at his wife.

"Mother of God," said O'Reilly, "surely you could have something stronger today?"

The minister shook his head and tutted.

"Makes you wonder," said O'Reilly, "why the Good Lord bothered with his first miracle."

"And what would that have been, Doctor O'Reilly?"

"In Cana of Galilee. As I recall, His Sainted Self didn't turn the water at the wedding feast into orange juice. It was wine."

The minister seemed to take the ribbing in good part. Fair play to him, Barry thought. Then the minister said, "Very well, Doctor. If you insist. Two small glasses of red wine, please."

"Good man ma da," said O'Reilly, clapping the minister on the shoulder. "Come on, Barry. I'll need a hand to carry it all."

Barry shrugged at Patricia and mouthed, "I'll be back in a minute."

"Lord," said O'Reilly, "she's not going to run away. And Patricia?"

"Yes, Fingal."

"Keep that seat on the corner beside us for Kinky. I see her heading this way."

Barry had to run to keep up with O'Reilly, who, as was his wont, went straight up to the head of the queue, raising not a single protest from those waiting. He gave his order to Willy Dunleavy. "And make sure my Black Bush is a double. Do you hear?"

Barry squeezed past Maureen, Seamus, and baby Barry Fingal Galvin.

"How's about ye, Doc?" Seamus said. "This is our last hooley in Ballybucklebo. The three of us is off to America on Monday."

"I'm grand, thanks, and good luck to you there, Seamus. Maureen. I hope you make your fortune, and maybe you'll come back and visit one day."

"We'll be back, Doc, right enough," Seamus said. "It's tough enough having to go."

"I know how you feel," Barry said. "Now, if you'll excuse me, I have to give Doctor O'Reilly a hand."

He moved to O'Reilly's side, took a tray of full glasses, and headed back to the table.

Kinky was seated in the corner, beaming mightily as she adjusted her new hat.

Barry handed out the drinks, then took his seat beside Patricia. He raised his glass to her and whispered, "To the new scholarship winner."

She smiled and toasted him, but said quietly, "No, Barry, just 'to us.'"

He felt her hand take his under the table.

"Excuse me, Doctor Laverty," Kinky said. "Himself is blethering away to that nice Dublin lady, but when you've a wee minute will you tell him what a great success my new hat is?"

"Of course, Kinky."

She held one finger to her lips then said, "*I* know very well why none of the rest of the ladies have new ones . . ." Of course she did. O'Reilly had told her the whole story at lunchtime yesterday and asked her to keep it to herself. "Flo Bishop bought one in Bangor, but the rest are in their old ones, so mine's the envy of all."

"I'm pleased."

"And there's one more wee thingeen I've to tell you."

"And what's that?"

"That friend of yours, Doctor Mills, phoned just before I left for the church . . ."

Barry's fist tightened around his glass.

"And he said for to tell you . . ."

But Barry couldn't hear her words. The air was rent by the music of the pipes, the battering of the drums, and the howling of Arthur Guinness who had crept under the table at O'Reilly's feet.

"That tune's called 'Marie's Wedding,'" O'Reilly roared over the din.

Barry didn't care if it was the tune the old cow died to. He wanted to hear what Kinky had to say.

Some chance.

Donal Donnelly led the procession. Behind him came the Highlanders, kilts swinging, bags inflated, cheeks red and bulging, foreheads sweating, fingers fluttering over the chanters. Two tenor drummers whirled their woolly-headed drumsticks. Side drummers played paradiddles and rolls. A man Barry didn't recognize had taken Seamus Galvin's place as big drummer and was whacking away.

Behind them came the donkey, resolutely pulling the little cart where the marquis perched. Looking solemn in his morning coat and top hat, he was every inch a peer of the realm. Sonny seemed bewildered by all the fuss, but Maggie, her white wedding dress shining in the sunlight, had a smile from ear to ear.

Behind ran the children, skipping over the grass. One little boy—Barry thought he recognized Colin Brown—was happily turning cartwheels.

Sonny's five dogs appeared from wherever O'Reilly had left them and ran jumping and barking beside the cart.

Barry wanted to talk to Kinky, but until the pandemonium died down, he was going to have to wait.

43

Let's Have a Wedding

Boom-boom. Boom-boom. The big drummer gave the double beat to signal the end of the tune. The wailing of the pipes died, and for the first time in that noisy gathering silence fell. The sun warmed Barry, and the aroma of roasting pig tickled his nostrils.

The marquis dismounted and stood to hand Maggie down from the cart. Barry smiled when he noticed that her now thrown-back veil was held in place by a demure circlet of artificial lilies of the valley, but in the circle, front and centre, was a wilted orange nasturtium. The day Maggie MacCorkle *doesn't* have a dead flower in her hatband, he thought, will be the day the sun fails to rise.

She must have owned a set of dentures because, although Barry had never seen her wearing them before, today her smile was flawless. Her cheeks, which he had once thought looked like dried prunes, were full and shining. And someone had done a remarkable job of hiding the fine brown moustache that lurked under her makeup.

The marquis led Maggie and Sonny to the head table. Maggie fussed with her gown, and Sonny stood behind her chair waiting until she seemed to be comfortable before taking his own seat. Then he sat, with the erect posture of a regimental sergeant major.

The moment the marquis took his place and the bridal party was settled, a roar of cheering filled the air and sent a flock of jackdaws whirling and cawing from the tops of the elm trees.

Barry sat beside Patricia as the rest of the crowd found seats. The hum of conversation was more muted, and he'd no difficulty hearing Patricia whisper, "She looks lovely."

It was true, he thought, even if Maggie was in her sixties.

Sonny seemed uncomfortable in a morning coat, presumably lent by the marquis. It was at least one size too large, but he wore it with his usual understated dignity. He was bent, smiling at his five dogs who were clustered round him, vying for their master's attention. Barry watched him pat each one in turn. He couldn't hear whatever endearments the old man was murmuring to the friends he hadn't seen since he'd been admitted to hospital, but Sonny's eyes glistened. He even had a pat for Arthur Guinness, who had joined the canine celebration.

O'Reilly said, "You'll be pleased to see them." Sonny looked up and smiled. "Can you get them in under the table, Sonny? It's time to get the business started. And you, Arthur Guinness, you great lummox, sit."

It took a while to get the dogs settled.

Barry leant over and tried to attract Kinky's attention, but she was deep in conversation with the middle-aged woman sitting opposite her. The woman was unknown to Barry. He overheard snippets of their conversation.

"Have you heard the latest about Miss Moloney?" the stranger asked.

Kinky, who had been told the full story by O'Reilly, looked suitably innocent. "I have not."

"It's wonderful what modern medicine can do." The stranger oozed confidence in her information, but lowered her voice so Barry had difficulty making out her next words. "They took her up to the Royal, and she had that marvellous operation . . . the one where they remove the *entire* brain and then put it back." Her eyes widened.

"Aye, so? The whole shebang, is it? Tut-tut," said Kinky, wonderingly. Then she caught Barry's eye. As he laughed out loud, she did a masterful job of keeping a straight face. "Well, well, there's a thing. We'll just have to be very nice to the poor *sean-bean*—the old woman—when she comes back to Ballybucklebo. I think I'll bake her a cherry cake. Maybe some of the other ladies will be able to make something too."

Barry couldn't hear the reply because O'Reilly was on his feet, pounding a fork on an empty water glass. "I want your attention. Your attention," he roared, in his quarterdeck voice. "And that includes you, Donal Donnelly."

"Sorry, Doctor."

"Now, my lord, ladies, and gentlemen . . . and that *doesn't* include you, Donal Donnelly—"

He was interrupted by laughter and had to wait for it to subside.

"I've been asked to compere this afternoon's festivities, where we're here to celebrate the wedding of two of Ballybuckebo's finest residents."

"*Hear, hear!*" someone yelled, as applause started.

O'Reilly battered the glass. "But be that as it may, if you don't stop interrupting, I'll never get finished . . . and none of us'll get fed. So everyone hold your wheest, and pay attention . . . and that *does* include you, Donal Donnelly."

More laughter.

"Saving the reverend's presence, because it's usually his job"— O'Reilly bowed to the minister—"I'm going to tell you the order of service. We'll start with grace, then we'll eat. There's a buffet set up beside the bar, and I want this done all shipshape and Bristol fashion. None of your Ballybucklebo scrums. None of this charging about like the Gaderene swine. Head table first, then each table in turn, starting with the one on my right. Is that clear?"

He paused until a murmur of approval had died down.

Barry smiled, but he glanced at Kinky and wished O'Reilly would get a move on. He really wanted to put his concerns aside and enjoy the occasion, and he'd be able to do that with much more enthusiasm once he knew what Jack had had to say. It was the uncertainty that was so hard to take. He concentrated on what O'Reilly was saying.

"Once you've all been fed and watered, there'll be a bit of a pause, and then some speechifying. Not much, I promise, because I know some of you will have serious business to attend to." He lifted his glass.

"Now you're talking, Doctor," someone yelled.

"I'll call on each speaker, and I have advice for them. I want every one of you to stand up, speak up . . . then shut up. Be like Fergus Finnegan, the jockey. Short. Very short."

"Good things come in small bundles, so they do, Doctor," Fergus yelled back, "and the bigger they are, the harder they fall."

The allusion to O'Reilly's size was not lost on the crowd, and there were more roars of laughter and a few loud whistles. Fergus rose and bowed to his supporters.

"One to you, Fergus," O'Reilly conceded, and waited for silence. "I'm done now," he said, "so I'll ask you all to rise and bow your heads while the reverend says the words." He turned to the minister. "If you please, sir?"

Barry stood with everyone else and waited until grace was finished, then immediately leant over the table. "Kinky? Kinky?"

"What?"

"What did Doctor Mills say?"

"He said, Doctor Laverty, for to tell you he was very sorry, so—"

"Sorry?" Did that mean Harry hadn't found anything? Barry felt a trickle from under his armpits, and although the sun was drowsily warm it hadn't made him sweat until that moment.

"He'd been up all night. He'd slept late, but he was on his way to see your other friend, and he'd come straight on down here after. Is that all right, sir?"

Barry sighed. "Fine," he said. "Thanks for telling me."

"Doctor Laverty?"

"Yes?"

"You look like a man who's got his fingers stuck in a milking machine and the suction pressure on full. I told you you'd hear what you want to, so just you bide, and be patient."

He stared at her. He had never seen her look so serious. "I'll try to," he said. And by God, he would. He'd be an idiot to be the only misery-guts in the whole of Ballybucklebo today, and there was something about Kinky that he didn't understand. It beggared all logic, but he was willing to take her word that all would turn out for the best.

"Good, so," she said. "Now run along and get you that nice Miss Spence a bite to eat."

"I will."

Kinky sniffed. "Mind you. In my opinion that pig could have done with another half hour's roasting."

There hadn't been much conversation at the head table as the meal was eaten. O'Reilly, napkin tucked under his collar, had headed back to the buffet for a second helping, and he, Barry thought, was a man who'd not long ago taken Kitty O'Hallorhan to the Old Inn at Crawfordsburn for lunch.

O'Reilly burped. "Excuse me," he said. Then he turned to Barry. "I'm going to give them ten more minutes for the ones who were served last to finish eating." He glanced at his glass. "I seem to be dry. Can I get you anything?"

Barry shook his head.

O'Reilly rose. "Stay, sir," he said to Arthur as he headed for the bar.

Barry pushed his plate away and said to Patricia, "Would you like to meet the happy couple?"

"I'd love to."

"I should warn you: Maggie's a bit different. The first time I met her she was complaining of headaches."

"I don't see anything different about that."

"Two inches *above* the crown of her head?"

"What? Are you serious?"

"Absolutely. Come on, let's go and have a word."

Patricia rose and together they moved along the table.

"Excuse me," Barry said. "Maggie, Sonny, may I present Miss Patricia Spence?"

Sonny stood, and bowed. He took Patricia's hand in his and bent over it, planting a kiss one inch above it. "Charmed, Miss Spence."

He'd have been right at home at the court of Louis XIV of France, Barry thought.

"So *you're* the one I've been hearing about," Maggie said, head cocked to one side, eyes narrowed, as she regarded Patricia with a frankly appraising gaze. She grinned. "You're even prettier than I heard tell. You've been the talk of the village, you know."

Barry had never seen Patricia discomfited before. She blushed and stuttered as she said, "Th . . . thank you, Maggie."

"Aye," said Maggie, "but beauty's only skin deep and it'll fade." She pursed her lips. "If he's in love with you, he must have fallen for your eyes. They're lovely, and *they'll* last, so they will." And her own eyes sparkled.

It was Barry's turn to blush.

"I think, Doctor Laverty, this young lady's too good for you," Maggie said.

"I'm sure you're right, Maggie," Barry said, as he looked at Patricia. He didn't have time to say more.

O'Reilly was back and on his feet, ringling-dingling his fork on a glass. "Pay attention. I know some of you are still eating, but it's time to let the dog see the rabbit and get things moving along. Those of you on your feet, take your seats."

Barry led Patricia back. As he sat, he noticed a slurping noise coming from beneath the table. A quick glance beneath let him see a contented Arthur Guinness with his tongue darting in and out of a bowl of dark liquid that Barry knew was Smithwick's beer. So O'Reilly *had* pardoned the wellie-napper.

The glass was jangling again. Barry sat up and heard O'Reilly say, "Right then. It's time to get on with the proceedings, but before we do, I want to say on behalf of everyone here a huge thank-you to the marquis of Ballybucklebo for allowing us to use his grounds."

The roar from the crowd was deafening.

"I agree," said O'Reilly, "but now with no further ado I call on His Lordship to propose the toast to the happy couple."

O'Reilly sat, and the marquis rose. "My lord . . ." He pretended to frown. "Hold on a minute, that's me I'm talking to, and you all know what talking to oneself is a sign of."

Loud laughter.

"I'll start again. Ladies and gentlemen, we have all known Maggie

MacCorkle and our friend Sonny for many years. Sonny: chess player, expert on Middle Eastern pottery, and . . ."—he looked straight at Bertie Bishop—"Norman land titles."

Barry looked over, saw the councillor scowl, and saw Mrs. Bishop fetch him a ferocious dig in the ribs with her elbow.

"Maggie: cat fancier; mistress of Ulster's most belligerent feline, General Sir Bernard Law Montgomery; window-box gardener *extra-ordinaire*; and—some of you may not know this—winner of the silver medal in the All-Ireland springboard diving championship in nineteen twenty-two."

Barry certainly hadn't. Neither by the look of amazement on his face had O'Reilly. Nor judging by the gasps of amazement had many of the villagers.

"And here she is, once again taking the plunge, but this time . . ." —he inclined his head toward Sonny—"I think she's won the gold."

No one laughed. No one cheered. Instead the sound of hands clapping in sincere agreement was loud and prolonged.

"Now, I want to take Doctor O'Reilly's advice and be short. Congratulations to you, Sonny, and every happiness to you, Maggie." He raised his glass. "I'll ask you all to charge your glasses and rise with me and drink a toast. Long may they be happy together and the sun shine every day on their marriage. To the bride and groom."

"To the bride and groom," roared the chorus.

O'Reilly called, "Sonny will now reply on behalf of the happy couple." He tapped Sonny on the shoulder. "On your hind legs, Sonny."

Sonny rose. O'Reilly sat.

Barry looked at the older man, pulling with one finger inside his one-size-too-big collar. Sonny stood with an erectness that belied his years and exuded the sort of bearing that came naturally to a reigning monarch.

"My lord . . . and I'm *not* talking to myself, ladies and gentlemen. I've very little to say on behalf of . . . my wife and I . . ." He smiled down at Maggie.

Barry saw both of them blush.

"But there are a number of people I should like to thank. First, like

Doctor O'Reilly thanked him, I want to thank His Lordship for his generosity to me in so very many ways."

There was polite applause.

"Next I want to thank Councillor Bishop . . ."

Barry heard a communal in-drawing of breath. Everyone present knew of the long running feud between the two men, the dispute over Sonny's roof that had caused Maggie to refuse to marry him until the roof was repaired.

"No. No," Sonny said. "The councillor *is* repairing my roof, for which I am very grateful, and I trust that from now on he and I can let bygones be bygones." He looked straight across to Bertie Bishop.

"Finally," Sonny said, "I want to thank Maggie MacCorkle for waiting for me for all these years and finally consenting to be my wife . . ."

Maggie certainly had waited. Barry knew that. It could happen. He looked at Patricia and wondered what she was thinking.

"And for bringing with her such a wonderful dowry."

Barry frowned. Surely that old custom had died out years ago?

"I am, of course, referring to the donkey and the pig. Maggie and I were driven here on one half of the dowry . . ." He paused and surveyed the crowd; then his leathery, usually serious face split into an enormous grin. "And you greedy buggers have eaten the other half."

The cheers and laughter were deafening as Sonny sat.

Before O'Reilly could speak, Maggie had risen. Barry could see some of the older attendees frowning. In Ulster the bride was meant to sit demurely by her new husband's side and say nothing. But then Maggie, at least as much as Barry knew her, had always seemed to make her own rules. "I know, I know, I'm meant to keep my trap shut, but His Lordship proposed a toast to both of us, and don't I have a mouth too?"

"And sure don't we know that, Maggie?" a heckler called. "Isn't it usually going up and down between your ears like a skipping rope?"

General laughter.

"Be that as it may, I want my turn to thank His Lordship and . . ." She gritted her false teeth, and Barry could see her hands clenching by her sides. "And Councillor Bishop. If he hadn't fixed Sonny's roof,

I'd still be alone with my cat." Then she grinned. "I've advice for some of youse." She let her gaze fall on Barry and then turned to O'Reilly and Kitty. "Sonny and me are a pair of stubborn 'oul goats to have fallen out over a stupid roof. We waited far too long. Don't you young folks be as daft as us."

Barry glanced at Patricia, who was looking, with one eyebrow raised, at Maggie. He saw O'Reilly frown and stare at the back of Kitty's head, and he would have given a day's wages to know exactly what Patricia *and* Fingal Flahertie O'Reilly were thinking at that moment.

Maggie bent and planted a wet kiss on Sonny's forehead. "I still love you, husband," she said. Then she sat down to a round of applause that made the previous bout of clapping sound as faint as tiny ripples on a shingle beach.

O'Reilly was on his feet, waiting for silence. "Well done, Maggie." He held up his hand. "I promised you this would be short, but a little bird has told me that one or two among us could use a moment's respite." He paused and looked at Archie Auchinleck and his son, who both had several empty Guinness glasses on the table in front of them, "And I confess that includes myself. His Lordship says to use the facilities on the ground floor. Go on off all those that need to, ladies first, and we'll reconvene in ten minutes."

O'Reilly left. Arthur Guinness stuck his muzzle out from under the table and put one paw on Barry's thigh.

"Don't you bloody well dare, dog," Barry said sternly.

Arthur heaved a sigh and trotted off after O'Reilly.

Barry was aware of someone standing behind him. Turning, he saw Donal Donnelly, bareheaded and with the top three buttons of his uniform tunic undone. Julie MacAteer, looking pale but happy, stood by his side.

Barry rose. "How are you, Julie?"

She smiled at him. "Well on the mend, thanks, Doctor."

"Good."

"I just wanted to say thanks . . ."

"No need."

"And cheerio for a wee while. I'm going down to Rasharkin for a couple of weeks to see my folks." She looked at Donal. "And when I get back him and me have to make our plans."

"Good for you," Barry said, thinking that Kinky's song had been right, even if the particular wedding had already been arranged.

"I hope I'll be seeing *you* when I get back, Doctor?"

"So do I," he said, knowing she'd take the remark as simple politeness and not a reflection of his uncertainty about following Patricia to Cambridge, or his worry about the postmortem findings. "Just don't get wed too soon after this one." He picked up his whiskey. "What with the ta-ta-ta-ra two weeks ago and now today, my liver's going to need a while to recover."

Donal laughed, then asked, "Can I introduce Julie to Miss Spence?"

"Of course, Donal."

"We met this morning, Miss," he said. "This here's Julie MacAteer, so it is."

"Pleased to meet you, Julie," Patricia said.

"Likewise," said Julie, and then she bobbed. "If you don't mind me saying so, Miss," she said shyly, "I think your man Percy French must have had you in mind when he wrote that wee song, 'The Star of the County Down.'"

Patricia laughed. "I'm very flattered you'd think that, Julie, but I don't have 'nut brown hair,' and I'm certainly not in 'my two bare feet.'"

Barry knew the song well. He supposed everyone in County Down did.

> "From Galway to Dublin town,
>   No maid I've seen like the fair *cailín*,
>   that I met in the County Down."

He looked at Patricia, and for him every word rang true.

"We'd best be running along, Doctor," Donal said.

Barry was so intent on admiring Patricia that he barely noticed them go, nor did he see O'Reilly return.

"Barry?" O'Reilly asked, "have you seen Arthur?"

"What?"

"Arthur?"

"He trotted off after you."

As if to answer O'Reilly's question, there was a frenzied cackling from the brushwood beneath the elm trees, and a single cock pheasant rocketed into the sky, its short wings blurred in the speed of their beating, its green head flashing emerald in the sun. The pheasant curled away in the swooping flight of its kind to disappear over the topiary animals.

"Huh," said O'Reilly. "That's where the damn dog is. In that covert."

O'Reilly moved to stand behind the table, lifted his fork, and began belabouring the glass. "Welcome back. Now shut up and pay attention. Next on the agenda," he roared, "I'll ask Councillor Bishop to come up here."

There was a muted muttering while the councillor stumped to the head table. A voice called, "What about the Duck then?"

The councillor stood with his legs braced apart, hands gripping the lapels of his black suit jacket. "My lord, ladies, and gentlemen," he intoned, as if addressing the county council. "Unaccustomed as I am to public speaking . . ." He paused as if waiting for laughter, but it failed to materialize. "One of youse asked a very important question . . ."

"Aye. What about the Duck?"

"I have," said Bishop, stealing a glance at O'Reilly, "been giving this matter serious consideration, so I have. I have listened to your concerns, and I'm going to take the sound advice of Doctors O'Reilly and Laverty, so I am."

"To run away off and chase yourself?"

Barry had to admire Bishop's aplomb.

"No," he said, smiling. "I'm a bit on the heavy side for running."

That did provoke a few chuckles.

"So I've made up my mind, and I've told Willy Dunleavy he and his family can have the lease for another ninety-nine years."

There was absolute silence.

"Did youse hear what I said? I'm going to—"

The cheering drowned out Bishop's next words.

Barry saw the little man puff out his chest like a pouter pigeon. "So there," he said, "and if Sonny's ready to bury the hatchet, then so am I."

The cheering increased.

Bishop bent down, and he and Sonny shook hands. "And that's all I have to say, except that my toasts will be to friendship, so . . ."

"Bertie. Bertie." Barry turned to see Flo Bishop on her feet waving at her husband. "Bertie, it is not all you've to say. You promised, and I know you promised, you did so, when we was down in Bangor on Thursday, and it was at the hat shop, and . . ."

Barry distinctly heard the councillor whisper, "God, will that woman never shut up?" He raised his voice. "Right. Right, Flo. I did near forget. I'm sorry." He pointed at Barry. "My Flo's been awful sick, and it's a very rare thing she's got. I know because Doctor O'Reilly said he'd never seen a case, and we all know he's a very learnéd man . . ."

A rumbling of agreement could be heard.

"But our Doctor Laverty here, he sussed it out in no time flat, and he's her fixed up right as rain, so he has. Flo and me's very grateful, Doctor."

The hush had descended again, and Barry could feel many eyes boring into the back of his neck.

"I know I said my toast was going to be to friendship, and of course to Sonny and Maggie," Bishop said, "but I'll ask youse all to rise . . . and drink to our two doctors as well."

"Aye, to our doctors *and* to the Duck. God bless them and all who sail in them," the heckler shouted.

Barry chuckled at the addition of the traditional blessing given to a ship as it was launched at the Belfast shipyard, but he was flattered to be mentioned in the same breath as the public house.

"Well done, Bertie," O'Reilly said, as Bishop went back to his place to the sound of cheering. "And," said O'Reilly, "that leaves one last speaker before we can get down to the serious business of the day. Will you welcome, please, Donal Donnelly?"

"Jesus," the voice yelled, "after the lord mayor's carriage comes the smell."

Donal, kilt drooping more than usual, buckteeth splendid as he grinned, came forward and made the obligatory introduction. Then he said, "First of all, me and Julie want to thank Doctor Laverty too. Youse all know what he done for her . . ."

There was a muted round of applause.

"But most important, me and the Highlanders, and a brave clatter of the other lads, and a wheen of the wives here have a wee present for Sonny and Maggie. Would youse two stand up, please?"

Sonny gave Maggie a puzzled look, shrugged, stood, and then helped her to her feet.

"On behalf of the village of Ballybuckebo, it gives me great pleasure to give you the key to your new and fully furnished house that we managed to get finished this morning." He handed a huge artificial key, crafted from cardboard or plywood and covered with silver aluminium foil, to Sonny.

Barry saw the look of sheer amazement on Sonny's face, and if his eyes had been damp when he'd been reunited with his dogs, tears now ran freely down his cheeks. Barry felt a lump rising in his own throat, dashed the back of his hand across his eyes, and thought, How could any young doctor in his right mind think of leaving Ballybucklebo? He saw how Patricia was looking at him, forced a grin, and directed his attention to what Donal was now saying.

"Here you are, Maggie." Donal gave her a real set of keys. "I'm giving these to you because as any of the married men here'll tell you . . . they may be the legal heads of the household, but they all know who really wears the trousers, so they do."

There was a moment's silence. Barry saw Mrs. Bishop nudge the councillor in the ribs, and he could have sworn he heard Bertie Bishop saying, "Yes, dear."

The wave of laughter started low, and grew and grew as a tidal wave gathers strength as it nears the shore. The racket engulfed the crowd. There were catcalls and piercing whistles. One of the pipers, unbidden, launched into an impossibly fast strathspey. Children yelled. Barry saw one little girl, obviously terrified by the pandemonium, burst into tears and bury her face in her mother's skirt.

Sonny's dogs burst out from under the table, yipping and barking. The old spaniel raced in tight, hurried circles chasing its own tail.

Barry's earlier question about whether the wedding festivities would match up to those of the Galvins' going-away party had been answered, very much in the affirmative.

He moved to tell Patricia what he thought, but a hand on his shoulder made him turn to find himself staring up into the open, country face of Jack Mills. "Sorry I'm late, mate, but better late than never."

44

The End Is Where We Start From

"Jack." Barry stood up, his hands sweating, as he stared at Jack's face for any hint of what the news might be. "Have you seen Harry?"

"Och, aye. You'd have to feel sorry for the poor bugger. He looks like the wreck of the *Hesperus*. That flu's a nasty one."

"I'm sorry about that. Did he have the report?"

"Aye." Jack's face was expressionless until he eyed the half-full wine bottle and grinned.

Patricia, who had been following the conversation, a puzzled look on her face, reached for a clean glass and handed it to Jack. "Here."

"Ta, Patricia." He grabbed the bottle. "Nice to see you. You're looking gorgeous."

"*Jack*. The report." A cloud had passed in front of the sun, and in its shadow Barry felt chilled.

"Right enough." He fished an envelope from the inside pocket of his jacket and handed it to Barry. "Have a gander at that while I'm pouring." He lifted the bottle.

Barry grabbed the envelope. He knew how Patricia had felt when her examination results arrived. He barely had the strength to open the bloody thing, but he ripped the flap open, fished out a form, unfolded its two pages, and began to read.

Major Fotheringham's name and identifying information headed the pages. Next came the histological report. Barry scanned the first page, which described *polymorphocytic infiltration and lymphocytic aggregation, atheromatous plaques, platelets, fibrin, and eosinophilia of the myocardial fibres.*

He flipped over to the second page to the section headed Summary.

There is striking evidence of atherosclerotic occlusion of three of the four major coronary arteries . . .

He lowered the paper.

He was having difficulty focusing on the typing, but he raised the sheets and read on: *. . . and extensive damage to the myocardial muscle supplied by these vessels.* There was more, but he dropped his gaze to the final section, Conclusions.

Cause of death: Massive coronary occlusion of sufficient magnitude to result in sudden death prior to the formation of obvious macroscopic pathological changes.

He reread the words, brighter now on the page since the cloud had moved away from the sun. Major Fotheringham had died of a coronary, a condition that had nothing whatsoever to do with his earlier cerebral haemorrhage. Barry exhaled. No physician could have saved the man's life. He tucked the report into an inside pocket.

"You all right, Barry?" Patricia stood by his side. She was frowning.

"What?"

"Are you all right?"

"Fine. Yes, thanks. I'm fine."

"Good, because you went white as a sheet."

"I . . . I've been waiting for this report. I'll tell you what it's all about later, but I've been waiting for it for the last two weeks." He grabbed her and hugged her. "As Donal Donnelly would say, 'it's the best thing since sliced pan.' "

"So that's two of us with things to celebrate, isn't it?"

"Damn right it is." He kissed her, not giving a tinker's damn who saw. "Now," he said, "I have to go and tell O'Reilly. He's been waiting too."

"Go ahead. He's over there with Kitty, but come back and tell me soon. I'm dying to hear."

"I'll be back." Barry started to walk to where O'Reilly stood deep in conversation with Kitty O'Hallorhan. He heard Jack call, "Good news? Harry told me what it said."

"It's exactly what I wanted to hear. Why the hell didn't you tell me at once if you knew?"

"And spoil the surprise? Don't be daft, and it was worth it just to see that idiotic grin on your face."

"You bugger," Barry said. "I've been on eggs about this." But he couldn't be angry with Jack. He couldn't be angry with anybody. "Now, I have to go tell O'Reilly."

"Do me a favour before you go?"

"Sure." Barry realized that keeping O'Reilly waiting now didn't really matter, and it would give Barry a few moments to let the news sink in.

"See that stunning redhead over there? The one with the amazing green eyes?"

"Helen Hewitt?"

"Introduce me, like a good lad."

"She's one of my patients, Jack."

"Not one of mine. Come on. Introduce me." He headed towards Helen.

Barry said to Patricia, "Back in a jiffy. I promise I will explain." He followed his friend. "Jack, I should tell you; Helen has a mind of her own."

"It's not," said Jack, "her mind I'm interested in. Have you seen her legs?"

Barry had a mental picture of Miss Moloney's hats battered beyond recognition. "On your own head be it, Mills, but you have been warned." He coughed. "Excuse me, Helen, may I introduce you to an old friend of mine, Doctor Jack Mills?"

Jack bowed slightly. "Helen," he said, "the face that launched a thousand ships."

Barry heard Helen's laugh, heard her say, "Away off and chase yourself. You're full of it."

Barry shook his head, laughed, and made a beeline for O'Reilly, past Highlanders piping for dance sets, past kids and dogs chasing each other. Sonny's five dogs were clustered around O'Reilly and Kitty. There was no sign of Arthur Guinness. Nor of Sonny and Maggie.

They must be in the Big House getting changed into their going-away clothes.

Barry was still laughing when he arrived where O'Reilly and Kitty O'Hallorhan stood close together, O'Reilly's arm round Kitty's waist. Barry waited for them to finish speaking.

Kitty chuckled. ". . . And then you put me out the fifth-floor window of the students' residence in the sling of that friction rope-and-pulley fire escape device . . . and it only reached to the second floor."

"With you hanging in it like a great big spider, between the devil and the deep blue sea," O'Reilly said. "At least the warden didn't catch you." O'Reilly cleared his throat and took his arm from her waist. "Just . . . h-hem . . . talking about old times," he said. "What can we do for you, Barry?"

"Fingal, Jack Mills brought me the PM report."

O'Reilly's shoulders stiffened. "And . . . ?"

"Massive silent coronary."

"Bloody marvellous. Wonderful. Tough on the major, but that's life." He grabbed Barry's hand. It must have been a reflection of O'Reilly's pleasure because his grip was the car-crushing one Barry remembered from their very first meeting. "Bloody marvellous." He pumped away with all the vigour of a cowman at a dry cattle-trough pump. "We'll see the widow tomorrow. I told you, she'll keep her promise now we have the facts. No lawsuit. Jesus Murphy, I'm delighted for you, son."

"I'm sure you'll explain all this in a minute, Fingal," Kitty said.

"I will, by God, but first this calls for a jar. Whiskey, Barry?"

"Just a small one, but later. I've left Patricia all on her own, and I promised I'd explain to her what this is all about."

"Right." O'Reilly took command. "You wait here, Kitty. I'll get the drinks. Barry, you bring Patricia over here. She'll want another wine." Without waiting for an answer, he charged off singing to himself a lyric Barry recognized came from *The Mikado.* "The threatened cloud has passed away . . ."

"You've known him for years, Kitty. Was he always like this?"

"Worse," she said. "He's mellowing with age."

She really had the most delightful smile.

"I'd better go and see Patricia," he said. "And thanks."

"What for?"

"You know." Barry hesitated. He knew he meant for being with Fingal, but baulked at saying so.

"Get on with you," she said, clearly having understood his meaning. "We're just old friends."

Patricia was waiting where he'd left her. "Sorry about that," he said.

"Terrible," she said, with a grin. "Leaving a helpless maiden all on her own. I'm waiting for the explanation."

"It's a long story, but between the jigs and the reels of it, that report I just got has saved my bacon. You know O'Reilly has offered me a partnership after one year as his assistant?"

She nodded.

"It looked as if it was going to fall through."

Her eyes widened. "You told me, but I thought it was all straightened out."

"I was threatened with a lawsuit."

She shuddered. "Good God. When?"

"Last week."

"You never said anything about it." She frowned. "You might have told me."

He shook his head. "No. You'd enough on your plate."

"The exam?" Her cheeks reddened.

Barry held up both hands. "There was nothing you could do. I had to wait for the results of a postmortem."

"Because . . . ?"

He explained.

"And you just got the results a few minutes ago?"

"That's right."

"And it's not your fault, is it?" She kissed him. "Wonderful. So you can stay?"

Should he tell her he'd been thinking of leaving anyway, of looking for a post in Cambridge to be near her? No. "Yes," he said. "I can stay."

She kissed him again. "I'm very happy for you."

He looked into her eyes. "But what about us?"

"Us?" She didn't answer at once. Her brow wrinkled. She ran one hand over the top of her head. "I love you, Barry. I really do."

"And I love you, Patricia. You know that, but three years is a hell of a long time."

She took his hand. "We both have our careers to think of. We're both of us far too young to get married, if that's what you have in mind."

It was. The second he'd understood the import of the pathology report, he'd made up his mind to propose. At least Patricia had spared him the shame of an outright rejection.

"I know all that," he said, "but—"

"There aren't any buts, Barry. Listen. If you love me as much as you say you do, you'll wait. Some people do, you know."

"Sonny and Maggie?"

She nodded. "Deep down they must love each other very much, and I *know* how much I love you, Barry Laverty. I'll come back to you. Never worry about that." She came closer, flung her arms around his neck, and kissed him, harder than she had ever kissed him before, as if there was more anger than love in her lips. She was smiling, her dimples deep when she pulled away. "Of course I will. Don't you *ever* doubt it."

He laughed, kissed her, and said loudly, "I believe you, Patricia. I love you, and I don't give a hoot who knows."

He was going to say more but was interrupted by cheers and the clattering of tin cans on gravel. The marquis' Rolls-Royce, strings of cans and old boots tied to its rear bumper, had been drawn up to the portico of the big house.

"Come on," he said, "we have to go and see the happy couple off."

He took her hand and led her across the lawn. They arrived just in time to see the marquis walking down the broad front steps. He was leading Sonny, now dressed in a neat, double-breasted grey suit, and Maggie in a heather-mix twin set, smart pleated wool skirt, and a straw hat with a single rose in the hatband. She carried her bouquet.

Well-wishers lined the steps.

Maggie hesitated, then threw her bouquet at the crowd. Barry wished Patricia had been the one to catch it, but the roar of approval from the crowd, and the look of bewilderment on O'Reilly's face when it flew straight to Kitty O'Hallorhan, made up for his disappointment.

Sonny helped Maggie into the back of the Roller, and the marquis, as befitted his position of best man, drove them away, accompanied by the clattering of the cans and the music of a single piper. Why the man was playing a bagpipe version of "Rock around the Clock" was beyond Barry.

"Tell me again, how long did you tell me Maggie had waited for Sonny?" Patricia asked.

"More than fifteen years," Barry said without thinking.

"Now there's a thing," she said, cocking her head slightly to the side, one eyebrow raised and a smile on her lips.

And Barry heard the unspoken promise and slipped an arm around her shoulders. "Indeed it is," he said.

He heard O'Reilly call, "Barry, get over here this instant." He was summoning Barry and Patricia with a roar and a come-hither wave of his hand.

O'Reilly was sitting with Kitty and Mrs. Kincaid. Barry had forgotten that there were drinks waiting for Patricia and him. Taking her hand, he walked to the table, then held Patricia's chair until she was seated. He noticed that Arthur Guinness had made his way back from the covert and lay under the table, slurping from his stainless-steel bowl.

"Here you are." O'Reilly handed the wine to Patricia and the whiskey to Barry. "*Sláinte.*"

"*Sláinte mHath,*" Barry replied, standing behind Patricia with a hand on her shoulder.

"Right then," said O'Reilly. "The jollifications here are really going to get going now, but I've a half-notion you youngsters might like to slip away?"

Barry glanced at Patricia, who smiled up at him.

"Good," said O'Reilly. "In that case, I'll take call tonight."

"Thanks, Fingal." Barry set his glass on the table and stood back to allow Patricia to rise, but he was halted when O'Reilly bellowed, "Not yet, you goat. You've not finished your drink. And before you gallop off, I've a job for you."

Barry shrugged and picked up his whiskey.

"Now," said O'Reilly, "if I'm going to take call, I'll need to be near the phone." He looked directly at Kinky. "Do you think, Mrs. Kincaid, you could put together a bite of supper for Sister O'Hallorhan and me?" He didn't wait for a reply but turned to Kitty. "You might like to see how an old country GP lives?"

"That would be lovely." She nodded her agreement. "But I'm not sure I could eat anything else."

"Supper is it?" Kinky asked, staring straight at O'Reilly's straining waistcoat buttons. "I can do that all right. I've all the makings of a wonderful salad, so."

Barry had to smother a laugh.

O'Reilly grunted and bent down to reach under the table. Still bending, he fixed Barry with a stare. "Now, Doctor Laverty," he said slowly. "I've not asked you about your plans for the future, but I'm going to take a chance now. In view of your recent news, will you be accepting my offer?"

"I will, Doctor O'Reilly, and thank you."

"Grand, so. Grand." Kinky's chins wobbled as she laughed.

"And," O'Reilly continued, "I assume you'd like to work unsupervised?"

"Well, I . . ." It certainly was what he'd been dreaming of two weeks ago as he watched the seagulls spreading their wings above the foreshore of Ballybucklebo. "Yes, Fingal. You would be right."

"Good. Because I've your first independent case for you, Doctor Laverty."

Barry felt a glow in his cheeks and pride in O'Reilly's obvious confidence. He glanced at Patricia. He'd rather be taking her somewhere at once, but if there was a patient to be seen . . . He was relieved to see her nodding at him. "Who is it, Fingal?"

"Not who . . . what." O'Reilly guffawed as he straightened up. Then he pulled a single Wellington boot from under the table and thrust it at Barry. "You find a home for that bloody thing, Doctor Laverty . . . and you'll not have me breathing down your neck while you do."

AFTERWORD

by

Mrs. Kincaid

I suppose I shouldn't have agreed to do this the last time, because here I am at it again, but Doctor O'Reilly says my recipes were appreciated by the readers, so. And sure, appreciation is better than imitation as a sincere form of flattery.

Himself and that nice Sister Kitty O'Hallorhan are in the upstairs lounge listening to some awful caterwauling. He says it's an opera called *Le Nozze di Figaro,* whatever the divil that means. Something to do with weddings, he says. I've had my fill of those today. My feet hurt with all that standing around, and my jaw's near cracked with all the smiling I've had to do for people who've been admiring my new hat. Still and all, it was nice of young Doctor Laverty to get it for me. I've it back in its box ready for the next go-round when that eejit Donal Donnelly and wee Julie MacAteer tie the knot.

I'm just glad to be here in my own kitchen with my feet up. My ankles swell, you know, and it doesn't hurt to give them a bit of a draining. I'm sitting at the table with a pen in my fist, thinking about what I should give you this time by way of instructions for cooking.

Jesus, Mary, and Joseph, would you listen to that coming from up there? They call that woman a soprano? If you'd like my opinion, I think if she stopped standing on the poor wee pussycat's tail it would stop yowling, so. Lady Macbeth thinks the same as me, I can tell you that. She's under the table with her tail over her ears. The wee dote.

The row would distract a body from her task, but I'll have to make a start. I think I'll take Doctor O'Reilly's advice and give you the recipes for some of the meals I've been putting on the table in the last couple of weeks, but if you don't mind I'll not say nothing about pigs on a spit, roasted whole. I doubt there's much need for that in America. Anyway, His Lordship's cook wouldn't take my advice. It *could* have done with cooking for another half hour.

So. Let's see. Where'll I start? At the beginning, Kinky Kincaid. That's the place. Here you are then. I gave the Doctors an Ulster breakfast at the start of the story. Everything in it is well known but perhaps not the soda farls. I'll start with the recipe for them and then a few of the other things you'll have read about if you've got this far in the book.

Ulster Recipes

Soda Farls

1 pound all-purpose flour
1 teaspoon salt
1 teaspoon baking soda, heaped
10 to 15 ounces of buttermilk

Sieve the dry ingredients into a bowl. Then add enough buttermilk to give a soft, but not sticky, dough. Turn onto a well-floured board, and shape into a round cake about 1½ inches thick. Transfer to a floured baking sheet, and mark into 4 to 6 wedges (farls). Bake at 400° to 425° F for 30 to 35 minutes. The farls can be separated once the soda bread has cooled.

If preferred, the farls can be cut into wedges and cooked on a floured, gently heated griddle. This is the more traditional method.

Sherry Trifle

sponge cake or pound cake
raspberry jam, seedless

2 ounces sherry

8 ounces fresh or frozen raspberries (no need to defrost)

2 bananas

10 ounces custard

(I make my own custard:

2 egg yolks

2 tablespoons sugar

1 cup of scalded milk)

But if you can get it Bird's custard is grand

whipped cream

2 ounces flaked almonds, lightly toasted (omit if any of the diners is
  sensitive to nuts)

Break the cake into pieces, then spread a little jam on each. Put them into a large glass bowl. Then sprinkle the raspberries and sherry over them, stirring to let the sherry be soaked up.

Slice the bananas, and set the slices evenly over the raspberries. Pour 10 ounces of custard over the top. Spread the whipped cream evenly over the custard, and sprinkle on the flaked almonds. Chill for 3 to 4 hours before serving.

MOCK TURTLE SOUP

This recipe will feed 4 to 6 people but, och sure, the way himself eats there might just be enough for himself and young Doctor Laverty, so.

1 large onion, finely chopped

1 tablespoon butter

2 tablespoons olive oil

2 pounds meaty oxtails

1 garlic clove, mashed

3 whole cloves

¼ teaspoon thyme

1 bay leaf

¼ teaspoon allspice
1 tablespoon flour
3 cups hot water
3 cups chicken stock
1 cup peeled, chopped tomatoes
salt and pepper
½ thin-skinned lemon, chopped with the rind still on
1 tablespoon parsley
2 hardboiled eggs

Brown the onion in the butter and oil. Add the oxtails and brown them slightly. Add the spices and herbs. Stir in the flour until it bubbles. Add more butter and oil as needed. Pour in the stock and hot water. Bring to the boil. Then add all the other ingredients except the eggs. Simmer for 2 hours. Take out the oxtails, and cut off the meat and the marrow. Discard the bones (Arthur Guinness is very partial to them in this house), and put the meat and marrow back in the broth.

Serve into individual bowls, adding coarsely chopped eggs and a teaspoon of sherry to each bowl. Garnish with parsley.

That's it then. I'm off to my bed. I know I'm going to be busy tomorrow, and it looks like I'll be cooking for two, now Doctor Laverty has agreed to stay on . . . at least until he gets a place of his own with that Patricia Spence of his. Lord knows when that'll be, her off to Cambridge and all. Och, but sure the course of true love never did run smooth.

And if that fellah Patrick Taylor gets round to spinning more yarns about us folks in Ballybucklebo, and he's not showing any sign of drying up yet, before you know it I'll be back at this table writing more myself, so.

Until then, always remember, *is fearr an tsláinte ná na táinte*—health is better than riches—and you'll not be healthy if you don't eat right. I just wish I could persuade himself to eat a toty-wee bit less.

Slán agat.

Farewell,

MRS. KINKY KINCAID
Housekeeper to
Doctor Fingal Flahertie O'Reilly, M.B., B.Ch., B.A.O.
1, Main Street
Ballybucklebo
County Down
Northern Ireland

Author's Note

Doctor Fingal Flahertie O'Reilly and the denizens of Ballybucklebo first appeared in 1995 in my monthly column in *Stitches: The Journal of Medical Humour*. It was suggested that these characters might form the foundation for a novel.

I had just finished a thriller, *Pray for Us Sinners*, and was beginning to construct its sequel, *Now and in the Hour of Our Death*, but found myself hesitating to delve once more into the misery of the Ulster Troubles. The idea of writing something lighter was appealing, and so *An Irish Country Doctor* took shape. The good folks at Forge had sufficient faith in this work to commission it and its sequel, *An Irish Country Village*.

Like *Only Wounded* and *Pray for Us Sinners* and more recently *Now and in the Hour of Our Death*, the Laverty-O'Reilly novels are set in the northeast corner of Ireland. But unlike my other works, which I strove to make historically accurate, these stories have taken some liberties with geography.

The setting is a fictional village, the name of which came from my high-school French teacher who, enraged by my inability to conjugate irregular verbs, yelled, "Taylor, you're stupid enough to come from Ballybucklebo, pronounced Bally-buckle–*bo*, not 'boo.'"

Those of an etymological bent may wish to know what the name means. *Bally* (Irish, *baile*) is a home or townland—a mediaeval geographic term encompassing a small village and the surrounding farms; *Buachaill* means "boy," and *bó* is a cow. In *Bailebuchaillbó*, or

Ballybucklebo—the townland of the boy's cow—time and place are as skewed as they are in Brigadoon.

Since the publication of *An Irish Country Doctor*, I have been amazed by the number of my Ulster friends who insist on trying to pinpoint Ballybucklebo as a real village in North Down. It is clear that the old Irish pastime of chasing moonbeams is not yet dead.

I have been at pains to use the Ulster dialect. It is rich and colourful, but often incomprehensible to one not from that part of the world. For those who may have some difficulty, I have taken the liberty of appending a glossary (page 421), but I have been sparing in my use of the Irish language as it is not spoken by most of the citizens of Northern Ireland.

Sadly, although the Ulster folk still use their colourful idiom, the rural Ulster I have portrayed has vanished. The farms and villages still look much as they did, but the simplicity of rural life has been banished by the Troubles and the all-pervasive influence of television, which was not seen in colour in Ulster before 1967.

The automatic respect for their learning shown to those at the top of the village hierarchy—doctor, teacher, minister, and priest—is a thing of the past, but men like O'Reilly were common when I was a very junior doctor.

I was a very junior doctor at a time when, only five years earlier, the link between thalidomide and birth defects had been established. In 1963 the first cadaver kidney transplant had been performed in Leeds, and in 1965 cigarette advertising was banned from British television. It was not until 1967 that Doctor Christiaan Barnard gave Louis Washkansky the first heart transplant. We had to wait until 1978 for the birth of the world's first baby conceived by in vitro fertilization.

Diagnostic tests were rudimentary, both in the laboratory and in imaging departments. Not until 1979 was Godfrey Hounsfield awarded the Nobel Prize for the invention of computerized axial tomography, the CAT scan. The eighties, the decade that saw the identification of the AIDS virus, was also the time lasers began to appear in operating rooms.

By today's standards the practice of modern medicine in the 1960s was in its infancy, and much depended on the clinical skills of the Doctor O'Reillys. And on that subject, may I lay to rest once and for all two questions I am frequently asked by readers of my columns in *Stitches*? Barry Laverty and Patrick Taylor are *not* one and the same. Doctor F. F. O'Reilly is a figment of my troubled mind, despite the efforts of some of my expatriate Ulster friends to see in him a respected—if unorthodox—medical practitioner of the time.

Lady Macbeth *does* owe her being to a demoniacally possessed cat, Minnie, and Arthur Guinness owes his to a black Labrador now long gone who had an insatiable thirst for Foster's lager. All the other characters are composites, drawn from my imagination and from my experiences as a rural GP.

PATRICK TAYLOR

Glossary

The Ulster dialect, properly called Ulster-Scots, is rich and colourful but can be confusing. In my mind I hear the expressions used by my characters as clearly as if I were living back in the north of Ireland, and I have tried to reproduce their idiom as accurately as possible. I was, after all, immersed in the northern speech patterns for thirty years. For those unfamiliar with Ulster-Scots, however, I have taken the liberty of appending this short glossary.

Like all patois, Ulster-Scots is not one bit shy about adopting useful phrases from others. For example, the reader should not be surprised to find examples of Cockney rhyming slang here.

acting the goat: Behaving foolishly.
apples and pears: Cockney rhyming slang for stairs.
argy-bargy: Voluble disagreement.
arse: Backside (impolite).
aunt Fanny Jane, my: Nonsense.
away off and chase yourself: Go away.
away off and feel your head: You're being stupid.
away on: I don't believe you.
bamboozle: Deliberately confuse.
banjaxed: Exhausted or broken.
banshee: Female spirit whose moaning foretells death.
barmbrack: Speckled bread.
bashtoon: Bastard.

beagle's gowl: Very long way; the distance over which the cry of a beagle can be heard.

bee on a hot brick: Running round distractedly.

bigger fish to fry: More important matters to attend to.

bit my head off: Expressed anger by shouting or being very curt.

bloater: Salted and smoked herring.

blow you out: Tell you to go away.

bob, a few: One shilling; a sum of money.

bodhrán: Irish. Pronounced "bowron." A circular handheld drum.

boke: Vomit.

bollocks: Testicles (impolite). May be used as an expression of vehement disagreement or to describe a person you disapprove of; for example, "He's a right bollocks."

bonnet: Hood of a car.

boot: Trunk of a car.

both legs the same length: Standing about uselessly.

bowsey: Dublin slang, drunkard.

boys-a-boys, boys-a-dear: Expressions of amazement.

brass neck: Impertinence, chutzpah.

bravely: Feeling well.

buck eejit: Imbecile.

bun in the oven: Pregnant (impolite).

cailín: Irish. Pronounced "cawleen." Girl.

call the cows home: Be ready to tackle anything.

capped: A cap was awarded to athletes selected for important teams. Equivalent to a letter at an American university.

caubeen: Traditional Irish bonnet.

casualty: Emergency room.

céili: Irish. Pronounced "kaylee." Party, usually with music and dancing.

champ: A dish of buttermilk, butter, potatoes, and chives.

chemist: Pharmacist.

chiseller: Dublin slang, a small child.

clabber: Glutinous mess of mud, or mud and cow clap.

clatter, a brave: A large quantity.

colloguing: Chatting about trivia.

conkers: Horse chestnuts. Used to play a children's game.

cow's lick: Tuft of hair that sticks up, or hair slicked over to one side.

cracker: Excellent (see also *wheeker*).

craking on: Talking incessantly.

crúibins: Irish. Pronounced "crubeen." Boiled pigs' feet, served cold and eaten with vinegar.

cure, wee: Hair of the dog.

dab hand: Skilled at.

damper: Device for restricting the flow of air to a coal or turf fire to slow the rate of burning.

dander: Literally, horse dandruff. Used to signify either a short leisurely walk or anger. For example, "He really got my dander up."

dibs: A claim upon.

didny; didnae: Did not.

divil: Devil.

divil the bit: None. For example, "He's divil the bit of sense." (He's stupid.)

doddle: A short distance or an easy task.

dote: Something adorable.

dote on: Worship.

do with the price of corn: Irrelevant.

drill-the-dome boys: Medical slang, neurosurgeons. See also *nut-cracker*.

drouth, raging: Pronounced "drewth." Alcoholic.

drúishin: Irish. Pronounced "drisheen." Dish made of cows' blood, pigs' blood, and oatmeal. A Cork City delicacy.

dulse: A seaweed, which when dried is eaten like chewing gum.

eejit: Idiot.

egg-bound hen: A hen with an egg that cannot be laid stuck in the oviduct. Applied to a person, it suggests extreme distress.

fag: Cigarette.

fall off the perch: Die.

fenian: Catholic (pejorative).

field, the: A place where Orange Lodges and bands congregate after the Twelfth of July parade.

finagle: Achieve by cunning or dubious means.

fit to be tied: Very angry.

flying: Drunk.

fornenst: Besides.

foundered: Chilled to the marrow.

full of it: Being either stupid or excessively flattering.

gander: Take a look at.

get (away) on with you: Don't be stupid.

get on one's wick: Get on one's nerves.

give over: Stop it.

glipe, great: Stupid or very stupid person.

gobshite: Dublin slang used pejoratively about a person. Literally, dried nasal mucus.

good man ma da: Expression of approval.

grand man for the pan: One who really enjoys fried food.

great: The ultimate Ulster accolade; can be used to signify pleased assent to a plan.

grotty: English slang. Run-down and dirty.

guttersnipe: Ruffian.

hairy bear: Woolly caterpillar.

half-cut: Drunk.

hand's turn: Minimum amount of work.

having me on: Deceiving me.

head staggers: Making a very stupid decision. Literally, a parasitic disease affecting the brains of sheep and causing them to stagger.

heart of corn: Very good-natured.

heifer: Young cow before her first breeding.

hirstle: Chesty wheeze.

hit the spot: Fill the need.

hobby-horse shite, your head's full of: Literally, sawdust. You're stupid.

hold your horses: Wait a minute.

hooley: Party.

hoor: Whore.

houseman: Medical intern.

how's (a)bout ye? How are you? Or good-day.

humdinger: Something extraordinary.

I'm your man: I agree to your plan and will follow it.

in soul, I do: Emphatic.

in the stable: Of a drink, already paid for before being poured.

jar: An alcoholic drink.

jaunting car: An open, high, two-wheeled vehicle. The passenger accommodation was two benches, arranged along either side so the passengers sat with their backs to the cart bed. By the 1960s it was rarely seen except in the most rural parts of Ireland or as a tourist attraction.

jigs and reels, between the: To cut a long story short.

knackered: Very tired. An allusion to a horse so worn out by work that it is destined for the knacker's yard, where horses are destroyed.

knickers in a twist, in a knot: Anxiously upset.

knocking: Having sexual intercourse.

Lambeg drum: Massive bass drum carried on shoulder straps by Orangemen and beaten with two sticks, sometimes until the drummer's wrists bleed.

length and breadth of it: All the details.

let the hare sit: Leave the thing alone.

like the sidewall of a house: Huge, especially when applied to someone's physical build.

liltie: A madman. An Irish whirling dervish.

load of cobblers': In Cockney rhyming slang, "cobblers' awls" means "balls." Used to signify rubbish.

lough: Pronounced "logh," almost as if clearing the throat. A sea inlet or very large inland lake.

lummox: Stupid creature.

main: Very.

make a mint: Make a great deal of money.

moping: Indulging in self-pity.

more power to your wheel: Very good luck to you; encouragement.

muggy: Hot and humid.

mullet, stunned: To look as stupid or surprised as a mullet, an ugly saltwater fish.

Mullingar heifer, calves like: Cows from Mullingar were said to have very thick legs.

my shout: I'm buying the drinks.

near took the rickets: Had a great shock.

no dozer: Clever.

no goat's toe, he thinks he's: Has an overinflated sense of his own importance.

no spring chicken: Getting on in years.

not as green as you're cabbage looking: More clever than you appear to be.

not at myself: Feeling unwell.

nutcracker: Neurosurgeon.

on eggs: Extremely worried.

Orange Order: Fraternal order of Protestants loyal to the British crown.

orange and green The colours of Loyalists and Republicans, respectively. Used to symbolize the age-old schism in Irish politics.

ould goat: Old man, often used affectionately.

out of kilter: Out of alignment.

oxter: Armpit.

oxter-cog: To carry by supporting under the armpits.

pacamac: Cheap, transparent, plastic raincoat carried in a small bag.

Paddy hat: Soft-crowned tweed hat.

pan loaf: Loaf of ordinary bread.

Paddy's market: A large, disorganised crowd.

peat (turf): Fuel derived from compressed vegetable matter.

penny bap: A small bun, usually coated in flour.

petrified: Terrified.

physical jerks: Gymnastics.

piss artist: Alcoholic.

poke: Have sex with; a small parcel.

pop one's clogs: Die.

poulticed: Pregnant, usually out of wedlock.

powerful: Very.

power of: A great deal of.

quare: Ulster pronunciation of queer. Very strange.

raring to go: Eager and fully prepared.

recimetation: Malapropism for recitation.

registrar, medical: Trainee physician equivalent to a North American resident.

rug rats: Children.

run-race: Quick trip to, usually on foot.

script/scrip: Prescription.

scunner, take a scunner at or to: Dislike someone intensely and bear a grudge.

semi: Semidetached house. Duplex.

sheugh: Bog.

shit, to: To defaecate.

shite: Faeces.

shufti: Army slang. A quick look at.

skiver: Corruption of "scurvy." Pejorative. Ne'er-do-well.

skivvy: From "scurvy." Housemaid.

sliced pan, best thing since: Presliced, then wrapped, pan loaf was reintroduced after the Second World War. To be better than it was the acme of perfection.

slip jig: Traditional dance.

snotters: Runny nose.

soft hand under a duck: Gentle or very good at.

solicitor: Attorney, but one who would not appear in court, which is done by barristers.

sore tried by: Very worried by or very irritated by.

spavins: A disease of horses resulting in a swayback.

sponge bag: Toilet bag.

stays: Whalebone corset.

stocious: Drunk.

stone: Measure of weight equal to fourteen pounds.

stoon: Sudden shooting pain.

stout: A dark beer, usually Guinness.

strong weakness: Hangover.

take a gander: Look at.

take your hurry in your hand: Wait a minute.

taste, a wee: Amount. Small amount, not necessarily edible.

ta-ta-ta-ra: Dublin slang, party.

thick: Stupid.

thick as champ: Very stupid.

thon: That.

thrapple: Throat.

throw off: Vomit.

toty: Small.

toty, wee: Very small.

turf accountant: Bookmaker.

up the spout or pipe: Pregnant.

wean: Pronounced "wane." Child.

wee: Small, but in Ulster can be used to modify almost anything without reference to size. A barmaid and old friend greeted the author by saying, "Come on in, Pat. Have a wee seat and I'll get you a wee menu, and would you like a wee drink while you're waiting?"

wee buns: Very easy.

wet (wee): Alcoholic drink.

whaling away at: Beating.

wheeker: Very good.

wheen: A large number of.

wheest: Be quiet.

wheezle: Wheeze in chest.

whippet: Small, fast, racing dog, such as a mini-greyhound.

willy: Penis.

won't butter any parsnips: Will make absolutely no difference.

you're on: Agreed to, or to indicate acceptance of a wager.

your head's cut (a marley): You are being very stupid, and your head is as small and as dense as a child's marble.

your man: Someone who is not present but is known to all others there.

youse: Ulster plural of you.

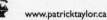